Liz Ryan's Novels

'Captivating . . . Brings a freshness and verve to the boy-meets-girl story. The Ryan twist on fictional romance invests the rosy garden of love with some of the sharpest thorns.'

Justin McCarthy, Irish Independent

'Vivid and witty . . . great charm.'

Brenda Power, Dublin Sunday Tribune

'Immensely readable.'

San Antonio Express News

'Will delight the reader who has already devoured Maeve Binchy.'

Liverpool Echo

'Very well written . . . cracks along at whippet-like pace.'

U Magazine

'A big, fast-moving story, lit with terse insights.'

Dublin Evening Herald

'Liz Ryan is smart and funny and she writes well.'

Irish Times

Also by Liz Ryan in Coronet Paperbacks

Blood Lines
A Note of Parting
A Taste of Freedom
The Past is Tomorrow

About the author

Liz Ryan has been a journalist for many years, and a regular contributor to many magazines and radio programmes.

The Year of Her Life

Liz Ryan

CORONET BOOKS

Hodder & Stoughton

First published in Great Britain in 2001 by Hodder and Stoughton
First published in paperback in 2002
by Hodder and Stoughton
A division of Hodder Headline
A Coronet paperback

A CIP catalogue record for this title
is available from the British Library

ISBN 0 340 76878 9

Printed and bound in Great Britain by
Mackays of Chatham plc, Chatham, Kent

Hodder & Stoughton
A division of Hodder Headline
338 Euston Road
London NW1 3BH

ACKNOWLEDGEMENTS

Diamonds aren't a girl's best friends – girlfriends are! My brilliant collection, starring Mary Davin-Power, Sharon Plunkett, Anne Rooney, Sheila Desamais and Jeannette McAteer, is world class. Endless kisses for all your support, moral and logistical, and special thanks to Philip Nolan too even though he's a guy, he sparkles! Thanks to my mum Lil Greenhalgh for putting up with all the anti-social schedules, to Eithne for packing a hundred dishes and to all those lovely friends who, by word or deed, helped to get this book written. You are just wonderful and I love you to bits.

JANUARY

Lola.

    Lola Cola.

    Lo-la *Co*-la!

    Rah-rah-rah!

    Lauren Kilroy studied her Ferragamo shoe and frowned. Try again.

    Lo . . . la . . . Co . . . la . . . Alo . . . ha . . . Cue swaying dancers, palm trees and Hawaiian music.

    Zzz.

    Well, if she was at her best she wouldn't bloody be here, would she? Wild horses wouldn't drag her into a doctor's waiting room if there was any way out of it. Especially one as dated and dilapidated as Dr Mallon's, in this sinking suburb where someone was probably, right now, slashing the tyres of her BMW outside. There wasn't even any *Hello!* magazine or *VIP* to distract her with news of Posh and Becks; Dr Mallon's patients read *Woman's Own*, *National Geographic* or some dog-eared rag called *Horse & Hound*. To Lauren, a horse was something that ran unseen races at Leopardstown while she entertained her corporate clients in the hospitality marquee. Get near one, and it would bite off the sleeve of your Louise Kennedy suit up to the elbow.

    Not that she wanted to entertain any clients today. She'd had to do it, over a launch lunch for forty-six at Guilbaud's, but what

I

she really wanted to do was go home, slide between her Kelly Hoppen sheets and sleep for Ireland. Sleep for months, for years, for gold medals. Stifling a yawn, she tried to get her head back around the Lola campaign, but how could anyone concentrate in this awful environment, with two hideous little boys on either side of her, one snivelling and scratching, the other pulling and tugging at his distracted, messy-looking mother? Consulting her watch, she battled an urge to get up and march into Dr Mallon's consulting room, tell him to get a blasted move on. It was six forty, and she was supposed to be meeting Jordan at ten to eight in the foyer of the Gate Theatre. She had absolutely zero desire to see Chekhov's *Seagull*, or Chekhov's thrush or magpie for that matter, but opening nights were important. You went to them whether you—

'Mrs O'Shaughnessy?'

Dr Mallon's head appeared briefly around the door, and the woman with the whiny kids stood up to shepherd them through it. Good. That only left herself and some mousy-looking man who'd held the door open for her as they arrived simultaneously. Since she'd stepped into the waiting room in front of him, that put her before him in the queue. Next.

A clock, twelve minutes slow, ticked over the mantelpiece, and with some impatience Lauren wondered why on earth Dr Mallon – or his overweight, breathless wife – didn't do up their tattered old Victorian house. Since her first visit here as a child thirty years ago, she didn't think even the magazines had changed. Certainly the carpet hadn't, or the silk-striped wallpaper or the box of toys that was meant to amuse waiting infants. Even she knew that little girls didn't play with rag dolls any more, and boys didn't read the *Beano* or the *Dandy*.

Not that she knew much else about children, except that she didn't want any and hadn't time to in any case. Not even if Jordan were – well. Jordan had his own life, and she had hers, and the situation suited both of them just fine. He'd pass out cold if he could see where she was now, demand to know why she hadn't gone to some proper doctor, preferably a Mr, on

Fitzwilliam Square. Someone with an Armani suit, Kurt Jackson painting in the foyer and Jaguar parked outside the front door. Dr Mallon wore a cardigan and corduroy trousers, and didn't even have a receptionist.

But Dr Mallon, she reminded herself, saved my sister's life. Caoimhe would be dead now if he hadn't spotted right away that it was incipient meningitis. She was only five weeks old then, and now she's twenty-seven, and it's an unwritten rule in our family that we all go to Dr Mallon. Not that he's likely to be in practice for much longer, he must be at least sixty, and soon we can all find ourselves new doctors, shiny ones with wide-screen televisions in state-of-the-art waiting rooms. Not that Mother will, of course, she'll manage to dig up some other old doddering geezer who'll take up wherever Dr Mallon leaves off. Dad never goes to the doctor anyway. But Caoimhe and I will be free, our debt of loyalty will be paid. About time too. Even if Dr Mallon is a good doctor, and I can trust him to fix whatever the hell is wrong with me, he's had his day.

I've had mine, too, right now. I don't want to go to the theatre. If Jordan hadn't already got the tickets I'd call him on his mobile and tell him—

'Lauren?'

Startled, she snapped her head up, realising with horror that it had actually begun to sag, that she'd been nodding off. Deliberately not looking at the man whose turn it arguably was, she stood up, smoothed her skirt and followed Dr Mallon briskly into his surgery. She was in a hurry. And, although she'd somehow never dared say it outright, she wished Dr Mallon would call her 'Ms Kilroy', in front of other people at least, as befitted a thirty-two-year-old businesswoman. Advertising *executive*.

Dr Mallon's surgery was as frayed and faded as his waiting room, with an old leather couch, a fringed Foxford rug, an oak filing cabinet spewing manila folders over its brass handles. At sixty-something, the man had clearly missed the computer era, and Lauren sighed inwardly.

'Please. Sit down.'

The doctor's watch – not digital, but with Roman numerals – slid down over his forehead as he gestured to the chair in front of his ancient oak desk, and it struck Lauren that his wrist was thin, his still-abundant hair now totally white. When he smiled his face seemed to fragment in wrinkles, and his blue eyes were more azure than cobalt. He really was getting on. Seating himself slowly and rather heavily behind his desk, he glanced down at the handwritten file which already lay open on it, and then seemed to change his mind, divert direction.

'So' he began pleasantly, looking back up at her, 'how are you?'

'I don't know' she replied, 'that's what I'm here to find out.'

He nodded, but still didn't pick up the file, which presumably contained the results of the blood test he'd sent her for ten days ago. The one that would explain why, at thirty-two, she felt ninety-eight. Probably stress, he'd said, which was what happened to people who worked fourteen-hour days and then raced off to play squash or catch planes to New York. Or it could be anaemia. Iron would cure that, plus a few 'proper meals' of cabbage and liver, not microwaved or rushed in some restaurant, but eaten as nature intended. Dr Mallon was a resolute believer in nature, and Lauren thought she would sooner starve than swallow one mouthful of either liver or – uughh! – cabbage. She eyeballed him.

'Have my results come?'

She knew they had, but a small tremor shot through her as she tackled the question head-on. Jesus, what if there was actually something wrong with her! But Dr Mallon hadn't seemed unduly alarmed after examining her last week, only delivered a mild and rather tedious lecture about her 'generation', which ran itself ragged, and its diet which was 'rubbish' and its women who were 'neurotic' about their weight. In fact Lauren didn't consciously diet at all, because she so rarely got to finish a meal anyway. She was five feet seven inches tall and a magazine chart had informed her that eight stone one pound was quite within normal range for her height.

Dr Mallon exhaled a small sigh and smiled again, in a rather exasperating way that made her suspect he'd be patting her hand any minute now, telling her she really must start getting more sleep. Which she would, if she *could*!

'Yes, they have. But first, tell me, how are things at work?'

'Frantic' she replied with what she supposed must be naked impatience. 'But you know they always are, I told you that last week . . . I'm working on a new campaign for a low-cal soft drink, you can see it for yourself on television in April, if I can get the damn jingle sorted in time!'

And get out of here in time for the theatre, she thought, which I won't if you're going to start into my work. I'll be late and Jordan will be drumming his fingers and we won't be let in until after the first act – for God's sake, Dr Mallon, please stick to the point and write me a prescription and let me get out of here.

'April' he repeated, slowly, maddeningly. 'Hmm. I see. And your parents? Young Caoimhe? Are they well?'

Jesus! 'Yes, thank you, they're very well.'

He eyed her mildly, but somehow quizzically, in a way that forced her to elaborate. But her conscience was clear about her parents, whom she dutifully took to lunch every other Sunday at a hotel in Howth. A horrible hotel, but she'd had to grit her teeth and give in, after they'd toyed with their designer food at a much classier, more expensive venue in town, and hardly eaten a bite. At least they ate their plain chicken and potatoes in Howth, which meant their mouths were full much of the time and the strain of conversation was eased.

She'd been taking them to the Howth hotel with clockwork regularity for three years now – except if abroad or working weekends – and she didn't want to think about it much less talk; the repetition, the dullness, the numbing predictability of the whole routine. Her parents, Eoin and Betty, absolutely loved routine.

'Good. And your – um – boyfriend? What's his name again, Joe?'

Lauren winced. *Joe?* As in Soap? Dr Mallon somehow made her beloved, her best boy, sound like a truck driver.

'Jordan. Jordan White. He's in good health too, thanks.'

'I'm glad to hear it. Remind me now, what is it he works at?'

Definitely, she thought, you're losing it, Doc. You asked me this ages ago and I told you at the time, five years ago when you put me on the pill. At least the one bright spot in all this is that I can't be pregnant . . . can't be ill, either, or you wouldn't be rambling like this, you'd be rushing me into hospital.

Feeling vague relief mingling with frustration, she answered his question. 'Jordan is a judge. A criminal court judge.'

'Ah, yes. That's it. I knew it was something that keeps him very busy.'

Inexplicably the words hung on the air, and Lauren looked at Dr Mallon sharply. What are you suggesting here, old man? That you know Jordan is married with a wife and two children, and that *that's* what keeps him busy?

Well, even if it's true, it's none of your business. Besides, I'm busy myself. And women of my age don't have boyfriends, by the way, they have *partners*.

Nettled, she consulted her watch for the second time.

'Dr Mallon, I'm very sorry, but I'm really in a tearing hurry this evening. Could we possibly just – you know—?'

A tad guiltily, because she knew he meant well, she rolled her index fingers rapidly one over the other, to convey getting on with things. In response he lifted his glasses from where they lay, put them on and finally picked up her file.

'Yes, Lauren, of course we can. I'm sorry if I seem to be delaying you, but it's just that your parents are such old friends, and I've always had a special interest in Caoimhe, as you know.'

Yes. Caoimhe was his baby all right, and he always enquired quite justifiably about her with a mixture of pride and interest. But could we leave Jordan out of the picture, and move along?

Dr Mallon frowned at the file, put it back down again – oh, *God!* – and clasped his hands, thinking for some seconds before he spoke.

'Before we discuss the results of your blood test, Lauren, would you mind if I asked you a personal question?'

'Well, I – no, not if it's relevant.'

Surely that, she thought, would keep him to the point. But there didn't seem to be any speeding him up. Jordan was going to be fuming.

Dr Mallon cleared his throat. 'This – er – ahem – this boyfriend of yours. How long have you been with him now?'

'Five years. It's on the chart. My contraceptive history, I mean.'

'Yes. So it is. That's a long time these days for a young woman to stay with one partner! But I – ah – do I gather that you have stayed with him? Exclusively?'

Lauren blinked. What was that supposed to mean? 'Yes. Most certainly. Jordan and I—'

'Let me guess! You're getting married?'

Dr Mallon looked almost eager, and Lauren recoiled. 'No. Not at all. We're very happy as we are.'

His eagerness suddenly seeming to wane almost into sadness, Dr Mallon leaned forward, and faced her frankly.

'Are you? Are you sure, Lauren?'

Yes. Yes, she was very sure, and not a little angry. 'I am, absolutely! Why on earth do you ask?'

'I ask because . . . because after five years, I would like to see this man make a commitment to you. If he could. But I get the impression that he can't. Am I right about that, Lauren? Please correct me if I'm not.'

Mystified, and abruptly unnerved by the strange turn this meeting was taking, Lauren gazed at the man, and he gazed back.

'Can you tell me I'm wrong?'

She wished she could, if only to counter Dr Mallon's apparent clairvoyance. But: 'No. You're not wrong. It – it just isn't a problem for us, that's all.'

Dr Mallon removed his glasses and steepled his hands to the bridge of his large, uneven nose, letting them dangle between his fingers.

'Then, Lauren, it is about to become a problem. I'm very sorry to have to tell you this, but you have hepatitis.'

Hep – atitis? What was that? She'd read something about it in the papers, but it didn't register. She felt punched. Felt the room go ice-cold, her body freeze.

But it was January, and Dr Mallon's heating system wasn't up to much. In fact he couldn't be up to much himself, despite all he'd done for Caoimhe, if he thought she actually had some definite malady, as seemed to be the case. There was nothing wrong with her that a long, decent night's sleep wouldn't cure, maybe a few vitamins. Stock still, she sat staring at him, defiance instantly welling up.

'Dr Mallon, I think you must be mistaken. I'm simply a bit tired, that's all.'

'Yes. I know you are. It's called TATT – "tired all the time". Very common. Only, in your case, there's a reason for it. You have, according to these laboratory results, hepatitis.'

At first it still didn't register. And then, very gradually, it did. She felt a slightly manic inclination to laugh.

'Oh! I'm with you now! One of the guys in the office had hepatitis last summer, after he drank something weird on a trip to Rio! But I didn't think it was contagious, and anyway he's better now—'

As she spoke Lauren's mind zipped back to what Dr Mallon had said a minute ago, and giddy relief flowed through her veins. He'd effectively asked her whether she'd been sleeping with anyone else besides Jordan, which must mean he thought she'd slept with Paul from the office.

Except that he didn't know Paul, or know that he'd had hepatitis – what? A, B, C? Apparently there were different kinds, and Paul had had a mild one. Anyway, she had not slept with him, had any physical contact with him whatsoever. So there. Dr Mallon was mad.

He regarded her in silence, evidently waiting for the shock to sink in. But she was over it now. The diagnosis was wrong.

He sighed, stood up and plunged his hands into the pockets

of his fawn lambswool cardigan. 'Lauren, I know this is not what you came here expecting to hear. But the very sad news, which it is my duty to break to you, is that you have hepatitis C, a very serious form of this disease. It affects the liver, and I am going to have to refer you to a hepatologist. A specialist.'

She leaped up in turn, and heard her voice shrill as she faced him. 'But I can't have! You're crazy! How could I have got it? I haven't been to any of the countries where people get these things, I haven't been sleeping with anyone bar Jordan—'

'No. I've known you long enough to be sure you haven't. But – but Lauren, I strongly suspect that Jordan has been sleeping with someone besides you.'

Her head whirled, the room eddied around her.

'J – Jordan? But he—'

'He has a wife. Please tell me the truth, Lauren. He has, hasn't he?'

It seemed to take her an hour to find her voice. 'Y – yes, he has, but he doesn't sleep with her! They live separate lives, have done for years, only stay together for the sake of—'

'I know. The children. Do you happen to know when the last one was born?'

'It was born seven years ago, two years before I met him!' She knew she was shouting, but couldn't stop.

'And there have been no more since?'

'No! None!'

'You're totally sure?'

'Of course I am!'

Dr Mallon sighed. 'Then perhaps his wife had a transfusion for some other reason. I'm sorry to distress you, but I have to tell you that he's the only source of infection I've been able to come up with since getting these results. *You* haven't had a transfusion, and I think it might have been in the newspapers if Judge White had been involved in any accident that would have necessitated his having one.'

Oh. Could Dr Mallon know more about this man, this

9

relationship, than he'd been politely pretending? Defiantly, Lauren stared at him.

'Dr Mallon, you don't know everything about everyone in my life.'

'No. But I do keep my finger on my patients' pulses, in more ways than one. I've had mine on yours since the day you were born, even if I haven't always let you know it. You can be a little – tricky, sometimes.'

Fighting to steady herself, she sank abruptly back into her chair. 'Dr Mallon, I – I'm not quite sure what's going on here. I simply can't imagine how I could have hepatitis. But if you're sure I have, I – I'd like you to please explain it to me properly. What kind is it, what do I have to do to cure it?'

Sitting in turn, he spoke as if to a distressed, irrational child. 'It's hep C, which as I've told you affects the liver. We'll need further tests to determine how badly yours is damaged. If it's not too far gone, you may well stand a fighting chance. You may not even feel particularly unwell, could continue to work part time for some months yet—'

Part time? Some months? Lauren clutched at the edge of his desk, letting her hair swing over her face, feeling faint and sick.

'Would you like some water? Should I open the window?' Anxiously, gently, he reached his hand to her. Swaying slightly, she recoiled.

'No, I—' Her breath expired, she felt as if the doctor were holding a pillow over her face. After a few moments, she forced words out in a whisper.

'Are you trying to tell me that this – illness – can be – ultimately – *fatal*?'

He must have had to do this before, she realised, and that was what was enabling him to do it now as he looked briefly away, and then swung inexorably back.

'Lauren, life is ultimately fatal. It's merely a question of the speed at which it moves. Some people drive Ferraris, others drive Puntos—'

'And what,' she gasped, 'am I driving?'

'I'm afraid,' he said candidly, 'you are driving a Ferrari. At a hundred miles an hour. There is very little that can be done about hep C.'

'But – but drugs – surgery – surely—'

'Yes, well, interferon is a drug that can sometimes help, up to a point. But its side effects are daunting. The only surgical option would be a liver transplant, if one were available, but you'd be low-priority because the new liver would stand such a high chance of becoming infected in turn.'

He added something else, something sympathetic or soothing, but her mind squealed to a stop. No! No, no, *no*!

This couldn't be. It just could not be. This happened to other people. Not to thirty-two-year-old women who had it all, had a quality of life envied by everyone, boyfriends who adored them and gave them ruby bracelets for Christmas. Trips to New York, Singapore, Paris, loft apartments and Gucci watches, a BMW waiting outside the door to drive home in. Didn't Dr Mallon understand that Elliott Johnson had retired from Axis Advertising only three months ago, personally nominating Lauren Kilroy to partnership in his place, and that she, Lauren, was now earning £100k a year with senior responsibility for the Lola—

She slammed the flat of her hand down on the desk.

'OK. Just tell me. Who's the guy and where do I find him? What does he do to sort this out and what does it cost? I'm in the VHI on Plan E, insured to the hilt for whatever it takes.'

Dr Mallon surveyed her as if scrutinising a painting. Or a statue.

'Lauren. I don't think you're quite taking this in yet. I don't think you're hearing what I'm saying to you.'

Saiv Lovett rarely had to wrestle with her dogs, but she was almost yanked off her feet now as they strained at the leash, their paws scrabbling frantically on the frost as they came within sight of the house and began to bark. First Elmer the labrador, whose bark was big and deep, then Duster the Old English sheepdog, who sounded like a cannon and would put the heart sideways in anyone who didn't know him.

'Cut it out, lads! What's the matter with you?'

Their hysteria only intensified, the noise punched a hole in the black night, and Saiv felt the hackles rise on the back of her neck as they dragged her up the laneway so fast she had to use her heels for brakes. There must be someone at the house. Either someone they knew, or – a burglar? It was an old house, with rattling sash windows even a child could smash in a flash, and she still hadn't got round to putting in the alarm everyone said she should. She hated alarms, which were always going off by mistake and driving people – nuts.

But now, swinging open the heavy rusty gate, she wished she had some form of defence, because the dogs' bark was a lot worse than their bite, they were so sweet-natured they'd end up making a burglar a cup of tea. Could there really be one? Despite the clarity of the night she couldn't see a thing, the dogs were spinning round so madly her legs were entangled in their leashes and she yelped as the gate slammed back on her hand. With that, Elmer sprang free and hurled himself forward.

There was a terrified scream, and a thud.

Saiv ran forward, making a mental note to buy a mobile phone as well as alarm. In the dark, Elmer seemed to be devouring someone who was lying in the mud under him, writhing and shrieking, not realising that he had no intention of ripping their throat out. He was a huge labrador, but all things considered, Saiv thought a burly policeman would be better. If only she could call one. Tentatively, she peered at the roiling mass, unable to see where dog ended and human began.

'Elmer! Heel! Now!'

Reluctantly, Elmer paused in his ministrations while Duster bayed at the moon, yowling lunatically. Bending down, Saiv pushed Elmer off and peered at the body underneath, which to her surprise was wearing a short tight skirt, glossy tights and one dangling, muddy stiletto.

'Jesus! Lauren!'

No answer, only some noise between a sob and a grunt. Horrified, Saiv reached down, took Lauren by the hand and hauled her to her feet, astonishment swirling with a desperate desire to laugh. That would be a designer suit Lauren was wearing, presumably, but now it was only fit for the dustbin. Looking round, she spotted the other shoe lying on the gravel by the front steps, left Lauren tottering while she retrieved it, and handed it to her with a sheepish grin.

'Here. Sorry. They thought you were a burglar.'

When she found it, Lauren's voice was arctic. 'Call the fucking savages off and get me inside.'

'Yeah, OK. Calm down. If I'd known you were coming – what in God's name are you doing here anyway, out of a clear blue sky? It's nearly ten o'clock, I haven't seen you for months—?'

Lauren didn't answer, and Saiv glanced sidelong at her as they mounted the steps and she rummaged for her key. In the light of the full moon, lacing through the bare branches of an overhanging beech, Lauren's face was deathly pale. The dogs had really scared her, and Saiv felt contrite. But that was why Lauren always phoned well in advance of her rare visits, so that the dogs could be shut away and no damage would be done to her impeccable outfit, her immaculate person. Never, in the fourteen years they had known each other, had she ever arrived unannounced before.

Inside, the elderly house was at least warm and bright, if not tidy, and the dogs shot off to their bowls in the kitchen while Saiv led Lauren into the sitting room where she'd left the fire burning. Removing the fireguard, she stoked it, threw on a couple of logs and went to light various lamps around the room, sweep enough clutter off the sofa that Lauren could sit down.

First, she expected her to request a clothes brush so she could remove the mud from the back of her suit, pick her way through the mess to the bathroom to repair the hair which, undeniably, was now fifty quid's worth of coiffure down the tubes. Saiv never ceased to wonder at the amount of money Lauren spent on herself, even if it was necessary, as she maintained, for business purposes.

But Lauren didn't say anything about the state to which the dogs had reduced her clothes, didn't whip out comb or lipstick or anything; she merely sank down on the sofa, still ashen and trembling, and looked at Saiv with – oh, God – tears gleaming in her eyes. Guiltily, Saiv went to her and squeezed her shoulder.

'Sorry, Laurie. That was a bit of a wild welcome. Let me get you a glass of wine—?'

Another lengthy silence, slightly unnerving. And then Lauren spoke in a very low voice.

'I don't want wine. I want brandy. A large brandy.'

Saiv smiled at that. Lauren always assumed that everyone had a fully stocked drinks cabinet at all times, complete with ice bucket, cocktail shaker, coasters and swizzle sticks. But at least there was some brandy, Metaxa that someone had brought from Greece last summer . . . taking two glasses from the sideboard, Saiv dusted them surreptitiously on the sleeve of her sweater and filled them with a good inch of Metaxa apiece.

'Here. That'll put you right, and then you can tell me what you're doing out in the wilds of Meath in the dark of a winter's night . . . how are you, anyway?'

Lauren raised the glass, stared into it and then stared at Saiv.

'I'm dying.'

Saiv grinned. 'Well, I presume it's a hangover in the best possible taste! Long lunch, was it, a drop too much Dom Perignon?'

'No. I mean I really am dying, Saiv. Dying as in hospital. Funeral. Cemetery.'

Her voice was toneless, and Saiv pushed her sandy curls back from her face as she sank into an armchair by the fire and reached for her glasses. She didn't bother with them out walking, because she liked the surreal fuzz myopia lent to the trees and fields, but now she wanted to see her friend clearly. She'd often suspected that cocaine or other such substances percolated in the world of advertising, but – surely Lauren wasn't on some kind of trip? She looked ghastly, and sounded deranged.

Slugging a mouthful of brandy, she sat back and surveyed her.

'Laurie, I have to tell you, albeit not for the first time, that I haven't the remotest idea what you're talking about. But if it's a joke it's not funny. Please clarify.'

Sitting on the edge of the sofa, Lauren clasped one hand round the knees of her laddered tights, lifted her glass with the other and emptied it.

'I have hepatitis.'

Saiv gaped. 'What?'

'Hepatitis C. The fatal kind, Dr Mallon says. I left his surgery about two hours ago. Then I called Jordan, but his mobile was switched off. He's at the theatre. Then I thought I'd drive into town and drag him out of the theatre. And then I – I decided I wanted to see you instead. I know it's late and you always walk the dogs at night but I . . . I . . .'

Just in time, Saiv jumped out of her seat and flew to Lauren, got her arms around her as she burst into tears. Never, not since Isaac Hyland dumped her at the end of their first year in college, had she ever seen Lauren Kilroy shed a single tear.

'Oh, Laurie, oh, my God . . . I thought you were joking, or drunk or high or something . . . oh, *Jesus*—'

Individually, like icicles, tears fell and soaked into the smooth fabric of Lauren's skirt. And then she gasped, buried her face in Saiv's shoulder and sobbed uncontrollably, digging her scarlet fingernails into the back of her sweater.

'Oh, Saiv . . . wh . . . what am I . . . what am I going to *do*?'

Lauren felt so light, Saiv thought as she held her, it was like holding a handful of dust; but her heart was pounding as if it would explode. Her own heart was racing too, and she drew a deep breath, forced down a sharp rising spike of panic. Normally she was the messy one, as dishevelled and laid-back as Lauren was sleekly controlled; but under what Lauren called her 'hippy chaos' lay infinite reserves of calm, serenity and inner order.

She was going to need them all to deal with this.

For some time she continued to hold Lauren, stroking her dark glossy hair, rocking her like a mother while the tears cascaded into her shoulder, saying nothing, letting her body language do the talking. Out in the hall, she was distantly aware of the grandfather clock ticking quietly, rhythmically, until finally, with deep resonance, it struck the hour. Ten o'clock.

Ask not, she thought, ask not.

Eventually, much later it seemed, Lauren lifted her head, and Saiv slid a forefinger under her chin, raised it until their eyes were level.

'All right. Let me look at you.'

Like a child Lauren sat obediently still, allowing Saiv to inspect her in silence, and Saiv realised what she was waiting, yearning to hear: 'But Laurie, you look fine, there can't possibly be anything the matter with you.'

Saiv wished she could say it, longed for the airy nonchalance with which Laurie herself often told the odd little white lie. But it was one of the greatest differences between them: while Laurie bounced over any rocky terrain she encountered in life, Saiv was cursed with a need to dig deep into it, analyse it, get at the truth. And the truth now was that her friend, whom she had not seen for two if not three months, looked haggard, wretched, dreadful.

Maybe it was just the unprecedented mess her face was in, the blodged mascara and erased lipstick, foundation the tears had washed away? Saiv sat back, and considered.

'First, go to the bathroom. Wash your face, comb your hair and fix your make-up.'

'What?' Drawing back in turn, Lauren looked resistant; but her voice had no fight in it.

'Go on. There's a reason. I want to see how you look under normal circumstances.'

Getting to her feet seemed to take huge effort. But finally she made it, reached for her abandoned handbag and left the room without a word. Gazing after her, Saiv found that she was trembling.

Lauren? Kilroy? Hepatitis?

Oh, no. Not Lauren. Not the Lauren whose laughter rang bright as a bell at every party, the brazen brat who told porkies and got arrested for speeding, pulled deals and drank champagne, blew a hundred quid on a bottle of perfume and sported two elastic bands on the beaches of Barbados. Zing! Saiv could still hear the twang of the bikini strap the day Laurie had bought it, twirling it over her head as she grinned and swore Jordan would love it. Not that Lauren.

Not even the earlier Lauren, the one she'd met in the canteen queue at UCD one bright spring day in 1986, during the brief phase when Lauren was flirting with studying. Flirting with William Shakespeare, which gave her the chance to flirt with Isaac Hyland, and fall in love with him, and get her heart broken by him. There'd been a new Lauren after that, tougher, harder, shinier; but the early incarnation had been standing behind Saiv Lovett at the cash register, waiting to pay for her lunch, when the notoriously scatty Saiv Lovett had discovered she'd left her purse in her locker, and had no money to pay for her vegetarian pasta bake. Mortified mumblings had ensued, until suddenly Lauren intervened, stuck out her hand with a fiver in it.

'Oh, here, take this, you're holding everybody up!'

Gratefully Saiv had taken the money and been extricated from the acute embarrassment only a myopic, amnesiac nineteen-year-old could experience. It had seemed natural to head for the same table with their trays after that, and get talking about their so-called studies. Saiv's were genuine, she was immersed up to her neck in history, Italian and the philosophy in which, today, she held a doctorate. Lauren's were fake as a three-dollar bill, she merrily asserted; she was only doing English because Isaac was doing it, and French because she was determined to ransack the shops of Paris some day (an ambition she had spectacularly achieved), and philosophy because 'that's what everyone does in first year, isn't it? Boring old twaddle, but they have to pass you, because there's no such thing as right or wrong answers. I'll be dropping it next year.'

'Oh, but you can't' Saiv had protested earnestly, 'it's absolutely fascinating. It enables you to look at the world in a whole new way.'

Lauren had cocked her head and looked at her as if she were already eccentric, which most people now reckoned she actually was. 'Lose those vile specs' she'd said, 'and the world might look at *you* in a whole new way.' Saiv should have been offended, she supposed, but somehow she wasn't, because Lauren's laugh was so blithe and friendly. And Lauren had waved away the fiver, too, when she'd tried later to reimburse it. By the end of term they were inseparable friends, and people called them the odd couple.

Meanwhile, after attending innumerable rugby matches and by dint of cheering louder than anyone else, Lauren had finally caught the notice of Isaac Hyland, on whom she'd had her sights trained since day one. Nowadays Lauren was a striking, elegant woman – or had been until today – but then she'd simply been pretty, a healthy extroverted teenager, secretly conscious of not being so very much different to thousands of others. Bagging the beefy, cheery prop forward had been a huge notch in her belt, and she'd fallen into bed with him while she, Saiv, was still labouring under the illusion that relationships had something to do with Dante's poetry and sandalwood-scented candles.

'But' Saiv had breathed, aghast, 'you're surely not going to *sleep* with him?'

'I am' Lauren had replied, 'going to fuck him absolutely senseless. Cross-eyed. Up, down, back, forth and sideways.' And, while Saiv was still clutching her chest, she had. Four months later, after an incandescent romance, Isaac ditched her overnight, in a way that was the emotional equivalent of pushing her off the Cliffs of Moher. Saiv sometimes thought since then that, while Lauren's body had been found, her soul never had.

Of course that explained the year of frozen celibacy afterwards, all the guys to whom she'd subsequently given the heave-ho before they could give it to her, and finally, nine years later, the absolutely foul Jordan White. The Jordan White who, while Lauren was with Dr Mallon tonight, had been at the theatre. Saiv felt she could have written the script.

And now, what was Jordan White going to make of this drama? Hepatitis. . . . could Lauren possibly be exaggerating, was this another of those ploys for attention she was prone to make when she was feeling low or neglected? Not that Lauren ever admitted to feeling low; on the contrary, she became more glittery than ever. That bright glitter was probably what kept Jordan attracted to her, as well as the need Saiv suspected he could detect underneath, and the power it offered him.

God, she thought, I loathe that man. No wonder Laurie keeps us apart. But he loathes me too, because he knows I see right through him. I don't even need to put on my glasses to do that, any fool could see him for what he is. Anyone at all, except Lauren Kilroy who . . . if she really is ill, is going to need him. Need him badly, in a different way to the one he exploits, a way he never bargained for.

If he lets her down, I'll kill him. I will make his life a living hell, a misery from here to eternity.

But she can't be ill, can't be 'dying'! She must have got different kinds of hepatitis mixed up . . . when she comes back we're going to have to talk this through and iron it out. She's only thirty-two, the youngest partner at Axis Advertising and so proud of her promotion – God, who'd ever have thought anything would come of that? One day you're a penniless student, bored in a philosophy class, dreaming up a competition slogan to try and win a car. Next thing you're snapped up by the agency that's running the competition and you have a salary as well as a car, your studies are out the window. Your parents, who've slaved to put you through a year of college, are heart-broken – and then, barely tolerated. Your whole life is on fast-forward and you're making as much money as your own father. You're turning into a Barbie doll and starting to seriously believe that a soft drink or a new brand of tights can actually change people's lives. Worse, you're persuading *them* to believe it.

And yet, for some strange reason, you still stay sporadically in touch with your old pal, who's now a cranky spinster living with her dogs in a tatty farmhouse miles from 'civilisation', writing a book that's going to sell five copies. I stay in touch with you, too, because you make me laugh and take me out of myself, and I still owe you a fiver you won't take. But I've never really understood why you stay in touch with me, Laurie; we're different as chalk and cheese.

I'm just glad you chose to come to me tonight, instead of going to Jordan White, and I'm waiting intrigued to hear why you did it.

When Lauren came back into the room she looked, Saiv thought shocked, like some kind of medieval Japanese madam. The lines and layers of make-up she had applied merely heightened the porcelain paleness of her skin, the angularity of her bones; it was as if she were wearing a transparent mask. Yet she managed to smile, wryly.

'Well, you haven't changed! Why does everything in your bathroom have to be called Simple, or Gentle, or Eco-something? Where's the Issey Miyake perfume I gave you?'

Saiv swallowed, and waved a vague hand. She didn't wear perfume, and the gift had, um, travelled further afield. But then the gift she'd given Lauren in turn, a wonderful book called *Captain Corelli's Mandolin*, had probably been relocated too. Try as she might, she couldn't get Lauren to read anything more demanding than a designer label.

So why, every birthday, did they keep on giving each other things they'd rather have had themselves? With a jolt Saiv wondered; really it was a form of imperialism, as if each was trying to colonise the other. Next birthday, she thought guiltily, I'll give her something she – *next birthday*?

Getting up, she refuelled the fire, replenished the brandy and handed Lauren her refilled glass. 'Now. You still look awful, so get this into you and tell me what exactly in God's name is going on.'

Lauren twirled the brandy, took an old rug off the sofa and, to Saiv's surprise, draped it over her knees. Could she simply not bear to look at the ladder in her tights, or was she cold? With this fire blazing?

'I'm not sure whether I'm allowed to drink brandy.'

'What? Since when?'

'Since Dr Mallon told me tonight that my liver's fucked.'

Saiv clenched the stem of her glass, and forced her voice into big-sister mode.

'Lauren. Listen. I think there must be some kind of mix-up. I know you like your jar, but alcohol gives you cirrhosis, not hepatitis.'

'Yeah. Well. That's the zillion-dollar question, actually, Saiv. What, or who, has given me hepatitis?'

'What kind of hepatitis? A, B, C?' Even as she said it Saiv shuddered; the contaminated blood that had quite literally got into circulation gave people hep C, which was what had killed a woman called Bridget McColgan and been the subject of ongoing litigation ever since. But Lauren, to her knowledge, hadn't been anywhere near hospitals or transfusions.

'Hep C. The . . . the one that kills you.'

So. She hadn't been hearing things, the first time Lauren had said it. She had not imagined that this thin and tired, but otherwise healthy young woman, had gone out to her doctor tonight and received a death sentence.

'But – this is impossible. Out of the question. Where on earth would Dr Mallon think you had got it?'

Abruptly, Lauren put down her glass, leaned back and gazed at the ceiling. 'He seems to think I might have got it from Jordan.'

Jordan? But this was getting ludicrous, insane. Saiv had seen a photograph of a perfectly healthy Judge Jordan White in the *Irish Times* barely a week ago, alongside a report of a rape trial in which he had controversially insinuated that the victim's attack had been more to do with sex than violence. Jordan White was a fascist lunatic, but he was a lamentably healthy lunatic.

'Lauren . . . I have to say this is all terribly puzzling.'

Despite herself, Lauren laughed briefly. Saiv had such a sweet way of understating things. Her idea of drama was an abandoned puppy.

'It certainly is. I plan to cross-question Jordan about it as soon as I see him. Under oath.'

With a resounding clang, the penny dropped. So that was why Lauren had not gone straight to Jordan? Because, conceivably, *he was her killer*?!

But that still didn't explain . . . 'Laurie, how could Jordan have hepatitis C? He hasn't had any injury that you've told me about, no blood transfusion that I know of.'

'No.' Lauren exhaled with slow, infinite care. 'He hasn't had an injury or a transfusion. What Dr Mallon seems to think he might have had is sex with his wife. Or someone else.'

Saiv could not have been more stunned had the roof fallen in. Naïve as she notoriously was about men, and much as she disliked Jordan, even she didn't think he was total bastard enough to – dear God. After five *years* with Lauren? Five years of allegedly undying devoted love, frustrated only by noble duty to his innocent children?

Saiv looked at the poker by the fire and, as a pacifist, found herself surprised by her next thought: if this is true, I will take that red-hot poker and ram it up his arse until it emerges through his nose.

'But he – she – his wife – could she have had anything . . . ?' Saiv's mind was spinning, unable to envisage all that must be going through Lauren's.

'Dr Mallon mentioned something about a baby. That she might have had a baby, and been given blood.'

'But you said – you always said—'

'Yes. I said what Jordan said. That he wasn't sleeping with anyone else. He told me so five years ago, and I've had no reason to wonder since.'

'Oh, Lauren. This can't be right. There must be some other explanation.'

'Mmm. There's drugs. Contaminated needles. But I don't use them. Nor does Jordan. As a judge, he'd be ruined. That only leaves the wife, hooked on heroin, or a second mistress somewhere. Or, as Dr Mallon said, maybe a baby.'

Suddenly Lauren sighed, so sharply that Saiv thought she must be in pain. Well, of course she was in pain. Pain and shock and . . . this was too much for any one person to cope with, even for both of them between them. Lying back on the cushions, Lauren looked like an empty laundry bag. Only then did it hit Saiv: how *long*? If she's dying, how long has she got?

Jesus. I can't ask her that. But I have to know.

'Laurie, look. Dr Mallon is old and maybe getting a bit doddery. I think you should consider finding a second opinion. Did he even say anything about treatment?'

'He mentioned some drug, which apparently has hideous side effects and only works up to a point. He wants me to see a specialist to see whether it's worth trying. The specialist can also tell me, in passing, roughly how long I've got. Dr Mallon gave me a ballpark figure of at least a year. Hardly less, he said, likely more. The specialist can be more accurate.'

'Then you'd better . . . would you like me to call him and . . . arrange it for you?'

'*No!*' Without warning Lauren jumped to her feet and stood staring down at Saiv. 'Dr Mallon said he'd set up a consultation, but I don't want one! I don't want to be told the date of my death! I won't go to see him!'

'But – oh, God, Laurie—'

'Yeah. I'm in denial. That's what old man Mallon said. Perfectly normal, extremely common. Some people take weeks or months to get their heads around stuff like this. Some attack it like a space programme, others never deal with it at all. Well, I can't face it, OK? Call me chicken if you like, but – Saiv, I *can't*! Not now, not tonight, not until I've seen Jordan and—'

Her face crumpled, and at that moment her phone rang from her handbag. Saiv thought it sounded somehow menacing and macabre; also that it was probably Jordan.

She reached out and grabbed Lauren's arm to forestall her from answering it. 'Let it ring, Laurie. You can't speak to him now, not until – I think you should let me get you some hot tea and food and stay here for the night.'

Lauren never stayed at the dilapidated house, which was 'out in the sticks', had spiders and dodgy plumbing as well as two dogs and an unnerving quantity of books, which she always said made her feel as if she hadn't done her homework. But she couldn't drive home tonight, not in the state she was in, with two brandies under her belt to boot. As the phone kept ringing, Saiv reluctantly braced herself for a row.

But then Lauren bent down, reached into her bag and switched it off.

They stayed up all night, getting slowly, resolutely drunk, sometimes even laughing amidst the tears. Although their lives had diverged radically since their student days, and many of their attitudes too, somehow they still always connected when they saw each other, when Lauren deigned to visit the 'awful' farmhouse or Saiv, on her rare visits to town, dropped in to Lauren's metallic, minimalist apartment, each gasping and laughing at the exploits of the other. Saiv's latest 'exploit', taking a year off her university lecturing job to write a book, had sent Lauren spinning with horror, she just couldn't imagine how anyone could live on fresh air for a year.

'Or less than fifty grand anyway, minimum.'

Saiv had grinned at that. 'I don't even earn fifty grand when I'm working! But I'll get by . . . I have that bit of money from my parents.'

Her parents had died in an air crash while she was finishing her doctorate, and Saiv had shared a small legacy with her two brothers, and never boarded an aircraft since. Not even to visit her beloved Italy, where as a student she had spent a memorable summer au-pairing for an opera singer, nor to return to India where she had later back-packed for six months, taking odd jobs along the way before starting her 'proper' job. Lauren didn't think lecturing in philosophy was any kind of job, she thought it sounded like a total drag; and now writing a book was even worse. Yet she had offered to contribute to Saiv's project.

'I'll bail you out when you get stuck. Meanwhile, here's a few quid to get you started.'

On the spot, she'd reached for her chequebook and Saiv had had to do battle to persuade her she'd be fine, would survive without help, touching and generous as the offer was. Lauren had tossed her hair.

'You'll starve, you'll see. But give me a shout when you do and I'll fill your freezer full of smoked salmon. And foie gras!'

That was four months ago, and so far Saiv was staying financially afloat, because her needs had always been modest. Unlike Lauren, all she needed was 'a bed over her head', household basics and her ancient, rattling Citroën. Only after she'd left Lauren, that day back in August, had she realised that Lauren hadn't asked what the book was about. But still she felt a glow of tenderness for the support Lauren had offered; money was simply the medium in which she operated. Besides, it'd take a year and a day to explain a book about Jean-Jacques Rousseau to anyone; Lauren probably thought he was a French fashion designer. Saiv had laughed as she was leaving the apartment, and Lauren had kissed her on both cheeks as was her work-acquired habit.

'Madness, of course, but good luck with it. Who knows, maybe it'll be a smash hit and make a millionaire of you!'

'Ha! It's not that kind of book, Laurie. It'll end up in three university libraries under a pile of dust. But the important thing is, I want to write it and I'm going to write it.'

Lauren had cocked her head, gazed at her askance and whirled back to the 'real' world of advertising. Advertising had never convinced Saiv to buy anything in her life, and she was deeply suspect of the way it fed on people's insecurities, but she'd never said this to Lauren. Lauren had chosen it, and it was not in Saiv's nature to be judgemental.

Nor was it in her nature, now, to force Lauren into discussing her illness only hours after discovering it. They both needed time, she felt, to simply let it lie between them, untouched, until they could face it. But she was curious to know why Lauren had not rushed straight to Jordan, for either consolation or confrontation.

Lying back on the sofa, plucking at a thread of the old plaid rug that clashed comically with her sleek suit, Lauren intently examined a cobweb on a cornice.

'Because I . . . I just couldn't. I simply didn't know where to start, what to say.'

'But Laurie, he's going to have to know. Whether he's responsible or not, he's certainly involved. At the very least, even if he had nothing to do with – with infecting you – he's going to be devastated. He could put his arms around you and give you all sorts of comfort I can't.'

Lauren sighed. 'Yes. He could. But—'

'But what?'

'Oh, Saiv . . . it's so hard to explain. You've always had this dewy-eyed idea of romance. You think love is the kind of thing you give your dogs, hugs and cuddles and walkies in the woods . . . but that's not how Jordan sees it.'

'Then how does he see it?'

'He sees it as a – an upbeat kind of thing. He doesn't believe in people burdening each other with their problems, he thinks it's everyone's duty to be on good form, smiley, sociable, blithe spirit kind of thing.'

'Blithe – spirit? Laurie, you're terminally ill! Or so Dr Mallon thinks anyway, although we're going to have to see further about that. Anyway, Jordan could hardly expect you to come bouncing out of his surgery with a diagnosis like that – or did he think you'd just gone for a routine consultation?'

'No. I thought I had. But Jordan doesn't know I've been to

the doctor at all. I was to meet him later at the theatre and I didn't see any point in telling him that I had an appointment . . . I'd just been tired, that's all.'

'But if he knew you'd had a blood test, then surely he must know?'

'I didn't tell him about that either. It – it was trivial, at the time.'

Saiv was bewildered. What kind of relationship was Lauren in, exactly, after five years? One that had still got no further than dating, going to parties and social events? And sex . . . ? Silly as she knew she was, Saiv still clung to the belief that sex wasn't worth having without love. Which explained why she wasn't sleeping with anyone herself; but Lauren claimed to be wildly in love with Jordan. It hardly seemed possible, after all this time, that the feeling could not be mutual.

'Laurie, it sounds to me as if – as if there's been some kind of breakdown in communication here. You should have told Jordan all this, at the outset!'

'Should I? Do you think so, Saiv?'

Lauren looked genuinely curious, her green eyes bright with . . . what? Saiv couldn't make out what she was thinking.

'Of course you should. I'm not mad about Jordan White, as you know, but he is a human being and – and your lover! A lover implies love! And love implies concern . . . doesn't it?'

Lauren studied her brandy, contemplating its depths in silence for a few seconds. 'Yes. It does. It's just that Jordan has so much else to concern himself with . . . I don't tell him everything that's going on in my life and he doesn't tell me everything that's going on in his.'

You can say that again, Saiv thought with a rush of fury that went against her grain; it seems there might be a hell of a lot he doesn't tell you.

'Well, you're going to have to tell him now.'

'Oh, Saiv . . . how? How am I going to tell him this terrible thing? I know I have to do it, and I will, but *how*?'

There was a plea in her voice, almost a desperation, that Saiv found disturbing. Lauren was not a woman to ask for advice if she didn't need it, and rarely seemed to think she did. Saiv hesitated.

'Well, if I were you I'd just sit down with him, somewhere quiet where you won't be disturbed, and explain what has happened. He'll surely understand how upset you are, and angry too if you have reason to be angry. You must find out, Laurie, whether you have or not. If you haven't, then you're going to be relying on him a lot over the next . . . months or . . .'

Her voice trailed off, and they looked wretchedly at each other. Lauren's stare was so acute that Saiv flushed uncomfortably, and strove to divert the painful subject. Sitting there in her hand-knitted sweater and long blue skirt, curls askew and legs looped over the arm of the chair, she thought suddenly what an incongruous contrast she must make to her svelte, manicured friend, whom she only saw four or five times a year.

'Laurie. Tell me something? When you left Dr Mallon tonight, was I the first friend you thought of? Or did you contact any of the others first?' There were several, whom Saiv had met occasionally over the years, bright glamorous girlfriends like Lauren herself, who 'did' lunch with her, went to the races or shopping in London. She seemed to particularly recollect a financier called Adèle and a television producer called Gemma.

Lauren put down her glass and pondered the flames of the fire. 'Well . . . I did call Gemma, but her phone was busy, and then I remembered that she had a phone conference tonight with someone in America, it was scheduled late because of the time difference. I suppose I could have called Adèle, only she has her son to stay on weekends, was picking him up from her ex – sorry, Saiv. I guess this is a huge whammy to hit you with.'

Saiv felt mixed emotions. She was very glad Lauren had come to her, but hoped it wasn't just because good old Saiv Lovett would be sitting there with nothing else to do, nobody else to see. Which happened to be the case, but it was by choice; she cherished her solitude.

'Yes. It is a huge "whammy", as you call it. But I'm glad you came here, Laurie.'

She was very surprised when Lauren reached out, took her hand and squeezed it, briefly but hard. 'I am too, Saiv. You've always been the calmest, most restful person I know. And the most honest. I hesitated at first, because I knew you'd tell me what you thought rather than what I wanted to hear. But maybe it's what I need to hear. Gemma would probably have said oh, bullshit, you can't be sick and Jordan can't be involved, let's put on a video and cheer you up. Adèle might have even laughed it off, said antibiotics would fix me and it served me right for going to an antique like Dr Mallon. But that's what worries me – Dr Mallon might be old and shabby, but somehow I have faith in him. He saved Caoimhe at the speed of lightning, when speed was essential. I know it's years ago, but a lot of people still go to him. I'm kind of superstitious about him, have never dared change doctors.'

'Mmm. Well, you'll still need to see a specialist, as he says, but I think your instinct is probably right. If you believe in Dr Mallon, stick with him. How is Caoimhe, anyway?'

'She's fine. But she's in Vancouver with her family. This isn't the kind of news I want to break over the phone to her. Not until – not unless I have to. D'you mind playing sister to me in the meantime?'

'No, Laurie. Not at all. In the circumstances, it's an honour.'

Saiv half smiled, torn between fondness and anguish for her friend. In many ways Lauren was a flighty friend, capable of cancelling a date if something better came up, given to eternal chit-chat about nothing, starry-eyed over Jordan White and very, very conscious of clothes, cars, money, status and appearances. She could, Saiv thought wryly, be *deeply* shallow. And yet there was something so endearing about her, something in her fragility, her quest for acceptance, her mad generosity. Saiv thought she was a classic case of arrested development, a person who'd never grown another moral, intellectual or emotional inch after prematurely quitting college. But maybe, deep down, she felt college had been too much for her, too daunting? She certainly strove hard enough to pretend it had merely been a bore, and that her subsequent

career was far more rewarding. Which depended on your definition of rewarding. Not everyone wanted to live like a looper out
in the wilds of Meath, on herbal tea and bananas, with two dogs
and a lichen-green bath. Sometimes, Saiv Lovett had even been
known to talk to her plants.

From nowhere, the full weight of Lauren's news hit her
like a hammer, and she yearned to howl. She did *not want* this
giddy, gossipy, brass-brazen friend to die. This old friend,
who'd lent her a fiver when they'd been so young. Who was
yet so young, in ways that had nothing to do with Clarins or
Lancôme. Who'd yet to get her loan back, and had offered
another.

I'm going to do this, Saiv thought with clarity, and fierce
resolution. If Lauren is really ill, I'm going with her, wherever
she may be going, whatever strength it may take. It's going to be
horrible, heartbreaking and a huge responsibility, but I'm
choosing it. I'm doing it.

But . . . 'Laurie, it's way after four. You're exhausted. I
think—'

Lauren jumped upright, looking white, and appalled. 'Four!
Jesus! I've to get to the office – it's miles – my clothes—'

Rising, Saiv gathered up the glasses, cups and plates, noting
Lauren's virtually untouched supper. Not that she'd nibbled
more than half a sandwich herself, stifling nausea.

'Laurie, it's Friday night, or Saturday morning. You don't
have to go to work. Even if you did, I wouldn't let you. You're
staying here with me for the weekend.'

'But—'

'The whole weekend. We have a lot of thinking to do. Apart
from how to tackle Jordan, we need to figure out the best way to
handle your parents, if or when it has to be done. We also need
to suss out the medical situation – I have an encyclopaedia and
then we can look up the internet. And most of all we need to
think and talk about *you*.'

Lauren clutched the rug. 'Me? Oh, God, Saiv, I'm so busy! I
have a hundred and one things to do before I—'

'Yes. You have. And we need to sort out what they are. In order of priority. Our first is to get you some sleep.'

'But I'll never be able to sleep! I'm totally hyper! I can't!'

Quietly, Saiv looked at her. 'You can. The spare bed is soft and the pillow is filled with lavender, I'll put a hot-water bottle in and your body will take over from your mind.'

'Lavender! You're barking louder than your dogs! Besides, I haven't any—'

'I'll lend you some clothes. Not fashionable, but they will keep your notorious modesty intact. I know you're terrified of staying in this decrepit little dump, but I'll keep the dogs under control and the temperature at a hundred degrees, I'll make you hot nourishing meals and take you walking somewhere that will deeply soothe your spirit, if you'll let it. I will mother you like a baby, if you'll let me.'

Pleadingly, they looked at each other. Saiv saw that Lauren was within one step of bolting, but somehow she knew she wouldn't do it – because where, then, would she go? Back to her empty apartment? To the home of Jordan White, complete with wife and children? To the friends who wouldn't thank her for interrupting their beauty sleep, disrupting their day? To her all-consuming office, deserted for the weekend?

Lauren paused, handbag already in hand; and then she slumped back onto the sofa, looking unprecedentedly meek. Saiv saw what shock and stress had done to her, that she was on the verge of collapse. But still she rallied, just marginally, with a flicker of her nonchalant self.

'All right. Lock me up and throw away the key. Give me a flannel nightie and a mug of cocoa. I am resigning myself to a weekend from hell, and on your head be it.'

Saiv beamed and patted her hand, and silently wondered what in Christ's name you did next, when your dying friend put herself in your hands for a whole weekend. When she had no idea how many of them she might have to spare.

★　　★　　★

Awaking next morning with a jolt, Lauren sat up and groped for her watch, astonished to discover that it wasn't morning at all, it was nearly two o'clock. What?! How had she slept so long, so instantly and so deeply? She couldn't even remember falling asleep, had the impression that she had more fainted than fallen, virtually into a coma. And then it hit her.

Hep C. I crashed out after telling Saiv that I'm very sick, and then staying up all night talking about it. This isn't my bed, it's Saiv's and I'm here in her house in the middle of nowhere. I have hep C and Jerome Mallon says I got it from Jordan White.

Maybe. Or maybe not. Jerome Mallon is going on no information whatsoever, nothing more than some speculative hunch. There's no evidence. Which Jordan would say means there's no case.

God, please don't let me die. If you're up there, don't let any of this be real. Let it all be some crazy mistake. *Please*.

Is that by any miracle a bathrobe hanging on that hook, or is it a sheep? Saiv should be shot for the things she wears. I want my own robe. My turquoise silk. I want a hot shower with rivers of Lancôme milk, a torrent that will wash this nightmare out of my mind, out of every pore in my body. It isn't a nightmare. It's a hallucination. I'm temporarily insane. It's that ghastly brandy last night. I'll call Jordan as soon as I get my game together and everything will be fine. Just let me get up and check in that mirror that I'm still alive.

Yes. Well. If you could call a lemon alive, then that's what I am. My tan must be fading. Christmas in Florida seems like years ago. But it's only three weeks. I don't suppose Saiv has any fake tan? Ha! She's more likely to have carrigeen moss in her bathroom, or extract of managed-species seahorse. Thank God Jordan can't see the way I look right now. But I wish he was here. I love him and I miss him, I've never had any reason to doubt him. He'll take me in his arms and – where's my phone?

Rummaging in her bag, she dug it out and checked her messages. Two from Jordan: one last night, rather irritably wondering where she was, another this morning while she'd been sleeping, softer in tone. Why hadn't she turned up at the theatre, or called or been contactable? What was wrong? Please call him ASAP – well, not just this minute, because he was at home, but maybe early on Sunday when the children were being taken to church and it would be 'safe'. Instantly Lauren's heart lifted and she tucked tomorrow morning into her mind as something to look forward to, a bright window in the darkness that was pushing its way into her life. Jordan would repel it, sort out this whole bizarre thing. Feeling faintly surreal, she threw on the bathrobe and made her way out to the kitchen, where there were sounds and smells of life.

Saiv stood at the table, fully dressed, laying out the makings of brunch. Gingerly, they looked at each other, and Saiv smiled.

'Hi. So you got some sleep, finally?'

Lauren pushed her hair off her face and curled her toe, with a subconscious shiver, around a breadcrumb on the floor. The tiles felt gritty, and cold.

'Yeah. I guess I was shattered. Sorry for keeping you up so late.'

'Oh, it doesn't matter. I don't keep regular hours any more. Sometimes when I'm writing I hardly know what day of the week it is.'

'Oh . . . the book. How's it going?'

'So far so good. I got three hours done this morning.'

Saiv smiled again, and Lauren frowned. Saiv had been writing while she was sleeping? Was Saiv not supposed to be worrying, fretting, pacing round the kitchen table wondering how to make everything better? Well, she thought, that's lovely. Her dying friend is lying comatose in the bedroom, and she's working on her book as if nothing was wrong.

Nothing *is* wrong. I'll stay here until I get my head around all this, catch up on my sleep, and by Monday everything will be normal again. I won't even think about it in the meantime. Not any more than I can help. It would be stupid to get all revved up over something that's going to have a perfectly rational explanation, in the end.

Saiv seemed to be thinking the same thing, because she took bacon and sausages from under the grill and served them up with an aura of perfect calm, poured coffee and sat down to eat.

'Here, have some mushrooms with that. The toast's just popping. I hope you're hungry.'

Amazingly, Lauren found that she was hungry. And that was a good sign, wasn't it? If she was ill she wouldn't be able to look at this food, on its muddle of mismatched plates, and those horrible bowls of dog food lying on the floor. Uughh.

'Would you happen to have any orange juice?'

Saiv pushed a bowl of fresh fruit across the table. 'Sure. Help yourself. The squeezer's on the worktop – sorry, I forgot to do them.'

Lauren blinked. She never had to do this at home, because her fridge was always full of ready-squeezed cartons from a company which was amongst Axis's clients – oh!

'Lola!' she yelped.

'Who?'

'Lola! Cola! Our new client – I'd earmarked today to think about their campaign. It's airing in April, we're under pressure.'

'But' Saiv said, not unreasonably, 'today's Saturday. Don't you get weekends off?'

'Yes, but I don't take them! Not when – there are so many low-calorie products out there, we're going round the twist trying to come up with a new angle on this one.'

Saiv suppressed a grimace. Did it matter when the world got its new cola, would there be a revolution if the ads were not blaring by April? 'Laurie, for God's sake. You had an appalling shock last evening and your blood sugar's probably lower than the Atlantic at ebb tide. Eat your breakfast and forget your work.'

Lauren whipped round, orange in hand. 'Oh, I see. You get your work done, but mine doesn't matter, is that it?'

Stung, Saiv was about to retort when, in the nick of time, she copped on. Lauren was in shock. Wired to the moon. She might or might not want to talk about her diagnosis today, but meanwhile anything could trigger an explosion. This was going to be like having a stick of gelignite in the house for the weekend.

'Yes, of course it matters. Calm down. I just think you should give yourself a break, that's all, in the circumstances. Make some space for Lauren Kilroy.'

'Huh! You're always saying I make too much space for Lauren Kilroy, that I think too much about myself. As I recall, you once called me a – a narcissist.'

Oh, boy. 'Yes, well, I was only talking about your beauty routine then, the amount of time you spend at the hairdresser or gym or massage parlour. Or manicurist or sun salon. Anyway, today we're going to do something that will make you look and feel better than any of those things.'

Lauren whizzed the oranges vehemently, carried her glass of juice to the table and plonked it down, seating herself confrontationally. Well, Saiv thought, it's a good thing I didn't want any juice, isn't it?

'What are we going to do?'

'Go for a walk.'

'A *walk*?'

'Yes. A long one, up to the hill of Tara.'

'Saiv. Forget it. I don't do *walks*.'

Saiv savoured a mouthful of sausage, and poured more coffee. 'Well, you're doing one today. Exercise releases endorphins – natural hormones that will make you feel up, more able to cope with – this – uh – situation.'

As abruptly as if a switch had been clicked, Lauren beamed into her juice. 'Jordan called. Twice.'

'Oh. And?'

'And I've to call him back. Tomorrow morning, while his wife takes the kids to church. When he hears what's happened, I'm sure he'll ring Dr Mallon and get this whole mess sorted out.'

She nodded vigorously, and Saiv saw that she was waiting for some kind of agreement, affirmation. Instead, Saiv thought of a question: if Jordan and his wife lead separate lives, why does she have to be out of the house before Laurie can speak to him? After five years, doesn't Mrs White know her husband has a mistress, maybe even have a lover of her own?

With an effort, she laid her palm on Lauren's hand. 'Maybe he will. It could all be a – a mix-up at the lab, or a computer error. I wouldn't think Dr Mallon is great with computers, at his age?'

Lauren's face fell, unexpectedly and pitifully. 'Actually, Dr Mallon doesn't have a – a computer.'

Damn. Damn, damn, damn. 'Oh. Well, I'm sure the laboratory has one. They're all so short-staffed, it would hardly be surprising if there'd been a mistake. Alternatively, Dr Mallon might have confused your file with someone else's.'

Lauren considered. 'Yes. Everything's stuffed into this old filing cabinet, he could easily have taken out the wrong paperwork. Phew! What a relief, if he has!'

She smiled hugely and Saiv smiled with her, wincing inwardly. It wouldn't be great news all round, if someone else had what Lauren thought she had. But, if it came to that, she'd rather it wasn't Lauren. Selfish, shallow, maddeningly lovable Lauren.

Was that a terrible thing to think? To wish Lauren would get a reprieve while some arguably better person, maybe the parent of young children or some socially valuable contributor, was doomed instead? There were people out there, tons of them, who lived genuinely valuable lives, doing medical research or nursing, environmental studies, running animal sanctuaries, mothering families . . . while Lauren Kilroy went shopping and sang the praises of something called Lola Cola.

It was not a pretty picture, on the surface. But who was to say, to judge? Lauren could have potential, she could grow, maybe do wonderful things in the future. Or she could stay exactly as she was; funny, flippant, pretty and pointless as a butterfly. She might live to be a hundred without ever saying or doing one worthwhile thing.

Did butterflies have the same rights as every other species? Was just about anyone else not of more consequence than Lauren? Here was the woman who thought happiness came in a jar or a beribboned box, and didn't give two hoots whether anyone else got any or not. For sure, she must be heartily wishing that her diagnosis actually did belong to some unlucky other person, no matter who. She'd probably even pass it gladly over to Saiv Lovett, whose silly old philosophy book was never going to net her the kind of big bucks to be made out of fizzy cola.

'Saiv, are you listening to me?'

She shook her head. 'Sorry. What?'

'I said, d'you think old man Mallon really has flipped? Got me crossed with someone else?'

Her hand tautened on her coffee mug. 'It's a possibility, Laurie. I don't want to get your hopes up, but . . . why don't we just wait until Monday and then start seeing about a specialist, h'mm? I know you don't want to see one, but—'

'But Dr Mallon said I don't have to! Not yet, not until – unless – I start getting symptoms! He said this thing could lie dormant for years, if I have it at all – Saiv, specialists send you to hospitals for tests and all sorts of horrible stuff, then if there's bad news they give it to you and you've got to live with it, maybe for ages or maybe for – I don't want to know! Not as long as I don't have to!'

Saiv saw agitation swirling like a geyser, terror rising rapidly to Laurie's smooth, formerly unflappable surface. She felt a punch of pity, and sadness and not a little confusion.

'All right. Let's play it by ear. Have you any symptoms so far?'

'No, only being tired, which is hardly a big deal. I've been working too hard.'

Saiv thought of her Christmas holiday in Florida, but said nothing. Let her talk.

'And I'm a bit pale. Off-colour. But Dr Mallon said that might not be jaundice at all, I could just need a bit of iron. I'm going to start eating cabbage and every other gruesome thing that gives you iron. I'll be right as rain, you'll see.'

Childlike and defiant, Lauren's voice rose, and Saiv surprised herself by suddenly wanting to hug her. Take her on her knee, almost, and rock her and say there, there, everything's going to be fine. Don't cry, Laurie, don't cry.

I'm losing it, she thought. A shrink would say that I'm transferring from my four-legged friends to my two-legged. Say I should get a life and wean myself off a woman who, if the chips were down, would eat me for breakfast.

But she looks so lost.

Pushing back her chair, Saiv stood up. 'If you can be, Laurie, then you will be. Now, before it actually does rain, get dressed and get a move on. We're going to Tara.'

Lauren pouted, but then trotted obediently off to do as she was told, and Saiv saw that she was grateful for the distraction. Anything, even a walk, was better than ringing up Dr Mallon to confront him and find out that no, he hadn't made any mistake at all.

It was a volatile day, steel-grey showers mixed with sudden bursts of light and tentative rainbows, huge dark clouds and tiny white ones scudding over the plains of Meath, green and flat for miles in every direction. As they tramped through the wet grass, Lauren plunged her hands into the pockets of Saiv's borrowed raincoat and groaned.

'I don't see any flaming hill.'

'You will.'

'Yeah. When hell freezes over, which I already have.'

Turning, Saiv laughed at the spectacle Lauren presented; clumping along in boots that were too big for her, with a hood pulled down over her eyes against the rain and sulky rebellion in them, she looked like a disgruntled legionnaire on a forced march. Or a kid whose lollipop had been locked away pending better behaviour.

'Oh, look, Laurie . . . the rainbow, see it, arching up out of those trees? Isn't it gorgeous?'

'It's a fucking rainbow.'

'Oh, Laurie! Open your eyes!'

'Yeah, and when I shut them again it'll be gone. That's what rainbows do. Vanish. You're such a romantic . . . why can't we find a pub and get some Irish coffees or something? I'm not well. I'm getting pneumonia out here.'

'Well, that'll take your mind off your hep C.'

Lauren gasped, and Saiv did too, stunned by her insensitivity. And then, to her vast relief, Lauren laughed. Roared with laughter, and clasped her shoulder.

'Wow, you don't take any prisoners, do you? You should be in the army, Sergeant-Major Saiv Lovett. This philosophy stuff is just camouflage. You're tougher than your bloody boots.'

As she said it she looked frankly into Saiv's face, and they exploded in laughter again, as one. In that flash Saiv saw two things: the way to deal with Lauren's alleged illness, and her friend's hugely extenuating sense of humour. She'd never have expected anyone to laugh at such an awful joke. Yet Laurie was laughing loudly, even if there was a tinge of hysteria to it.

'What do I get at the end of this goddamn walk? A medal pinned to my chest?'

'Yes' Saiv retorted, 'if I can find your chest. It doesn't win any medals in itself, does it?'

Lauren grinned again. Her underwhelming dimensions had been a butt of jokes at college, until she'd bagged Isaac Hyland who said he much preferred slim women to bosomy ones like Saiv. So there, now! Even if Isaac had ditched her, he'd still fancied her. Just as Jordan White now fancied her.

'Saiv . . . what am I going to do about Jordan?'

Saiv walked on, thinking about it. Her instinct was that she was walking on eggshells . . . yet she wondered whether Lauren might respond better to more robust treatment. After all, she wasn't officially an invalid yet – and, even if she were, she didn't normally pull punches with people herself. She hadn't been made a partner in Axis for nothing.

'I think . . . I think you're going to tell him straight out what

Dr Mallon told you, and then take it from there. A lot will depend on his response.'

'Yeah, but . . . you don't really think he could have anything to do with it, do you?'

Lauren sounded tentative, eager to hear the rebuttal she would believe if Saiv offered it. It would be a comfort, and something to briefly hold onto. But then it could be cruelly snatched away, too, and Saiv wondered how she'd deal with that on top of everything else.

'I'm not sure, Laurie. You do have to remember that he is married. Whether you like it or not, he still is.'

'But only in name! What d'you mean?'

'I mean . . . that . . . if it's only in name, why can't you phone him right now, or whenever you like?'

Lauren stopped dead, and leaned up against a beech tree, pulled at its bark heedless of the nail polish which, Saiv noticed, was getting damaged.

'Because' she whispered as if they were actually there, 'of the children.'

'Oh, Laurie. I know this is a bad moment, but – you might save yourself a lot of grief if you'd only wake up and look around you. How many married men do you see leaving their wives, their comfortable homes? You read far more women's magazines than I do, you know the story-board. It rarely has a happy ending.'

'But Jordan *loves* me. That's the difference in our case.'

Oh, God in heaven! How could this smart, savvy, worldly-wise woman be so blind? If you applied one ounce of reason, of any rational process, it simply wasn't possible. Lauren was being deliberately obtuse, and it was making her exquisitely vulnerable.

But she was doing no more than millions of other women, reposing faith in a man to make her happy, rather than in herself. Saiv was firmly convinced that only one person could make anyone truly happy, and that person was yourself. A man could enhance happiness, extend and develop it, but he couldn't create it. Lauren wore Jordan on her arm like a diamond bracelet, and yet he was not fully part of her life, nor prepared to be. Could he possibly be just for show, the youngest appointee to the Criminal Court? Certainly they made a handsome couple, even if his appointment had been linked to influential political friendships, but did love come into the pretty picture at all?

Well, they would soon find out.

'Laurie, tell me something. What do you want out of this relationship, at the end of the day? What do you really want?'

Lauren flinched, but didn't look away. 'I just want Jordan,' she sighed eventually. 'Just Jordan.'

'Not a home with him, or children or grandchildren? No family gatherings or anything of that nature?'

'Saiv, I have my career! Even if I wanted any of that, I haven't time for it.'

'No. Not now, maybe. But if time were precious – as it may come to be – would you want to spend it exclusively with him? Or he with you? If Dr Mallon is right and you do have to – to pick certain priorities – would Jordan be top of your list?'

Lauren gazed down into the wet grass. And then up into the wet branches. And then peered into the distance.

'Ah! There's the hill! I can see Tara now! Come on, since you've dragged me all the way here we may as well climb it, and the view had better be as hot as you promised.'

Dropping the subject of Jordan like a hot coal, she marched on, and Saiv marched behind her, suddenly infuriated. Lauren had started the conversation, and now she was ending it the moment it no longer suited her to continue. What was the *point*? It was like trying to reason with a child. Or a butterfly, fluttering around the flame of a candle.

Walking swiftly ahead, propelled by rage, Lauren was seething too. What the hell, she asked herself, does Saiv Lovett know about anything? She hasn't even dated a man for years, she thinks it's better to moulder away than settle for anyone who isn't perfect. Maybe Jordan isn't perfect. But he's better than playing solitaire out in the sticks. And how dare she talk to me about children, *grand*children, when I might not be going to live long enough to have any? How dare she?

As for Jordan – is it his fault that he has a family and cares about it, won't just walk out and abandon anyone? He wouldn't be a judge if he had no morals, if he could do something like that. He is a good man and he worships me and, if by any long shot I do turn out to need nursing, he'll stand by me. He'll be there holding my hand every inch of the way through. Who'd do that for Saiv, huh, if she were ill? Who? She lives in a dream, knows nothing about the real world whatsoever. This Rousseau guy is the closest she's ever going to get to a man.

I'd pack up and leave right now, if I had anywhere else to go, anyone else to turn to. But as soon as I call Jordan tomorrow, I will have.

It was pouring rain and they were driven into a pub after all, a mercifully warm one with a coal fire, but not many customers at this early hour of the evening. Its quiet stretched between them like a bridge across a churning river.

Picking up her drink, Saiv put it down again and decided to be blunt. 'Look, Laurie. Either I can humour you because you're unwell, or I can talk straight and tell you what I think. Which do you want?'

Uncomfortably, Lauren studied a coaster. Bulmer's Cider. She wouldn't mind getting the account for that, and jazzing up their coasters. But you had to pitch before you could score.

'I don't honestly know, Saiv. I'm so mixed up. I thought I'd rather be with you than with Gemma or Adèle, but now I – I just don't know!'

'Well, decide.'

'God! D'you have to be so hard?'

'You can be much harder, when you want to be. You cancelled our last lunch date because Jordan suddenly had an hour to spare.'

'Yeah, well. I don't get to see him as often as I'd like, do I?'

'Do you get to see me as often as you'd like? H'mm? Can I just drop everything and drive into Dublin whenever it suits you?'

'No, but you're – different!'

'I'm not different. I'm your friend and I deserve respect if nothing else. My time is just as valuable as Jordan's. Or yours.'

She let that lie on the air between them, and Lauren mentally picked at it. What does she mean? That my time is more valuable, now, than I'd realised? That I have to choose how best to use it? She's a cruel, callous bitch.

And she might be right.

Oh, why are we fighting? I'm too tired. That walk was absolutely exhausting.

'OK. We'll book another restaurant and have lunch out soon. My treat. Anyway, we're here now, aren't we?'

'Yes. And since we don't often get much time together, I'd like it at least to be constructive. So answer my question.'

'Oh, all right! I suppose a professor of philosophy has to know something about something. You can give me – ideas, OK? But not advice or zany stuff I can't handle. Especially not to do with men, since you know nothing about them.'

'Ah. So you can be tough and nasty but I can't, is that it? Sorry. Either it cuts both ways, or neither.'

'Saiv, I don't know what's come over you. I've never heard you sound like this before. So – so *clinical*.'

'Well, maybe I've never had to be like this before. It isn't every day friends come to me with a sob story like yours. If you want the truth, I'm as confused as you. I don't know *what* line to take. One minute you're crying, then you're laughing, then you're sulking and taking offence. I know you're upset, but I can't spin round in circles with you. I have to get some kind of grip on this whole thing.'

'Yeah, well . . . I suppose somebody has. I won't take offence again if you'll promise to be gentle and consider my feelings.'

'I'll consider them. But only if you'll consider mine too. You don't have to be sick to be hurt, you know.'

In mutual silence, they gazed into their glasses. And then, slowly, Saiv smiled. 'You never had any feelings before, that I knew of.'

'No. Well, now I have, OK? Just for the moment. I'll be getting rid of them as soon as possible.' Lauren grinned in turn, and the tension between them relaxed as the barman came over, idly wiped the table and asked whether they'd like anything else. Wickedly, Lauren inspected his faded dishcloth, the pub's faded wooden floors and aura of rustic somnolence. 'Yes. We'd like two glasses of champagne, please. Chilled. Preferably Taittinger.'

The barman stood back in alarm, and Saiv laughed aloud. How could anyone resist a friend like this, who within twenty-four hours of her doctor's deathly diagnosis was ordering champagne? Lauren's expression was full of comic defiance; yet as the barman went off to fetch their bubbles Saiv wondered how long it could last. Sooner or later, reality was going to kick in, bursting Laurie's bubble with a bang.

The air must have done her good, Saiv thought with satisfaction as Lauren helped prepare supper – well, chopped a handful of herbs – chatting about things they had done or seen years before, apparently keen to put the current situation on hold for a few hours. Saiv didn't mind what she talked about so long as it distracted her, gave her breathing space. In between reminiscences she slipped out to the dogs, who were confined to the garden for the duration of Lauren's stay, with consoling tidbits. 'Don't worry' she promised them, 'it's not forever. She's only staying the weekend.' They looked at her accusingly, and scuffed at the earth, but there was nothing for them to wreck; it was more of a meadow than a garden.

When she came back indoors Lauren was tracing lines in the chopping board with the point of her knife, apparently lost in thought, one half of her hair tucked behind her ear and the other dangling across her cheek, softly illuminated under a pool of overhead light. I must, Saiv silently conceded, get stronger bulbs one of these days . . . meanwhile, let's light a few candles.

'D'you remember' Lauren asked without looking up, 'when I told you and my parents I was quitting college? Everyone went berserk.'

'Yes. With good reason. You'd have got your degree if you'd given yourself half a chance.'

'Nah. I wouldn't. I wasn't motivated enough.'

'You were just at an awkward stage, that's all. Not really sure what you wanted to do with your life.'

'Maybe not. But I knew quick enough once I got offered that job! Was that a lucky break or what?'

Chucking tomatoes into the blender and whizzing them, Saiv glanced at her. Did she sound as if she could be seeking some kind of approbation, confirmation that she'd made the right choice?

'I've never been sure. I suppose most people would say it was. Not many girls of barely twenty land jobs like that, with lots of money and travel. You've been to some fantastic places.'

'Mmm. Even if sometimes it's only airport, taxi, hotel, conference and back again, I have. But Eoin and Betty, or should I say Moan and Batty, still go on at me about it. You'd think I'd deserted a convent to run a brothel, to listen to them!'

'Well, maybe they wanted you to get more education than they'd had themselves.'

Lauren looked up. 'Live their lives through me, you mean? Hah. Tough luck. I reckon Dad was just jealous that I was earning more than him.'

'Could you blame him! You weren't even half his age. But he probably just wanted the best for you.'

'And what would that have been? I don't even know what I'd have done with a degree if I'd got it. And what's wrong with advertising, anyway? It's a sight more fun than doing eternal exams and burying myself in books the way you do – honestly, I don't know how you stand this life of yours!'

Vaguely, Lauren waved her knife around the room to illustrate Saiv's unspeakable life, and Saiv laughed.

'It suits me. But I know it wouldn't suit everyone.'

'You're telling me. Teaching the same stuff over and over, and now digging up this old French bloke who's been dead for donkey's years . . . who's going to read your book, when you ever finish it?'

'I'll finish it all right. But I haven't given the slightest thought to who'll read it. It's simply a challenge, to stretch my mind and see what new ideas I can come up with about someone already well documented. It makes me think and if it makes anyone else think that'll be a bonus. It's fun, in its way.'

'Fun?' Lauren looked aghast. 'Is that what you call fun? Will you even make a penny out of it?'

'That's not the point! If I'm lucky it might break even, pay for the time it's costing to write. But Lauren, money isn't everything. I know you think it is, but it isn't. Not to me, at any rate.'

'But what has anyone got without it? Money's very important. Especially to a woman. It buys independence and freedom and—'

'And you can become a slave to it.'

'Rubbish.'

'Oh, yeah? Could you live for one day without your expensive toys? Your swish car and clothes and apartment? Jewellery, cosmetics, furniture – I'll bet you spend more on your hairdresser in a week than I live on.'

Lauren grinned. 'And so what, if I do? I'll tell you straight, Saiv, a good cut and some highlights would take years off you. And a decent outfit or two, some shoes . . . do you even possess a pair of high-heels?'

'For what? Walking the dogs?'

'Answer my question. Do you?'

'Yes, I do, for your information. One pair, which I haven't worn since I can't remember when.'

'You need to get out more.'

'I get out every day.'

'Oh, Saiv!' Lauren laughed outright, and Saiv was glad, even if it was at her expense. 'Walking the dogs isn't *out*! You're hopeless!'

'What's hopeless about exercise and fresh air, beautiful scenery, living my own life in my own way? What, would you mind telling me, is so much better about dashing to an office every day, to be inspected by everyone to see whether you're keeping up to the cutting edge and wasting hours on petty politics, with a master plan for flogging cornflakes, or baked beans or plastic products to pollute the environment?'

'Uh, oh. Here we go. The eco-warrior rides into battle.'

'Don't get me started. At least I don't spend an hour stuck in traffic every morning, emitting mountains of carbon dioxide, and another hour again every evening . . . I'd go mad if I lived a life like yours.'

'Then we're quits. It's very kind of you to have me stay for the weekend, but frankly I won't be sorry to get back to my lovely apartment and wide-screen television – do you even have a television? Where is it?'

'It's in the living room. A small one. I hardly ever use it.'

'But surely you watch *Friends*, sometimes? Or *Coronation Street* or *Big Brother*, *Ally McBeal*?'

'I don't even know what those things are, apart from *Coronation Street* which I've accidentally seen once or twice in the homes of people who hadn't the manners to turn off their televisions when they had visitors.'

'Ooh! Aren't we prim!'

Saiv stirred the pasta and smiled into it. 'If you say so. I just prefer reading to television, that's all. It's not against the law.'

'But don't you ever want a change of scenery? Wouldn't you love a night out – dinner at a decent restaurant, drinks and dancing at a nightclub?'

'I'd sooner slash my wrists than go to a nightclub. Remember you once dragged me to some awful dive when we were students, and I hated it even then?'

'I remember. The Pink Elephant. You slipped off home after barely an hour and left me to—'

'Carry on snogging some total stranger! My idiot parents brought me up to think sex came after you got to know someone, not before, and I've never been able to rid myself of the quaint idea since. But you were never burdened with that belief, were you?'

'What's that supposed to mean?'

'Oh, here, open that bottle of wine and admit it – you were sleeping with Jordan White before you even knew his second name.'

Damn! Cursing herself for her stupidity, Saiv could have bitten her tongue off. Jordan was the very last subject she'd wanted to raise.

'Yes, well, it was instant chemistry. His career was taking off like a rocket, the same as mine, we had a lot in common.'

'Right. You were two brash, shameless, self-seeking, go-getting—'

Lauren lifted the corkscrew aloft. 'Adventurers! We just wanted an adventure, at first . . . d'you remember he was a barrister then, all over the shop with that libel case of his?'

Saiv remembered, and thought she probably wasn't the only one who did. Jordan had been the prosecuting barrister in a libel case against a newspaper, netting unprecedented damages for his client and causing a furore over freedom of the press. Impressed by his hard-hitting case, the judge had awarded a quarter of a million against the *Clarion*, which continued to hotly insist that every word it printed had been justified. Whereupon the judge, who as it happened was a friend of Jordan's father, had delivered a scathing lecture about the iniquity of the downmarket tabloid media. Next day, neither the judge nor Jordan White had been popular in the downmarket tabloid media.

'I remember! He was a rising star and you just couldn't resist hitching your wagon to glamour boy, could you?'

'*Au contraire*. He hitched his to mine.'

Well – whatever. Saiv couldn't deny that Lauren and Jordan

were well suited to each other. Or had been, up to now, in many respects. For Laurie's sake she'd tried to like him, and even after she'd failed she'd never openly criticised him. There was nothing to be gained by alienating her friend, who'd been happy with Jordan since. Saiv could never have managed such a relationship herself, with its restraints and clandestine parameters, but it seemed to suit Lauren's busy lifestyle. She'd never appeared to want any more than Jordan could offer.

They looked at each other, and then Lauren looked away, began busily pouring wine.

'Tell me where you keep your plates and I'll set the table.'

Saiv told her, and as she put them out she began to talk about her sister Caoimhe, whom she missed since Caoimhe had married a Canadian two years ago and moved to Vancouver.

'Every woman should have a sister, Saiv, don't you think?'

'Well, yes, if possible, it would be nice! I never had any . . . is that why I put up with you, I wonder, brazen hussy and all as you are?'

She thought Lauren would laugh. Instead she nodded, quite firmly.

'It must be. I can't imagine why else you would.'

Serving up the pasta, Saiv was astounded.

Next morning, after a fitful sleep far shallower than the previous night's, Lauren awoke agitated and perspiring, feeling as if her limbs were moulded into Saiv's soft, sagging mattress.

Jesus, she thought, would the woman ever go into Habitat and buy herself a decent bed. I'm not staying here again tonight. I have to get home and sort out my clothes for work tomorrow. I have to get the car washed and work on Lola, I have to do something with my hair and—

I have to call Jordan.

Hauling herself upright, she looked around her in the curtained gloom. It was a cold Sunday morning, made for sleeping late, but already she could hear the dogs running around outside, and the steady click of Saiv's keyboard from somewhere inside. *How* could Saiv be writing, she wondered again, how can she be doing this to me? *I'm* the one in need of attention, not Jean-Jacques bloody Rousseau.

Unless this is her way of coping? Is she trying to pretend nothing's happening, nothing's wrong? It's not like Saiv to hide her head in the sand. But maybe writing clears her mind or something. Either that, or – or her work must be as important to her as mine is to me. But I get paid properly for mine, I have something to show for it! She's mad. Totally off her trolley.

I'll have a shower, and then I'll call Jordan. I can't think any further about any of this until I do that. He'll put my mind at rest, and then maybe we'll even get together this evening if he can get away for an hour. He could come over to the apartment and . . . God, I need a hug. I really, really need to see him, be with him.

Shivering, she got up, draped herself in the shaggy bathrobe and made her way out to the bathroom; Saiv's accommodation did not stretch to guest showers en suite. When she got there the water was barely lukewarm, depleted from Saiv's own shower earlier, she supposed, and she tripped over a couple of books lying open on the floor. Picking one up, she peered mystified at its title: *Zen And The Art Of Motorcycle Maintenance*. Was Saiv planning to buy a motorbike? The ludicrous vision made her grin in spite of everything, and she flicked through the pages at random: but it seemed to have nothing to do with motorbikes at all. Instead there was stuff about some guy called Phaedrus, who from what little she could make out had completely lost his marbles.

Either that, or Saiv had lost hers. The other book was even weirder, written by some Greek who must be dead at least a zillion years, and she snapped it shut with defeated impatience. God, these bookworms were for the birds! It would answer Saiv better to go out and buy a whole new stack of big, thick, fluffy towels, and get this bathroom done over while she was at it. It looked like a cross between a warehouse and a library. Picking her way through the clutter, Lauren took a tepid shower, brushed her teeth and hair, and made her way back to the bedroom.

Now? Should she call Jordan now, before she got dressed? Have breakfast first? Talk to Saiv, see what strategy she recommended?

No. Saiv doesn't like Jordan, does she? She can't stand him, she'll only tell me to be firm with him and . . . I have to do this on my own. Be decisive, and get it over with. I'm going to feel a million miles better after I've done it. Why am I even hesitating? It's all a stupid mistake and Jordan will know that straight away. He'll tackle Dr Mallon and straighten everything out.

Not allowing herself to think further, she clenched her fist, unclenched it and sat down on the bed, plunged her hand into her bag where her mobile lay waiting. Drawing a deep breath, she took it out and stabbed in the number. After only two rings, it was answered.

'Jordan?'

'At last! Lauren, I've been worried sick! Where are you?'

'I'm in Meath.'

'Where?'

'Meath. At Saiv's house. I'm staying with her for the weekend.'

'But darling, why didn't you tell me? What happened on Friday night? I waited for you at the theatre, missed the first act—'

Exhaling, Lauren sat back on the bed, a smile of relief spreading across her face. Jordan's voice sounded so warm, so concerned, exactly what she wanted and needed to hear. Needed badly.

'I couldn't make it. Something came up. It's so silly, completely outlandish really, but I—'

Waahh! On the other end of the line, there was a piercing wail, and the slam of a door. And then a woman's voice, loud and distinct.

'Jordan! We had to leave, right in the middle of mass! I can't get her to stop crying!'

Another wail, high-pitched and prolonged. The baby screamed again, and Lauren leaped back, dropping the phone as if electrocuted.

FEBRUARY

'Oh, Laurie, come on. Please?'

'No. I'm sorry, Saiv. I just can't spare the time.'

'Laurie, you must! You've been working yourself to the bone when you should be on sick leave—'

'I'm not sick. I feel perfectly OK.'

'*Lauren*—'

'Maybe next week, then, or the weekend after. I'll try to make a window.'

Exasperated, Saiv steeled herself. She was not letting Laurie win this battle again. Not after a whole month.

'Look, Laurie. If you don't come out here then I am coming in there. To Dublin, to your apartment. Now. Your choice.'

There was a lengthy and somehow peevish silence. But Saiv Lovett was famous for keeping her word, and Lauren Kilroy knew it.

'Oh . . . all right, if you must. But I'll be busy, you'll have to amuse yourself. I can't cook either, as you know, so don't expect Mom's apple pie. We'll have to eat out.'

'We'll eat out tonight, if you like, and then I'll cook tomorrow. I'll stop off at Smyth's farm and pick up some organic produce.'

'Oh, Christ! Not rabbit food!'

Saiv nodded adamantly into the phone. 'Yes. Maybe even a rabbit. I'm on my way.'

Loud sigh. 'Well, if you must. Don't say you weren't warned.'

'I'll bring my suit of armour. See you round seven.'

Hanging up, Saiv whistled low in satisfaction. At least when she saw Lauren she'd be able to assess the state of her, both physically and emotionally. Right now, she thought she was still actually reeling more from the blow of discovering Jordan's new daughter than the blow of Dr Mallon's bombshell, but how she was coping with both was beyond her. Whether she liked it or not, she was having company for the weekend. Much as Saiv detested Dublin, she couldn't stand the suspense of not seeing Lauren any longer, her nerves were on the verge of snapping. And, if there were any legal way of doing it, she would bring a shotgun to Dublin with her, for the express purpose of blowing Judge Jordan White's head off from close range.

Of course it was inevitable. Of course the bastard had been two-timing both his wife and his mistress. Naïve as she was, Saiv had not been remotely surprised to discover that. Her shock had been entirely attributable to the look on Lauren's face when she came into the kitchen, that Sunday four weeks ago; it was the look of someone caught in an explosion, someone who had stepped on a landmine and instantaneously lost a limb. Barely vertical, Lauren had clutched a chair, swayed, and sunk speechless into her friend's arms.

But even had she been able to speak, it would not have been necessary. Saiv had guessed immediately what had happened, in outline if not in detail: either Jordan hadn't wanted to hear that his mistress was ill, or he had in some way caused her illness. Or both. As it turned out, Jordan had got a screaming shock in turn, when Lauren had finally found the strength to confront him a week later, and tell him about her hepatitis. Yes, he admitted under pressure, the screaming baby had been his, his wife had been planning to visit its grandmother after church and then been forced by its cries to change her mind, to bring it home. The baby, whose name was Darina, had been the product of a one-night stand, he asserted; he and his wife had just had a little too much to drink one night, that was all.

Saiv had gasped on hearing that. Surely a judge didn't behave like a drunken teenager? It was probably another lie, but she'd seen that Lauren was clutching at it, yearning to believe it. In any event, Jordan had nearly fainted on hearing Dr Mallon's theory, which was that Lauren's hepatitis could have been transmitted through him, via a contaminated transfusion given his wife during childbirth. Yes, his wife had been given blood as a matter of fact, but—!

Then, Lauren had told him, he'd be well advised to get his wife to a doctor. Clearly she was infected too, and didn't yet know. He might have hep C himself, or be a carrier – must be a carrier, even though science didn't seem to be entirely sure how this whole thing worked. At any rate, he was in major trouble, and had better get his ass in gear pronto. Yelping in panic, beside himself with horror, Jordan had gone racing off home, and that was the last Lauren had seen of him. Not one call, since then, not one word of apology, or concern, or comfort. Not one whisper.

As she marched around the house throwing weekend supplies into a holdall, Saiv fumed, thinking that she had a damn good mind to blow the whistle on Jordan White, leak the story to a newspaper or radio station. The still-smarting *Clarion*, she knew for sure, would be thrilled to get its hands on it. Judge White in love triangle, mistress contracts hepatitis! Wife gives birth to secret baby! Wow. That would blow him out of the water. Saiv could never remember feeling such a thirst for vengeance in her life. And she'd do it, in a flash, if only Lauren would let her.

But Lauren wouldn't let her. Lauren had locked the door on the whole affair and thrown away the key, gone off to grieve in private, mourn the betrayal of five years of her life and love. Refusing Saiv's pleas to come and spend another weekend in the healing quiet of Meath, she'd said she needed time on her own, and was way too busy besides, which Saiv took to mean that she was throwing herself into her work when she wasn't well, should be resting and recuperating from two mortal blows. Instead she was working like a demon, telling none of her colleagues anything about either one, running ragged from enormities that simply seemed outside her powers of comprehension. When Saiv suggested getting mad, getting even with Jordan, it was as if roles were reversed; normally she was the calm one and Lauren was the livewire, but now, when she was incandescent, Lauren was provocatively, infuriatingly silent. Saiv still hadn't given up her campaign for justice, but she thought it might be going to take time, because, against all the cosmically long odds, Lauren showed signs of still being a little bit in love with the gruesome man. Just a little bit, a lethal bit.

God in heaven! Hepatitis was nothing at all compared to the illness, the incurable lunacy of love, if Lauren could still cling to it under these damning, incontrovertible circumstances. Was she crazy, was she actually certifiable? Saiv thought she must be, and resolved to have another go at her now, this weekend at her apartment. No doubt Jordan White already had a fair helping of punishment on his plate, with his wife under a sudden potential death sentence, his own status in question and his love affair in smithereens; but what Saiv could not forgive was his lack of remorse, his failure to tell Lauren he was sorry or find out how she was doing.

That, she thought seething, is absolutely beyond the bounds of decency, way outside the pale. That is what is driving me to desperation, and to Dublin. I hate going there, hate these sorties out into the bright lights and the teeming city . . . into reality. But if it's the only way of seeing Laurie and making her see sense, then that's where I'm going. I've never got involved in a fight in my life, but by Christ my knuckles are bared now. That man is not getting away with this and that is all about it.

Saiv was stunned when, two hours later, she arrived at Lauren's apartment in Temple Bar. A vast penthouse, coolly decorated in tones of white and ivory, it seemed to float around Lauren, mocking her pallor, her almost palpable fragility. In the month since they'd seen each other, someone had carved out Lauren's features, chipped into her bones with a chisel . . . apart from crucifying her emotionally, Jordan had also deflected her from her original intention of challenging Dr Mallon's diagnosis. It had been a wavering intention to begin with, because she dreaded confirmation, and now she said she couldn't face doing it. She'd see him later, and then a specialist if warranted. Looking at her, Saiv thought it was warranted, and rage fought pain in her heart. All of this, she thought, *all* of it, is Jordan White's handiwork.

'Hi' Lauren said, tossing back her hair, still wearing the suit in which she'd arrived from work. 'How are you?'

How was *she*? Lauren always politely asked, but rarely waited for the answer, dying to gallop on with news of her own. Saiv felt thrown, lost for words.

'Well? Cat got our tongue? How's the opus magnum coming on?'

Opus? So, Lauren did remember something from college, after all? Saiv reflected. 'I'm a bit bogged down at the moment. But writing a book is a marathon. I'm nowhere coming in behind the leaders yet, but there's still a long way to go.'

'Uh-huh. And how's the other book, the one you were reading? *Zen's Motorbike*?'

'Zen's what? Oh! That's just fireside philosophy, the kind of thing people read in the bathroom.'

'Saiv, do yourself a favour. People read the sports section in the bathroom. Someone should anchor you to real life with a rope. Anyway, I hope you've brought your glad rags, such as they are. I've booked Bruno's.'

'Oh. Trendy?'

Lauren waggled the side of her hand, her sleeve swimming on her wrist. 'So-so. But he's a doll. French. You'll love him.'

'I'd rather he aspired to love me, and all his customers.'

'Customers? Saiv, they're clients! Don't you dare use that word in public or I'll kill you. Now, sit down and let me get you a drink, since you've come all this way. Dom P OK?'

Nodding, Saiv waited while Lauren popped a cork in her brushed-steel kitchen and emerged carrying two crystal flutes.

'There now. France's finest. Drink up.'

Normally indifferent to whether she drank from a mug or a tumbler, Saiv couldn't ignore the beauty of the twinkling glass in her hand, refracting points of light around small, lazily rising bubbles. This, undeniably, was what was meant by quality, craftsmanship in a material item; the crystal was spliced into perfect little diamonds, each one faceted so that there was always a brilliant point. The glass felt weighty, assertive and very classy. And the champagne tasted wonderful in it, so good she wanted to savour it slowly, in tiny sips. Lifting it, she raised it to Lauren.

'Here's to you, Lauren Kilroy. I have to admit you have exquisite taste.'

In everything, that is, except men. What on earth does a woman like you, a *lady*, see in a man, a *creep* like Jordan White? Everything in this apartment is so carefully chosen, so top of the range, how could your taste have lapsed so abysmally in him? Was it his social status? Did the fact of his being a barrister actually cut ice with you, did you get hooked when he became a judge? Could you be so impressionable, so easily bought?

If that's the case, then you're an idiot. A simple, feather-headed little fool. We have nothing in common, and it's a mystery what I'm doing here, what we could possibly see in each other . . . except that, for some inexplicable reason, I love you as much for your weaknesses as for your strengths. On the plus side, you're bright, dynamic, hard-working and fun; on the minus side you're a snob, intellectually lazy and totally myopic about men. In business you're as steely as your kitchen, but in person you're just a kid trying to impress the grown-ups. You know I hate socialising and yet you've chosen this fashionable restaurant tonight, which I'm sure I'm going to loathe; I could kill you for doing it and yet you'll try to rip the bill out of my grasp when it comes, refuse to hear of letting me pay my own way. Which I can do, you know, and would like to do. It'd be a pleasure to treat you if only you'd ever let me.

Why can't you ever relax, and stop trying to impress everyone? Hey? Why?

And why can't you choose your men the way you choose your crystal, not just for looks but for solidity, finesse, character? Jordan White is just a million quid's worth of Woolworth's, a shiny bauble that snaps under the slightest pressure. Just a cheap bauble, that has cost you so dearly. It breaks my heart to see you looking like this, and if I ever get the chance I will kill him. Or worse.

'So we decided that billboards might work after all . . .'

With a jolt, Saiv snapped out of her reverie, realising with a flash of frustration that Lauren was actually talking about work, as if it mattered. How could it, to a woman ticking off her time in weeks and months, maybe a year or two at most? What did she want, her epitaph up on a *billboard*?

'Uh-huh. And what else have you been up to lately?'

Twirling her drink, barely touching it, Lauren reflected. 'Well, I went to London on Tuesday, just for the day, we did a presentation for the Arcos account—'

'I mean, apart from work! Don't you have a life?'

Even as she said it Saiv wondered; was this Lauren's way of keeping everything at arm's length, at bay? Did she think that, by acting normally, she could stay normal?

'Of course I have – a more exciting one than yours, too! Come on, let's go round to Bruno's and get you into circulation. It's always crammed on weekends.' Abandoning her drink, she got up and fetched their coats, and Saiv followed her out with trepidation, wondering whether the entire night was going to be filled with trivia, a busy exercise in self-deception.

The restaurant was indeed packed, and Lauren was seized by a beaming Frenchman the moment she walked into it, air-kissed on both cheeks, showered with compliments on how well she looked. Almost everyone was dressed in black, and Saiv shivered, knowing it was de rigueur but thinking it looked funereal. Without any thought of being non-conformist, she'd chosen to wear pink herself, because it was a wintry night and pink made her feel warmer. With a small smile, she wondered now whether it might almost cause a scandal, whether Lauren's unfashionable friend would be the talk of every table.

Their meal took ages to get under way, because Lauren was distracted several times by people who came over to say hello, and twice she got up to visit others in turn. Starving, Saiv eventually begged her to at least look at the menu.

'Oh, why don't you order for me . . . I'll just have soup and a salad.'

Was that all? 'OK. And to drink?'

'Mineral water. But you have wine if you like.'

With an airy smile she vanished over to the far side of the room, leaving Saiv to mull on whether she just wasn't hungry, or was losing her appetite, or watching her health. When she comes back, she thought, I'll probe a bit, try to find out.

But when Lauren returned she plunged into gossip about the acquaintances around her, relating anecdotes that were amusing but maddeningly irrelevant: what did it *matter* that the man on table five was sleeping with the woman on table two, unknown to either of their partners? Was it not, in fact, slightly sad and distasteful? Battling impatience, Saiv thought that this kind of thing was one of the many reasons why she wasn't married.

The world was full of people like these, who found the concept of fidelity as funny as it was unsophisticated, who blithely embarked on affairs without either the sensitivity or the intelligence to foresee the pain they were inevitably going to suffer and to cause. And what was the point of a partner who wasn't, as Lauren might say, a 'designer original', exclusive to one special person alone? I might be a country hick, Saiv supposed, but if this is city life they can keep it. It all sounds so *brittle*.

But finally, after much fluttering and waving, Lauren settled down, and Saiv looked frankly at her.

'So, tell me how you've been. Really been . . . I could murder Jordan White for what he did to you – does he know for sure, now, he's a carrier?'

She nearly fell off her chair when Lauren's face lit up.

'Actually, I was wondering whether to tell you . . . you're so weird about these things. Jordan called me this evening just before you arrived.'

Saiv didn't know whether to be relieved or horrified. For Laurie's sake, if it would make her happy – but what did the man want?

'Did he? About what?'

'Well, about us, obviously! He said he was sorry for not doing it sooner, but he's had things to take care of . . . he's missing me.'

'I dare say he is. It must be rough out there in the jungle.'

'Oh, Saiv! I know he behaved badly, but he'd had a nasty shock. It's just taken him a bit of time to – to adjust, that's all.'

'Laurie, the man gave you hepatitis C and then ran a mile when he was accused of doing it, on top of fathering a child with his allegedly estranged wife. To call that behaving badly is putting it very mildly.'

Lauren fiddled with her fork. 'Yes, well . . . he says he's very sorry and he wants to talk about it.'

'What? You – you're not going to see him, surely?'

'Yes. I am. I know you won't understand this, but part of me still loves part of him. I miss him terribly and I – I think he deserves a chance to put his side of the story.'

'*What* side? Do the facts not speak for themselves?'

'Oh . . . you could look at it like that. But I don't. I want to see him and sit down calmly and—'

'And try to patch things over? Get *back* with him? Is that what you mean?'

'I don't know. All I know is that we had a row, and I can't bear to end our five years together this way. Even if – if it's not possible for us to go on, I'd at least like us to part on friendly, civilised terms.'

Saiv gaped. 'Lauren, you are a front-line volunteer for unhappiness. This man has you hypnotised in some way. I think you need to see a – a psychiatrist.'

'Oh, Saiv, don't start! Jordan made me very happy for five years and—'

'Did he? Did he really? Can you swear with your hand on your heart that he truly gave you everything you wanted, cherished you, always put you before himself?'

'Yes, as much as anyone could, he did.'

'And you never wanted anything more from him? Commitment, or the comfort of being with him whenever you wanted to be, or the right to play an active part in his life?'

'I did play an active part in it. He told me I was the most important person in his whole world.'

'Except for the children. And the on-off wife.'

'Saiv, children are different! He's responsible for them.'

'And for your illness.'

Lauren drew back, and looked distressed. 'Maybe. But if I am seriously ill, then I don't want to – to be ill on my own. This is a terrible thing for all three of us – me, him and his wife. If she's ill too, I want him to look after me the same way he'll look after her.'

'Do you think he has that much devotion to go round?'

'I hope he has. Anyway, there's only one way to find out. I told him he could come to my apartment next Wednesday night, and we'll talk about it. After all, he didn't know his wife was infected, did he? It wasn't deliberate, and it's not his fault.'

Saiv despaired. Completely despaired, and felt like crying. If she thought Jordan could contribute one iota to whatever might be left of Lauren's life, make her happy in any real way, she would say yes, go ahead then, see what he has to say for himself. But instinct told her, shouted at her, that the man only wanted to salve his conscience, and would make Lauren desperately unhappy. He would steal precious time from her, and then, almost certainly, leave her to die alone.

The thought enraged her, overwhelmed her with misery. Reaching across the table, she took Lauren's hand, and held it.

'Lauren, don't do this. Please. For my sake, if not for your own. I am imploring you as an old friend not to see Jordan again.'

For a moment, for one split second, it nearly worked. Lauren paused, gazed at her silently and intently; and then she withdrew her hand, shook her head.

'I can't. I'm sorry, Saiv, but I can't not see him. If you want the truth, I am addicted to him. I know it's insane, but there it is. Maybe some day, if you ever fall in love, you'll understand.'

Wretchedly, Saiv pushed away her plate, unable to finish her meal, and they sat looking at each other, mutually beseeching. Each sensed the other's pain, and longed to ease it, but there was nothing either of them could do. Polarised, they sat for a long time, studying the minutiae of each other's faces.

Saiv slept late next morning, until suddenly Lauren burst in on her, smiling like a sunrise.

'Hi. Shake a leg, and let's go shopping!'

'Uhhh . . . it's Sunday, Laurie. The shops aren't open.'

'Sure they are! From noon! You haven't been to town for ages, there must be heaps of stuff you need. Brown Thomas have the most gorgeous new bed linens and bath stuff—'

Saiv sat up, groping for her glasses, ruffling her hair. 'I have buckets of sheets and towels. And I didn't come to Dublin for *stuff*, I came to see you. Gave up two days on my book as a matter of fact. Can't we just stay here and talk? There's a lot I'd like to—'

'Oh, yak yak yak! We did enough of that last night. C'mon, let's blitz BT. And Pia Bang and Monica John.'

She's fencing, Saiv thought. Fighting me off; after last night, she doesn't want to be alone with me again. Doesn't want to face anything. We'll go out and buy tons of things we don't need and today will be a totally frivolous day. Wasted, as if she had thousands of them to spare. But, if that's how she wants to play it – well. I don't have any right to make life harder for her than it already is. And she loves shopping, it'll be fun for her.

'OK. You can buy and I'll watch.'

'Oh, no! I'm going to get lots of lovely stuff for us both! You know what I just realised recently?'

'What?'

'That you can't take it with you! Money is there to be enjoyed! Carpe diem!'

With an incredibly airy grin, she twirled off to get dressed, and Saiv lay back on crisp white pillows, surveying the matching duvet cover, feeling like a model in a magazine feature. Everything in Lauren's apartment was so perfect, it was almost terrifying. Wondering how the dogs were getting on with their sitter, she got up and braced herself for shopping. If Lauren could be dragged into Dunne's, she might invest in a couple of lightbulbs.

It was a beautiful sunny day with hints of spring in it, and by the time they went outdoors the streets were already thronged; Saiv was amazed by how young everybody looked, how many tourists jostled around squinting at maps. Out in Meath, only old people were left, and her village had yet to welcome a black or oriental resident. Thinking that maybe a day in Dublin would be a novelty after all, she let Lauren lead the way, hoping she wouldn't wear herself to a thread.

'Now! Shoes! Let's look in here!'

Four exhausting hours later, laden like mules, they tottered to the top of Grafton Street, and Saiv whimpered for mercy. 'Oh, Stephen's Green, thank God . . . let's go in and sit down for a minute?'

Lauren grinned. 'OK. Will I get you some bread to feed the ducks?'

'Oh, ho ho, very funny.'

As it turned out the ducks were so stuffed with the bread of countless children that they could barely waddle, and Lauren and Saiv sat looking at them, laughing at the antics of some remarkably determined kids.

'Aren't they sweet?'

'Yeah, I guess. But I couldn't eat a whole one.'

Saiv smiled; Lauren's views on children were long established. Which, in the circumstances, might be just as well. At least that won't be ripped from her too, she thought, that's one sorrow saved. How awful for the kids, if she had any. How do people *cope*, when they lose someone they love? I thought I'd go to pieces, when Mum and Dad died. I cried every night for nearly a year, it was like having every limb amputated. And Lauren rang me every evening. Every single evening, to talk about parties and soccer matches and things that seemed to have nothing at all to do with it. Didn't have. But it was her voice that mattered, the thought, the comfort.

'Laurie?'

'Mmm?'

'Have you seen your parents lately?'

'Last week.'

'And did you – mention anything?'

'Nah. They'd probably just say I'd brought it on myself.'

'Oh, Laurie!'

'Well, they would. Anyway, there's no point yet, is there? It might just be a false alarm.'

'Don't you want to know?'

'No. Not yet. I – I'd like it if you'd just let me take things at my own pace, OK?'

Saiv considered. In Lauren's shoes, she'd have gone much further by now, got the facts and – and how the hell did she know what she'd do? How could she tell what Lauren might be thinking or feeling, who was to say what she should do? What anyone would do, staring death in the face? Now that she thought about it, very few people would have the courage to square up to it; most would probably back off as Lauren was backing. Which she had a perfect right to do. Maybe, if by any miracle Jordan did turn out to be supportive, she'd be better able to handle it then.

'Yes. OK. I won't nag . . . as a matter of fact I think you're handling things very well.'

Lauren whipped round to her, looking half pleased, half apprehensive. 'Do you?'

'Yes. I can't begin to imagine how you must feel when you're on your own, but when you're with me you're great.

Even on the phone, you don't cry, don't whinge . . . but you can do any of those things if you want, at any time. Meanwhile, you're bright and cheery and keeping busy, which must be a huge effort, and I think you're wonderful.'

Visibly pleased, Lauren moved closer to her, stretching her arm along the top of the bench so that it touched Saiv's back. 'Thanks, Saiv. Thanks for saying that. It means a lot.'

'Mmm . . . tell me something. Am I still the only one who knows?'

'Yes. For the moment. I'm keeping it on a need-to-know basis, don't want everyone fussing around me like a clutch of mother hens.'

'Not even Caoimhe?'

'Especially not Caoimhe. She's so far away, it would only torment her not to be able to be here with me. But she has her job and a young baby. She'd want to drop everything and come racing home, which wouldn't be fair to her or to her family.'

'No. Well . . .'

'Well, why don't we go home and try on our new finery!' Saiv smiled. 'I only bought a pair of socks.'

'Yeah, but remember that cashmere cardi I got in two colours? One's for you. The pale green. And the teak photo frames from Zouk? They're for you too. You can put my picture in them and admire me when I'm gone.'

Out of nowhere, tears rose and glimmered in Saiv's eyes, and she was unable to speak. Lauren's generosity was perpetual. And it was the first time she had alluded to going, to actually being gone. Stricken, Saiv thought what life might be like without her, feeling as if she were glimpsing the depths of a dark, abandoned canyon.

The intercom buzzed, and Lauren took a deep breath, a long look at herself in the mirror before responding to open the door downstairs. Saiv had unexpectedly phoned a few minutes earlier, to wish her well for her meeting with Jordan if she must do it, although what she personally would like to do required a razor. Astonished by her vehemence, Lauren had said she could handle the encounter, not to worry, and gone to put on her warpaint. Jordan liked make-up, especially glossy scarlet lipstick.

'Hello, Jordan. Come on up.'

He came into the apartment with a smile and the scent he always wore, of money and power. Both hands were full: one with a giftwrapped bottle and the other with a dozen dark, perfect red roses, not yet fully open. Looking at him as he reached to kiss her, Lauren thought how well he looked at forty-three; maturity suited him, gave authority to his bearing. Although she was wearing stilettoes he was still taller than her, and the hair that had once been nearly as dark as her own now had a nice, commanding touch of grey to it. Accepting his kiss, which was hampered by his cargo, she took the flowers and bottle from him.

'My favourites. Thank you. Let me put them in water.'

While he seated himself in the lounge she found a vase in the kitchen, arranged the roses and unwrapped the bottle. Vintage burgundy, 1985. How nice, she thought, the perfect present for a woman with hepatitis. He'll be enjoying this on his own.

'So' he called, 'how have you been?'

She smiled as she came back out to him, carried the vase to a table. 'I've been very well, considering. How have you been?'

'Oh . . .' Loosening his tie a little, he lay back on the sofa, waved a hand with vague impatience. 'Busy. The damn rape trial is dragging on forever. Her counsel's wound up like a cuckoo clock. Sometimes I think lady lawyers were sent to try me – ha!'

Smiling at his little joke, she went to sit beside him. Patting the cushions, he made space for her, and took her hand in his.

'Look, Lauren. I know you've been a bit – um – upset. But it's all been a shock for me too, you know. We – I – didn't plan this baby, and I thought it would be easier if you didn't know about it.'

She nodded. 'Yes. For both of us.'

'Lauren, I was only thinking of you! There was nothing you

could do about it, and I didn't want you upset over a – a stupid accident, that's all.'

'Mmm. We seem very accident prone lately, don't we?'

He sighed. 'Yes. It's been no fun for – for anyone. I've been distraught about this illness of yours . . . but you mustn't panic. I've made some enquiries and it seems the prognosis can be quite good for a long time, for lots of people. Besides, you're a born survivor! I want you to see a specialist and start doing whatever it takes.'

'I will. In a while. When I'm feeling a bit stronger.'

He looked sidelong at her. 'Oh, Lauren, don't start going under, please. You've always been strong as steel. It's one of your most attractive features. Weepy little women are so – so not you.'

'No, well, you needn't worry about that. I'm not going to cry all over you.'

Looking relieved, he put his arm around her and drew her to him, kissed her hair. 'That's my girl. I know it – it must be difficult for you, but you'll cope, you'll see.'

'Mmm. I think I will, if you help me to.'

'Yes . . . well . . . things are pretty hectic at home at the moment, as you can imagine, but when they settle down maybe we . . . can . . .'

His sentence trailed off, and he pulled her closer to him, ran his hand over her cheek, looking into her eyes. 'God, you look beautiful tonight, not ill at all . . . why don't we open that bottle of wine, h'mm, and get comfortable, just forget the whole problem for the moment?'

'Forget it?'

'Yes, well, there's nothing we can do about it tonight, or until you pursue the medical options open to you. Meanwhile, it's been so long since we were together . . . I've missed you so much.'

His voice was low, his look intent, with an intimacy in it that made her spine shiver. He was, and always had been in her eyes, an almost dangerously sexy man. Even when she wasn't in the mood for sex, which was very occasionally the case, he had a way of alluring her, seducing her. Fingering his tie, a silvery silk one she had brought him from Charvet, she gazed into the dove-grey depths of his eyes. Large, deep eyes, charged with some hypnotic power.

'Mmm . . . all right, darling. Let's open the wine and talk over a glass.'

Getting up, she went into the kitchen and opened it, brought him a large glass filled precisely one-third full, with some water for herself.

'Aren't you having any?'

Shifting on the sofa, he gazed at her speculatively, and she shook her head as she sat back down beside him. 'No. It was sweet of you to bring it, but I think maybe I'd better not.'

He looked disappointed. 'Oh, well, if you're sure . . . if I say so myself, it's a very fine burgundy.' Suddenly he smiled. 'Do you remember the time we went to Burgundy, that long weekend visiting all the chateaux?'

'Yes, of course I do. It was lovely.' The memory came to her as if from outer space, aeons ago; they must have visited at least twenty chateaux, where he'd sniffed and sipped as he was doing now, appreciatively swilling wine round his mouth, nodding in satisfaction. He was something of a connoisseur, entered into long conversations with sommeliers, read tasting notes as avidly as if they were thrillers. Not that he read thrillers, or many books for that matter, with such a heavy workload. Yet he liked books, liked to be given leather-bound classics for the library shelves in the home Lauren had never seen.

Putting down his glass, he removed his jacket, under which he wore a fine, very white linen shirt, and replaced his arm around her.

'I think maybe I'm going to have to take you to France again soon.'

'Are you?'

He ran his finger under her chin, and smiled into her eyes.

'*Ah, oui.* Madame needs a little break. I will take her to Paris and pamper her, make her feel wonderful.'

She snuggled closer to him. 'Can you get away?'

'For you, I can do anything. Maybe we could go at Easter . . . if you make an appointment at Chanel, or whichever designer you like, I'll buy you a new summer wardrobe. You wear your clothes so wonderfully . . . I like this little number.'

She was wearing a thin black blouse, and he fingered it, his eyes never leaving hers as he kissed her lips very slowly, very carefully. He was, she'd often thought, the greatest kisser in creation; unhurried, building up the blaze languidly, as if to music. Again she felt a little shiver, and he slipped his hand under the blouse.

But . . . 'Oh, Jordan. I'd really like to talk to you before . . . before we . . .' Slightly baffled, she pulled away, wondering what she was doing. She had only agreed to see him tonight, nothing more; they were supposed to be discussing her condition, and his new baby. The baby that didn't seem to bother him nearly as much as it did her.

Insistently, frowning a little, he pulled her back to him, raising a quizzical eyebrow. 'Lauren' he whispered into her ear, 'let's relax. Let's just be together, and love each other a little . . . you do know how much I love you, don't you?'

She thought about it, and nodded. 'Yes, Jordan. I do.'

'Well then, come here and give me a kiss.' Without warning his hand was inside her blouse again and his tongue was in her mouth, drawing her to him in the way she had never been able to resist.

But something in her was resisting now, for the first time ever. She needed to talk to him, and she couldn't do it with his tongue in her mouth. Again, she drew away, sitting up and pushing back her hair.

'No, Jordan. Please, not yet. Not until we – there are some things I want to ask you about – in the long term—'

With a sigh, he sat up in turn, keeping hold of her hand. 'In the long term, Lauren, as I've told you before, the children will be grown up and then I'll be free for you.'

That wasn't what she meant, but now that he mentioned the children it struck her that, with a new baby, he was projecting further ahead than ever. Not that she'd ever asked him to leave his family, or wanted him to do such a thing, but she had assumed that, when the boys were teenagers, he would have a lot more free time for her. Now there was a girl as well, only a few months old. She felt as if time were turning into space, into distance.

'Jordan, I – I'm not thinking quite that far ahead. I can't afford to. I'm thinking of maybe this time next year, if I . . . if my condition . . . deteriorates.'

For a few moments he was silent, speculative, wearing the ponderous look that unnerved barristers in court. And then he squeezed her hand. 'Lauren, don't worry. You're young and fit and I'm sure you're going to be alive and well for a long time yet. But if a time should ever come when you need care, you mustn't worry. I'll look after everything. The best clinic, the best doctors, the best money can buy.'

Reassuringly, he smiled at her. But she didn't smile back. 'Jordan, I won't need money. I have my own, and am insured from here to eternity – literally! I just want to know that – that you'll be around for me then, beside my bed, holding my hand.'

He stroked her hair, breathed into it. 'Darling, of course I will. Total support. You can count on me. But Lauren, I can't bear to talk about this . . . the idea of ever losing you is so painful . . . you can't imagine what I've been going through.' With a sound halfway between a groan and a sob, he buried his face in her shoulder. 'Please. Let's not think about it any more for now. Let me just show you how much I love you.'

Softly, suddenly, he was pushing her down into the sofa, stretching out on top of her, his hands burrowing into her clothing. Writhing, she tried to push him off, but he was very heavy, and insistent.

'Jordan, please! I'm not in the mood at the moment.'

'Then let me put you in the mood.'

His voice was muffled, his weight pinning her down, crushing her bones as he fumbled with the tiny buttons of her blouse, and suddenly every nerve in her mind and body stood on end.

All right, Jordan. If this is what you want, then let's do it. Let me give you what you're asking for, my love. Let me get in the mood and do what we have always done best, you and I.

Exhaling, she lay still under him, feeling his heart begin to race, to thunder in his chest as he seemed to fill with lust, swell with it. Sex had always been so very important to him, the lynchpin that held their relationship together. Thoughtfully, she wound her fingers through his hair, curling little strands of it into her grip.

'Jordan,' she whispered.

'Mmph?'

'Why don't we go to bed, and get more comfortable?'

Lifting his face, he smiled at her. He loved her bedroom, where she kept a variety of the sex toys he liked, and had that wonderful wide brass bed.

'That's my Lauren. God, you are so gorgeous.' Getting up, he bent down, scooped her up and carried her in his arms to the bedroom, laid her down on the billowing white duvet. Smiling up at him, she slowly, seductively fingered her blouse and peeled it off while he watched enthralled, his eyes eager as a child's for the treats that would be coming next.

'Let me' he begged, 'do the rest?'

Archly, she winked wickedly at him, and he flung himself down, rolling her out of her remaining clothing and then tearing off his own, his nakedness revealing his desire, his unprecedented impatience. For a long moment she studied him, smiling, teasing in the way that always promised they were about to have a very, very good time together. Propped on his side, he studied her in turn, devouring her body with his eyes, licking his finger and stroking it, arousing her to a point at which she felt jet-propelled.

'Now' she said in the clear, commanding voice he liked, 'on your back, man, and let me take charge of you!' Beaming assent, he did as he was bid, flinging off the duvet to lie on the sheet looking up at her, entirely in her hands. But instead of lying with him she got up and went to a chest of drawers, swaying her hips as she went. When she came back, she was carrying a handful of gauzy, glossy silk stockings.

'Lie still, now.'

Bending over him, she placed a kiss on his forehead, her breasts brushing his chest as she reached for his wrists, and raised his arms over his head.

'I think you'll agree, Jordan, that you've been rather a naughty boy lately, haven't you?'

Thrilled, he concurred that yes, he had. He was very sorry, and deserved to be punished. Slowly, but firmly, she took one of the stockings, wound it round his wrist and tied it to the bedpost. He adored this game, which they had played many times before, and gazed up at her with something close to worship.

'And the other.'

Obediently he let her tie the other wrist too, and then his ankles as well, one to each brass post until he was immobilised, stretched taut like a human X. She grinned.

'Well now, Judge Jordan, I hope you're comfy. Let me check.'

Walking round the bed, she inspected each of the knots in turn; although the stockings looked flimsy they were silkily strong, wound several times and tightly tied – not enough to cut off his circulation, but certainly enough to keep him where he was.

'H'mm. I think we can do better than that, don't you?'

Quizzically, hopefully, he looked at her, wondering what new twist she might have in mind this evening. Usually sex started at this point, but . . . God, she was the most marvellous mistress in the world!

'Yes ma'am, I'm sure we can! Do your worst!'

Strolling out of the room, she was absent for some minutes, but eventually returned, wearing something on her wrist that looked like a chunky bracelet. It was a roll of duct tape, left behind by the caretaker after a recent plumbing repair. Taking it off, she begain to unpeel a length, and tried to tear it with her teeth. It wouldn't give.

'What's that for?'

'You'll see. Just a little precaution so we don't disturb the neighbours.'

A pair of nail scissors stood in a glass jar with other paraphernalia on her dressing table, and she took them, cut the tape and came back to him, stretched the length swiftly and firmly over his mouth. It was very sticky, and adhered beautifully.

'Mmph!' He shook his head, and laughed with his eyes; she must be planning something fabulous if she felt there was need to stifle his cries.

'Now, let's see how you'd look with a little make-up.'

Make-up? That sounded a little weird, but somehow erotic too; she'd never been as kinky as this. Stretched and silenced, he lay in a state of extreme agitation as she took her box of cosmetics and busily began to apply eye-shadow to his eyelids, the brush tickling and teasing flirtily to a point at which he could hardly contain himself.

'Blue would suit you, but the closest I have is this sage green, d'you like it? . . . and a little blusher . . . I know! You'd look sweet in my gold earrings, let me get them!'

Out of nowhere they appeared and were clipped to his ears in a flash, large fan-shaped things that pinched rather painfully. His eyes widened, registered pain, and he shook his head as vigorously as he could.

'No? Do they hurt? Oh dear.'

But she didn't take them off, and at that moment something changed in his face, began to express faint but rising alarm. Standing back, she put her finger under her chin and surveyed him thoughtfully.

'Now, what else? You look very pretty, but there's still something missing.'

He was beginning to sweat and, she noted, panic a little. Panic just as she had done herself, that night in Dr Mallon's surgery.

'Oh, yes. I have it. The roses.'

Out she marched to get them, and back she came with the whole vaseful, removing one to see whether its thorns were still on. They were.

'Now, Jordan, a little pain is good for the soul. You're going to have to be a brave boy.'

He began to thrash and heave, his face suddenly frantic, wildly funny under its grotesque make-up: but she didn't laugh. What was that he had said again, about rape having nothing to do with violence? With her fingertip, she stroked the point of a thorn.

'Ooh. Sharp. Nasty.'

And then, without warning, she stabbed it into the soft flesh under his ribs. There was a muffled yelp, and she took another rose, lifted her hand high and flayed him with its stem, leaving a superficial but bloody streak down the inside of his left thigh. And another, and another, alternately flaying at speed and puncturing at leisure, until his bouncing body was scored all over, droplets of blood flying in every direction.

'Tsk. What a mess. My good sheets will be ruined. Does it sting? Let me get some iodine.'

His eyes rolled huge and incredulous in his head, terror gushed from every pore, the whole room seemed to throb with horror. Unmoved, she fetched a bottle of iodine from the bathroom, poured it liberally onto a chunk of cotton wool and dabbed it on all the cuts, taking care not to miss any of the more sensitive areas. Sweat flew from his head as it churned from side to side, his eyes clenched shut, his screams filtering faint but high-pitched through the tape. Finally, after a full ten minutes, she stood back.

'Now, Jordan. I hope I don't go through pain half as bad as

that from this infection you've given me. But then you've had so much pleasure too, not only from me but from your wife as well, the night you made that baby.'

His eyes were bulging almost out of their sockets. Casually, she took her robe off the back of the door and wrapped herself in it.

'I think I'll take a shower now, and get dressed. I'm going out for the night. Tomorrow night too, actually. I might treat myself and stay at the Merrion. But don't worry. I'm going to call someone to come and release you. On Friday. A photographer. From the *Clarion*.'

'Jean-Jacques' Saiv muttered to the screen in front of her, 'I love you dearly, but today you are driving me nuts. You're supposed to absorb all my concentration, distract me from everything else, but right now you're nothing but a pain and a nuisance. I'm ditching you, and going out for a breath of air.'

Clicking off her computer, she sat irresolute for a moment, and annoyed. Why couldn't she focus? Why did her mind keep swinging back magnetised to Lauren, and Lauren's meeting with Jordan, and Lauren's perfect, provocative apartment? While in it she'd felt as if she were in a hotel, edgily on her best behaviour, but in retrospect there must have been more to recommend it than she'd realised, because she couldn't put it out of her head. Those crisply sparkling sheets . . . when she'd got back to her farmhouse, which unlike Lauren she didn't own but only rented, she'd inspected all her sheets and found them wanting. Clean, certainly, but faded and threadbare. Until now she'd always found faded old things appealing, mellow and restful, but today she felt an inexplicable urge to go out and buy something brand new. New just for the sake of it, the fun of it, as if she were a normal person who worked hard and deserved reward. But even the very thought gripped her with guilt.

Why? Why did she find it so difficult to spend anything on herself, indulge to even the smallest degree in the things others enjoyed, revelled in? Staring at the blank screen, she sat thinking about it. Could her disdain of the material world – the thought was ludicrous – possibly be related in some way to disdain of herself? Was she going a bit barmy, turning into some kind of spinster hermit?

It sounded nonsensical, and she wished she could lose the feeling, forget the indecent luxury in which Lauren lived. Maybe, if she simply went to a chain store and bought one fresh, inexpensive set of new bed linen, she could settle down and get her mind back onto the far more important, interesting question of Rousseau – whose view it happened to be that human beings were corrupted by their quest for acquisition. Did a new duvet set count as 'acquisition'?

Yes, if it wasn't only a duvet set. If a duvet set might lead to a new bed to go with it, new curtains, new flooring . . . God only knew what she might start wanting next. On leave from her job, she was tied to a tight budget, and it would all get out of hand. All her life Saiv had guarded against ever letting anything get out of hand, especially her finances, because somehow she'd sensed from a very young age that she was always going to live alone, with nobody to lean on in a crisis. How could she have known such a thing, from the age of four or five? Was it somehow connected with never having played with dolls, never being drawn to the domestic games other little girls loved? Was it to do with being short-sighted, having got glasses when she was nine, a barrier already imposed between herself and the boys who, as everyone chanted, didn't 'make passes at girls who wore glasses'? Or was it her love of the books which, her brother Tom had once told her, scared off all his friends, who'd never ask a bookworm out on a date? Loftily she'd replied that she wouldn't be interested in those brain-dead boys anyway; but the memory had lingered, insinuating itself into her consciousness, reinforced at school where the 'cool' crowd lived for discos, made fun of anyone who liked to read or study.

Of course that had all been a long time ago, she'd grown and gained her independence since then, eventually made friends with like-minded adults. But she'd never shed the feeling of being somehow unlovable, the kind of girl who'd always have to fend for herself. No man was ever going to do it, protect her in any way, and so she'd gradually created a world of her own, one she controlled and adamantly defended, and today Lauren was the only one of her friends who wasn't an academic, a writer, thinker or teacher of some kind. Lauren was the small, single chink in her armour.

Oh, blast Lauren! Lauren hadn't even answered her phone calls yesterday; a recording had requested voicemails at both her home and office, and now Saiv couldn't get on with her work for thinking about a silly woman who, despite all advice and pleas to the contrary, insisted on seeing the autocratic, selfish man she called her lover. The one who'd made her ill, and made a baby with his wife. Even if her own love life was empty as a drum, Saiv still thought she'd rather be alone than be involved with someone like Jordan White.

I'm not buying any goddamn new sheets, she thought with sudden resolution. But I can't write any more this evening, either. I think I'll walk the dogs down to the village and pop into the shops, just get a pint of milk and a bottle of Jif for the bathroom. If Lauren comes to stay again I – God, why is she doing this to me? I'm not running a guesthouse, she can take me as she finds me. But I need milk anyway, and some air.

'Come on, lads, look lively! Walkies!'

The dogs came bounding out and she found their leads, snapped one on each collar, threw on a trenchcoat and headed out to the village. It was only about four o'clock, but already the sky was darkening, filling with big knuckleduster clouds that blacked out the remains of the light, sweeping along on a hefty wind. Pulled by the dogs, she walked swiftly, down the long muddy drive and out onto the road, which had a footpath and was lit by street lamps just coming on, glowing orange. It had been raining and the occasional passing car sprayed her with slush, but still she was glad to be out, even looking forward to her first human contact of the day. Sometimes, immersed in her work, she wrote all day and then ate dinner alone; although her friends phoned they hadn't asked her out since she began her book, because she'd told them she wouldn't be available. Jean-Jacques Rousseau was consuming all her energy, she didn't have enough left for socialising in the evenings. But a few words with the shopkeepers hardly counted as socialising; it would just be nice to see faces and hear voices.

Voices! Grinning to herself in the dark, thinking of Joan of Arc, she wondered whether she really was going a bit nutty, whether maybe she should drop into the pub and hang out for a bit; it was a small friendly pub where a woman alone could feel comfortable. It even let dogs in, if they behaved themselves, because this was farming country and so many people had them. But let's get the few groceries first, she thought, as the lights of the main street began to appear and people became visible, shadowy but definitely there. Heading for the all-purpose grocery store, she shortened the dogs' leads as she pulled up her collar; it was very cold and the shop lights burned like beacons, warmly welcoming. Things would be quiet enough at this time of day, before the commuters started coming in for their frozen pizzas and lottery tickets en route home from Dublin; four o'clock meant housewives and pensioners, and a bit of leisurely chit-chat. Saiv was surprised, as she approached the store, to see that it appeared to be busy.

When she went in it was thronged, so crammed that she could hardly see Mrs O'Neill, standing stalwart and looking somehow barricaded behind her counter. What was going on, could all these people possibly need pints of milk at once?

'Disgusting' a voice was shrieking, 'absolutely revolting.'

Saiv recognised it; it belonged to Máire Finnerty who ran a B & B at the far end of the village. Standing solid as a pillar amidst the surging throng, which was buzzing like a beehive, Máire was waving a furious finger aloft, her face red and puckered as a raspberry.

What was disgusting, revolting? Baffled, Saiv followed Máire's gaze, which was impaled on something she couldn't see, obscured by the number of people milling around it. Glad she'd tied the dogs outside, because they'd get excited in this atmosphere, she made her way curiously over to the edge of the seething little crowd and peered through it, feeling steamy heat rising after the cold outside.

'Outrageous! Did you ever – obscene, that's what it is! Grotesque!'

Yelps of indignation, some laughter too, rising on a wave of communal horror. Ducking under someone's elbow, Saiv wriggled her way through until she could see what it was they were all gasping at.

And there, pinned on top of a stack of newspapers that had evidently just arrived, lay the supine, naked, gagged, flayed and bound body of Judge Jordan White. Even if she hadn't recognised him Saiv couldn't have missed the screaming headline, two words in best tabloid tradition: 'White Blackened!'

Stunned, she felt as if someone had flung a bucket of boiling water over her. Jordan! White?!? Involuntarily she wrenched her gaze away, and then looked again; the picture did not disappear. Forcing herself to look properly, she registered it as if witnessing some demonic aberration, some horror created by the hand of hell. In the middle of the lewd, lurid photograph there was a little heart-shaped blob, just big enough to cover Jordan's crown jewels, with the word 'censored!' stamped on it. Feeling faint, Saiv stood rooted to the spot.

'Disbarred!' somebody bawled. 'Hanging's too good for the likes of him!' The crowd seemed to concur, there were nods alternately shocked and sad, angry and militant. Saiv couldn't say anything, all she could do was stand there staring, digesting, disbelieving. Somebody tapped her on the shoulder.

'Don't buy it, Saiv. It only encourages them to publish this kind of thing.'

Dazed, she turned into the face of Oonah Ruane, a local farmer's wife known as the best jam-maker in the county, whose produce won medals at every fair. Since she'd been working from home Saiv's acquaintance with the local people had improved, because she saw more of them, and in slow motion she nodded now at Oonah.

'You're right. I suppose it . . . does.' Faintly, she wondered, but her gaze was riveted, she couldn't wrench her eyes off the appalling picture, which occupied the entire front page. Another voice piped up.

'And why shouldn't they be encouraged? Isn't this freedom of the press? Haven't we every right to know what's going on? This man is depraved! He – he's a sex maniac, sick and twisted! He has no business to sit in judgement on anyone!'

The voice belonged to Terry Flahavan, owner of the garage where Saiv bought her petrol and got her Citroën fixed. After a pause that felt about a month long, she found her own voice.

'Y – you have a point, Terry. But – but where on earth did they get this picture?'

'That's what I'd like to know!' Red-faced, he snatched up a copy of the newspaper and waved it under her nose. 'Found in a Dublin apartment, that's what it says here, bound, gagged and beaten after some sex game went wrong! "Judge White was badly dehydrated and in need of medical attention . . . had no comment to make to our reporter or photographer after they arrived following a tip-off from an unnamed caller . . . but it is understood that his resignation is to take immediate effect."'

Suddenly Terry exploded in laughter. 'I'll say! That's him down the Swannee, and no loss either! Pompous git, never did like the look of him nor the sound either, all his political cronies . . . well, he can kiss them goodbye after this. Wouldn't be surprised if he has to leave the country.' Chortling hugely, he tipped his cap to the two incredulous women, tucked the newspaper under his arm and marched off to pay Mrs O'Neill for it.

Reeling, Saiv stared at Oonah, whose reaction seemed to be taking a different tack. 'W – what do you make of this, Oonah?'

Deliberating, Oonah glanced briefly back at the photograph, inexorably still there even as fingers plucked copy after copy from the stack, and winced. 'Well, I don't think they should

LIZ RYAN

have printed such a dreadful thing, after all there are children to consider, you couldn't leave the likes of this lying round the house . . . and he has children himself, I always thought Judge White was a nice decent family man, so young to be rising so high . . . but. Well. Really. I'm very shocked. It's a sad day for this country if that's the way our judiciary behaves. Very, very sad.'

Looking as disappointed as a child who'd just discovered the truth about Santa, she wandered away, leaving Saiv still standing agog as someone else took her place, his jaw dropping as he snatched up the *Clarion*.

'Jesus! Is this what the country's coming to? Pornography in the courts, in our family newspapers? I'd shoot a bastard like this if I got hold of him – Mrs O'Neill, you must protest!'

Mrs O'Neill nodded wretchedly as she took the man's money from him, and Saiv hesitated, surveying the *Clarion* again with utter distaste. It was horrendous, unspeakable and utterly gross. And, she promised herself with wild elation as she picked up a copy, she was going to have the picture framed.

The phone was ringing when Saiv finally got home, delayed by numerous people on the way who were all dying to discuss the shocking news. It transpired that she was the only one who hadn't known Judge White had been missing all day Thursday, and everyone looked bemused to discover that she'd heard nothing of the security panic, seen no television at all. Feeling sheepish, she picked up the phone.

'Hi! Fancy a Chinese tonight?'

'What?' It sounded like Lauren, but it couldn't be. Not sounding so nonchalant. Not in the midst of this mayhem.

'Spare ribs, chow mein? I thought I might drop out to see you, and bring rations for the peasants while I'm at it.'

Saiv stood stock still, forcing herself to think straight. If Lauren had yet to see the *Clarion* . . . oh, dear God. But – 'Laurie, I—'

82

Nonplussed, she fell silent. If Lauren hadn't seen the paper, she must be crazed with worry, wondering where Jordan was. When she did see it, a bombshell was about to explode in her face. Desperately, Saiv tried to stall for time.

'Yes, OK, come on out, only, uh, there's – that is – um—'

'Huh? What are you babbling about?'

'Oh, Lord . . . Laurie, the most awful thing has . . .'

She couldn't find words, and was bewildered when Laurie suddenly laughed.

'Ah! You've just seen the *Clarion*!'

God almighty, Saiv thought, the whole village has seen it, probably the whole country. But—

'Have *you*?'

'Yeah. Great, isn't it? Old Jordan's well and truly up the creek without a wetsuit. Got his birthday suit, though.'

Lauren collapsed in laughter, and Saiv struggled vainly for comprehension. Lauren thought this was *funny*?

'But what—?'

'Happened? I'll tell you when I see you. Bye!'

Airily she hung up, sounding as if she hadn't a care in the world, and Saiv put down the phone with the most horrible sense of creeping, dawning suspicion. Surely Lauren couldn't – hadn't – anything to *do* with this? Surely she wasn't heading out here in search of a bolthole, a place to hide out until the fuss died down? But Jordan White was her boyfriend, her lover of five long years, her idol! She *couldn't* have anything to do with it.

Could she? Removing her coat, staggering into the kitchen where she realised she'd clean forgotten to buy the milk, Saiv sat down on a chair, took out the newspaper and laid it on the table, aghast as she studied the picture clearly, fully. Jordan's body was covered in angry-looking welts, his wrists and ankles were blue at the points where he was tied, and his eyes were manic, frantically imploring the photographer not to do it. Imploring in vain; the *Clarion*'s sales would make up the shortfall from the fine he'd once imposed on it. Whether you approved or not, there was no way you could walk away from this issue without buying it.

It was a lewdly depraved scene by any standards, and in the circumstances – a judge, no less, AWOL and then found tied to a brass bed – there was going to be massive political fallout from it. It would be talked about for weeks, in private and in public; Jordan White was completely, totally, irrevocably ruined. Professionally annihilated, socially destroyed. It was, almost literally, a crucifixion.

Saiv slammed her hand down on the paper and was engulfed in laughter, wishing she'd bought a hundred copies.

'So I just left him there, and checked into the Merrion.'

'You fool! Why didn't you come here to me, or stay with Gemma, or Adèle?'

Lauren waved a chopstick. 'Couldn't traipse all the way out here, because I had to be at work next morning. Didn't want to stay with anyone and have to talk about it, or pretend nothing had happened. It was bad enough in the office yesterday, when the news broke that Jordan was missing and everyone started in on me with questions and sympathy. I told them I'd broken up with Jordan, actually, and couldn't imagine where he was. Everyone kept bringing me cups of tea and saying how sorry they were, no wonder I'd been looking under the weather lately . . . really I should get an Academy award for my performance.'

Lauren grinned so wickedly that Saiv had to grin in turn. 'But what if Jordan tells the police that it was you?'

'And next thing the newspapers are doing a follow-up story on his terminally ill mistress? I'd say he'd sooner slash his wrists.'

'But he'll have to tell them something, surely?'

'He'll let it be quietly understood that he was under pressure and, um, strayed away from home on Wednesday night. Of course the police will track down ownership of the apartment to me, but Jordan's a bastard, not an idiot. He'll call in a few favours and get the whole thing hushed up, wait and see.'

'But doesn't the *Clarion* know it was you?'

'Yeah. Sworn to secrecy. I cut them a deal for anonymity in return for the scoop – I'm not an idiot either!'

'And what about his wife? His *children*?' Thinking of them, Saiv cringed.

Lauren scooped up another mouthful of chow mein, and reflected. 'H'mm. He has a problem there all right. Obviously the baby's out of it, but the boys will get a gruesome time at school. If I'd thought of them in time – but now the damage is done, and the White family is just going to have to live with it. As I lived with them, in a manner of speaking, for five years. It was always the children this and the children that. They were his excuse for everything. Now he's damn well going to have to find an excuse for *me*, to *them*. I'd say he could be looking at a helluva bill for treats and prezzies over the next few years.'

'Oh, Lauren! Be serious!'

'I'm perfectly serious. He'll eventually buy his way back into their affections. Maybe even into the wife's.'

Lauren arched an ironic eyebrow, and Saiv wondered at her blithe tone. Somewhere deep under it, she must be bubbling with bitterness, vibrating in the void of Jordan's loss. Much as Saiv detested the man, she had never doubted that Lauren, in her carefully casual way, loved Jordan as much as it was in her power to love anyone, since Isaac Hyland.

'If I were Mrs White I'd pack my bags and – no, actually, I wouldn't. I'd throw *him* out.'

'Yes, well, she might. My guess is that she knew about us all along, but it suited her to stick with him for the lolly and the status. Now that they're gone she might not find him quite so attractive. On the other hand, they do have a new baby to consider, don't they? A baby she possibly had on purpose, to pin him for as long as possible. She won't want to be stuck on her own with three children and no maintenance from her abruptly unemployed husband. Maybe she'll pack him off to South America to start a new life and send money home from there?'

Saiv sat mesmerised. Were there really people out there who

thought like this, worked this way? Marriage sounded even worse than politics, with people using and abusing each other all over the place . . . even using babies. Part of her was thrilled by what Lauren had done, by the sheer audacity as much as the justice of it; another part was absolutely appalled. She would tell Lauren so just as soon as she could be sure she wouldn't get another fit of laughter.

'But what triggered it, exactly? I thought you worshipped him, was petrified you were going to take him back in spite of everything he'd done.'

Lauren gulped some water, swallowed it slowly, considering. 'I think I probably was. My head said no, you fool, don't, my heart said yes, do, you adore him. And then – I think it was the wine that set me off.'

Saiv's eyes widened. 'You mean you were drunk?'

'No. Not in the slightest. I mean he brought me a bottle as a gift – me, with hepatitis, a damaged liver! I suddenly realised he'd brought it for himself, couldn't have been thinking of me at all. Then he started prattling about taking me to France, as if France was going to solve everything, as if I – I could be *bought*. Well, maybe there was a time when I could have been, before Dr Mallon started getting in the way with his "come in number ten, your time's up." And then the last straw was when he – he wanted to have sex.'

'Sex?'

'Yes. You must have heard of it. It's what consenting adults sometimes do when—'

Saiv laughed. 'Oh, all right! Get to the point!'

'Jordan, in the midst of my trying to discuss my illness and my dubious future, started pawing me and then made a lunge at me. It was as if someone had snapped on a light, I suddenly realised that he didn't want *me* at all, only my body. Saiv, I just can't describe how I felt. Used, dirty, betrayed, like a piece of meat being toyed with by a dog. What's more, he was getting kind of heavy, and I actually found myself feeling a little bit afraid of him. I've no idea how far he would have gone, against my will, but I didn't want to find out. And then suddenly I felt this absolutely electric surge of anger, and my mind clicked into gear. Since I wasn't strong enough to fight him off, and words didn't seem to be working, the only option was to distract him . . . lure him, you might say, seduce him into a sense of security. We'd fooled around before, so he – hah! – he trusted me.'

Fooled around? Saiv decided she didn't want to think about that. But Lauren was a revelation, and she was fascinated.

'So you – uh – tied him up?'

'Yeah. At first he loved it, and then . . . oh, Saiv, you should have seen his face when he realised! Talk about one picture being worth a thousand words . . . that was when I thought of calling the *Clarion*. Needless to say, they were ecstatic. But I didn't do it until this morning, because I thought it would do him good to stew first for a while.'

Yes. Jordan had indeed stewed, for about thirty-six hours according to the newspaper. His condition, when discovered, had been pitiful. Decency prohibited disclosing the details. Cupping her chin in her hands, Saiv mused on it.

'Well . . . can we say with certainty that you two won't be getting back together, then?'

Throwing back her head, Lauren laughed euphorically. 'No, I don't think the United Nations could fix this one! I feel so – so liberated, right now, as if I'd had a conversion on the road to Damascus. But maybe later on . . . well . . . you know, it's hard enough to face being ill without having to face it alone. I haven't quite thought what I'm actually going to do without Jordan, swine as he is.'

Instinctively, Saiv bridled. 'Lauren, you are not alone. You are my friend, for some reason I've never known, and I will be with you every inch of the way. If your illness is confirmed, that is.'

Lauren looked at her, and she looked hastily away, wanting to disclose neither emotion nor the thought which had recently been flitting round the edge of her mind. If Lauren couldn't face phoning Dr Mallon, should she do it for her? Call him secretly, and only confess if the news were good? It was a bit brazen, but then Lauren herself was brazen as brass, as had been spectacularly proven today. Thinking of what she'd done, Saiv was filled with admiration, and wanted to hug her.

But Lauren looked abruptly muted, lowered her long, lush eyelashes.

'I know you will, Saiv. But thanks for saying so.'

In silence they looked at each other, until suddenly Saiv couldn't stand it. Normally she savoured silence, but this one was so charged she felt she would snap.

'So, I'm harbouring a criminal, huh? A kidnapper, for the weekend?'

She laughed lightly, and Lauren smiled. 'Looks like it. I've come better prepared than last time. Mace spray for the dogs, heated rollers for my hair, earplugs so the fucking birdies don't interrupt my beauty sleep.'

'Mmm. Well, it's only a humble cottage, and I know you hate the countryside, but I hope you'll be comfortable.'

Rather oddly, Lauren looked at her. 'D'you know, Saiv, I do feel comfortable. You – you're kind of soothing to be around.'

Unused to compliments, Saiv blushed. 'Well, I won't be around all the time! I have to work on my book tomorrow.'

'Yeah. That's OK. I've brought my briefcase to do some work myself, on the Lola campaign and some other stuff. I won't disturb you.'

Saiv found Lauren deeply disturbing, but not in the way she meant. If only she'd face it, she thought, then we could face it together . . . but maybe she's faced enough for one day.

As if reading her thoughts, and determining to prove her wrong, Lauren leaped up. 'Come on! Let's find your pathetic little television, and watch the news! I want to see what the nation is making of the tragic plight of Jordan White.'

Agreeably Saiv switched it on, and Lauren sat avidly watching the story unfold, laughing at some bits, nodding vehemently at others, correcting the reporter in places. In turn Saiv sat watching her, noting her clenching fists, her flinching emotion when Jordan was filmed driving stony-faced into his home.

Oh, Laurie. You did such a brave and outrageous thing to that man, the kind of thing I'd never have the guts or imagination to do. You seize every chance, you live life so large, I wish you could have lots more of it. But what is this going to cost you? How are you really feeling, how are you going to cope without the man you should have been able to count on? You have such vitality, but do you have the resources to go on alone, down this dark tunnel? Is there any substance there, under all that sassy style?

At that moment a small tear rolled down Lauren's cheek, and Saiv reached out to her in alarm. But impatiently, defiantly, Lauren brushed it off.

'Isn't this great? Some day when it's safe you can tell the dinner-party anecdote of what Lauren Kilroy did to Jordan White, and you can say I laughed till I cried.'

MARCH

The entire half-acre of grass around the cottage was dusted with daffodils, and the sun was warm enough that Saiv could sit outdoors, drinking her morning tea as she savoured the lovely view. Up in the neighbouring farmer's field the lambs were so exuberant they looked as if the farmer had furnished them with skipping ropes, and Saiv laughed as they belted around bleating, the more daring ones venturing as far as the ditch to inspect her from closer quarters. It was a wide ditch, too deep for them to cross, but still Saiv kept Elmer and Duster under tight control at this time of year; although they were friendly they were still dogs, and nature was nature. But it was in benign mood this morning, tickling the land with soft sunshine that hinted at summer, soaking into Saiv's shoulders, warming her in mind and body. It was nearly ten o'clock, late to be still idly breakfasting, but she was enjoying her little bit of leisure, thinking how lovely it was not to have to jump into her car and dash breathless to college, to lecture a bunch of seething students who were far more interested in the Spice Girls than Sophocles. If the college was any nearer Saiv would have cycled there, but it was bang in the middle of the suburbs, where she had absolutely no desire to live.

Anyway, she didn't have to go there today. Her colleagues had thought she could bang out her book during the long vacations, and they also thought she was writing it to notch up academic status, but both views were way off the mark. She'd started it last autumn, but had soon realised it was a full-time project that couldn't be fitted in around the 'day job'; it had swiftly swallowed all her time and attention, the only way to tackle it was by complete immersion, not just the writing itself but the research, which consumed hours in libraries and on the internet. But now she was nearly halfway through, completely engrossed, loving the absorption of it. Loving these little moments, too, that were the bonus of working at home; if it was sunny you could steal a few precious minutes outdoors, draw breath and simply *be*. Saiv thought she'd rather be sitting here now, under this blue sky listening to the birds, throwing crumbs to a robin, than anywhere else in the world. It wasn't dramatic scenery, in fact it was just a green field with a few trees around it, but it filled her with a deep, satisfying sense of peace. Unlike Lauren, she felt no need to fill every waking moment with frantic activity, didn't want phones ringing forty times an hour or e-mails pumping in like rising tides; to Lauren these things were confirmation of her importance, but to Saiv they were simply stress. College was like that, full of rush and stress, and she wondered how she would ever return to it in September.

Oh, well. She would worry about that *in* September. For now she was content to live life one day at a time, working at something she was loving, in a steady rhythm of her own choosing. And there was a sense of achievement, even if it couldn't be measured in any of the ways Lauren measured it. Her project was costing her money, not making it, her publisher was some little outfit based in the wilds of Kerry, she was never likely to become either rich or famous; but she was doing her own thing, and that was what mattered. Every day she learned something new, stretching her mind as far as it would go, weaving a world that seemed far richer, deeper, more engaging than the real one, which looked increasingly superficial whenever she emerged blinking into it. In recent times she had discovered that it didn't matter at all if she missed the news for days or even weeks at a stretch, that it simply shrieked on from one crisis, one war, one disaster to another, and after a while they all began to look and sound the same. Of course some things still touched her, particularly famine or the suffering of children, but so much else, she suspected, was hyped out of all proportion, feeding the insatiable public appetite for activity. It was as if millions of people couldn't bear to sit still for one moment, hear a second's silence or rest easy in peace; everything had to be go, go, go. Was there anyone out there who'd sooner look into their own soul than into a television screen, listen to a bird singing if they could have Boyzone blaring?

'Saiv,' Lauren had said to her one day recently, 'you're going Amish. You'll end up plaiting your hair and knitting your own pasta, driving round in a horse-drawn buggy.' She'd laughed, uncaring; nobody was going to dictate how she lived, certainly not a magazine or an advertisement or a politician, anyone who regarded the rest of humanity as mere fodder for the achievement of their own ends.

Not, naturally, that it wouldn't be nice to have someone here beside her sharing this beautiful morning, the view, the day ahead. There was a fine line between solitude, which she prized, and loneliness, which loomed rather alarmingly in the long term. But at least being an adult meant not having to date anyone you didn't like, not acquiring an indiscriminate partner simply for the sake of having one. Lauren couldn't understand how anyone could live alone, and since burning her bridge to Jordan she'd been jumpy as a cat, but Saiv thought her attitude neurotic.

'Why can't you just relax and enjoy your own company for a while? Be kind to yourself instead of expecting someone else to be?'

Impatiently, Lauren had glared at her. 'Saiv, a woman without a man is like a fish without a bicycle.'

Such graffiti-type remarks made Saiv laugh; Lauren seemed to think always in terms of poster slogans. And yet, she felt sorry for Lauren if that was what she really thought. Not only because Lauren was missing Jordan so acutely, but also because she was now caught in such a predicament. She couldn't risk getting into any new relationship with hep C, breaking the news to some horrified man who might promptly abandon her.

So she was flirting instead, going out with anyone who asked her and then ditching them after they'd taken her to whatever party or event she wanted to attend; despite all Saiv's pleas her social life was more hectic than ever. Where she was getting the energy Saiv couldn't imagine, but she prayed it wasn't from the same source she knew some of Lauren's colleagues got it. There was a kind of desperation about Lauren these days, as if she were trying to pack a dozen lives into one, and her definition of 'living' meant attending every party in town. With all her heart Saiv wished she'd slow down, sit back and take stock, but she didn't nag, because somewhere at the heart of the whirlwind she sensed fear. Even after having faced up to Jordan White's venality, Lauren still couldn't face up to herself, or to the illness she seemed to think might evaporate if she refused to confront it. Saiv thought she was like the little Dutch boy, plugging the dam with his thumb.

A small breeze began to rise, cooling the warmth of the sun, and Saiv got up, decided to have a second mug of tea indoors. Lately she'd got into the habit of checking websites before she started writing each morning, scanning to see whether there might be any new bit of information to be gleaned about hep C. But no dramatic revelations had been forthcoming, all she knew for sure was that it was still something of a mystery disease, transmitted in various ways, affecting different people in different ways. Some were acutely ill, some died, some lived normally for years without even knowing they had it. There was even a D strain now as well, and an E, fuzzing the picture and baffling the scientists.

Boiling the kettle, she stood gazing out the window, wondering. Was it time to take matters in hand, finally phone Dr Mallon as she'd often thought of doing? It was something she'd have to approach cautiously, lest he think she was doubting his professionalism, and even at that he might – quite rightly –

refuse to disclose any confidential information. He would undoubtedly refuse. But all she wanted from him was confirmation: yes, the diagnosis is correct, there hasn't been any muddle or mistake. If she knew that for sure, she felt that maybe then she could make some kind of progress with Lauren, gently, gradually get her to accept the truth and start acting accordingly. If she knew for sure her days were numbered, would she want to spend the remainder of them at that advertising agency, working herself to the bone, going out with men whose names she could barely remember? Would she still shop as if there were no tomorrow if she knew there actually *was* no tomorrow?

Maybe she would. Saiv knew her values weren't everyone's, and that they especially weren't shared by Lauren, who'd panic if every waking moment wasn't filled with people and activity. In ways she was spinning round on a hamster wheel, but it was her wheel, her choice. Any yet . . . Saiv smiled to herself as she thought of the gifts they gave each other on birthdays and at Christmas. Maybe sometimes you had to bite the bullet, give a friend something you'd hate yourself, if you thought they'd love it; only rarely could you risk introducing something new to them.

On the one hand, it might be kinder to simply let Lauren be. On the other, Saiv found herself still clinging to hopes of conversion, of showing her friend that there were other, more satisfying ways to live a life, of getting so much more out of it than anything to be had from a shop, a party, a passing whim.

But then, she'd had a passing whim herself. She'd been briefly affected by Lauren's affluence, hadn't she, thought of treating herself to some lovely new linens? And she hadn't even dared tell Lauren, who'd have been delighted, insisted that she do it, because there'd be such pleasure in conversion for her too. In various small ways they'd been pushing and tugging at each other like this ever since they'd known each other, and although neither of them was gaining ground it lent a certain bite to their unlikely friendship. We're like Mormons, she thought, or those other sects, forever knocking on doors in the remote but perpetual hope of letting the light shine in. It's a silly crusade, egocentric too, we should simply respect each other's choice of lifestyle . . . but I suppose the opposite side of the coin is that we want to share the things we each enjoy, enrich the other with them. At least we've never had a row over it, or let it damage our relationship, and I hope it never does. For all her silly faults I love Laurie, and she . . . she's been gravitating to me a lot lately, so she must see some attraction in me. I'm glad somebody does, even if it's not a man. Sometimes I think how nice it would be to have a man around, a sexual friendship. But I'm damned if I'll ever doll up and bat my eyelashes at anyone the way Lauren does. If I ever meet anyone he'll have to take me as I am – which I suppose means I never will. They all want dolly birds, glamour girls, and I'm just not cut out for that.

Anyway, am I going to ring Dr Mallon or not? Should this be Lauren's decision, to make as she chooses? I wish she'd do it, lift the suspense, take her head out of the sand. But since she won't . . . at least *I* could get the facts straight. Even if I didn't tell her, I'd have information to go on. I'd know how to play things, and how much urgency there might be in them.

Yes. OK. I will call Dr Mallon. The worst he can do is tell me to mind my own business. But . . . I won't do it right now. Not when Laurie's insisting it's my turn to visit her, that I go to Dublin so she can treat me to a birthday night out. The weekend would be ruined, and so would the birthday, if I had to set off with bad news. God, am I really going to be thirty-four tomorrow?

Yes, I am, and I won't think of it as getting older. It's an achievement. Another year survived, enjoyed in so many ways. The only thing I haven't done, that I'd really like to do, is go back to Italy. But I haven't the time or the money for that. And since I can't fly, it'd be a nightmare trek on ferries and trains.

Oh, face it, Saiv Lovett. If you expect Lauren Kilroy to face up to something so much worse, you've got to face up to the fact that you're chicken. Thousands of planes fly millions of miles every week, yet you haven't the guts to go on one, because your parents were so unlucky nine years ago. Flying is normally the safest form of transport, and all the statistics show that you're just chicken.

And maybe that's why you haven't got a man, either, to share this lovely day, or your birthday, or anything else. You like to think you're different, that you won't settle for anyone less than special, but Lauren would say you're just a common coward, defending yourself with your dogs and your books. Locking yourself in your room like a child, and refusing to come out in case, God forbid, there might be a bogey-man outside. You're pathetic.

Look at Lauren. She got hurt once, didn't she? Hammered senseless by Isaac Hyland? But she got up and dusted herself off and went back right into the fray. She faced up to that much.

But then that's her natural arena. She's so attractive. She's pretty and she knows how to dress, has charm to burn, whereas you can't even cope with contact lenses. Can't talk about anything that didn't happen a hundred years ago, can't handle the rough-and-tumble of everyday life. Maybe much of it is banal, but it's *reality*. You're just terrified of letting it get too close, of having to climb down off your bloody high horse and be *human*.

That's what's wrong with you, isn't it? Either that, or Lauren is right and you are going Amish, will end up in a home for the bewildered. So, what are you going to do about it? If Lauren isn't going to be around forever, you won't always be able to live vicariously through her. Do you still want to be here on your own when you're eighty, waiting for Godot?

What do you want, huh? Sooner or later it's going to be decision time, for all you know you could get suddenly ill too, discover that your own time is limited. Lauren's not unique, it happens to hundreds of people every day of the week. Your own parents were cut short virtually in mid-sentence. And your brothers live miles away, are not going to be around if you ever need someone to hold your hand.

So who is, eh? Jean-Jacques Rousseau? Unlikely as any other

guy is to show up, you can definitely count him out. He may be fascinating but he is not living, breathing flesh and blood. So don't try escaping back to your computer to hide behind him.

Try going to Lauren tomorrow, and letting her take you out on the town, and being open to whatever happens. If nothing else, it'll be a novelty.

'So there you are, you see. Just as I said.'

'Nothing happened? Really? I was sure the police were going to come banging on your door, charge you with false imprisonment and march you off to jail for what you did to Jordan.'

'Hah! I'm not going to any jail that doesn't have a boutique and a gym and catering by Patrick Guilbaud!'

Lauren grinned widely, and Saiv admired her perfect, expensive dental work. She hadn't had teeth like those at college. Then, she'd been pretty, nothing more. Now she was gorgeous, gleaming with the expensive burnish of everything money could buy: dentistry, clothes, cosmetics, the admiration of colleagues who only knew the new Lauren, the one who'd invented herself overnight at the age of nineteen. Her body is beautiful, Saiv thought, and her soul is in cold storage. Is that one of the reasons why, until recently, we saw each other so rarely? Because I'm the only person who knows who she used to be?

She's buried the old Lauren very deep. But I know the old Lauren and I've never been able to let go of her. She knows me, too, and has never let go either, not even after I went 'weird', as she calls it. We're gluttons for punishment, but we're hanging in, hanging onto that indefinable intimacy. I wish she wasn't so indiscriminate, nowadays, in her friendships, and I suppose she wishes I was less discriminate in mine.

But there we are. You can't have everything, and she's still got something. I know she has, under all that powder and varnish, all this impeccable, impenetrable décor. I might be myopic, Laurie, but I'm not obtuse, and I'm good on intuition.

'So . . . how are you feeling?'

'Great. Never better, never busier.'

Saiv stifled an urge to scream. 'Well, you certainly look great.'

Lauren beamed. 'D'you think so?'

'Yes. That suit is fabulous, cerise suits you so well – I don't know how you always manage to look so perfect.'

'Saiv, *chérie*, appearances are everything. I spend two grand a year on dry-cleaning, as much again on accessories, probably the same on hairdressing, manicures . . . looking good doesn't come cheap, but it's vital.'

'But what's the point of earning so much if you have to plough such a chunk of it back into work, into impressing colleagues and clients?'

'Oh, Christ. You just don't understand the first thing about business, do you?'

'I suppose not. The logic eludes me, it seems so pointless . . . anyway, I meant how are you feeling about Jordan? You're not sorry you did it, are you?'

'No. I am missing him like mad, but I am not repenting. He finally pushed me a bridge too far. I just . . . he's sort of left a space in my life, that's all. Of course I could fill it up in a flash if I – well, let's just say I'm taking a breather. I only go out with low-risk guys at the minute.'

Saiv blinked. 'Is there such a thing?'

'Oh, sure. I've even gone to parties with a few gays. At least they're a laugh.'

Saiv pondered it. 'Well . . . I know you were mad about Jordan, but I must admit I can't see you sitting at home moping.'

'No way. I leave the sitting at home to you. But not tonight. What about coming to this little launch party with me, it's only cocktails, and then maybe we'll see a movie? Your choice.'

'Is that a trade-off? If I go to some cocktail thing, we can go to the IFC afterwards?'

'The where?'

'The Irish Film Centre! It's one of the few things I like about Dublin. They show wonderful European and South American films—'

'Oh, Jesus! In black and white, with subtitles, two people and a dog staring at a wall for two hours? Saiv, gimme a break!'

Saiv pouted slightly. 'Well, you did say I could choose. It's my birthday.'

'Yeah, but – there's a great thriller on at the Savoy. Bruce Willis is in it.'

Saiv was on the point of protesting when the thought struck her: how many more films might she get to see? Am I entitled to waste her night on something she'll hate, if her nights are numbered?

'All right. Let's do a different deal. We'll go to the Savoy tonight if you'll drop your plans for a restaurant lunch tomorrow, and we can go on a picnic instead.'

'A picnic? Saiv, are you mad? It's March!'

'I know, but the weather's wonderful . . . I'd love to go to the Wicklow mountains, since we don't have any mountains in Meath.'

Lauren hesitated, and Saiv saw in her face that she didn't want to do it. But, unexpectedly, Lauren shrugged.

'Oh, very well. Another forced march up a bloody mountain. I'll go if we can drop into Avoca Handweavers on the way – and that shopping gallery at Powerscourt.'

'Both?'

Firmly, Lauren eyeballed her. 'Yes. Both.'

'Oh, all right then! You win.'

'No, *you* win.'

Briefly, there was a flash of mutual resentment. And then, simultaneously, they laughed.

'You're such a bully.'

'You're such a bore.'

'What time's the cocktail thing?'

'Now. Six thirty. For God's sake go and put on something

decent, you can borrow my new Louise Kennedy if you promise not to get tractor oil on it.'

The drinks party was ghastly, crowded, sweltering and noisy, and Saiv felt strangled in the outfit she had mistakenly borrowed. But, insisting she looked great, Lauren led her up to a group of acquaintances and then left her with them, while she pirouetted off after a passing photographer. A large sweating man eyed Saiv, and smiled.

'So, you in advertising too?'

'Er, no.'

'No?' He looked incredulous, as though nobody could possibly not be. 'What d'you do, then?'

Saiv cringed, felt like something exposed from under a rock. 'I – I teach philosophy.'

'Huh?'

'But I'm on leave at the moment, writing a book.'

Already the man looked bored, but Saiv suspected he'd been instructed by Lauren to look after her, or be polite at least.

'What's the book about?'

'A philosopher. Jean-Jacques Rousseau.'

'Oh, yeah? Any money in it?'

God! Why was that everybody's first reaction? 'No,' she said, 'it's a labour of love. I'm simply enjoying doing it.'

Perplexed, the man gazed into his drink, which looked like whiskey. 'I see.'

No you don't, Saiv thought, you don't see or even want to see. You think I'm as dull as ditchwater, some little country mouse you can't get away from fast enough. The only thing you can see is that this suit's too tight for me and I can't fasten the buttons of the jacket, because I don't have a figure like Lauren Kilroy's, which you're ogling over my shoulder.

'Well, if I wanted to make money I wouldn't be writing about Rousseau, would I? I'd be churning out buckets of sex with a nice violent twist of a knife in somebody's back.'

Caught unawares, the man frowned, and then laughed. 'Yeah! That's the stuff to give the troops! Gotta think of the market, you know, gotta give people what they want.'

Oh, shut up, Saiv thought, you ignorant oik. Suddenly, sweetly, she smiled at him.

'So what do you think of Rousseau, anyway? Would you classify yourself as one of his "natural men"?'

'Eh?'

Was it the wine she was sipping, or what? Saiv didn't know what was emboldening her, carrying her over this precipice. But she plunged on. 'You don't know who Rousseau is, do you? You're wondering if he plays for Arsenal.'

Looking irritated, the man frowned again. 'Look, lady, I know who plays for Arsenal. And I bet you don't know who *they* are.'

'No. So we're quits. Horses for courses.'

'Right. Excuse me, think I see someone I know over there. Be right back.'

He clumped off, leaving Saiv on the fringes of a group which was paying no attention to her. There now, she thought, that's what happens when I let Lauren drag me along to these things. Horrible man. Still . . . I kind of enjoyed that. At least I spoke up and said boo.

Eventually Lauren came back, glancing at her watch. 'C'mon, time to go.'

'Oh? OK . . . but we've barely been here half an hour, we'll be early for the film.'

Firmly, Lauren steered her out. 'Saiv, half an hour is the allotted time for these things. You're never first to arrive and you're never last to leave.'

Saiv's coat was thrust into her hand, and she was still trying to figure it out as she was propelled through the door. 'But how can nobody be first? Or last? *Some*body has to be.'

'Yes, but not me. Or you. Now, let's go see Brucie.'

She simpered, and Saiv saw that the film was going to be as awful as, two hours later, it turned out to be. Bruce Willis, she thought, was to acting what Colonel Ghadaffi was to world peace. Within five minutes she'd worked out how the plot was going to end, which it finally did after trundling through every cliché in the history of cinematography. Yawning, she realised she'd dozed through long expanses of it.

'Well' she said as the cinema started to empty around them, 'I'd rather watch the grass grow. What did you think of it?'

Lauren's eyes were shining. 'I loved it. Bruce is so gorgeous.'

'But he has the personality of a log! Surely a pretty face can't hold you rapt for two hours?'

'Sure it can. Why not?' Lauren looked puzzled, as if she genuinely couldn't see why not, leaving Saiv wondering. Was Lauren really so adolescent, or was *she* the one losing the plot? Certainly she'd been out of step all evening. But, even if she'd loathed everything, at least she'd tried it, and Lauren was looking like a kid who'd been to a party.

Suddenly, Saiv was touched. For all her style and savoir-faire, Lauren did have a childlike quality at times, and it was so easy to please her, to make her happy. All she wants out of life, Saiv thought, is the simple things. It's a good job not everyone is like me.

Next day they set off on their picnic, and as Lauren swung her BMW jauntily out of its underground parking Saiv eyed her, assessing the colour in her face and the gloss of her hair, the vivacity in her eyes. Nobody would guess from her appearance that she was ill, only that maybe she needed to gain a little weight, and it dawned on Saiv that shedding Jordan White had done her good. The man, in every sense, had been corroding her. Even if she missed him, she was better off without him, and looked it.

But did she know it? Probably she didn't, yet: knowing Lauren she was more likely crying herself secretly to sleep by night while faking perky insouciance by day. She'd sooner shoot herself than ever let anyone see she was under stress, or unhappy with any aspect of her gilded life. That's why she's turning to me, Saiv thought: I'm her safety valve, the only person who doesn't inhabit her shiny, artificial world. To inspire confidence in business she has to appear confident, even when she's sick in body and sick at heart. Especially then. And the stress of that charade could make her even worse.

En route to Wicklow they stopped several times so Lauren could raid the shops, and Saiv surveyed her with wonder. How could any of this stuff matter to her? Did it matter, or was it just a distraction, one more way of keeping reality at bay? Even though they were on their way to a rural picnic, Lauren was elegant in palazzo pants and an angora sweater, made up so that her skin looked peachy, smiling at all the shop assistants as she waved credit cards, signed cheques with a flourish. In Avoca Handweavers she turned to Saiv looking baffled.

'This stuff is gorgeous. Don't you want to get anything?'

'No, not really. I'm on a tight budget, and don't need anything anyway.'

'Oh, come on! You're no fun at all. There must be something . . . what about that dress over there, that'd suit you?'

It was pretty. But – 'No. It isn't warm enough yet for summer dresses.'

'But it will be! Don't tell me there isn't one single thing in this whole shop you like?'

Looking around it, Saiv smiled. 'Of course there is. I like those earrings and the kimonos and the dresses, and those jackets and that patchwork eiderdown . . . I could go mad in here, if I was mad.'

Lauren stiffened, as if attuning her antennae, and ran her eye over all the items. 'Right. I'm going to choose for you.'

Before Saiv could stop her she sailed over to the stack of eiderdowns, selected a pale yellow one and shook it out. 'This one?'

'Beautiful. But not today. Not for me. Put it back.'

Lauren tucked it under her arm, marched onto the jewellery display and unhooked a pair of unusual earrings, small vertical amethyst rectangles anchored to graphite. Holding them up, she studied them against Saiv's face and hair, nodded, and turned to the assistant.

'We'll take these, please. And this.'

Saiv gasped. 'We will not! Lauren, stop it! What do you think I am, a millionaire?'

Lauren beamed; the assistant was already wrapping. 'I think you're thirty-four today. These are your prezzies.'

'What? Lauren, are you insane? These things are over two hundred—'

'If you don't shut up I'll get the dress as well.'

Horrified, Saiv fell silent as the transaction was completed, quaking lest Lauren carry out her threat. Finally, laden with bags, they left the shop, Lauren radiating triumph in her wake. Saiv didn't dare speak until they reached the car.

'Oh, God. You are lethal, Lauren. An absolute menace to yourself and everybody else.'

'Yeah. But you like them, don't you?'

Her smile was so eager, her tone so wheedling, that Saiv felt suddenly swamped with guilt for her ingratitude, and hugged Lauren to her, bags and all. 'Yes. I like them. I absolutely love them, and you for doing such a wilful, wicked thing.'

Lauren's whole face lit up, glowed with pleasure. 'Well, somebody's gotta do it. It'd be a cold day in hell before you'd ever dream of spoiling yourself, wouldn't it?'

Yes. Saiv conceded that it would. 'Only – Jesus – so *much* – you never do things by halves, do you?'

'Certainly not. I'm delighted we found things you really like.'

Saiv pondered that, as they got into the car, and took the point. Was Lauren starting to feel the same way she was herself, about taking account of each other's tastes? The eiderdown and earrings were both beautiful, but neither, she was sure, would suit Lauren at all. This was a gesture of sheer generosity.

'But you gave me a card at breakfast this morning, and sang happy birthday with a champagne toast!'

Starting the car, Lauren grinned. 'That was just to get you in the mood. I was sorry not to have presents ready then, but I thought for a change you might rather choose your own. Pity I can't giftwrap them – but the bags are nice, aren't they?'

Biting her lip, Saiv nodded. 'They're lovely, and I can use them again, too.'

'Ah, yes! Ever the eco-warrior! Now, how do we get to this damn mountain, have you any idea where it is?'

It was still quite a drive to the Featherbed, and while Saiv worked out directions from the map Lauren drove at rally speed, screeching round bends that twisted sharply upwards before levelling out, eventually, into moors. Saiv clutched her seatbelt.

'Are we in a hurry?'

'Well, it's nearly two, I don't want you accusing me of wasting daylight.'

'I won't accuse you of anything, if we get there in one piece.'

'Ha! This is a BMW, far too good for the likes of these little tracks! We'll get there – where exactly, anyway?'

The road was starting to smudge into wide expanses of spring colour, exuberant lime green flirting with flashes of mauve heather and lemony gorse; occasionally a sheep leaped out of a ditch and Saiv shrieked.

'Jesus—!'

Lauren laughed as she weaved around them. 'Chill out. If I hit one you can build a fire and barbecue it, get yourself another girl guide medal.'

Eventually, with relief, Saiv screwed up her eyes, thinking she saw the stream that was a thin blue line on the map. 'Over there. Pull in, and we'll walk from here.'

'What, with the coolbox?'

'I'll carry it, it's not heavy.'

'No, but my shoes will be ruined.'

Looking down, Saiv saw that she was wearing fine leather ones, with heels. 'Oh, Lauren! You idiot! They're for dancing!'

'Mmm. Well, you never know who you might meet, even

out here. So let's park as close as we can, I'm not trudging through any grass or muck.'

Nudging the car forward, she parked at last, as tightly as if in a Paris street, so close to the river they could hear it gurgling in the stillness when the engine was cut.

'Wow. It's quiet out here.'

'Isn't it? Heavenly. Not a soul around as far as the eye can see.'

Instantly, Lauren reached forward and turned on the radio. 'Music. We can roll down the window and hear it from wherever we're going to eat.'

Firmly, Saiv reached forward in turn and snapped it off. 'Laurie, we're out in the mountains. Silence is the whole idea.'

'But—'

'We can listen to music when we get home. Now, I'll take the coolbox, you just take the rug.'

Muttering, Lauren got out, took the rug and draped it on a rock barely ten metres from the car. 'This do? Here OK?'

'No! Further on, by the river!'

Briefly, Lauren looked mutinous. But then she picked it up, went on and did as she was told, laid it down again in a mossy hollow shielded from the breeze, filled with sunshine.

'Here. By the water, but not too damp I hope.'

Smothering a smile, knowing there'd be recriminations later about palazzo pants being ruined, Saiv admired the site with satisfaction. 'Perfect. A car could drive right by without anyone even seeing us! Get comfortable and I'll unpack the picnic.'

But no other car appeared; it really was an isolated part of the mountain, gleaming pristine under a vault of blue sky, untouched and unseen. The sun was warm if not hot, and Saiv glanced solicitously at Lauren.

'Warm enough?'

'Bloody freezing.'

'Hold on. I brought a spare sweater. I'll get it for you.'

It was a large loose Aran sweater, the kind Lauren wouldn't

normally even try on, but when Saiv brought it from the car she took it gratefully, and put it on.

'Phew. Great. Thanks.'

'You're welcome. And don't worry, you look fabulous.'

Surprisingly, Lauren didn't argue. Instead she sat on the rug, with her arms wrapped around her knees, watching Saiv unpack. 'What'd you bring?'

'Cheese sandwiches. Box of salady stuff. Hot coffee thermos.' She waved it aloft, and Lauren eyed it dubiously. 'H'mm. We could have had a proper hot lunch at Avoca. That's probably cold by now.'

'It's fine. Just forget Avoca and think mountain. Look at the view, smell the air . . . isn't it invigorating?'

Lauren wrinkled her nose. 'I smell sheep, or cows or something.'

'Yes, that's nature, and it doesn't cost fifty pounds a bottle!' Wriggling down beside her, Saiv sorted the food and stretched out on the square of rug Lauren hadn't commandeered. 'Here. Have a sandwich.'

Taking it between two fingers, Lauren eyed it cautiously, and Saiv waited for questions about mayonnaise, mustard, variety of cheese. But then, slowly and studiously, Lauren bit into it.

'H'mm. Not bad.'

Saiv thought it delicious, when she bit into her own; the fresh wild air gave every flavour an edge. Pouring coffee, balancing the plastic cups on a rock, she lay back and fell silent, chewing absently, peacefully. Lying back in turn, Lauren lifted her face to the sky, and closed her eyes.

'That sun is actually warm . . . lovely.'

Thinking that it wouldn't penetrate her make-up, which was probably packed with UVF filters, Saiv lifted her own face, knowing and not caring that it would freckle immediately.

'Mmm . . . this is the kind of spring day that makes you feel good to be alive.'

She said it carelessly, thoughtlessly, and then wondered

whether she should have. But Lauren didn't seem perturbed; idly plucking a long tuft of grass, she let it slide over Saiv's cheek.

'Tickle?'

'Ha! Yes, lay off. I'll spill my coffee.'

'Oh well, I'm sure there's more.' Again Lauren dangled the tip of the grass on Saiv's face, drawing it slowly over her nose, down to her ear and throat. It was a somnolent feeling, vaguely summery, and the silence seemed to expand around them like an inflating raft. Lying on her back, Saiv studied the sky until it got too bright, and then let her head roll sideways, feeling drowsy. Somewhere, very distant, she could hear a lamb bleating for its mother.

Beside her, propped on one elbow, Lauren remained silent, sipping her coffee intermittently, apparently aware of the peace and unexpectedly savouring it. Saiv couldn't remember her ever having sat so quietly for so long. Apart from the lost lamb, the only sound was the silvery brush of water over stone.

'That sun is so warm' she murmured at length, 'I'm half asleep.'

Lauren didn't answer, and Saiv stretched contentedly into a more comfortable position, her mind drifting like a balloon up into the blue beyond. It was a part of friendship, she thought, that two people could simply be, without feeling the need to talk. Losing hold of whatever she'd been thinking, about Thomas Hardy and his Dorset moors, she simply lay in the palm of nature, the soft warmth sinking into her body.

Later, when it eventually came, Lauren's question was very quiet.

'Saiv?'

'Mmm?'

'If you only had a year to live, what would you do with it?'

Oh. Was that where Lauren's mind had got to? Without reacting, without even opening her eyes, she mused carefully on it.

'I don't know. Maybe something indulgent, or maybe something worthwhile?'

'Which?' Lauren's voice was hardly a whisper, as if she were turned away, facing into the flickering breeze.

'It would depend.'

'On what?'

'On what I was doing to start with, I suppose.'

There was a pause. 'Would you . . . would you finish your book?'

Saiv was about to say yes, she surely would, when something caught her. Would she? She loved her book, but she loved lying here in the sun, too, basking in nature's bounty, idle as a lily of the fields. She could do a lot more of this, if she didn't have a deadline. Or she could go to Italy, for one last glimpse, if she weren't afraid of flying. But then what would be the point of being afraid, if you were dying anyway?

And was not everyone dying a little, every day? What was more important, to finish what you'd started, or savour what was left? Completing the book would mean not having time to see Siena, or lie out in the hot rich warmth of an Italian meadow. Or do any one of a dozen other things that might suddenly spring to mind, if time were running out.

'I – I'd have to think about it.'

'Then think, and tell me.'

Saiv opened her eyes, but found that Lauren was not looking at her. She was lying on her side, facing out across the moor towards the little river, the creamy sweater baggy on her slight frame. Saiv gazed up at the sky.

'I . . . I'd finish it at top speed, if I thought I could, if that would still leave enough time to go to Italy and find a home for the dogs and sort everything with my brothers and make a will and – God, there'd be so much to do!'

No answer. Slowly, Saiv sat up, and touched Lauren gently on the back. 'Why do you ask, Laurie? Are you all right?'

Even more slowly, Lauren rolled over, turning to look at her, and she saw that she was not all right. In her eyes, tears hovered like dewdrops.

'No. I'm not. I – Saiv, I'm afraid. I am so afraid.'

Her voice was muffled, but there was a quiver in it, one that cut Saiv to the heart. Putting one hand on Lauren's shoulder, the other on her face, she looked into her gleaming eyes.

'Of course you are. Of course you are, Laurie.'

As if she were her mother, she held her to her, and Lauren sniffled, letting a tear fall, trying to beat back the next. For a long time, neither of them spoke.

Eventually, when she felt she could trust herself, Saiv grasped her shoulder, hard. 'Laurie . . . please . . . you must see that specialist. You have to do it.'

Looking down, Lauren gazed into the grass. 'And if I do . . . what if he says no, I don't even have a year now, it's only nine months? Or less? Saiv, I can't face that. I can't.'

'But then you'd know where you stood. You'd be in control, at least.'

'Saiv, I'm in control of everything else, but I don't want to be in control of this! I don't want it to be – to be – *final*!'

Lauren pulled back, and Saiv looked at her, trying to think, trying to imagine. Could you force someone, prod them over such a precipice?

'All right. If you don't want to, it would be cruel of me to insist. But then . . . you've got to try to – to arrange your priorities, in some shape or form. Decide which things you really want, which matter. And which you can ditch. Maybe then you could stop wondering, wandering in the dark. You could enjoy life, whether it turns out to be long or short, live all you have of it.'

Another silence, bewildered and piteous, in which Saiv sensed all of Lauren's fear, felt it herself and was glad of sharing it.

'Will you do that much, Laurie? Will you try to figure out what you want, and aim to do it if you can?'

Lauren dipped her head. 'I – I'll try. I am trying. But I'm so confused. I thought I wanted Jordan, and now I haven't got him. I threw him away of my own free will.'

'Yes. You did. And you were right. I know it hurts, and you feel alone, but you're not as alone as you think. I'm here for you, and your parents would be too if only you'd tell them, trust them.'

'No. They wouldn't. They'd fuss and panic and blame me for it all.'

'Laurie, you don't know that! Sometimes people are much stronger than they think, when they need to be. You can do this, and maybe so can they.'

Almost pleadingly, Lauren looked at her. 'Do you think so?'

'Yes. I do. I wouldn't be saying it otherwise. Since you want my opinion, let me give it to you. I think you should confide in your parents, and I also think you should consider taking a break from work. You need to stand back and take stock.'

'But Lola – the campaign starts next month – we're up to our ears, we're talking big money! I can't drop out now, let everyone down!'

'All right. After the campaign, then. How long does it run?'

'Six weeks. Until the middle of June.'

'OK. Will you promise me you'll do it then?'

'Yes – but – we're into Krunchy Kornpuffs after that, working on it already—'

'Lauren! Are you *listening* to me? Or am I talking to that flaming sheep over there?'

Involuntarily, Lauren glanced at the distant sheep, and Saiv shook her, made her return her gaze to her own.

'Laurie, the world is afloat on cola, tunnelling its way through thousands of cereals! These things are not important, one more or less makes no difference! Advertising is not brain surgery, nobody's life is depending on it! Listen to me or I'll strangle you!'

Lauren jerked up, and abruptly clasped her hands around her knees, stared out over the undulating heather. 'All right. Don't shout at me, Saiv. I am listening to you.'

Saiv drew a deep breath. 'OK. Then do what I say. You have money, more than you need, you can afford to do it. You have that luxury, no dependents. So make the most of your freedom, your resources.'

Lauren seemed to think about it. 'No. I could take time out, couldn't I? I don't have any children to support or worry about. I don't have any partner, or any children.'

Saiv was slightly perplexed. Lauren sounded so sad, so wistful. Yet she'd never hinted at wanting children. On the contrary.

'Would you – have liked – would you like to have them?'

'I – I don't know. I'd hate to inflict this on them, hate to leave them all alone if I did have them. But if I were well—' Suddenly her fist clenched, her voice rose. 'Jesus! Why is it always the Jordans of this world who get to have children? Rotten bastards who should be castrated and not let have any?'

Saiv sighed. She sometimes wondered the same thing herself. But teaching philosophy made you . . . well, philosophical. 'I know. It never seems fair, does it? It's the master plan of some bastard deity, to try our patience and teach us strength. But if the world were fair maybe we'd be bored stiff.'

Lauren ripped up a fistful of grass and glared at it. 'If there's a god, or deity or whatever, I hate it for doing this to me. I hate him, or her or it!'

'I don't blame you. But even worse happens to others. At least you've got time to think, and act.'

'Yeah. A blink of an eyelid. That's all I've got.'

'Laurie, you don't know that! You might have years . . . but what you've got to do now is work on the assumption that time is finite, and use it accordingly. In fact that's what we should all be doing, since none of us knows for sure.'

Lauren pouted fiercely, furiously. 'Bugger this, Saiv. Bugger the whole bloody thing.'

Saiv laughed, and put an arm around her shoulder. 'Yeah. Bugger it. And beat it. Jettison the dross and make this a year to remember. The year of your life.'

Without warning Lauren whirled round, apparently thinking at speed. 'OK. I will. I'll take your advice and act on it. You were always the intelligent one, the one who got the exams and made me feel like a birdbrain. I just hope you're right this time, that's all.'

Saiv was astounded. 'I made you feel like a birdbrain? But you're the successful one, a wealthy executive, bright and beautiful – don't be ridiculous! I'm the one who feels stupid, lumpen and clumsy, when you're around!'

Open-mouthed, somewhat breathless, they stared at each other. It was some time before Lauren spoke again, quietly, sounding chastened.

'Well, I never meant to make you feel like that. I had no idea I did.'

'I had no idea I gave you an inferiority complex.'

Again they regarded each other, nonplussed. Overhead, the tiny dot of an aircraft caught the sunlight, winking, towing a twin white trail through the sky. Lauren looked up at it.

'I – I'll start making some changes, then. Start moving in a different direction, if—'

'If what?'

'If you'll come with me, meet me halfway.'

Saiv smiled, and held her hand, willing reassurance into her. 'I will, Laurie. I'll come all the way, however far it may be. Only—'

'Only what?'

'Only you've got to stop trying to – trying to buy my friendship! I know you're generous by nature, and I love the things you give me, but I – I feel smothered! And I can't compete, don't want a friendship that can be measured in material things anyway. You must let me stand on my own feet.'

Lauren's eyes widened. 'But you're broke, haven't a bean. I *want* to help.'

'I know you do. And I appreciate it. I'll call you if the bailiffs come knocking. But meanwhile, no more sneaky presents, OK, no more extravagant restaurants? I think a simple life might suit us both better for a while.'

Lauren thought about it. 'Oh . . . OK. If you'll let me give you just one more thing.'

'What is it? One what?'

But Lauren shook her head, looking slightly evasive. 'No. Don't make me tell you yet, or even ask you. Leave me alone for a while first, to see whether I can do any of the things you think I should. I'm not at all sure I want to do them. But if I do, and they work, there'll be a reward in it. For both of us.'

'A reward? Is achievement not its own reward?'

'Oh, don't start! I'm a thoroughbred filly, I need carrots dangled!'

Saiv tried to pursue it, but Lauren wouldn't budge, and she recognised the futility of persisting. Anyone who could tie up a judge, keep her illness secret from every colleague, every other friend, even her family, had the tenacity of a mule. All Saiv could do was hope she'd use it to maximum benefit, and live to see her own birthday in September, maybe even share another spring picnic this time next year, up in the hills under the warm healing sun.

Back home next day, Saiv awoke to the sound of pelting rain and a cold sharp wind surging through the trees; at this time of year you never knew what to expect. In Lauren's apartment the heating came on automatically in the mornings, but not here, and Saiv shuddered as she got up to light the fire in her bathrobe, get the back boiler going. For one fleeting moment she wondered again whether Lauren mightn't be right, whether there was a lot to be said for the comforts that money could buy.

Ah, you're going soft. That woman is corrupting you. Get a blaze burning and you'll be fine. At least you have lots of logs, you're not some OAP eking out her tiny supplies, blue with the cold. Get dressed and put the bloody kettle on.

She felt better after she'd done that, and was warmed by a sense of growing tranquillity as well. It was perfect weather for writing, she'd stay indoors all day, snug as a bug. Munching a piece of hot toast, she fed crusts to the dogs, wondering whether she was imagining the new feeling of affinity she intuited between herself and Lauren. For all the years they'd known each other, they'd never gone on a picnic before, done anything outdoorsy, and she'd thought that Lauren would hate it. But she hadn't complained nearly as much as expected, and in the end they'd lingered up on the Featherbed for hours, talking in murmurs, sometimes hardly at all, letting the vast silence swallow them up. It had been the kind of day that made you wonder whether there mightn't just be some kind of deity after all, one that was not entirely malignant.

Saiv didn't have any fixed religion, distrusted any dogma that required checking in your intellect at the front door. Having repudiated Catholicism, she'd explored Buddhism, and now she could see a case for Pantheism. If there was any kind of god, its handiwork was surely to be seen in the stars and the seas, the rivers and mountains. But anything ending in 'ism' or 'ist' was to be treated with caution, and she had no intention of ever enlisting in any kind of army. I'm a conscientious objector, she thought; all I want is to see everyone being as kind to everyone else as possible.

So let's practise what we preach, and dig out Dr Mallon's phone number. If I can get any kind of information out of him that will help Lauren deal with this nightmare, that'll be a good day's work already done. Where's the directory?

The phone rang several times, and she was on the point of wording a voicemail when, at last, it was picked up. Expecting a receptionist, she was surprised to get Dr Mallon in person, sounding harassed.

'Yes, can I help you?'

Automatically she felt herself clicking into professor-of-philosophy mode, the well organised academic who could track down facts and assert herself quite firmly when need arose.

'Good morning, Dr Mallon, my name is Saiv Lovett, I'm a friend of Lauren Kilroy's and I was hoping you could help me with an enquiry about her.'

'Yes, what is it?'

'It's her diagnosis. She tells me she had a blood test in January and the result you gave her indicated that she has hepatitis C.'

There was a pause. 'So what's your query, Ms Lovett?'

'My query is – well, I just want to double-check that it's correct. That there hasn't been any mistake or misunderstanding anywhere along the line.'

Another pause. 'I see. Well, you'll appreciate that I cannot give you any confidential information about a patient, madam.'

'Yes. I know that. All I need is confirmation of the facts, so I can help her deal with their implications.'

'And what makes you doubt the facts?'

'Nothing! I'm quite sure they're correct. It's just that . . . well, could there have been any confusion at the laboratory, any mix-up with labels or anything like that?'

A weary sigh. 'Ms Lovett, let me assure you that every care is taken in pathology. It's too important to get it wrong.'

'Indeed it is. But there was that case recently . . . blood for a baby in Galway going to Mayo by mistake.'

'I believe that error occurred at the train station, not the lab.'

God! Why was he being so defensive? Why did so many medics think they were above human error, an unassailable deity that never disclosed, never discussed anything? Lauren had given her to understand that Dr Mallon was quite a nice man, so why couldn't he just play ball, now?

'Dr Mallon, I'd really appreciate it if you could just pull up Lauren's file and double-check it for me. She's a friend and I want to help her. Just to make sure it's the right name on the right results on the right file. Please?'

'I beg your pardon? You're surely not suggesting there's any confusion *here*, in my surgery?'

'No, of course not! I just—'

'Well then, let me assure you that the results are correct. I've been in practice for forty years and I am not in the habit of telling people they have fatal illnesses when they don't.'

Saiv's heart sank to her boots. Fatal? For sure, then? And was he refusing to check his files?

'I see. Well, I know you have an excellent reputation, so can I safely assume that you've already verified the lab information yourself?'

'Ms Lovett, I always verify everything. Now, if you don't mind, I do have some patients waiting—'

'But — could you at least just tell me what I should do? What's the best way to care for Lauren, and get her to care for herself?'

'You should make sure she avoids alcohol, takes extreme precautions with hygiene, particularly dental, and gets plenty of rest. I've told her all this myself. But I can't do anything more for her until she agrees to see a hepatologist. Perhaps you can persuade her to do that.'

Saiv sighed. 'I'm trying to. Is speed vital?'

'That's what we won't know until she sees one. She doesn't have any acute symptoms, there could be grounds for optimism . . . but I can't tell you any more than that. If you want to help, then try to get her to see sense, and a specialist. Now, I'm sorry, but I have a child here who's just drunk a bottle of solvent.'

'All right — but Dr Mallon, would you mind just taking my name and number, so you can call me if anything new comes up or there's any change in Lauren's status?'

'Ms Lovett, that kind of call is normally made only to the patient directly, or to their family if the patient is incapacitated.'

'Yes, I know, but — she isn't very close to her parents, and her sister is in Canada — I'd really appreciate it if you'd just jot down my details.'

He couldn't refuse to do that much, she guessed, and grudgingly he did it, to the accompanying sound of a whimpering child. Feeling frustrated, and largely defeated, she thanked him and hung up.

Damn! She was sure he'd just scribbled her number to humour her, probably on some scrap of paper he'd lose before lunch. So much for the kindly, fatherly figure Lauren had long depicted; the man sounded more like a grouch, with that touch of arrogance that came, inevitably, from playing God, dealing out life or death diagnoses. If only he had a receptionist, maybe she could have talked her into checking the file: but he didn't seem to have one.

But he had sounded sure about the results. And he had a name, she knew, for reliability, accuracy, trustworthiness. He had saved Lauren's sister . . . he was, undeniably, a good doctor. Or had been at the time. Did that mean he still was? All doctors were under stress these days, their surgeries filled not only with ever-weirder cases but with hypochondriacs, people pursuing claims and compensation, people who saw them as social workers, miracle workers. Maybe Dr Mallon was worn out with it all, or maybe he needed a new pair of glasses, had started to squint at small print . . . Saiv didn't know whether he wore glasses, but she did know he was over sixty. He *could* have made a mistake.

But it didn't sound as if he had. Lauren wasn't a new patient. He was unlikely to confuse someone he'd known since she was a child with anyone else. If she were to be honest, Saiv knew she was simply grasping at straws, hoping against hope. All she could say was that she'd tried. And tried, apparently, to no avail. Feeling despondent, she went into her study and sat down at her desk, tried to start her day's work. But Rousseau's face kept turning into Lauren's, and by noon she was still staring out the window, watching the rain weep down.

APRIL

Lola! Cola! The name and logo blared from every billboard, shouted from every television, and Lauren smiled with a feeling of completion when her colleague Shane Jackson stuck his head around her office door, calling out congratulations on the run. Everyone was always on the run around here, no conversation ever lasted more than a minute, and even as she waved acknowledgement he vanished.

Still, it was done, and done well. The client was expressing something close to approbation, the creatives were perilously near to happy, the consumers would soon be swilling oceans of the stuff. There were even crates of it here in the office, in case anyone got thirsty – or cared to sample the product. Lauren shuddered. Most of these drinks were full of chemical additives and, as Saiv pointed out, one was much the same as another. Her only duty was to convince the public otherwise, which in this instance meant branding the stuff as both healthy and trendy, getting them to put their money literally where their mouths were. Personally, she only ever drank mineral water, and would sooner ingest paint-stripper than Lola Cola.

But it would sell. Everyone always wanted the latest thing. Sitting back on her swivel chair, Lauren allowed herself a moment to relax; but it was difficult to relax when the entire corridor outside was booming with the raised voices of Mike Danaher and Charley Keogh. The row seemed to be about a batch of posters which had come back from the printers with a misplaced apostrophe, and each was blaming the other for it. Even though the posters were for an account which had nothing to do with her, Lauren felt an automatic urge to get up, run out and intervene. After all she was a partner, everything concerned her ultimately. But, for the first time in her entire career, she didn't get up. Mike was a notorious bully who shouted over everything, and the suspicion struck her that a man who shouted as much as he did was possibly a man who didn't get a word in edgewise at home. Knowing his wife Joan, it was a plausible theory. As for Charley, his marriage had broken up recently; maybe he too was letting off steam. If they came to blows, murdered each other for that matter, she wouldn't particularly miss either of them.

What she should do, she supposed, was simply pack up her briefcase and go home, like everyone else, or to the pub. It was after six and she'd done her day's work, skipping lunch even though she'd been in since eight that morning. Swivelling in her chair, she gazed out the window and pondered her options.

Once there would have been no debate about it; she'd have gone to the pub, joined for an hour in the camaraderie, black jokes and blue humour. Being seen in the pub was particularly important for anyone who'd been promoted, lest they convey an image of getting too big for their boots. It was politically crucial to remain 'one of the lads', which meant sinking pints and swearing like a trooper.

Then, after an hour or so, the married people amongst the group would slide off home, amidst jokes about being hen-pecked and indentured slaves, while those who had 'no homes to go to' would drift off somewhere for communal pizza and more beer. Briefly, Lauren was tempted; since ditching Jordan she often felt her apartment ringing hollow in the evenings, lovely but empty. Not that Jordan had often been in it, but at least the phone would usually ring. Now that she was single, it rang less often, as if her solitude might be somehow contagious and she'd been put in quarantine. Nobody expected a busy female executive to be married, much less to have kids or domestic duties, but there was no doubt about it; you were perceived differently if you were partnered. Until this year, this month, she'd been on the other end of the telescope herself, baffled by any woman who couldn't drum up an escort even if he was just arm candy. Except Saiv, of course, who was as odd as two left feet.

Maybe, if she went to the pub, Shane Jackson would be there? He was a nice guy, married admittedly, but his wife was often in London on business from one end of the week to the other. Once, years ago before meeting Jordan, she'd even had a fling with him. Only a one-night stand, but he'd given her to believe he wouldn't be averse to repeating it, seemed disappointed that she wasn't interested. That had been in the days when it was her policy to cut and run, never get involved in anything that might turn into another Isaac Hyland fiasco. Now, she flirted with the idea of putting a smile on his face tonight.

But . . . no. Although she was feeling resolutely well, packed chock-full of every vitamin known to science, she just hadn't the energy for the complications that Shane might entail. What she did have the energy for, if the truth be told, was walking the two miles home.

Jesus. Was she losing her marbles? It must be the spring sunshine that was going to her head, stretching into the evenings now, illuminating the bursting buds on the trees outside. Or else Saiv had sabotaged her, with those barmy expeditions to Tara and the Featherbed, making her not only venture outdoors but actually breathe air that wasn't air-conditioned. An alarming novelty; and now it seemed to have affected her in some crazy way, given her a taste for more.

But I can't walk home, she thought. My briefcase weighs a ton and these shoes were not made for walking. Two miles, for God's sake, in Ferragamo stilettos? Besides, it'd be dark by the time I got there and . . . if I'd known how Temple Bar was going to turn out, I might not have bought an apartment there. It was touted as so trendy, Dublin's left bank, and now it's full of pubs and stag parties and drunks. The apartment's great, but I was a stupid sucker to fall for the area. There's no way I could walk to my building without getting hassled, maybe even mugged for my Gucci briefcase. I wouldn't be the first. Bloody hell, I'm not chancing that.

Well, then. I'd better just call Blue Cabs and tell them I'm ready to leave. At least they usually turn up pretty pronto, for a gold-card customer like me. What do I spend on them every year, exactly?

I've never worked it out before, but let's see . . . a fiver home every evening, a fiver in every morning, including tip. That's not much. But how many days do I work? Five days a week, forty-six weeks a year . . . two hundred and thirty days a year, multiplied by a tenner a day. Crikey. Is that really two thousand, three hundred quid, just to go to work and home again?

Well, I'd have spent even more on parking if I took the car, before I became a partner. Those spaces in the basement are five grand a year each. Now I'm a partner I'm entitled to one as part of my package, only then I'd be stuck in traffic, it's a nightmare since they installed that bloody bus lane. So I have to use taxis, which can zip along in the bus lane.

I suppose Saiv would say I could take the bus! And what does she know, with her bike and her rust-bucket old Citroën, out in the sticks? If I used public transport – when it's not delayed or cancelled or on strike – I'd be squeezed in like a sardine amongst all those people spitting and sneezing, chomping gum, steaming in damp raincoats, I'd arrive for work looking like something the cat dragged in. Besides, executives do not take buses. Bad for punctuality, bad for image. My credibility would be punctured overnight.

Still . . . two and a half grand a year, almost, for taxis? Plus clothes, plus hairdressing, shoes and accessories . . . I must spend at least as much again on those. More. Now that I think about it, it's costing me an awful lot to work.

But work is fun! I love it when things are busy and the adrenalin's flying, when Mike Danaher and Charley Keogh aren't screaming like fishwives, when everything's happening rat-tat-tat. When posters aren't screwed up or couriers aren't late or some idiot client isn't bawling like a baby . . . when we're working on some hot account like Lola Cola. Even if the stuff is rubbish, it's a big earner. Even if the world is full of it, there's always room for another brand.

Isn't there? Isn't that the challenge? Creating a demand for more in a saturated market? I wish Saiv would stop saying it's pointless. That makes my career sound pointless, *me* sound pointless.

I really wish she'd stop.

I really wish I could walk home.

I really wish there was somebody at home.

I'm no good at being single. Just not cut out for it. If it wasn't so infra-dig, so *studenty*, I might even rent out the spare bedroom, consider sharing the apartment with somebody. Only then, what if we didn't get on? What if I got a tenant and he or she was a slob, wrecking the place? Or throwing big drunken parties? Or falling behind with the rent, expecting charity? Finding a decent flatmate is notoriously not easy.

Which I guess leaves me here calling for my taxi, going home alone. Eating alone, sleeping alone.

Bloody hell. Is this really how my life is going to be, from here on in? Where is my life going, and for how long, how much of it have I got? Do I dare consult that specialist, and find out?

No. Oh, no. Not that. Not yet. As long as I'm feeling well I'm going to assume I am well. If my body needed help it'd shout loud and clear for it.

So why is it shouting for a walk? How have I got into a situation where I can't even take it for a walk?

How is all this happening, and why is it happening to me?

'So what d'you think, Elmer? Should I go to the meeting, or stay home and watch the programme?'

Elmer looked briefly up at Saiv from the hearth where he was lying, as if to say 'this really isn't my problem, lady', and returned to the rubber bone he was chewing. Damn you, Saiv thought, why can't you talk like a Christian being? Why do I have to decide every single thing for myself, run everything, do everything? I've been writing all day and my shoulders are killing me, why can't you get up and give me a massage, you stupid dog? I've a good mind to sell you to Securicor for guard duty. And Duster, too. Pair of useless mutts.

I should go to the meeting. It'll be interesting and some of my colleagues from college will be there, it'd be a chance to catch up. I haven't seen anyone for ages, had an intelligent conversation with anyone since I can't remember when. It's in the Aula Maxima which is a beautiful venue, and there'll be a cup of tea afterwards, human beings galore. I'm tired of only having canine company.

But . . . it's not often you get an hour-long programme on your favourite subject. If Jennifer hadn't called I wouldn't even have known the BBC was doing Italy tonight – not one of those dashes round ten holiday destinations in thirty minutes, but a proper, in-depth special on Italy alone. What a treat. If only I'd ever got round to buying a video I could tape it, go to the meeting and watch it later. Lauren has a video, I could ask her to tape it for me . . . but she might forget. Anyway I have nothing to play a tape on, I'd have to go to Dublin to watch it there, if Lauren didn't lose it in the meantime or wipe it or something.

Oh, all right. I'll sacrifice the meeting and stay home. Italy is irresistible. If I can't go there is person, this is the next best thing, let's open a bottle of wine, settle in and enjoy it. *Sì, signora, bella Italia, con una buona bottiglia di vino, andiamo!*

Digging out a hoarded bottle of Amarone, Saiv stoked up the fire, curled up on the sofa and switched on the documentary. Focusing on the Renaissance, it started with a long, luxurious shot of Michelangelo's David in Florence, a statue so startlingly lifelike she could trace each vein and sinew as the camera progressed slowly upward from the feet, exploring bones and muscles as it wended its way gradually up to the wide, staring eyes. Saiv remembered those eyes indelibly, with their mixture of defiance and innocence, and felt a wave of nostalgia sweep over her; oh, to see them again, for real! As a student she had been hypnotised, seduced by them, and now they called out to her again, beckoning, beguiling, eternally beautiful.

As a student of nineteen she had gazed into them for hours, gone back to see the statue again and again, jostled unheeding by the crowds outside the Uffizi Gallery, before rushing off to find an English-language bookshop where she had bought two volumes, an academic biography of Michelangelo and a captivatingly romantic one called *The Agony And The Ecstasy*. Both were still on her shelves, dog-eared from re-reading, and she still wept in her heart for Michelangelo, who'd had such a lonely, troubled life. So long, but so lonely, plagued with political problems, money worries and an extremely troublesome family. Staring rapt at the screen, she thought she could see some of his sadness, now, in David's incredibly compelling eyes.

The camera pulled back, panning slowly around the statue from every angle, and then moved on into the piazza, where the blessedly low-key narrator spoke for a few minutes about Michelangelo before setting off for the Casa Buonarotti, the sculptor's house. Saiv remembered that too, its thick walls, opaque sense of shadow even on a sunny day; it had been a blissful refuge from the heat outside, and she had nearly fainted with pleasure to sense Michelangelo's spirit still in it, see so many papers written in his hand. I was such an impressionable kid, she thought, but it was exactly the right time to be in Florence; I soaked that city up like a sponge and it's part of me to this day. Not that anyone might think it, to see me now.

The narrator lingered in the house until she felt she could almost smell its chalky, woody scent, before setting off to visit a Pietà by Michelangelo, one that had frustrated him so much he'd finally taken a hammer to it and hacked off Christ's left arm. Despite attempts at repair it was still scarred, and even all these centuries later, these hundreds of miles away from it, Saiv caught something of the rage and pain that had gone into it. Nobody, she thought, could create such a work without having experienced sorrow, without truly understanding the nature of it, the helplessness, the massive challenge. It's not Michelangelo's most beautiful statue but it is so moving, so poignant I can hardly bear to look at it. The poor man endured so much, Pope Julius and the rest of them drove him nearly out of his mind, and he must surely have shed salt tears over this. He knew the meaning of death, physical and spiritual. And yet he survived, lived and worked on until he was ninety, as strong as he was sensitive . . . can there possibly be anyone like him alive today, living a life like his?

The narrator didn't shed any light on that; instead he set out into the streets of Florence, stopping off in squares and on bridges that made her heart skip a beat, sipping a cappuccino en route to other statues. As the camera caressed them Saiv could almost feel their silky lustre on her fingertips, the marble warmed by the life the sculptor had wrought in it, by the hot sun burning down on it and the spectators thronging round, enthralled by it. Fleetingly, she wondered whether her book on Rousseau would ever affect even one person the way these people were clearly affected, and cringed. She had so much to learn, she saw with sudden awful clarity, about creating anything of enduring value. And then learning how to do it didn't guarantee the giving of life to it, the vitality that would make it sparkle, and survive.

At this point the programme, still tracking Michelangelo, cut away to Rome, and she was faintly relieved. The Sistine ceiling was one work that had not taken her breath away, because it was too high up to see in detail; she remembered having had a crick in her neck all day after having peered, frustrated, for ages up at it. Besides, it was a little grandiose, executed to the specifications of some pompous pope, its restored colours too vivid for her taste; she infinitely preferred the creamy statues or inky cartoons of the Casa Buonarotti. Would she prefer them still, if she went back to Italy to see them again? If she could get over this terrible terror of flying, and go? Although this was not a tourism programme it was sucking her in, hauling her heart back to Italy, making her curse the terrible handicap of her fear. She had flown to Italy that first time, five years before her parents died, but now even the thought of a plane left her quivering, shivering.

Provocatively, the programme returned to Florence, to the gilded splendour of the Baptistry doors, to the green awnings of the Ponte Vecchio and then up to the gleaming golden Duomo, from where the camera roamed out over misty views of the Tuscan hills, all the way to tiny, fairy Fiesole. Oh, God, she thought, this is torture. I am *aching* to go back. I thought I'd learned to live without Italy but I haven't, this is tearing open all the memories, it hurts just to look at it. I saw Florence, parts of Rome and Siena, but what about Venice? Verona, Urbino, Padua, Capri . . . ? Am I never going to see any more, is this as close as I'll ever get again? It's not enough. I am starving for Italy, drying out and desiccating without its beauty, its radiant smile.

The narrator was talking about Raphael now, and Leonardo da Vinci, as he ambled through galleries containing their works, and absurdly she found herself siding with Michelangelo against his two more elegant, glamorous rivals. Raphael was a peacock, she thought belligerently, and Leonardo was a butterfly who kept flitting from one project to the next, never finishing half of what he started. Neither of them could hold a candle to Michelangelo for sheer stamina, and didn't have to put up with half as much hassle. In fact Raphael caused him a lot of hassle . . . still . . . that is a stunning painting. And Leonardo's mathematical mind is astonishing, his inside-out handwriting like some kind of code. *He* thought man could fly. He didn't think about jumbo jets going down over the Canaries, he just thought, let's go for it, let's do it. He'd be thrilled to the bone and beyond if he had the chance of boarding a plane today, could see what his vision has led to. He'd be off like a shot. He was raring to go five hundred years ago, with just a pair of strapped-on wings. All of these people were so damn brave, in their various ways. They'd have loved television, but they'd have laughed at me, sitting here watching it instead of getting out and living it.

Living. Unlike Lauren, that's what I have the option of doing, if I had the courage. It's almost like flying in her face, insulting the gods, not to do it. I'm not under any death sentence and buying a ticket to Italy is not generally regarded as suicide. My own parents, killed and all as they were, would probably tell me to get up and go, get a life. I wish to God in heaven there were some way I could, because I want to see David again before I die, and the Madonna of the Steps, and all these other exquisite things. Home is lovely, but there's just so much more out there. So *much* more.

Glass in hand, Saiv returned her attention to the documentary, savouring every drop of it along with the wine, tasting Italy on her tongue, feeling it flow into her bloodstream. When it finally ended in a flaming sunset over the River Arno, and the Amarone was all gone, she felt bereft.

But she was glad she had partaken of it. Usually she didn't watch television more than once or twice a month, and had heard of tonight's offering entirely by chance, from a friend who'd taken the trouble to tell her. Now she was left craving more, wondering what Italy was like today, fifteen years after she'd first seen it. Was it still chaotic, did you still have to don armour to buy an artichoke, cultivate the patience of Job to tackle a train station? Of course you could go there by train and boat, and she'd checked that out, but it would take two days, nearly three, each way from Ireland and back. Almost a full week, wasted on logistics. A week that could be spent on the Piazza San Marco or the plains of Lombardy, sipping amaretto in the twilight, gliding in a gondola by moonlight.

Oh, she thought suddenly, bugger this. What'd be the point of a gondola, if I didn't have some handsome hunk to share it? Maybe Italy's gone off since I was last there, maybe the traffic is now impenetrable and prices are astronomical and it's all completely corrupt, mercenary, tacky? I might go back only to find my student self stone dead, my tastes different, the memories unmatched by reality. I might be sorry I hadn't just gone hill-walking in Wicklow.

Only . . . I want to see that Pietá again, and that David. I want to laugh my way across the Ponte Vecchio with the silver shining in the sun and ice-cream dripping down my front. I want to sit on the edge of the Trevi fountain listening to some idiot singing 'Three Coins' at the top of his lungs, like that American did last time.

Lauren has never been to Italy, has she? Only that day trip once, to Milan on business. Milan's not Italy. She should see the real Italy before she . . . before she . . . grows old. Even if she does survive and live to be old, that's no time to start slogging round in the heat, up all those steps and hills. Everything in Italy's on top of one or the other. It takes energy, stamina, agility to see it properly.

If she could do it, could I do it? If I braced myself to go, would she go with me? I'd absolutely love her to see it, it's so different from the world she lives in, that thinks an advertising poster is art! She'd be a different person if she could touch those statues, feel their glow, their life force.

Of course Lauren's idea of a holiday is a beach, a bikini and a trashy book. And blokes and bars and shops, shops, shops. She'd be a nightmare to travel with, we'd probably have a huge row every day. The whole thing might be wasted on her and I'd resent her for ruining it for me. And yet, I'd love to try. Physically she still seems able to travel, which might not be the case later on. What a screaming shame if she died without seeing that David, so many beautiful enriching things.

If she does die without seeing them, will it be my fault? I know she's well capable of doing anything she wants for herself, but this is the kind of thing that would never occur to her, and she'd need persuasion. It'd be my fault for not pointing it out, and not persuading her. At the moment I have neither the time nor the money to go, but the book should be finished in the summer and I'll have a bit of both then . . . she'll be due some time off, and money certainly wouldn't be a problem for her. But in another way it might be, because I'd want to stay in cheap *pensione* and she'd demand five-star hotels. There'd be rows and resentment over that. We might come back not speaking, and never see each other again.

Another excuse, then, for not going. There'll always be another one. What about the dogs? How could I bear to leave them for two or three whole weeks, steel myself to put them in kennels? Could I possibly do that? They'd pine horribly and I'd miss them dreadfully, feel so guilty. It would be wanton cruelty.

And this, I'm starting to suspect, is slowly becoming a serious problem. I started out chronically shy, and now my world is shrinking to the point where Lauren is the only one who can even drag me as far as Dublin. If I don't do something about it, there'll be a name for it: agoraphobia. I'll end up so reclusive it'll be an ordeal just to cross my own threshold, even walks in Meath or Wicklow will be out the window. What is wrong with me, why am I so scared of going anywhere, meeting anyone?

I can cope with work, because it *is* work, in a nice safe orderly academic institution. But even that . . . the students are becoming more boisterous every year, and they had some bearing on my decision to take a year off. Unless I get out and about this summer, interact with people however much I hate it, I might scarcely be able to go back.

Lauren would be the ideal person to travel with, from that point of view. She's so extrovert she'd chat up Genghis Khan and invite him to join us for supper. She'd be like a shield, if she came with me. And I would so love her to see Italy, share its joys. I wish it were in my gift to give it to her, like a present, it'd open up her world in one way and mine in another. I've only ever been in love once in my life, and that was with Italy. It's so robust, so charming and passionate and beautiful . . . everything, strangely, that I'm not. An attraction of opposites.

Italy, hopefully, will be around for a long time yet. But will Lauren? If we don't go now, will it be lost to us both forever? Is this our only chance?

But I can't leave the dogs. And I cannot get on a plane. The mere thought, even here in my own home, makes me feel sick to my stomach. I can't do it.

And there's your epitaph, Saiv Lovett. 'She couldn't do it.' Dear God, Lauren Kilroy is not the only one who is dying.

I'll ring him.
I won't.
I will.
You will not!

Pacing around her apartment, in such a mood she hardly knew whether to sit or stand, Lauren eyed the phone and agonised endlessly: if she rang Jordan, would he speak to her? Had she made a completely unforgivable mistake, that day she tied him up? Or had she done the right thing? At this moment she didn't think she had, because in spite of evertyhing she was missing him like an amputated arm. No longer there, he was ghosting agonisingly.

Of course he wouldn't speak to her. She had humiliated him beyond endurance. If he was still even in the country, the most she'd get would be a vehement invitation to fuck off. He'd often said he adored her, but . . . oh, sweet Jesus, why couldn't she get him out of her mind?

Because there was nobody else to fill it up? Because she was a fool, a mesmerised rabbit caught in the headlights of his bright smile? Because her vanity wouldn't let her live without his adulation? Because the street-smart executive was just a silly adolescent, her tongue hanging out for her heart-throb? I'll have to see a shrink if this goes on, she thought, I'll end up in therapy over this. I can cope all day at work but I cannot cope here on my own at night. I'll crack like a pane of glass.

What'll I do? I suppose Saiv would calmly sit down and read a book. Huh. The only book I've ever enjoyed in the last ten years is my chequebook. I bet hers will be the bore of the century, if it ever sees daylight. Still, at least it seems to keep her off the streets, keep her sane. I should get some kind of hobby like that, some kind of project. Join a class or something . . . yeah, right. Chock full of nerds in anoraks.

'That's it, Ms Kilroy, very good, just twirl that heap of clay once more now and then fire it in the oven, you'll have a lovely little flowerpot to take home.' Waahh! I'll swallow strychnine before I'll join any flaming class. I should have gone to the pub after all and got roaring drunk. Except that now I'm not allowed enough alcohol to fill a gnat's thimble. None at all, if I were to listen to that damn doctor.

Shag this for a game of soldiers. It's only seven o'clock. Three hours before I have to go to bed so I can get up again at six for work . . . what a huge chunk of my life work occupies. How on earth do people live without it? I'd go round the bend if I had many vacant hours like these. I'd ring Gemma or Adèle or someone for a chat, only . . . it's such a strain having to sound chirpy all the time, not let slip that I'm ill. But word would get round in a flash and they'd start rolling me in cotton wool at the office and Mike Danaher or someone would start a whispering campaign that I'm not up to my promotion, can't hack it any more. What a shower of bastards those guys are, always waiting to trip someone up and get their own foot in the door. Dealing with all the politics is nearly as much work as work itself.

What's on telly? Where's the guide? Let's see . . . cookery on RTE. Science on Channel 4. Something about sheep on UTV. A quiz on BBC 1 and some dreary documentary about Italian art on BBC 2. Is this rubbish what I pay good money for, huh, cable as well as licence? Honestly, when I think what it costs to run this apartment and now I can't even sit easy in it for one night.

What does it cost, exactly? Mortgage, phone, heating, electricity, bins, maintenance fees, Mrs Mop to clean one day a week? And flowers . . . I love filling the place with them, but they don't come cheap. I guess the whole caboodle must add up to the guts of twelve or fifteen grand. And then there's the car, another two or three grand for petrol, tax, insurance. Four grand, to be realistic. Nineteen, altogether.

Jesus! Plus taxis, clothes and all the rest. We must be talking twenty-five a year in total, to run Ms Lauren Kilroy. And that's out of my net salary, after PAYE, PRSI, VHI and whatnot. It's a helluva lot.

Well, I earn a lot. I don't know why I seem to have money on the brain tonight. Still – I really am a very expensive commodity. And yet here I am, stuck here on my own, feeling blue and lonely and . . . it's not fair. It's *outrageous*. Whatever they say, money does buy happiness. Or did, until now. God knows I work hard enough for it.

And yet there's Saiv Lovett, pauper-poor, no equity, with the brass balls to actually take a year *off*. She can't afford it, yet she's loving it, seems to love that rustic life of hers with all but chickens on the back of her bike. Is she really loving it, going nowhere, seeing nobody? She seems to be. Seems a sight happier than I am, at any rate. Which at this moment wouldn't be bloody difficult.

Let's put on some music. Loud. Or as loud as apartment rules permit. Bruce Springsteen. He'll drown out my sorrows, I won't be able to hear myself think. Which, above all, is what I want not to do. I haven't let myself stop to think since I was barely twenty and quit college to become a hot-shot career woman. I abhor navel-gazers and indecision and analysing and all that junk; life is for living, not picking at. I sank my teeth into it and never let go since and I'm damned if Dr Mallon or anyone else is going to rip it away from me.

But I'd have to think about that, if I didn't work till I dropped and now take a sleeping pill as well, every night. If I didn't take one I'd be awake till dawn, bawling like a baby or having more awful morbid thoughts about . . . no. No way. If I don't think about it then it can't happen.

It can't, it won't! I'm too young, not even halfway through my list of things I want to do! Get married, go live in a beautiful house in Dublin 4, maybe even bite the bullet and have a kid some day . . . ? What was it Saiv said, about how if she was in my boots she'd maybe want to do something 'worthwhile'? What did she mean by that? Wrap a tea-towel round her head and go play Mother Teresa?

Well, sorry, Saiv. We're talking Posh Spice here, not Mother Teresa. You won't catch me saving lepers or building orphanages. I'm selfish and shallow and there you have it.

But . . . what the hell am I going to do? I love my work and I don't want to give it up; but I don't want it to be the only thing I've ever done, either. Could it really be that I only have maybe eight *months* left, to cram everything in? Oh, no, oh, please – I don't even know what everything is! What am I doing, where am I going?

Maybe I do need to stand back, as she says, and think about this after all. I could take a break from work, just a few weeks' holiday – not now with things so busy, but when they're a bit quieter, in the summer? If I'm not going to get to Paris with Jordan, maybe I could go with someone else. Certainly not on my own. Who'd go? Not Gemma, because she's married, nor Adèle because of her child, not Saiv because we'd throttle each other. She'd have me traipsing round the Louvre, staying in a fleapit, making me walk everywhere as if God hadn't invented taxis. Besides, she won't bloody fly.

But some sort of break might help, if I can get someone. I wish Caoimhe weren't in Canada. I wish my mother was the kind of woman who . . . who I could communicate with. She's only fifty-four, she'd be well able for Paris, but she'd nag me from one end of it to the other. Nothing would be right, up to scratch, the 'way we do it at home'. She'd use the chance to tell me again how I threw my education away, let her down by not getting letters after my name. How Dad slaved to put me through that first year and then all his effort was wasted, came to nothing. With the unspoken implication that *I* came to nothing.

Oh, Mum. Why do things have to be this way? Why can't I call you and tell you the truth, that I'm ill and unhappy and terrified out of my mind, that I need you, need a cuddle as badly as when I was a baby? I really do, Mum. I'd go home right now and sob all over you, if I didn't think I'd never hear the end of it, if it wouldn't be another weapon for you to aim at me.

But it would be a weapon. You'd use it to take charge of my life and march me to doctors and do everything your way, with the silent insinuation that this, somehow, is all my fault. You wanted me to be perfect and can't accept that I'm only human, that an accident can happen to me the same as it can to anybody else. I wish I could talk to you, but I can't.

I can't talk to anyone, for one reason or another, apart from Saiv. She's barmy, but at least she's there, and she listens. She's been a very good friend to me since all this started happening, let me play everything the way I want to play it. Why can't you be a friend, Mum? Are we going to be antagonists till the day I die?

I'd hate to think that we are. But that day might not be as far off as we could normally expect. If it dawns, will your shock and sorrow be all my fault too, for not telling you? Another black mark in my blotted copybook?

It'll be an enormous blot, much worse than dropping out of college. Dropping out of *life*! Tsk, tsk. How can Lauren have been so remiss, how can she have done this to me and her father? Of course she always was so wilful, would never listen . . . silly, selfish girl.

Oh, God. Do I dare tell you, and Dad, when we go out to lunch next Sunday? That'd certainly give us something to talk about, for a change. I'd give anything to tell you, if I didn't think it would all end in recrimination and fuss and – after all that – no support whatsoever. I could end up feeling less loved than ever, on my deathbed, even less than I feel now.

Which, if you want the truth, is pretty unloved. Maybe that's my own fault, for hanging out with people who define friendship socially, financially, index-linked to perks and promotions? I've offended on that score myself, mea culpa, I admit it. It's taken Saiv, these past few months, to show me what real friendship can be. Real friendship, it would appear, is patchy and ragged and honest, a frayed old blanket, but warm when you need it. Compared to Saiv, my other friends look like taffeta; shiny and showy, but scratchy. Not what you'd call snuggle material.

And you're right, Mum. More of it is my own fault, too. I've been deliberately involving myself with the wrong men. A series of one-night stands, and then the heavily married Jordan White. I'm what you'd call a slut. But you don't know how it felt to be dumped by Isaac Hyland, how desperately determined I was never to go through pain like that again. I thought a married man would be safe. He'd have his own agenda and – and it never in a million years dawned on me that I might fall in love with him, or get hurt again after all. I was a fool.

You told me so, didn't you? And now if I tell you what's happened, you'll say it again: you fool, Lauren, you little fool! Married men are bad news as well as morally disgraceful, you could see it coming . . . that's why I can't tell you. That's why our relationship has disintegrated to the point where the only thing we can safely discuss is the weather. You're my Mum, but you know nothing of what I think, of what I feel, you don't really know me at all.

In some ways, I hardly know myself. Lately when I look in the mirror I see something missing. Is it you? Is it Jordan? Is it some invisible part of myself? What is it, Mum, and why can't I ask you to help me look for it? Under all these designer outfits, all this concealing make-up, I'm suddenly wandering in the wilderness, lost as a little girl. A little girl spending twenty-five thousand pounds a year on things which, now that she's got them, are not making her very happy. It's a lot of money, to be spending on toys.

Toys are amusing to a child. But not so satisfying to someone having to grow up in a hurry, assess her life like an adult. Only then, what is? What would make life richer, deeper, more meaningful? If I gave up my toys would I find out, or could I just be left with a handful of nothing?

That's the risk I'm so scared to take. I'll never admit that to you, never let you know I'm scared of anything. I'll go to my grave without ever telling you how scared I was of college, of not being as bright as people like Saiv, of failing my exams after Dad had invested all that hard-earned money in me. So I quit and you were furious and we never discussed why I did it. If I die within the next year, you won't have any difficult daughter to disapprove of any more, but you might not have anything to compensate you either, not one single memory to be proud of. You could be left holding the ashes of a daughter who had no substance, was only a handful of nothing.

It was the simplest of pleasures, but Saiv sat savouring the sun on her back, soaking it up as she worked out in the garden on her manuscript, correcting the print-out by hand in red biro. It was a dotty way to work, everything would have to be keyed back into the computer later, but she was enjoying it, feeling sensual satisfaction in the thick stack of paper, which was pinned to the table with a chipped old marble paperweight she'd once bought in some Roman market. Occasionally there was a flutter of wind, but otherwise the day was warmly serene, caressingly tender; at the end of the field the trees were bubbling with white blossom, apple and cherry, and she was vaguely aware of the dogs running around, digging and chewing on some old toy. But they were distant, part of the pastoral tableau which resonated with quiet; apart from a couple of idly chirping birds there was not a sound to be heard. Pausing to chew the end of her pen, she noted that the two lilac trees down by the ditch were on the brink, ready to burst into flower in just a few more days by the look of them, and the hawthorn bushes were draped in creamy drifts of lace. The whole field was surging with energy, and yet it was so still, so silent. Revelling in the beauty around her, in the absorbing rhythm of her work, she dipped her head back over her papers and resumed her scribbling.

'Well, do I have to knock the door down altogether, off its hinges or what?'

The voice shot across her bows like a bullet, so unexpected she gasped, jerking her hand so that the pen flew off the side of the page. Standing at the side of the house, resplendent in tweed cap and green muddy wellies, stood her brother Tommy.

Instantly, she registered annoyance, with a flash of guilt immediately upon it. She should, naturally, be pleased to see her brother – and her niece Gráinne, standing behind him, peering round the wall with a look that said sorry, didn't mean to disturb you. But she was disturbed, hated unexpected interruptions when she was working. Tommy lived on a farm in Westmeath, only dropped in four or five times a year and then usually on his way to somewhere else, but never phoned first. Sometimes she got the absurd feeling that he liked to catch her unawares, that it gave him some invisibly upper hand. Ever since they were children, Tommy had somehow conveyed that he had the upper hand, was bigger, stronger, smarter and, nowadays, considerably more successful. Despite his rough farmer's garb, his weather-rusty complexion and coarse countryman's ways, Saiv knew that the car parked now round the front of the house was a Mercedes, covered in mud to camouflage the profitability of his dairy farm. Farmers didn't show off their wealth – indeed they went to pains to hide it – but in Tommy's case there was plenty of it. He was one of those farmers who knew how to work the system, grab every available grant, cosy up to local politicians and take Brussels for a long-running ride. He didn't keep in touch with Saiv, but dropped in without warning whenever he wanted something, as was presumably now the case.

Recovering herself, Saiv stood up. 'Were you knocking? I didn't hear a thing.'

'Aye, we were. I said to Gráinne, ah sure, what's the use, that aunt of yours will be up to her neck in her oul books somewhere – didn't I, Gráinne?'

Gráinne, a tall strong sixteen-year-old with sturdily plaited hair and freckled face, nodded at her father with an easy grin. Although her strong personality equalled his, there was something more open about her, a kind of candour that Saiv had always liked. What you saw, in Gráinne, was what you got.

'Yes, Dad, you did. Right as usual.'

She grinned at Saiv, and Saiv grinned back; the girl seemed

to sense her father's deprecation of 'oul books' without sharing it. Saiv didn't see her niece very often, but when she did she always wondered where Tommy had got his likeable daughter, who resembled him only in stature and healthy, ruddy looks. She resembled her mother Margaret even less; Margaret was a small fussy woman whose only activities, that Saiv had ever been able to divine, were the endless cleaning of her house and the frantic climbing of Westmeath's social ladder. Saiv only ever saw her at Christmas, which was more than enough.

'Well, I wasn't expecting you, or I'd have listened out for the car . . . anyway, come on and sit down, I'll make some tea and you can tell me what brings you here.'

As she said it Saiv eyed Tommy, wondering what he wanted. Before she found out, she knew, there would be a good deal of palaver to be got through, interrogation about when she was going back to work and resuming 'normal' life; only dreamers and layabouts, in Tommy's view, skived off to write books, or even read them for that matter. Yet both Tommy and Margaret were keen on education for their children; education of the kind that would, in due course, accumulate money.

'Ah,' Tommy said, throwing off his cap and sitting heavily down on a rickety garden chair, 'we just thought we'd pop in on our way to Dublin.'

'Oh? What's happening in Dublin?'

'The Spring Show. Next week. We're going to the RDS on a bit of business, I have a few cows entered in a few categories and Gráinne here will be putting her horse over a few jumps.'

Going into the kitchen to make tea, Saiv got the picture. Tommy and Gráinne were going to suss out the lie of the land, make sure her horse got good stabling for next week's show-jumping event; she was a capable, confident rider whose bed-room in Westmeath was bedecked with rosettes. Tommy, naturally, liked her to win, and liked his dairy stock to do well too in the agricultural part of the show. Success was good for business. Stacking a tray with tea things, Saiv brought it out to them, cleared space amidst the papers on which she'd been working and sat down, trying to look sociable. Without ever putting it into words, Tommy had a way of making her feel anti-social. Nine years older than her, he was in his early forties, and had disparaged her academic interests ever since she'd gone to university at eighteen. Twenty-seven at the time, he'd said there was only one useful thing a girl could do at university, and that was get herself a rich husband, perferably one who played football and had a healthy taste for a pint of Guinness. When Saiv had failed to engage in this pursuit, he'd given her to understand that she had failed some vital exam, let the side down in some essential way.

So she was surprised, now, when he took up a handful of her papers and scanned a few lines of the top page. 'What's this?' he asked. 'A speech to the United Nations?'

'It's my book on Rousseau' she replied equably, 'you know, the one I've been working on since last September. It's nearly finished.'

Without bothering to read further, he put down the pages. 'About time too. A whole year, with no income! Will there be any money in it, if it ever sees daylight?'

God, Saiv groaned inwardly, if one more person asks me that I will murder them. 'I don't know' she said, 'but it's unlikely. I'm not doing it for money.'

Gráinne looked up. 'Then what are you doing it for?'

'I'm doing it for the sake of doing it, that's all. For the interest and challenge and pleasure.'

Gráinne beamed. 'See, Dad? She's doing it because she wants to. Because she can. I told you she'd stick at it.'

Swallowing a mouthful of tea, he grunted. 'Aye, and then she'll be going back to her job, and if you have a lick of sense you'll be going to university yourself in two years' time, missy.'

Saiv gazed at him, extremely surprised. Granted, his two sons were at university, but they were both there for reasons related to farming: eighteen-year-old Liam was studying hor-ticulture and nineteen-year-old Mark was doing veterinary studies. Surely Tommy hadn't already decided that young

Gráinne should go too, to catch herself that rich but elusive husband?

But even as she looked at her niece, Gráinne scowled. 'I will not. I told you, I'm leaving school after the Junior Cert this summer.'

Tommy flushed angrily, and Saiv saw that some kind of conflict was going on between the two; this was the first she'd heard of Gráinne wanting to leave school so early. Curiously, she studied the girl's intent face, which looked suddenly resolute.

'Are you, Gráinne? At sixteen? To do what?'

Before she could answer, Tommy spoke for her, his beefy face darkening ominously. 'To – to be a mechanic, she says! To train in Richie Crowley's workshop and then set up a garage of her own! Did you ever hear such nonsense! She has her mother's heart broken . . . speak to the girl, Saiv, and knock some bloody sense into her. She's driving her mother and me demented.'

Ah. Saiv sat back and digested it, struggling to suppress a smile. Tommy was neatly caught halfway between a rock and a hard place. Having always ridiculed his sister's academic career – because, maybe, he hadn't accumulated enough entry points for university himself? – he now wanted his daughter to do a degree. Do anything, Saiv slowly began to suspect, other than become a mechanic. Margaret would have a fit of the fainting flutters . . . probably was having one already. Which was the reason behind this visit; on the pretext of sociably seeing his sister, Tommy wanted to recruit support, knew that the girl liked her aunt. From being a kind of black sheep, Auntie Saiv had become a role model.

'Well' she said slowly, thoughtfully, 'what Gráinne does will depend, presumably, on what Gráinne is good at. What do you think you're good at, Gráinne?'

Tossing her plait over her shoulder, Gráinne leaned forward, and Saiv was struck by the sudden eagerness in her face, the way her eyes lit up and her voice became firm.

'I'm good at cars. Cars and tractors and all kinds of machinery. I'm good at science too, at school, maths and physics—'

'There you are!' Tommy interrupted. 'Maths and physics! The girl's born to be a doctor, or a dentist!'

Saiv smiled. 'Well, actually you need biology for medicine or dentistry. Tell me, Gráinne, do you—'

'Or a banker!' Tommy interrupted again. 'She's so good at maths, she could run the Bank of Ireland! Finance! The stock market! We'd gladly send her to UCD or even Trinity, cost us a fortune, but we'd do it if only she—'

'She wanted to? But does she want to?'

'No way' Gráinne interjected, sounding as heated as her father, 'I'm not interested in any of those things, I'm interested in machines! Engines! I want to have my own garage!'

Exasperated, Tommy spread his meaty hands before Saiv, his tone changing from commanding to imploring. 'Did you ever hear the likes? A girl? A girl of sixteen, with the whole world at her feet, who wants to quit school to become a grease-monkey? Tell her, Saiv. Tell her about university, about your students, about the careers they'll have when they graduate.'

Saiv couldn't suppress her smile. Clearly a 'grease-monkey' did not figure in Tommy's plans for his family, nor in his wife's either. He had come here expecting that, as a professor, she would be horrified, urge Gráinne to continue with her 'book learning' at all costs. But Saiv liked the girl, whose chrysalis young independence was almost tangibly struggling to emerge and assert itself. Becoming a mechanic would be tough, a physically demanding life with a lot of male rivalry and ridicule to contend with, but if it would make her happy . . . Saiv didn't even know whether there was any money to be made at it, but that was beside the point. What counted was Gráinne's apparent vocation, the work that could make her face light up and glow as it was glowing now.

'Well . . . actually, Tommy, not all of my students will have such great careers as you think. Some of them are already at university for the wrong reasons – parental pressure, or financial ambition, or indecision about what it is they really want. Some haven't found their vocations at all, some are bored, some are lost. There's a very high drop-out rate after first year. If Gráinne knows what she wants, is lucky enough to have a passion for mechanics, then you could save yourself a lot of money by letting her do it. She'll only end up doing it anyway, in the long run, so what's the point in delaying her?'

Appalled, he gaped at her. 'What's the *point*? The point is that she's only a child, doesn't realise how important a Leaving Certificate is these days, and a degree!'

'But you don't have a degree yourself. And you laughed at me for doing one. I really can't see why you're getting so het up, Tommy.'

He was furious. As his grey eyes snapped sparks at her, she could read every line of his anger in them, and didn't care. He was a snob, his wife was another, so what if they never spoke to her again? Undoubtedly she was risking her fragile relationship with them, but it was an unfulfilling, sporadic relationship anyway; for young Gráinne's sake she would gladly sacrifice it.

'Well' he breathed, 'you're a great help. Me only daughter, and you don't even want her to get a proper education. You, with education to burn – you should be ashamed of yourself, Saiv, for helping her to throw away her whole future.'

Sighing, she put down her cup and looked at him. 'Tommy, Gráinne's future lies in Gráinne's talents, in her ability to use them and enjoy them. It does not lie in wasting time on some irrelevant academic course, nor in a piece of paper to be framed for all to see. My classes are full of kids who don't want to be in them and I do not want to see any niece of mine as restless, as confused as they are. I know sixteen is very young to leave school, but—'

'But I'd still be learning!' Gráinne interrupted vehemently. 'Richie would be teaching me! He says he needs an apprentice and he'll take me on, I could go to the tech and do a night course—'

Tommy swung round to her. 'The *tech*? Are you mad? You could do engineering at UCD for God's sake, if you want to meddle with motors!'

'But' Gráinne persisted, 'you don't need to be an engineer to meddle with motors! I don't want to build bridges or lay pipes or design escalators, I want to work with cars! With my *hands*! Now, this summer, after the Junior Cert!'

Tommy looked ready to explode. Saiv knew that, if she were to play the family game right, she should support him, should recommend that yes, Gráinne study engineering and then, if she were still determined, go into the motor industry as some kind of designer or consultant, someone who wouldn't get her hands dirty. But Gráinne looked so passionate, so desperate to get as dirty as possible.

'Then – since my opinion is being sought – I think that's what you should do, Gráinne. If you have a dream, then you have something invaluable. Go for it.'

Gráinne smiled hugely at her, radiating gratitude, and Saiv was struck by the irony of it. She had pleaded with Lauren not to quit college; now she was advising her niece not to go there at all. But you couldn't live life by a formula; the world was full enough already of square pegs in round holes. She didn't want this lively, energetic girl to become another one.

Abruptly, exuding frustration and ire, Tommy stood up. 'Well, if that's the best you can do for your niece, then we'd better be going. All I can say, Saiv, is I'm very disappointed in you.'

Stung, she also stood up, glancing at Gráinne before facing him squarely. 'I know you are, Tommy. But then you've been disappointed in me all your life. I'm not wealthy, I'm not married, I'm not any of the things a respectable sister should be, am I? So one more disappointment will hardly matter. Anyway, it'll be worth it, if any good comes out of it for Gráinne. She's a bright girl, a lovely girl, and I'd like to see her happy.'

With a snort, he picked up his cap and flung it back on his head, stamped away round the side of the house to his car. She knew it would be a long time before she saw him again, and felt a tinge of sadness; other people seemed to get on so much better with their families, have warmer and more generous relationships. With their parents dead and their only other brother living in Kerry, it would be good if she and Tommy got on well, liked each other better. Did people only like you if you said what they wanted to hear?

As if confirming that they did, Gráinne threw herself at Saiv, embracing her with fervour. 'Oh, Saiv, thank you! I was sure you were going to say I should stay at school.'

Returning the hug, she murmured into the girl's hair. 'No, Gráinne. It would have been easier to do that, but I couldn't. Not when you clearly want to be a mechanic so much.'

Nodding as she drew back, Gráinne grinned at her. 'It's true what Dad says. You're your own worst enemy.'

Her own worst enemy? Caught unawares by Gráinne's words, Saiv gazed at the girl's departing figure, wondering what they meant. It wasn't the first time she'd heard the term; Lauren sometimes said the same thing, but . . . ?

So. OK. Maybe there was a grain of truth in it. Maybe the life she had chosen to live was obscure, perplexing to those who saw no point, no profit in it. Maybe she was a member of a dying breed who weren't obsessed with money or image or status, people who preferred to live a quiet interior life because they didn't much care for what was going on around them in the bustling, hustling world.

Maybe, if she had a lick of sense, she'd be better off ditching her precious principles, conforming and shaping up to what society evidently required? If she chose to do it, she could rise to a new 'image', polish up her Ps and Qs, wear and say and do everything that a woman of her age was expected to wear, say and do. She could conform, march to the drum, smile as if her lips were taped to her ears. She could even butter up her blasted brother and earn his approval, if she had any reason to believe it was worth earning.

But then she wouldn't be Saiv Lovett. She'd be Saiv Super-Nice, fawning and dissembling and plotting her soft, easy life. She'd be head of department at work, never at home because there were too many parties to go to, grants to go after, contacts to network.

She'd see a lot more of people like Gráinne. Only people like Gráinne, then, might not want to see a lot more of her.

Sighing, she thrust her hands in her pockets and whistled up the dogs, hustled them indoors still wondering: did she really never do anything the easy way? Was she her own worst enemy?

Lauren, she thought suddenly as she washed the teacups, is right. I've got to get out more. Got to stop analysing everything. When this book's finished I'm going to go – where?

I don't know where. Don't care. All I know is that, just for a while, I've got to get away from *me*.

MAY

No!

Lauren didn't know how it was happening or why it was happening. All she knew was that one minute she was sitting on the edge of her desk discussing television voice-overs with Shane Jackson; the next minute the room was spinning and the vertical blinds, through which the sun had been glinting, were turning into spears or railings of some kind. She was slumped in a chair without having any idea how she'd got there, and Shane's voice was washing through her head like waves through a cave.

'Deep breaths . . . come on . . . fresh air . . .'

Opening her eyes, she saw his agitated face, and some other face behind; her secretary Angie, clutching a glass, looking panic-stricken. Around them a gale was blowing, papers were flying to the floor; someone had opened all the windows. She attempted to sit up, and every drop of blood in her veins seemed to sluice away, every bone seemed to freeze to ice. Her teeth were chattering uncontrollably.

'. . . a doctor . . .' Shane was saying. With the desperation of a mountaineer clutching a ledge, she raised one arm, stiff as a sword, and impaled her fingernails in his shirt.

'No . . . no . . . doctor . . .'

He leaped back electrified, and it dimly registered that she had hurt him, done something absolutely appalling with her nails. Words of apology formed in her mouth, but her mouth had turned into a block of that stuff you planted fake flowers in . . . whatsit . . . the effort of trying to think was superhuman, so exhausting she felt her eyelids closing again, heavy as marble slabs.

When she opened them again the room was full of people, people whose names she should know. Her face was wet, her blouse was open at the neck and someone was holding her wrist.

'. . . very slow . . . ambulance . . .'

Was it only a dozen eyes that were staring down at her, or a hundred, a thousand? In all of them she registered rapt horror, a kind of breathless fascination that made her feel like an insect under a microscope, everyone waiting aghast to see what it would do next. Of its own accord seemingly, her wrist wrenched free of the hand that was holding it, and she gripped the arms of the chair, heaved herself upright.

There was a long, long silence.

'I – I'm all right' she whispered.

They stared at her; apparently the evidence was contradictory. Desperation gripped her, winched her into what she hoped was a more normal position. Gently, Shane put his hand on her shoulder.

'Lean forward, Laurie. Put your head between your knees.' As he said it he put his other hand on her hair, bent her down until it was sweeping the floor and she was noticing, for the first time, the minute yellow flecks in the grey carpet.

Uuhhh.

In this undignified position he made her sit for what felt like hours, inhaling, exhaling, until eventually she felt some rhythm return to her breathing, and only then realised that she had been gasping. As somebody put something warm over her shoulders, she also realised that she had been shivering, twitching like a puppet. A bolt of panic scorched her like lightning, she felt her temperature rocket. With a huge effort of will, she lifted her head and looked Shane in the face.

'Jesus' he said, 'you were white as paper, now you're roaring red. You are one sick little lady, Laurie. We're going to have to call that ambulance.'

'No' she croaked. Someone seemed to have pumped pebbles down her throat.

'Yes' he insisted. 'Either that, or if you can stand up I'm driving you over to casualty at Vincent's.'

Vincent's? Hospital? Panic revved in her mind like a jet engine.

'No' she blurted again, waving him away with her hand. 'No hospital. No doctor.'

Quizzically, he looked at her, frowning, and then turned to the massed people behind him.

'OK. Drama over. Let's all get back to our desks and give Lauren some air. I'll take care of her, she'll be fine.'

Reluctantly, murmuring things she didn't grasp, they melted away until only Shane was left, kneeling absurdly on the floor beside her, tucking her damp hair behind her ear with an air of concern. The kind of patient concern a parent might have for a child. She felt weak as a kitten, but she forced herself to listen, because her responses were vital. She was not letting herself be taken to any hospital.

'So' he said soothingly, cajolingly, 'what's the matter, Laurie? Why all this fuss about seeing a doctor, h'mm? Why won't you let me take you to Vincent's?'

Her temperature was equalising now, her mind beginning to reconnect with her body. 'It's nothing' she said, enunciating carefully like a drunk, 'just a little dizzy spell. Don't fuss, Shane, please.'

'I'm not fussing. I'm worried. That was more than a dizzy spell.'

'It was just . . . I should have had breakfast . . .'

He patted her hand. 'OK. Just sit where you are while I get Angie to make you some tea.'

Obediently she sat, gathering her wits until he returned with a hot mug, which tasted blissfully reviving when she sipped gingerly from it. Ah, better. Now she could speak. Warily, she looked up at him.

'Thank you. I feel much better.'

'Enough to come down to the car with me? Or we can take a taxi.'

'No, Shane, please . . . you're way too busy. All I need is a little lie-down, I'll go home for an hour.'

He shook his head. 'The hell you will. You're—' Abruptly, he grinned at her. 'You're not by any chance pregnant, are you? Not another one hiding it until the last minute?'

She knew what he meant. Pregnancy, in this office, was considered akin to larceny, anarchy, treason. She had no idea why she had a sudden overwhelming urge to burst into tears. All she knew was that she had to get out of here, be alone, crawl into her own bed and sleep till Doomsday.

Feebly, she mustered what she hoped was a reassuring grin. 'I'd better not be, or I'll be suing the manufacturers.'

Her tone made him smile, she saw the tension easing out of his face. He was a good guy, and she was grateful for his concern – but Christ, what a spectacle, what a scene! In front of everyone, they'd all come in to see what was going on . . . she'd never live it down, not unless she stood up now and went firmly back to work. But she hadn't the strength, and knew he wouldn't let her. Better just slink home, then, and come breezily back in tomorrow, pretending it had all been a mirage.

He made one last effort. 'Look, Laurie, I know it's none of my business, but we are old pals . . . I don't know what's wrong with you, but I'd like you to do something about it.'

'I will' she promised. 'I'll take the rest of the day off and, if I'm not right as rain by morning, I'll see a doctor. How's that?'

Dubiously, he grimaced. 'Let me drive you home, then, see you safely into your apartment?'

Yes. OK. If that would divert him from his goal, if they could go to Temple Bar instead of St Vincent's. Standing woozily up, she reached for her jacket, and he dived to get it, draped it solicitously around her shoulders. 'Come on, then. I'll tell Angie to cancel the rest of today. You look awful.'

She felt awful. Felt as if her light wool jacket was made of concrete, pinning her arms to her sides, imprisoning her. For a moment her breathing threatened to go hyper again, she swiped the back of her hand across her forehead to catch the beads of perspiration. Grimly, Shane handed her a handkerchief.

'Thanks. J – just aftershock.'

He took his jacket off the back of the chair where he'd parked it, threw it on and put an arm firmly around her shoulders, steering her out, stopping to have a muttered word with Angie, who nodded anxiously before beaming nonchalantly at Lauren. Again, she had the sensation of being a child amongst adults, that they'd all be talking about her shocking behaviour after she'd left.

Down in the car park he eased her into his car like a baby, throwing her bag and briefcase into the back seat behind. She had no memory of having taken them with her. Getting in on the other side, he patted her knee.

'All right?'

'Yes. You really don't have to do this, you know, I could have taken—'

'Jeez, Laurie.' He sounded exasperated. 'Put a sock in it. I know you better than most, remember? I know there's no way you'd have fainted, been out cold for ten minutes or agreed to go home, if you weren't feeling like hell.'

Ten *minutes*? Oh, God. She was dumbstruck. Inexorably, he continued. 'I also know there's something going on here. You've given up drinking, you never touch alcohol or go to the pub any more . . . before you passed out we were talking about voice-overs and you looked as if I was talking about spaceships from Mars . . . bet you can't repeat one word I said to you, can you?'

No. Wildly she ransacked her mind, but nothing came. Not one syllable.

'So. I have to conclude that something is the matter. I know it's not kosher to be ill at Axis, but I'm talking off the record here, just as a friend . . . d'you want to tell me what it is?'

Briefly, he took his eyes off the road to glance at her, and something in his friendly face very nearly undid her, made her want to bury her face in his chest and sob her heart out. Shane, I am dying, I have hep C, I am swamped with panic, exploding with it! She knew he was the one colleague she could trust, he would tell nobody, simply stop the car and let her howl all over him. Then, after much weeping and mopping, he would take her home and hold her in his arms, eventually put her to bed with a hot drink and – and an order that she must, absolutely must, see her doctor and the specialist.

If she told him she was very ill, it would be confirmed. She would be very ill. Lifting her chin, she smiled at him, as brightly as she could.

'I'm just on a diet. Maybe overdoing it a bit.'

He snorted. 'Lauren, you're what – eight stone, max? Don't give me that guff.'

This had always been one of the reasons why she liked Shane Jackson; he was bright, sharp, on the ball. Now she wished he were thick as a plank.

'Well, the diet must be working. Maybe I'll lay off it a bit.'

Drawing a deep breath, he drove on in a silence that said he didn't believe her. Feeling like a suspect in the witness box, she prayed for the journey to be over, the interrogation to end. Although he did not question her further, his silence spoke for itself, and she knew he was onto her.

At her apartment he parked on a double yellow line, helped her out, took her things, demanded her keys, let her in and insisted on coming up with her. Pleadingly, she insisted she'd be all right by herself. In response he gripped her arm and marched her into the lift.

'Now' he said when they were inside, 'where's your teapot?'

She couldn't bear it. His kindness, for some reason she didn't understand, was undoing her completely. If he didn't leave her alone she would collapse in a puddle on the floor, go to pieces entirely. 'Please, Shane' she implored him, 'go back to the office and get on with your day. I'll be fine, really I will.'

He looked hard at her, debating. 'Will you, Laurie? Are you sure?'

'Yes.'

He sighed. 'All right. This is your home I guess, I can't boss you around. I'll go if you want me to. But only on one condition.'

She cringed, knew what was coming.

Leaning forward, he unexpectedly kissed the tip of her nose, and caught his hand under her chin, forced her to look him in the eye. 'See a doctor, OK? Get help, for whatever it is.'

Meekly, she nodded. 'All right. I will.'

Not looking entirely convinced, he nodded in turn. 'Good. Because if this happens again I'm taking you straight to hospital myself.'

With that, he was gone. As soon as the door closed behind him, Lauren sank down on the sofa, fighting a rising mixture of nausea and panic.

Oh, Jesus. Oh, *Jesus*.

'Much ado' Lauren chirped brightly, 'about nothing. I'm telling you, I'm fine.'

Even over the phone, Saiv smelled a rat. Lauren always sounded nonchalant when she was telling whoppers.

'That's not what they said at your office. Angie said you'd gone home sick, that you'd fainted and looked awful.'

'Did she really? Then Angie can start looking for a new job. She has no business giving anyone such personal details.'

'Laurie, she was worried and she knows I'm your friend. You should have called me yourself – where are you now, what are you doing?'

'I'm in bed taking a little nap, or trying to, if you'd let me.'

A nap? The dynamo who couldn't sit still for two seconds? Saiv thought briefly about that. 'OK. Take a nap. I'll be there by the time you wake up.'

'What?'

'I'm coming in to town, to look after you! You can't be on your own.'

There was a pause. 'Saiv, don't be ridiculous. You're working. You have a deadline, remember?'

'Too bad. I'm on my way.'

'But—'

'But what?' Even as she said it, she could almost hear Lauren thinking.

'But . . . if you come here, you'll get no work done. Why don't I come out to you? That'd be much handier for you.'

Saiv considered. Was Lauren up to driving? And why, for the first time in her life, did she sound as if she actually wanted to come to the 'unspeakable' house out in Meath?

Saiv couldn't imagine. But she was prepared to let Lauren play this whatever way she wanted, so long as she wasn't alone.

'Well – if you feel up to it, then pack a bag and come for the night. If you don't feel like driving, take a taxi.'

'Good idea' Lauren replied unexpectedly, 'that's exactly what I'll do.'

Saiv was amazed. And relieved. 'Great. I'll make a pot of chicken soup and have it hot by the time you arrive.'

Rather weakly, Lauren laughed. 'Yes, Mommy. See you soon.'

Hanging up, Saiv frowned. Lauren hadn't even mentioned locking up the dogs, which was unprecedented, and she had agreed to let someone else do the driving. Normally she went everywhere except to work in her own car, as if primed for a quick getaway; it was some kind of control thing and this was the first time Saiv had ever known her to relinquish it. Whether she admitted it or not, she couldn't be well. Mulling perturbed on it, Saiv went to see about the soup and light the fire: even on a warm evening in May, Lauren might be chilly. Might have a temperature, need nursing.

It was nearly two hours later when Lauren arrived, and the minute she opened the door to her Saiv saw that something serious, something cataclysmic had happened. As usual, Lauren was dressed to the nines, in a cream gaberdine trouser suit with a coffee-coloured silk shirt, toting a designer-logo holdall, a carrier box of wine and a giftwrapped package that looked like chocolates, but her smile was very strained. Impulsively, Saiv embraced her in a hug.

'Come in! Come in this minute and get warm, get comfortable . . . let me look at you.'

Lauren flinched away, as if knowing her make-up wasn't fooling anyone, sensing that Saiv could feel her fragility. Warily, she eyed the two dogs on the floor by the fire.

'Will they take the arse off me?'

'No, there isn't enough meat on you – but I'll put them out, if you like.'

Lauren dropped her bag, handed the wine and chocolates to Saiv and sank down on the sofa. 'Oh, let them stay, so long as they behave themselves. This is their home, I suppose.'

As she said it she looked around her, and Saiv looked with her. As usual the sitting room was a bit chaotic, the faded rug littered with books and a couple of logs that had fallen out of the basket; several unframed paintings by an artist friend leaned askew against the wall waiting to be hung, and the boots by the door were caked in mud. The stained-glass lamp was glowing warmly, but distinctly dusty, and the bookshelves on the wall were sagging to breaking point. Beside Lauren's crisp suit, Saiv was conscious that her long rose-printed skirt and blue sweater did not cut the sartorial mustard. With an audible sigh, Lauren sat back deeper into the sofa and looked up at her.

'This is so – so –' She waved a hand, and Saiv supplied the missing word.

'Messy?'

'No! Well, yes, messy, but I was going to say homey. Warm, cosy.'

A compliment? And the dogs allowed to stay? Definitely, Laurie must be way under the weather. Solicitously, Saiv poked the fire and piled more logs on it, wondering how to probe for the information which she suspected would have to be extracted like aching teeth. Reaching down, Lauren lifted an open book off the floor.

'Yeats?'

'Mmm. I read him all the time, on and off.'

Raising the book, Lauren flicked through it, with the faintly surprised look of someone encountering an old, forgotten acquaintance. Years ago at college, she had expressed passing fondness for the romance of Yeats, before dismissing him abruptly as 'too complicated'. Saiv had never known her to read a poem since; but now she began to read aloud, a random passage about exhausted love, sounding almost wistful.

'Is this about Maud Gonne? Was that who he had in mind here?'

Saiv winced. How, of all the books to hand, had Laurie managed to light on this one? For all his romantic tone, Yeats was a realist, and could be morbid; the lines Laurie was reading had a bitter edge to them.

'What does he mean here, Saiv, huh?'

'Oh, don't mind him. He was just whingeing about getting old. Our Willie was never happy if he wasn't complaining about one thing or another.'

'H'mm. Thwarted love. I suppose Maud Gonne did him in, made him a bit crabby.'

Surprised, Saiv left the fire to its own devices and came to sit beside Lauren on the sofa, pulling her sleeves down over her knuckles. 'Maud Gonne? D'you remember about her? I thought everything you heard at college went in one ear and out the other.'

Letting the book slide to her lap, Lauren gazed into the flames of the fire. 'Yeah. I do remember. She wouldn't marry him, and he was fuming. Never got over it.'

Saiv smiled. 'No. Never did. That's male ego for you. Didn't stop him marrying someone else, though.'

'So he did. It's coming back to me now . . . they had kids later and all, didn't they?'

'Yes. He was quite a devoted dad. But he always carried a torch for Maud. It must have driven his wife demented.'

'Yes. Still . . . it's romantic.'

Lauren smiled vaguely, leaving Saiv foundering. Romantic? It would be more Lauren's style to say the guy had a nerve, should have got counselling for his obsession. Lauren, since leaving Isaac Hyland behind her, had been strictly pragmatic. Tentatively, trying to assess her mood, Saiv put a hand on her shoulder.

'How are you feeling, Laurie?'

Lauren whipped round to face her. 'I'm feeling perfectly well now. I had a rest and woke up right as rain. If I was any more right I'd be listing to starboard.'

'If you say so. Which you will say, whether or not . . . but you know, Laurie, you can let your guard down here. There's no need to pretend.'

Momentarily, she felt the shoulder muscles contract under her hand, Lauren's spine stiffen defensively. But then, lightly and gracefully, she got up, shrugged off her jacket, went to her holdall and extracted a warm, casual cardi. Slipping into it, she smiled airily. 'So, where's this chicken soup you promised? Still running round the yard, waiting for me to wring its neck?'

Laughing, reluctantly diverted, Saiv went to the kitchen to see about it. Ten minutes later, returning with a stacked supper tray, she found Laurie curled up on the sofa, burrowing into the cardi and the book of poetry.

'Welsh rarebit? Mmm . . . listen to this.' Cupping the book in her hands she began to read aloud, while Saiv distributed plates and mugs, attentively listening. It was a poem written in Sligo, one lucent summer's evening, in homage to two beautiful girls. Lauren sounded entranced.

Handing her a plate of toast, Saiv waited. It was quite a long poem, but Lauren read it through to the end, her voice trailing off until she was sitting in silence, dreamily, the words lingering like notes of music on the woody air. Saying nothing, Saiv sipped soup uncertainly, noting the translucence of Laurie's skin in the dusk, the low clarity of her voice. In the lowering twilight there was something mesmeric about her, something hauntingly sad.

But when she looked up, her eyes were eager. 'Is this about us?' she asked, 'are we the two girls Yeats is writing about, this evening?'

What on earth could be in her mind? Cautiously, Saiv reflected, smiling at the absurdity of the idea. 'Well' she said eventually, 'it is evening! And you're beautiful. But I don't think Yeats would include me.'

'Saiv' Laurie replied quietly, 'don't say that. You have your own beauty. You have your aura.'

'My *aura*? Of what?'

'Of peace. And contentment. Your tranquillity lends you beauty.'

Flushing, Saiv looked down, with a feeling of walking on glass. Lauren had never spoken to her like this before, never read poetry, never sounded so . . . so thoughtful.

'Thank you' she said finally, quietly. 'What else makes you think any of this, written eighty years ago, applies to us?'

'The bit about one of the girls being condemned to death.'

'Oh, Laurie! Yeats didn't mean literally, he meant spiritually.'

'He says she got a reprieve, but spent the rest of her lonely life amongst people who were – ignorant. People who'd read Lola Cola ads, and swallow them!'

Firmly, Saiv drew herself up. Lauren was maundering. 'Yeats' she said assertively, 'was talking about Constance Markievicz, who got involved in politics, went to prison and became a socialist. She spent the rest of her life working among the poor and the uneducated. Yeats, who was a hopeless snob, felt she was throwing herself away on people who didn't understand or appreciate her.'

'Was he in love with her?'

'Laurie, Yeats was in love with himself. He wanted women to stay young and innocent, like the portrait of Dorian Gray, reflecting only what he chose to see.'

'Oh. But . . . but Saiv . . .?'

'What?'

'I thought . . . I seem to remember hearing that you can – can interpret poetry in any way you want.'

Laurie sounded so tentative she had to smile, touched by the rare shyness in her tone. 'Yes, of course you can. It applies to different people in different ways. That's part of its charm, you can read it in any way you want.'

Lauren raised a hand to her hair, tucking it out of her way so she could look at the lines again, peer intently and curiously at them. 'Well – the way I want to interpret this is that the condemned girl got a pardon. But she wasted it, didn't make much of herself afterwards.'

'If that's what it means to you, Laurie, then that's what it means. But why are you so taken with it?'

There was a quizzical pause, in which they sipped their soup and nibbled at both toast and question, clearing space for Lauren to float whatever was on her mind. Eventually the words drifted out, tiny adventurers on her current of thought.

'I mean – Saiv, suppose I got a reprieve? A pardon, a stay of execution? Suppose I found out I wasn't going to die – or not soon, anyway?'

She looked so hopeful, suddenly, and so vulnerable. Something about her, this warm still evening, reminded Saiv of the Lauren she'd first known, the lovely Lauren flirting with literature, and life, and love. In her throat, something clicked and locked, making her voice husky when she spoke.

'I hope that will happen, Laurie. I hope that you will live a very long time, and always be my friend.'

Lauren's hand clenched on the book, some tremor seized her almost imperceptibly, and she did not look up.

'I hope so too, Saiv. I want you always to be my friend. I'm only now beginning to understand what that means . . . and how much it means.'

There was a long silence, in which neither of them dared say anything more. The fire crackled, the dogs snoozed, the room became a warm soft cocoon, sealing them into it.

Eventually, in the honey-gold glow of evening, Lauren found her voice. 'Where was I?'

'You were saying . . . suppose . . . you got a reprieve?'

'Yes . . . well, if I did, what would I do with it, Saiv? Would it be some kind of blasphemy to spend it at my brash advertising agency, peddling crass advertising for crass products to crass consumers?'

'Oh, Laurie . . . I . . . you have to earn your living.'

They were both, Saiv knew, finding this conversation very difficult. But it was not its apparent tangents that bothered her; she could handle those. What she could not handle, she realised with searing sorrow, was the thought of losing Lauren. Lively, laughing Lauren, who in a way sounded so lost already. Surreptitiously, she swiped her sleeve across her face.

Not seeing the gesture, studying the pattern in the Turkish rug, Lauren seemed to be rummaging inside herself, hauling thoughts out and tossing them around.

'My living? But is it what you'd call living, Saiv? Is it? Working, or conspiring as Yeats puts it, amongst people who could never write anything as beautiful as this – people who wouldn't even want to, would despise such "drivel". People living as I've been living, drifting on a shallow surface, none of us ever daring to look into our own souls. If we even have any souls. People writing ads for others who live the same way, whose idea of poetry is the jingles they hear and the slogans they read. People who'd much rather have popcorn than poetry.'

Saiv forced a laugh, which fell echoing to the floor. 'Yes, well, consumerism isn't a crime! You're not peddling drugs—'

'Aren't I? In a way, I think perhaps I am. It's my job to get them hooked. Hooked and hungry, for more, more, more. Spending way beyond what they can afford, getting into debt—'

'Laurie, not all the products you advertise are addictive. And you must have some worthwhile clients, selling things that people need.'

'Yes. A few. I guess.' Rubbing her knuckle under her eye, looking suddenly tired, Lauren sat thinking, counting off her clients in her head. 'Thanks, Saiv. I know you think my work is worthless, but thanks for being loyal, and pretending otherwise.'

'Oh, come on! What's got into you? You enjoy your work, you're very good at it and you earn your own independent—'

'Living? But am I living, or is this a form of dying? Is it enriching, or is it merely money? Have I wrapped myself in a layer of banknotes so thick I can't feel anything through it? Is that what you call a gilded cage?'

'Laurie, if you were half as bad as you make out, you wouldn't have been able to read Yeats the way you just did. You'd have dropped that book like a hot coal, not been open to a word of it.'

'Maybe. But Saiv, that is the first line of poetry I've read in – what? Twelve or thirteen years? I started out studying writers like Yeats, learning from them, and then – then I did a runner. I shut off that whole side of myself, have been running scared ever since.'

'Yes. You have. Why is that, Laurie? Was it because of Isaac?'

Abruptly vehement, Laurie nodded. 'Yes! He – he hurt me so badly, I wanted to cauterise the wound, seal it shut. Wanted to run a mile from anything emotional, anything romantic that I couldn't hold in my hand and have complete control over. Plus, I was afraid – I thought – thought maybe I wasn't bright enough to hack it. If I'd slaved hard enough I'd probably have passed my exams, but I'd never have *shone*. Never had the confidence to do the kind of thing you're doing now, living on fresh air for love of your vocation, not caring what anyone thinks of you or whether you'll succeed. I redefined my whole idea of success, moulded and shaped it to suit popular interpretation – to suit me, until Dr Mallon threw his goddamn spanner in the works.'

'But Lauren, not everyone has the—'

'Not everyone has the what? The talent? Saiv, talent isn't the issue here. You have the talent to write a biography of whatshis-name, I have the talent to write ads and flog products. What I don't have, in spades, is the courage or confidence to aim any higher. To take risks, or stretch myself, or – or live by myself, the way you do, in harmony. I panic if I'm not surrounded by people at all times, preferably admirers, boosting me, telling me how great I am. I need to keep hearing that, because I don't feel it. Don't feel I'm anything special at all.'

Putting down her mug, Saiv slid to the floor and sat cross-legged on it, wrapping her arms around her knees, letting the firelight flicker on her freckled face, her ungovernable wheat-blonde hair.

'But Lauren, you are special. To me, for a start. Undoubtedly to your parents too, if you could only trust them, let them into your life a little. To your sister, no matter how far away she is. I'm the one who effectively has no family, is special to nobody.'

Frowning, Lauren looked curiously at her. 'But your parents loved you, you have brothers—'

'Yes. One in Kerry who never bothers to see or even call me, one who uses me when it suits him, and resents me in some weird way.'

'Resents you for what?'

'For not – conforming! For not marrying, for going to college when he didn't, for encouraging his children not to conform to his wishes. Tom was here only the other day, and there wasn't one drop of love lost between us. Not one drop.'

'No? But if he called to see you, he must have wanted—'

'Yes. Wanted something. He always does. Otherwise I never hear from him, see him from one end of the year to the other. Only if I can be useful, which in this case I couldn't. In a way it's almost worse than having no family at all.'

Lauren bit her lip, chewing on this information. 'Bastard. He should love you dearly, and be proud of you. You're so – so honest. So good and caring, so warm.'

'And anti-social and awkward! Unglamorous, bookish, broke . . . not even a pretty face, to make up for being odd.'

Lauren groaned. 'Saiv, beauty is in the eye of the beholder. I tart myself up, work at putting on a pretty face. You let everyone see the real you. You can afford to do that, because you've nothing to hide. Nobody will ever be disappointed when they strip off the varnish to reveal the person beneath.'

Saiv laughed. 'Nobody wants to strip off anything! You might not have noticed, Laurie, but there isn't exactly a queue of admirers down to the garden gate.'

In response, Lauren got up, came to Saiv's side, bent down and suddenly swept her mass of sandy curls up off her face. 'Then let people see you! Why do you hide under this mass of hair, inside all these baggy clothes? People can only glimpse you, guess at you! You have gorgeous blue eyes but you wear those old glasses—'

'I can't see without them, or manage lenses.'

'Then get new ones, at least. Ease off the vino and pasta, lose a little weight. Get a nice haircut and treat yourself to a new dress for summer.'

'But who'd notice?'

'*You* will. You'll feel better and it'll show, give you a boost.'

Feeling that the conversation was wandering, yet reluctant to haul it back to its sombre origins, Saiv thought about it. Lauren wasn't suggesting anything radical, any make-up or disguise of any kind . . . she was just being a friend, taking an interest, trying to help. Gratefully, she squeezed her hand.

'All right. If you think I should.'

'Yes. Give it a lash! Try something new . . . actually, I've been thinking of trying something new myself.'

Interested, Saiv looked up, and Lauren let her hair fall back round her face, sat down on the floor beside her. It was, Saiv registered, the first time Lauren had ever sat on the floor. In pale cream trousers, too, that would surely get scuffed. For a few minutes they sat in companionable silence, watching the logs burn.

'So . . . tell me. What have you been thinking?'

'I – I've been thinking about what you said to me, that day up on the mountain. The bit about maybe taking a break from work.'

Saiv was pleased. 'Have you? God, Laurie, I'm glad to hear that. After what happened this morning, you've got to ease up. You've *got* to. You've been pushing yourself so hard, it's insanity.'

'Maybe I have. There's always so much work to be done. And since Jordan – since splitting up with Jordan, I hate going home in the evenings. That damn flat is so empty.'

Damn? Flat? Could she mean that magnificent apartment? Saiv was bemused, even if all its smooth white contours did make her think of an igloo. A gleaming, pristine igloo, that would ring hollow if you were alone in it, give you the shivers if you were ill.

'Well, you don't have to be alone. In fact I'd rather you weren't. After this morning's episode, I – I'd rather you spent a lot more time here, Laurie. I know it's not convenient for work, but you could come at weekends, let me look after you . . .'

The idea was only forming in her mind as she uttered it, but Lauren turned to her as if seizing on it, with unexpected gratitude. 'Oh, Saiv – could I? Wouldn't I be in your way? I know you work weekends, I'd hate to be a nuisance—'

'Don't be silly. I don't work every waking hour. Besides, I shut myself in my study when I need peace. You could just rest and – and read more poetry, if you want! I mean, if you don't mind the dogs and the mess and whatnot.'

Cautiously, Lauren eyed the dogs. 'Well, they don't seem to have eaten me so far . . . maybe we're getting kind of used to each other. As for the mess . . . in some odd way I can't explain, it's kind of a comfort. Especially when you're here at the centre of it, so serene, so – so motherly! This isn't just a house, Saiv. It's a home.'

Smiling, sceptical, Saiv arched an eyebrow. 'Is it? Well, I hope you'll still be as enthusiastic when you're cleaning out the grate in the mornings!'

She couldn't envisage Lauren doing it. But Lauren nodded nonchalantly. 'Oh, I'll manage that, just so long as I don't ruin my nails – Saiv, you are so sweet to offer me this. If you're sure you mean it, I would love to do it.'

'Then consider it done. You can bring some stuff and simply leave it here . . . move into the spare bedroom and make it your own.'

Lauren laughed. 'What, colonise your cottage?'

'Yes. It'll be fun to have you around, part of the time at least, and I'll be much happier that I can keep an eye on you. Which reminds me, what were you going to say about taking a break from work?'

Stretching, Lauren shifted into a more comfortable position, thinking for a moment, looking speculative when she spoke.

'Well . . . I know you probably reckon I haven't been listening to a word you've been saying, scarcely a syllable since – since the start of this whole wretched year. But I have. As a matter of fact I was toying with your advice when you rang me this afternoon.'

Saiv's heart flipped over with hope. The specialist!? Could Lauren be going to see him, at last? Oh, please. *Please*. With huge effort, she tried to sound calm.

'Oh? And?'

'And I had . . . an idea.'

An idea? Apprehensively, Saiv frowned. The specialist wasn't an idea, he was a must, at this stage, a pressing necessity. Keyed up, she waited to hear what the 'idea' might be; and then, maddeningly, Lauren appeared to change tack, started looking around the room for something.

'Where's that wine I brought? Why didn't you open a bottle with our supper?'

'Because you can't share it with me. There's no joy in drinking alone.'

'Oh, rubbish. I'll have a mouthful if you'll have a glass – go on, open it.'

Saiv hesitated, and hit on a compromise. 'No. But I'll make coffee and open the chocolates.'

'Oh – OK, then.'

Was she playing for time? Had she hoped the wine might smooth the path of least resistance, to whatever she was going to say? Somewhat suspicious, Saiv went out to make the coffee, and returned to find Lauren stretched full length on the floor, chucking the wrappings off the chocolate box into the fire. Beaming seductively, she lifted the box to offer it to Saiv.

'Here you are – have one.'

Pouring the steaming coffee, Saiv selected a chocolate; they were of a luxurious expensive variety she'd never have bought for herself. Lauren, and her endless treats!

'OK, spit it out.'

'What, the chocolate?' Cheeks bulging, Lauren grinned like a chipmunk.

'No, the idea! Stop stalling!'

Slowly, Lauren swallowed her chocolate and sipped the hot coffee, letting it cool for a moment while she marshalled her thoughts. Saiv got the feeling she was trying to choose her words as if formulating an ad, relying on them for their selling power.

'Well' she murmured at length, widening her eyes in the little-girl way that always worked on men, 'I have to confess that that was a rather embarrassing incident at work this morning. I don't want to make a habit of fainting all over the office.'

'No. But it was a warning, and you're going to have to do something about it. Going to have to go and see—'

'So,' Lauren continued implacably, 'I think maybe it's time I took your advice – and a holiday.'

Saiv didn't know whether to be disappointed or relieved. A holiday wasn't as good as a hepatologist . . . but at least it was a start. In the short term at least, it could only do Lauren good. Maybe when she came back, she'd be strong enough to start seeing sense.

'A holiday, huh? And high time too. You must be owed masses of time off.'

'Well, the Lola Cola campaign still has two weeks to run. But I could get away after that, in June.'

'Great. For two or three weeks at least, I hope. Where are you thinking of going? With whom?'

'Ah. Um. Well, that's the thing, actually.'

'What is what thing?'

'The destination. And the travelling companion. I'd been thinking of France . . . but then I decided no, France is so tied up with my memories of Jordan, it might be a bad idea.'

Saiv concurred with that. The last thing Lauren needed was to be distressed in any way. 'Right. Forget France, then. Where else?'

Looking rather evasive, Lauren gazed into her coffee. 'I thought maybe – maybe Italy.'

Saiv's heart skipped a beat. Italy! In a flash she could see it, taste it, feel it. She would give anything for Lauren's freedom to fly, to wake up hearing its heartbeat.

'That sounds fabulous. As I've often told you, Italy is magic. Sheer magic. Go for it, Laurie!'

Eagerly, Laurie looked up, noting the flush rising on Saiv's face. 'You think so? This has to be a careful decision, Saiv, because if I'm not . . . well . . . it could be my last holiday . . . for a while.'

Her last ever? That was what she meant, and Saiv knew it. Forcefully, she put down her cup and went to a bookshelf.

'Yes! I think so, Laurie, definitely! You'll adore it, I promise you – here, look, this is a book about it, it has everything – stunning cities, beautiful scenery, sunny beaches, fantastic food. Even history and culture, as a last resort! It's so romantic, you could hang out in the Giusti Gardens reading Yeats till your eyes water . . . oh, I would love to go with you! But – who are you thinking of taking, anyway?'

Putting down her cup in turn, Lauren ploughed on, looking suddenly determined. 'You, Saiv. I'm thinking of taking you.'

She whirled round. 'Oh – no! Laurie, I'm so sorry, but you – you know I can't. Not unless you'd be prepared to travel overland, which would take days and be far too stressful in your – your current condition.'

'It certainly would. That's why we'll have to fly.'

Twanging with desire, torn in two, Saiv threw herself down on the floor, nearly weeping with frustration. In another few weeks her book would be finished, she would have the time to travel and even some money, but – but. The thought of a plane was so terrifying she had to fight a surge of instant nausea, clutch at the leg of a chair.

'Laurie, I'm sorry, but I can't. I literally could not get on a plane to save my life.'

Slowly, Lauren sat up and looked at her. 'Couldn't you, Saiv? Not even – not even for me, this one time?'

'No! I know it sounds crazy, most people would think I'm completely irrational, but it – it's a *phobia*! It would be like parachuting or bungee-jumping off Golden Gate Bridge! Please don't ask me to!'

Lauren considered. Saiv did indeed took petrified, white at the mere mention of it. But she'd been thinking long and hard about this, about how imprisoned Saiv was by her fear. To release her from it, get her somehow over it and out, would be to leave her friend a legacy. To give her the gift of freedom, to use after she was gone, to live her hopefully long life to the full.

But Saiv was ashen, backing off as if Lauren were coming at her with a blowtorch. Lauren could see that her fear was very real, that she was asking her to do something almost super-human. Saiv, she was sure, would rather be locked in a cage with a starving lion.

'What if I drugged you?'

'D – *drugged* me?' Wild-eyed, Saiv was breathing shallowly, rapidly.

'Yeah. There's this stuff called Zimmer or Zovver or something . . . one of the guys in my office takes it for long flights.'

'It – Laurie, it wouldn't work. My body would fight it every inch and – oh, God, it'd have no effect and I'd be left up there, captured, hysterical! I'd jump out!'

Lauren stifled a groan. 'Saiv, you can't jump out of a plane, the doors are locked – don't be an idiot!'

'I'm not an idiot, you don't understand – my parents were *killed*!'

'Yes. I know they were. I know how you feel. Calm down. It's just that – that I know how much you love Italy. This could be my last chance to see it, and I'd give anything to share it with you. Anything, Saiv . . . I really would.'

Aghast, Saiv stared at her. Surely she wasn't – wasn't going to *blackmail* her? Heap guilt on her, for not doing this? But she couldn't do it, she couldn't! No matter how Laurie looked, with that awful imploring light in her eyes, no matter how ill she was . . . oh, Jesus.

'Laurie,' she whimpered, hearing her own anguish in her ears, 'I'd give anything too. But not this. Not this. I can't do it.'

In one swoop, Lauren reached out and grabbed her forearm. 'Saiv, you can! Come on! You must! It'll open up your whole world!'

Saiv snatched her arm away, feeling the imprint of Lauren's fingers.

'No! Laurie, some things are just too hard, impossible . . . you know they are! You're as terrified of seeing a specialist as I am of getting on a plane!'

It was out before she had time to snatch it back, and Saiv gasped in horror: like a deranged lunatic she had thrown down a gauntlet, which Lauren was picking up, examining even as she spoke. Taut as a violin string, silence twanged between them. And then, unbearably, Lauren's eyes filled with tears.

'Yes' she whispered. 'I am. I am totally terrified, and that's why I haven't done something I know is essential, crucial. But I'll strike you a deal, Saiv. If you'll fly to Italy, I'll see a specialist when we come back.'

Oh, no. Oh, *no* . . . trapped, cornered, Saiv felt the room swirling around her, as if Lauren were holding a pillow over her face. If she got on a plane, she would die. If Lauren didn't get help, she would die.

'Please, Laurie, please don't do this . . .'

'Sorry. But there's your choice. I haven't got forever while you hang around and think about it. It's literally now or never, Saiv. If you haven't got the guts to go, then I'm not going to face *my* death sentence. The chances of which, incidentally, are a lot higher than the chances of yours.'

As if Lauren were holding a gun to her head, Saiv said nothing, struggling for the calm that was normally her greatest defence. But her heart was hammering. The gods were already holding a gun to Lauren's own head – and yet she was ready to face them down, dare them to pull the trigger, if in return Saiv Lovett would board an aircraft? Speechless, frantic, she tried to buy time.

'But I – you're making – oh, Jesus, Laurie, haven't you ever been afraid to fly? Wanted to jump up and bolt before they locked the doors?'

'No. Why would I? Statistically I'm more likely to get savaged by a Doberman than—'

'But we – we can't go away together! We'd have rows over everything, where to stay and where to eat and what to see—'

'Yeah. I thought about that. And decided that democracy, foreign as it is to my dictatorial nature, is the solution. You choose everything one week, I choose the next.'

Shot down, Saiv groped for fresh ammunition, floundering until suddenly Lauren thumped the floor. 'For God's sake! You used to love to travel, you adored Italy, India too! I'm going to rehabilitate you if it kills me! I'm warning you, if you won't do it, then I won't go to the specialist.'

Saiv felt the room freeze around her, icy daggers shoot up her spine. Lauren was robbing her of all argument. Dipping her head, she let her hair swing forward to hide her face.

'All right' she whispered, 'I'll go. If you're going to force me.'

Lauren touched her shoulder. 'Yes. I'm going to force you. And you're going to love every minute of it. You've achieved contentment in your life, by tackling only the things you feel you can handle, but I want to see you *happy*. I want to see you all lit up the way you were when you came back from Italy last time. Ecstatic, glowing . . . *alive*, Saiv.'

'I am alive. Writing my book is making me very happy.'

'In its way. But it's hard work. In Italy you'll have *fun*. You'll laugh and sing, you'll dance in the fountains, sizzle in the sun, feel ten years younger—'

Saiv turned to her, looked into her eyes. 'And then, when we get back, you'll keep your promise? You'll—?'

Lauren nodded. 'Yes. If you'll do this, I'll do that. OK? Do we have a deal?'

Gritting her teeth, Saiv nodded in turn. 'Yes. OK. I have no choice, so you have a deal.'

She knew she sounded petulant, but Lauren laughed. 'Ha! Striking deals is what I do for a living! Nobody stands a chance against me! Now, let's start planning – when exactly will we go, to where? If you'll do a week of beaches I'll do a week of cities – Venice? Florence, Verona?'

Suddenly the names gleamed before Saiv's eyes, spun through the air as if Lauren were tossing diamonds in the air, and she felt a shiver of the purest delight, joy seizing terror by the throat.

'Oh, Laurie – you're going to have to haul me by the hair onto this plane! But if you can get me to any of those places I – I will never be able to thank you enough. Never. I've longed all my life to see Venice and Verona, go back to Florence . . . I can't explain why, but they draw me like a magnet. I *hallucinate* about them.'

'Then we're on our way. I know you're petrified, but you did say I should do at least one worthwhile thing with my life. This counts as worthwhile, doesn't it?'

Briefly, Saiv was silent. This wasn't what she'd had in mind at all. But – yes. Lauren was handing her the key to the world she'd been locked out of for nearly a decade, giving her a hugely generous gift. She must make it worthwhile.

'Yes, Laurie. You're a bully, a shameless manipulator and a blackmailer, but if you can do this I will be indebted to you for the rest of my life. I will owe you one hell of a lot more than a fiver.'

'Ha! You've never forgotten that bloody fiver, have you?'

Vehemently, Saiv shook her head. 'No, Laurie. I never have. And I never will. Your friendship is worth its weight in gold.'

In the rising summer heat the office steamed like a botanic glasshouse, there were days when Lauren felt light-headed, but she was determined not to faint again. Shane and Saiv were right: she'd been working too hard, was all, she needed a break and now she was going to have one. Exhaustion was the problem, not hep C, it was a wonder everyone wasn't having dizzy spells. Like a gladiator she fought off all thoughts of illness, of its outcome, of never seeing her beloved baby sister again if Caoimhe did not come home for Christmas. Logically, she knew it would make more sense to go to Canada than to Italy, visit Caoimhe and her family, the infant niece she'd never seen; but Vancouver was a full day's journey away, with a change of plane, and instinct whispered to Lauren that it would be too much.

Her body could cope with the short trip to Italy, but . . . what if she passed out on the long flight to Vancouver, with no Shane around to pick up the pieces? The prospect was unthinkable – and then, one clammy evening, she picked up the phone to hear Caoimhe's voice on the other end of it, bubbling with anticipation.

'Laurie! I just called to tell you that I'm coming to Ireland for Christmas! Yes, husband, baby and all! I've been longing to see you . . . you will be around, won't you? You're not planning to go away anywhere?'

'No,' Lauren said firmly, 'I'm not planning to go anywhere. I'm thrilled that you're coming and I – I'll be at the airport to meet you! I know it's seven months away, but now I can plan around it, it will be fantastic to see you after all this time. I can hardly wait!'

Like a drowning woman grasping at a log, she made up her mind that evening: I will live until Christmas at least. I *will*. I don't care what this doctor says when I see him, I will see my sister again and that's all about it. The Italian sunshine will see me through, all the way to December. That's far enough, and I won't think any further. I'll simply take one day at a time, get more sleep instead of socialising, eat all the right stuff and cram myself with vitamins. I will survive, I will be well.

Her days were busy, and she spent much of them fending off Shane Jackson, the only one of her colleagues who suspected the truth. Steeling herself, she lied with impunity, assuring him she was fine until she almost came to believe it herself, and grinned at her own powers of conviction. It was nothing to be proud of, but she'd always been an innocent-eyed, first-rate liar. She could spin night out of day, and she did.

Only at night, sometimes, when she was on her own, when the street below the apartment was full of vibrant, healthy young voices . . . the clear carefree voice that had once been her own . . . shutting the window, she shut them out, and found herself enveloped in loneliness. One night it was so bad she crumbled completely, and picked up the phone with tears in her eyes, her hand trembling on the receiver. It was mad, it was futile, but if she didn't make contact with Jordan, hear his voice at least, she thought she would lose her mind.

You ended it, she reminded herself. Ended it so that there could never be any going back. You slammed the door with total finality.

Yes, but I miss him now! I want him, I need him! He was a bastard but he was all I had . . . oh, Jordan. Answer the phone. Please answer me, speak to me.

No answer. It rang and rang, until the line went dead, stretching into infinity. Then she tried his mobile, and a recording told her it was out of service. Frantically, sobbing, she went down to her car, jumped into it and drove in demented pain out to his house in Rathfarnham, beyond caring what wife or child might open the door. As soon as she saw him, she would hurl herself into his arms, howl for help, for the all-encompassing warmth of his embrace. But when she reached his house in the purpling night it stood dark and silent, empty as an abandoned citadel, and there was a sign in the garden: 'Sold.'

No! Where was he, where had he gone? Wildly she tried to think of possible refuges, but she knew it was useless: she would never see Jordan White again. And he would never see her suffering, never know or care what had become of her. Laying her head down on the steering wheel, she wept until her throat throbbed, her eyes stung and her head felt as if it would explode.

Time passed without measure, until a long time later she finally sat up, chafed her aching bones and started the car. As she drove away she felt gutted, distraught; but gradually a tiny chink of light began to glimmer in her mind like a star. Somehow fate had arranged it that he had not been there to witness this humiliation, to spurn her, to snatch victory from the jaws of defeat. Somehow her memories had been left intact, and her involuntarily salvaged dignity; he would never know how low, how crushed she had been. In his mind she would remain the winner, the one who had walked away.

At home she found, for the first time since January, that she did not need or want a sleeping pill. Collapsing drained into bed, she was scarcely aware of falling asleep; all she knew was that, when she awoke next day, something had gone from her life for good. Some poisonous thing was expunged, lanced like a tumour, leaving her profoundly calm. Getting up, she gathered together every photograph of Jordan she possessed, in albums and in frames, tore each one into fragments and then, piling them into the kitchen sink, set fire to them. As they burned the acrid smoke filled her nostrils like incense, she watched like a high priestess attending a rite of cleansing, and knew that while she might often think of Jordan White again, she would never yearn for him with such throbbing intensity. Whatever little might be left of her life, she had freed it to go forward.

Later that evening, over a solitary supper, she opened the book of Yeats that Saiv had loaned her, reading an entire poem for the first time in longer than she could remember, her spirit diving liberated into every line, excavating the Lauren who had so long been lost.

I'll get drunk, Saiv thought wildly. I'll start getting systematically drunk four or five hours in advance, and then when we get to the airport I'll take two or three of those Zimmer things Lauren promised to give me. I'll take a fistful. I'll take the whole packet. I'll be unconscious.

And then, where will I be? Out of Ireland, for the first time in nine years . . . out of my home, out of my routine, away from my dogs. Out of my mind, worrying about them? Out of my own skin, for sure, the skin I've been hiding inside since . . . since when? Since my parents died? Or since I realised I'm an outsider, who will never fit in anywhere? I used to try, when I was younger, more adaptable, but it was useless. For some reason I was just born different, never had the same interests or skills as other girls. Never played with dolls, never enjoyed nightclubs, never learned how to flirt, never watched soaps or had that knack for small talk. I grew up thinking life should be an epic drama, panoramic and profound, and when it turned out to be mostly mundane I retreated from it, took refuge in a life that's gradually become almost monastic. A kind of second-hand life, lived through books; they've become far more real than reality. I left reality to Lauren, she brought news from the outside world, I never had to confront it myself. Only in my students, sometimes, and now I've even run away from them, maybe because they remind me of who I was before I realised I wasn't stunning, or beautiful, wasn't epic material after all. As the saying goes, 'those who can, do; those who can't, teach.' So I teach, and walk my dogs, and dream no more of Arabian nights, of Himalayan days, of great love or boiling passion.

Not at thirty-four! I wear specs, and they're not rose-tinted. All I see for sure is quiet routine, some kind of contentment, nothing sexy or sensational. It's wiser to recognise your limits. Let's leave the beauty and glory and drama to Italy, which does those things so well; after a couple of weeks I'll probably totter home shattered and longing for my little cottage.

I've wanted Italy for years, but now that Lauren's making me go there – it's unnerving. Not just the flight, but the chaos that lies beyond that; the noise and urgency and throbbing vitality, all those people surging and shouting. I'll be flattened, trampled underfoot.

But Lauren is going. Going for my sake, when it would be much easier for her just to lounge around some Club Med in the sun, or pamper herself at a health farm. She hates monuments and churches and art galleries, but she says she'll do them, invest her precious time in things that interest me. She's incredible, and I'd better enjoy this adventure whether I do or not. Better fit in with her too, make sure she gets to swim and dance and stay in swish hotels if that's what she wants. She might never get another chance.

What *is* it about Lauren Kilroy? How is she the one person who's managed to infiltrate my life, even to the extent of staying here, now, at weekends? She's the only person who's ever punctured my privacy, and I feel far more in tune with her than with my blood family. The thought of losing her is like – like being burgled. But she's the one who's being burgled, mugged! Oh, God, let this doctor save her, let him tell her yes, why didn't you come sooner, of course we can save you!

There must be a way. If this specialist says there isn't then I'll make her see another, and another . . . I may be philosophical about most things but I am not taking this lying down. She won't either, once she finally confronts it, she'll fight like a tiger . . . is fighting already, in so many ways. But they're small ways; she hasn't fully psyched herself up yet to face it head-on.

But she will. I'll have her to myself in Italy and I'll work on her, even if it's like converting a Muslim to Judaism, a vegetarian to beef. I'll get her sparring like a boxer, throwing punches, going as many rounds as it takes. She's lost her lover, misses her sister, doesn't communicate properly with her parents, so it falls to me. We were both in shock for a while, I think, but now we've got to absorb that and move beyond it. We've got to get active and take control of this nightmare.

Meanwhile, in just one more week, my book will be finished and I can put Jean-Jacques to bed. He's been fascinating, and I'm going to miss him. But now summer's coming and I have no further excuse: it's time to get out, as Lauren says, and meet some real people. Try as I might, I can't hibernate forever. To start with, there are kennels to organise and hotels to book . . . Laurie can book the flights, though. I'm not doing that. Oh, Jesus, the very thought!

Don't think about it. Just finish your book and pack your bags and *go*. Laurie has enough on her plate, she doesn't need you whimpering and whingeing when she's facing a much bigger challenge. So just shut up and do it, OK?

As they say in America, just *do* it.

JUNE

'Champagne' Lauren announced triumphantly, and a cork popped like a bullet. Saiv jumped as if shot through the head.

'No – Laurie – I've already had two vodkas—'

Lauren beamed. 'Have you really? And now champagne, and then a couple of Zimovane in the taxi. You'll be so out of it, people will think you're being drugged and abducted, sold into white slavery. I'll have to check you in at the airport in case you tell them you're the emperor of China.'

Saiv spiralled unsteadily onto Lauren's immaculate white sofa – God, how did she keep it so clean? – gazed at the proffered glass, gulped, and snatched it. Agog, Lauren watched while she swallowed its contents in one long swift draught, hiccuped, and held it out for a refill.

'Wow. Do I gather that madam is a trifle nervous?'

Hysterically, Saiv clutched at the arm of the sofa, digging the nails of one hand into it while she grasped the glass in the other, lifted it aloft and emptied it a second time.

'No, no, not at all. I'm just a raving alcoholic. I'll never forgive you for this, Lauren Kilroy.'

'For what? Opening champagne to celebrate your finished book and our departure on holiday? I think congratulations are absolutely in order.'

Looking manic, Saiv stared wild-eyed at her. 'Laurie, it'sh not working. I'm shtill shtone cold shober.'

Lauren grinned. 'Are you? Then here, you'd better have one more for the road. Give Mummy your glass.'

Obediently Saiv held it out, and once more the froth foamed to the top. Before it could settle, the glass was empty. Never in her life had Saiv drunk so much so fast. And then a hazy thought struck her.

'Are you shupposed to mix them?'

'Mix what?'

'Drink and drugs?'

'Uh – no. Probably not. But in this case we'll just have to improvise . . . I have the Zimovane in my bag. I'll give you one when we get in the taxi and another when we're in departures. You'll sleep like a baby all the way to Venice. OK?'

'Mmm. OK.' With detached interest, Saiv noted that her legs were turning into toothpaste and her heartbeat was at Olympic sprint speed. The bottle was three-quarters empty and Lauren's glass was three-quarters full. This seemed to signify some interesting mathematical equation, but she couldn't quite grasp what it was.

The doorbell rang, and she leaped three feet high, spilling what was left of her champagne over the rucksack at her feet. 'What'sh that?'

'It's Blue Cabs, I'd imagine.' Serenely, Lauren went to the intercom, told the driver they would be down in a minute, and wheeled her elegant Samsonite suitcase to the door. 'OK, let's see, tickets, passport, currency – you got everything, Saiv?'

Dumbly, Saiv nodded at her, looking stricken. 'Y – yesh, I think sho, but – but but Laurie – maybe we won't go—'

Grimly, Lauren marched over to her, picked up the dripping rucksack with distaste and shoved it into her hands. 'Here. Take your Gucci luggage and get your ass downstairs.'

Saiv froze. Ignoring her, Lauren cleared away the drinks, checked the apartment over and picked up her lightweight Burberry coat. Saiv was wearing what appeared to be the contents of an Oxfam sack.

'Right. Let's go.' Clamping one hand on Saiv's shoulder, she steered her to the door, opened it and ejected her. Then, wheeling her own bag, she summoned the lift. Saiv felt an absolutely imperative impulse to run.

'L – Lauren, lifts give me claustrophobia—'

Without reply, Lauren pushed her into it, punched the buttons and stood in grim silence while they plummeted to street level, where the waiting driver took charge of their luggage. Lauren opened the door of the cab.

'Now. In you get.'

Desperately, Saiv opened her mouth to explain that she'd changed her mind, wasn't going. But her mouth didn't seem to be working, and next thing she was sprawling on the seat with the sensation of having been upended into it. As soon as the car moved off, Lauren opened her bag and extracted a small packet.

'Here you are. Sweeties.'

In one swoop Saiv grabbed the pill and swallowed it. Her whole body was clenched with such terror that, when they stopped at a traffic light, she reached for the door handle. But Lauren's fingers tightened on her wrist, pinned her in place.

'Hold it right there.'

Saiv felt like crying. But as they inexorably wended their way to the airport she realised that any struggle would be useless, not only because Lauren was imprisoning her but also because her body was swirling with chemicals; it was as if she'd been given an epidural for an impending operation. She was awake, but she couldn't feel her legs.

At the airport Lauren assumed command, steering their loaded trolley with one hand and Saiv with the other, even fishing her passport out of her pouch-belt for her at the check-in. The clerk smiled at them, and when Saiv smiled woozily back her jaw seemed to lock, leaving her with an inane, zombie-like grin.

'Is your friend all right?' the clerk asked solicitously.

'Oh yes' Lauren assured him breezily, 'but she – she's a Gaelgóir. Doesn't speak a word of English.'

Bemused, the clerk glanced at Saiv's passport, which was not in Irish. For an awful moment it looked as if he might be going to pursue the matter, discover that Saiv was drunk and refuse to let her board. But finally, with a shrug, he handed over the boarding cards. The woman looked too out of it to cause any trouble.

'Now,' Lauren muttered, 'straight into departures, and I'll give you your next pill.' Like a robot Saiv let herself be led away, weaving slightly, with the impression that she was Mary Queen of Scots being marched off to the executioner.

'Don't let this plane be delayed,' Lauren implored the ceiling, 'just for God's sake let it go on time.'

Saiv wished it would be delayed, preferably by a couple of months. But she couldn't say that, because her jaw was still etched into what she suspected was a truly spectral grin. Oh, well. Suddenly she had an urgent longing to stretch out on the row of seats and have a little nap.

'Saiv,' Lauren said, prodding her sharply, 'you're keeling *over*. Sit *up*.'

Somehow she did, and remained approximately vertical until, to her horror, the flight was called. There was no escape. They were going to have to actually board this aircraft, and fly in it. Her fingers curled around the underside of the seat and embedded themselves in it.

'Saiv, stand up. Get up, take my arm and walk.'

'I – I can't. Laurie, I – I can't move.'

'Do it' Lauren hissed, 'or I'll tell them you're pregnant and get them to put you in a wheelchair.'

Staring, Saiv remained seated, glued. Abruptly, Lauren seized her under the elbow, yanked her to her feet and dug her knuckles into her back. 'Move. Keep moving. Through those doors and down that ramp. Left-right-left-right-that's-it-keep going—'

Somehow she did, goose-stepping like a soldier on parade, vaguely aware that she must look odd, because people were grinning as they swept by. Talking, too, quite casually, as if they were not all going to their doom. At the door of the aircraft, the steward greeted them.

'Good morning, ladies. What seat numbers do you have?'

'Fourteen and fifteen,' Lauren bleated. The steward peered at Saiv.

'Are you – are you feeling quite all right, madam?'

'Mnf' she mumbled. Lauren beamed at him. 'She's fine. She's just – just been to the dentist. Nasty extraction. Local anaesthetic.'

'Ooh,' he breathed with a camp smile, 'you poor dear. Let me help you.' Plucking at her sleeve, he led Saiv down the aisle, deposited her in the inside seat, strapped her in like a baby and patted her hand.

'There we are. You just relax now and I'll come back and see how you are when we're airborne.'

*Air*borne?! Saiv tried to open her mouth to scream, and once again Lauren's fingers dug into her wrist like pincers.

'You heard the man. Relax.'

Nodding like a puppet, Saiv sat bolt upright, grasping the armrest, battling for breath. As the cabin crew counted heads she felt a tidal wave of terror rearing up; as they went to close the doors she fumbled with her seatbelt, rose and went to race for escape.

'Saiv' Lauren whispered, pleasantly, 'if you don't sit down I'm afraid I'm going to have to slap you across the face. If you do sit down, you'll be out cold within five minutes, and then we will be in Italy.'

Hyperventilating, Saiv hesitated, and Lauren shoved her down, buckled her back in. There was a dreadful whirr of igniting engines, and the pilot came on.

'Good morning, ladies and gentlemen, I'm Captain O'Neill and . . . today our route will be taking us out over the Irish Sea and . . . not expecting any weather problems . . . flying at thirty-three thousand feet . . .'

Lauren glanced at Saiv. She was ashen. Pityingly, she smiled at her. 'Now, don't panic. You've got this far. You'll be grand.'

The engines revved, the plane swung round and began to taxi. At the top of the runway it stopped, and Saiv whimpered like a puppy. Sweat was pumping down her face. With a sudden surge, the plane moved off, gathering horrific speed. And then, smooth as silk, it left the ground.

Lauren turned to look at Saiv. Her head was lolling back, her mouth was open and her eyes were closed. Emitting a deep gurgling sound, she snored loudly and departed for Italy, completely crashed.

'Laurie' Saiv breathed, 'I've died. Died and gone to heaven.'

For a moment Lauren did not reply, sitting considering in the bow of the boat, her face tilted under the molten sky.

'Yes' she said at length, 'you've gone to paradise by plane, and I've gone with you! This is – is truly exquisite.'

No photograph, not even a painting, Saiv thought, could have prepared them for the ghostly, glimmering beauty of Venice, the mirage-like vision gliding into view. As the vaporetto neared land they were silenced, embraced in the beckoning aura of the city called La Serenissima, the swirling water washing their minds empty of all else. Even Lauren looked radiant, disbelieving as the breeze ruffled her hair.

'Saiv, this – this is *ridiculous*! This is *Dis*neyland!'

Her face filled with delight, and Saiv clutched at her arm. 'Oh, Laurie . . . thank you. Thank you so much for making me come here. I have never in my life seen anything so entrancing.'

Lauren laughed. 'No! And I've never seen anything like you, conked out on that plane, *snoring* for Chrissake. So much for abject terror. I had to practically carry you off like a sack of spuds.'

Saiv looked sheepish. 'I – I can't actually remember much about it. I didn't really snore, did I?'

'So loudly that the man behind complained. Talk about embarrassing. I told him you had a sinus problem.'

Euphoric, Saiv splintered with laughter. 'You lied and bullied and chivvied every inch of the way . . . you were fabulous. You are the only person who could ever have done it.'

Smugly, Lauren grinned. 'Well, now we're here, let's make the most of it. As you know I can barely tell a cathedral from a palazzo, but I have to admit this is something else.' Raising a finger, she pointed to a looming golden mass, majestically floating into view. 'What d'you reckon that gizmo might be?'

'Lauren,' Saiv enlightened her incredulously, 'that's San Marco.'

'Huh?'

'San Marco! St Mark's Basilica gizmo!'

'Oh. Right. Cool colours, eh?'

Speechless, Saiv didn't reply, her eyes ravenously devouring the gilded sheen of the domes, the glow of the coral-tinged stone, the undulating reflection on the lapping emerald lagoon. Trailing her fingers in the water, she let her mind drift out to it, reaching for this magnificent sight, this memory that would stamp her soul for as long as she lived. Slowing, the little steamer chugged to its landing point, drawing her into the heart of the silent city, the depths of her dreams.

But other passengers were chatting, reaching for bags, disembarking with the eager spring of gazelles onto the landing quay, and Lauren nudged her: is this where we get off?

Reluctantly, Saiv roused herself. Travelling from the airport by boat on choppy water, coupled with chemical residue, was so disorientating she staggered to her feet, barely able to dredge up her first words of dormant Italian to the boatman. *Per favore, dov'è l'albergho Fiorita, è lontano?*

A torrent of words poured back, and she floundered as if drenched, unable to grasp a single quicksilver syllable.

Lauren laughed. 'Lost, are we?'

Flushing, Saiv nodded. No brownie points for this bewildering beginning. Should they get off, or not? Before she could decide, Lauren grasped her suitcase and gestured to her to follow. 'Come on, jump, quick before he takes us onto who knows where . . . this looks pretty central, we can walk a bit if need be.'

She leaped off and Saiv followed hastily, nearly missing her step and falling into the water. The Zimovane was still in her system, and she spun giddily as Lauren groped for the paperwork in her pocket, consulting it briskly.

'Hotel Locanda Fiorita, Campiello Novo . . . OK, where's that?' Unfolding a map, she held it out and they peered at it together, mystified. Venice appeared to be something of a maze. Lauren looked up, looked around, and then with a determined smile she marched up to a man walking by with a dog. Saiv waited, and there was some exchange of bilingual pleasantries, stabbing at the map, gradually enlightened response on both sides. Apparently, without having a word of Italian, Lauren was getting somewhere.

'Now!' she beamed as the man moved on, 'there's a helpful chap! We got off at the wrong stop all right, but we can walk, it's only about ten minutes from here.'

'How do you know? Did he speak English?'

'No, not really, but he – he got the idea, and so did I. Shake a leg, Saiv, I'm dying for a shower.'

Airily she picked up her bag and strode off, leaving Saiv to follow bemused. How did Lauren manage these things, how did she always somehow attain her goal? It was impossible to imagine her being lost for long, here or anywhere. Despite what she was saying about a shower she still looked as crisp as when they'd set out, not a wrinkle, not a smudge; no evidence of illness or frailty at all. Sticky in her own clothes, feeling her hair curl into corkscrews, Saiv marvelled at what sheer chutzpah could achieve.

The hotel, when they found it, was tucked into a tiny square, small and cute as a button, with geraniums edging every window. Saiv thought it looked adorable, and Lauren cocked her head, assessing it.

'Well – I don't think there's any danger of running into Jerry Hall or Madonna here, but I guess we'll just have to slum it.'

Then I must go slumming more often, Saiv thought as they entered the fresh, pretty lobby through a twinkling glass door that opened off the sunlit courtyard. Taking charge, Lauren strode up to the desk and introduced herself to the receptionist who, she apparently assumed, would be both thrilled and honoured to see her. So it turned out; two minutes later the man was handing her a key with his best wishes for a delightful stay in Venice.

'It's a wonder,' Saiv observed, 'he didn't give you his phone number as well. You charmed him footless. I don't know how you do this stuff.'

'You smile,' Lauren replied as if to a dimwitted child, 'and simply look as if you know what you're doing. It's not exactly rocket science.'

No, but . . . as they made their way to their room Saiv felt a surge of gratitude to her friend, who had steered her here the whole way from Dublin, through not only the dreaded flight but the airports at both ends, the connections to and fro, the street directions and now the checking-in. Whatever the state of her health, she was still so capable, so cheerily confident, so plugged-in to life's flashing switchboard.

Their twin room was shuttered against the sun, but scarcely had she set foot in it than Lauren had the folding system sussed, letting enough light into the room that it was illuminated without being dazzling.

'There we are! It's not the Ritz, but I reckon it'll do . . . what d'you think?'

Saiv sat down on a bed and surveyed her surroundings, the pale yellow walls rising into a beamed ceiling, the window with its view of tangled vines framing the little square beyond, and thought it was miraculous. In a city notoriously hard to find any accommodation in, Lauren had managed to locate a gem.

'It's perfect. You're a genius, and so you get first crack at the bathroom. I'm just going to sit here for a few minutes and . . .'

'And sober up! How's the head?'

Curiously, Saiv touched her hand to it. 'Still attached to the rest of me. Did I really do it, Laurie? Did I actually travel on a plane, and survive? Did I really *fly*?'

'Like Peter Pan' Lauren assured her. 'See. I told you there was nothing to it. Lot of fuss about damn all. Where's my bathroom kit?'

Clicking open her case she began to rummage for it, and Saiv continued to sit, surveying her until she vanished into the shower. How she had done it, how she had boarded that aircraft was still beyond her, but one thing was for sure: she never could have done it without Lauren Kilroy. And now it was over, it was accomplished. Dizzy with relief, she stretched out on the bed and lay contemplating the ceiling, hugging their joint achievement to her like a gift from the gods. To many people it would sound so small, look so ludicrous, but to her it was huge. After all these years she was back in Italy at last, and her joy was infinite.

Now, she thought, I know the meaning of the word renaissance, and it's not confined to art. Michelangelo doesn't have a monopoly on rebirth.

In retrospect that first day seemed like a dream, and they were into the next before Saiv fully regained command of herself, resolving to retrieve her tattered Italian and communicate with this sunnily sparkling country. Over breakfast in the hotel courtyard, she did verbal battle with the waiter, refusing to be vanquished into English, insisting on her cappuccino and cornetto and frutta fresca.

'Just one cornetto,' Lauren carolled, laughing, 'fruit's enough for me.'

The waiter went off to get their order, and Saiv frowned at Lauren's opaque sunglasses. 'Oh, come on, have a croissant, fruit's *not* enough.'

Lauren shrugged. 'Sure it is. I won't be hungry till lunchtime. Now, give me the guidebook and let's see where to start.'

'Why don't we just wander? For an hour first, anyway, to get the feel of the place?'

'Because we only have five days in Venice, and all this stuff you want to see is only open during the day. We can wander in the evenings.'

Yes, Saiv supposed, that sounded sensible. But, eager as she was to visit San Marco, the Rialto, Murano and everything else, she didn't want to set up any frantic itinerary that would exhaust Lauren. Reflecting for a moment, she hit on a compromise.

'Then let's take a vaporetto trip along the canal first, and get our bearings.'

'OK. I wonder if there are any shops along the way?'

Saiv choked with laughter on her cornetto. 'Oh, Laurie, you're incorrigible! Nothing you can buy in Venice could possibly compare with the things you can simply see . . . even Mastercard won't buy these masterpieces.'

Lauren pouted. 'Damn Italians. Why can't they just wrap the whole caboodle and put it in a carrier bag?'

Saiv drew breath to start in on a speech about the priceless value of art, and suddenly slammed to a stop, her spirit soaring up to the turquoise sky. Despite their different attitudes to what constituted a holiday, she sensed that she and Lauren were going to have lots of fun here, and a truly rewarding time together. The time of their lives.

Gulping her coffee, she pushed back her chair and stood up, lightly touching Lauren's shoulder. 'There will' she promised, 'be shopping, and Harry's Bar, and gondoliers clenching roses in their teeth, and everything you could ever want. Trust me, Laurie. You'll have the time of your life in Italy.'

Standing up in turn, Lauren slung her bag over her shoulder, coolly chic in a summer shirt and miniskirt, graceful as a Gucci model. Opening her mouth she started to say something, but then paused irresolute, and something flashed through her face. Something that told Saiv, in that split second, how much she had unwittingly offered her friend, the magnitude of those few simple words.

Groping to rescue the moment, she was forestalled by a tiny chiming sound, and Lauren reached into her bag to answer her mobile phone. Even when she was away from it, it seemed the world of advertising could not manage without her for five minutes. Grimacing, Saiv resolved that somehow it was going to have to.

Venice took longer to master than expected. At first they were enthralled by the glory, the drifting grace of it, the flashing sun enticing them into every corner, revelling and exclaiming. 'It's like a Russian doll' Lauren pronounced in the Palazzo Ducale, 'another layer and another and another.' And so they carried on, chipping away at it, navigating shadowy squares and labyrinthine streets, dipping into cafés 'for petrol' as Lauren put it, emerging again into the hazy white heat. Often, Saiv asked whether Lauren was tiring, but always Lauren said no, let's keep going, what's next?

Sometimes Saiv caught her yawning in a church or gallery, gazing sceptically up at the more overblown paintings, statues, frescoes, sneakily sitting down whenever a chance arose. But time and again she shook her head: no, I'm fine, I can rest later when we go to the beaches. Meanwhile, you guzzle these galleries, get your fix!

Saiv was getting her fix with a vengeance. Only now did she realise the depths to which she had immured herself in Ireland, sheltered in the academic life which, she began to think, was only a life on paper. Even her work on Rousseau didn't make her feel as she was feeling now, tingling and blooming, the parched leaves of her being unfolding like a watered rose, coming into colour. I'm falling in love, she thought, this is better than sex! Better than any I've ever had, anyway, far more fulfilling and more exciting. I could *eat* Venice, it's so rich, so sumptuous! I don't quite know yet how I'm going to do it, but I'm never letting go of Italy again.

Her delight propelled them through museums, towers, basilicas, on foot and on boats, losing their way and finding it again, taking tours, wandering solo, darting in all directions.

Each evening they were exhausted, but after a shower they went out again, for cool drinks on one of the piazzas. Everywhere, music trickled on the air; many of the waterside cafés had little orchestras after dusk, the sweetness of one violin competing irresistibly with the next.

It was heavenly. But it was difficult too, at times, to cope with the surging crowds everywhere, that jostled Lauren and made Saiv feel as if she were suffocating. So much to see, so many people pushing to see it! One evening, overcome with a kind of prickling panic, she had to leave Lauren abruptly and flee to the hotel courtyard, where she sat down alone under a rising sliver of moon, breathing deeply, getting a grip. Amidst the magic, she had felt a faintly lurking menace.

'Sorry' she apologised when eventually she returned to their room, feeling calmer. 'I just got this – need for air – it's my claustrophobia—'

Lying on her bed reading a book, Lauren looked up. 'That's OK' she said, 'take it easy. I know you need time by yourself now and then.'

'Thanks. I do. It's nothing personal. This city is just so crammed!'

'Yeah. With people like us! I was glad of the break myself.'

'Were you?'

'Yes.' Languidly, Lauren let her book slide to the floor, where Saiv was surprised to see its upturned cover: Emily Dickinson's poetry. But how awful, how morbid! And how unlike Lauren, who normally flicked through *Hello!* magazine. Where had she got hold of this, and why?

'It was in the hotel library,' Lauren explained off-handedly, and said no more. For a moment Saiv stood aghast, thinking of the first line that came into her head: 'Because I could not stop for death/He kindly stopped for me . . .' And then she grasped Lauren's hand, hauled her upright.

'Come on. Out for dinner. One of those fun restaurants with music and smart-ass waiters and lots of people.'

'Lots of people? But I thought you—'

'Lots' Saiv repeated firmly, and led her off with barely time for a slick of lipstick.

At random they found a busy bistro, but it was full; would they like to book a table for later? Yes, Saiv asserted, they would. Meanwhile they'd go and have drinks at – she groped for somewhere glamorous that Lauren would like – at the Gritti Palace.

On the way there Lauren's phone rang twice; it was an hour earlier in Ireland and her office was still going strong. Saiv gritted her teeth and prayed for a big notice in the Gritti Palace, banning mobiles. When they reached it she was relieved to see Lauren's eyes light up, assessing its opulent, gilded lobby, distracted. This was her kind of turf and Saiv noted the immediate lift of her chin, the sassy way in which she sailed in, saluting the doorman as if she were a regular. You could take Lauren Kilroy absolutely anywhere, Saiv thought, ruefully wishing the same could be said of herself. Her casual clothes felt like dusters in the elegant atmosphere, whereas Lauren was a grace note, contributing to the sense of style, making her feel like a waif by comparison – or worse, Lauren's mother. The mother Lauren seemed to feel she didn't actually have, when the chips were down.

Gingerly, she lowered herself onto the edge of an armchair while Lauren sank into a sofa, and a waiter rolled up as if on castors. *Buona sera*, what a beautiful evening, and what could he get the ladies to drink? Stifling a giggle, Saiv suppressed the sudden temptation to say she'd have a Bud by the neck.

'A glass of Moët, please, and a small mineral water' Lauren replied demurely, and Saiv blinked as the uniformed man went smartly off to fetch it.

'Moët? Is that for me?'

'Yes, I think so, don't you? Sorry I haven't got any Zimovane to go with it, but I hope you'll enjoy it just the same.'

Saiv crackled with laughter. 'I'll try! God, I'll be a drug addict by the time we get home, have to go straight to John of Gods.'

'Well, it'll be worth it. Even if I did have to drug you, I got you here, and you're loving it, aren't you?'

'Yes. Yes I am. Absolutely adoring every minute . . . and you, Laurie? I know it's been all churches and art so far, but—'

'But' Lauren replied unexpectedly, 'they're magnificent. I'm learning something new every day.'

Saiv sat back. 'Are you really? About what, precisely?'

'Oh . . . about the way people see things. Painters, and the people who enjoy their work hundreds of years after they've died . . . the paintings just live on forever, don't they?'

'Yes. The good ones do. The ones that connect with – with people's spiritual hunger, feed their souls.'

Lauren plucked at a cushion. 'Mmm . . . like Lola Cola posters, huh?'

Saiv laughed, but Lauren didn't, turning instead to coolly accept their arriving drinks and, while Saiv rummaged hastily for her purse, motion the waiter simply to leave the bill on the table. By the time Saiv found the means to pay it, he had gone.

'You're so cool! Why do I get so flustered, in places like this?'

Lazily, Lauren smiled at her. 'Because you need more practice at them, that's all. There just aren't enough five-star hotels out in wildest Meath . . . if you'd come into Dublin more often I'd train you like a puppy.'

Puppy. Briefly Saiv thought of her dogs, and felt a tug. And then, lifting her glass, she decided not to think about them. They were in Ireland, and she was in Italy, and that was that. Sitting back, she sipped her champagne.

'So, what were you saying? About enjoying the art, when I thought you'd be bored stiff?'

'No. I'm not bored. I'm not impressed by all of it, either. But some things . . . you can't help but be touched by some of these Madonnas, can you? They're so – so young, so tender.'

'Yes . . . it's not the religious aspect, it's the – the wistfulness. Or the humility. The look that seems to wonder, how can this be happening to me, how can I be the mother of this unique child? Sometimes they look almost psychic, as if they know He's going to die.'

As soon as she said it Saiv could have strangled herself, but

Lauren didn't flinch, only smiled a fraction. 'Yes. Talk about one picture being worth a thousand words. Too bad our gung-ho lads can't convey the message as succinctly . . . if Tintoretto were alive today I'd offer him a job at Axis in the morning.'

Taken unawares, Saiv caught the blade of irony in her words, and was bemused. It was the first time she had ever heard Lauren make fun of Axis, that all-important hub of the known universe.

'He might,' she smiled mischievously, 'turn it down.'

'Yeah. Or we might not be able to afford him. He might feel that no amount of money would pay him to plug our jammy, whammy pop-tarts.'

Saiv entered into the sardonic spirit, intrigued to find Lauren in this irreverent frame of mind. Was advertising not her god, was she not dutifully genuflecting tonight?

'Oh, I don't know . . . if you promoted him to one of your car accounts, he'd soon be driving a Mercedes of his own.'

'Yeah. Tintoretto on wheels, Tintoretto on the telly!' For a moment Lauren sat gazing into her glass, twirling it slowly, contemplating the bubbles. 'Poor guy'd be burnt out at thirty.'

'Well, some of these painters were, you know. Even five hundred years ago or more, they had their problems. Michelangelo was an absolute hostage to fortune, his bosses had him driven demented, his brother kept running up bills . . .'

Lauren arched an eyebrow. 'Really?'

'Really and truly. It was a nightmare. How he painted as he did, amidst all the mayhem, is a mystery. As for his sculptures – we'll see some of those if we get to Florence, and you will be awestruck. They're celestial.'

'Are they? Are we going to Florence?'

Cautiously, Saiv eyed her. Not wanting to overload their schedule, they'd agreed on these five days in Venice followed by five days on the beaches of Rimini, and left the final five blank to fill in as they chose. She would adore to go to Florence, but Lauren might have had enough art by then, start pining for the shops of Milan?

'I don't know. Let's play it by ear, and see how we feel?'

'OK. Tell me more about Michelangelo.'

'More?'

'Yes, more! Was he as good a sculptor as, say, Yeats is a poet? Does he grab you by the throat and say hey, what are you doing with your crummy little life, when you could be doing *this* with it?'

Astonished, Saiv groped at the folds of velvet under her, wondering what on earth had got into Lauren. Lauren who only knew of one Italian artist: Versace. Lauren who'd taken the money and run, years ago, as fast as her feet would carry her from anything that required thought, or study, or sensitivity.

'Y – yes,' she answered eventually, 'he was. He is. He does.'

'Tell me how. You know him, tell me what he says to you.'

It sounded almost like a demand. Lauren was not humouring her, not idly indulging her interests; she sounded as if she genuinely, almost urgently wanted to know. Saiv closed her eyes, and thought for a while before replying.

'I think' she began, 'that what Michelangelo says to me is . . . is keep going. Everyone will knock you for trying to do anything out of the ordinary, but don't listen. Don't worry about popular opinion, or money hassles, or impatient avaricious bosses . . . just keep going. If you do, you won't always succeed, but if you succeed even sometimes, on your own terms, your life will be a success. Your life might not be worth a damn to anyone else, but it will be worth something to you. Your work, whatever it is, will have worth.'

Lauren was studying her, listening intently, and Saiv wondered whether to go on, to tell her a little about Contessina and Ludovico, about the barmy Pope Julius, the crushing struggle to excavate marble and the scandalous, clandestine study of . . . oh, Christ, oh no. Not that . . .

'Did he do Madonnas?' Lauren interrupted, saving her.

'Yes' she breathed, relieved. 'There's a heartbreaking little one called the Madonna of the Steps, in his own home, the Casa Buonarotti, it—'

As if the chandelier had crashed down, Lauren's mobile

suddenly shrilled into the hush that had grown between them, and they both shuddered in shock. But in two seconds Lauren had composed herself, was answering it.

'Yes' she purred, 'no, no, don't worry, it's only seven here . . . it's in my desk, Bill, top left drawer, Angie will have a back-up on disk . . . how are things back on the ranch, anyway?'

Saiv sighed, and then began to slowly fume. Were they, or were they not, on *holi*day? What was the bloody point, if everyone could still get *at* Lauren, pursue her to the ends of the earth? Frowning, she waited impatiently, until at length Lauren hung up. But the spell was broken, they might as well be sitting in the Shelbourne in Dublin. Apologetically, Lauren smiled soothingly.

'Sorry. Damn twits can't find anything.'

'Why don't you switch it off, and let Angie cope?'

'It's six in Dublin. Angie's gone home.'

'Then let them wait till morning.'

'But—'

'But you're *away*! Not available!'

'Saiv, I'm an executive. Always available.'

'What, like Lola Cola, on tap round the clock?'

Lauren grinned, and groaned a little. 'Saiv, it's expected. That's just the way things are.'

'Then you don't own your own life. They do.'

'Saiv, look. We're sitting here in the Gritti Palace, drinking insanely expensive drinks, on our way to a delicious dinner and then maybe . . . who knows what? A nightclub, a gondola trip – what do you think is bankrolling all this?'

'I don't know' Saiv muttered mutinously, 'because I'm here too, somehow affording it as well, even though I don't have a mobile.'

'But it's your first holiday in years. Normally, as far as I know, you throw whatever you earn into animal sanctuaries, live on a tin of Whiskas and a pint of milk. When you're not taking time out to write waffle and live on even less.'

Saiv gasped. 'Waffle?!? I beg your pardon, it's no such thing! That book is valuable to me, whether anyone else likes it or not!'

Waving her glass, Lauren laughed at her outraged expression. 'OK, OK, calm down, Michelangelo. Let's finish our drinks and go eat. Better pay this expensive bill too I suppose.'

Recalling that it was she who had suggested the treat, Saiv dived on her purse and began to extract notes from it, squinting at all the zeros on the bill, trying to work it out in Irish terms. When she looked up, Lauren's American Express card lay on the salver, and the waiter was swishing to pick it up.

'Laurie, no! I invited you—'

'Saiv' Lauren sighed, uncrossing her slim legs and standing up, 'I really do think it's time you got yourself a credit card. People don't produce fistfuls of grubby cash in the Gritti Palace.'

Off she waltzed, and Saiv scrambled after her, fulminating. She just wasn't the sophisticated type, and sometimes Lauren made her feel like a complete country bumpkin. Which had its charms, at home, but was somehow maddening here, in what Lauren called the 'real world'.

After dinner they decided, following some debate, to take a gondola trip, romantic cliché and all as it might be. Not that there was much romance, as Lauren remarked, in two girlfriends going together; yet it started out limpidly wonderful, on ochre-tinted water under a molten scarlet sky. It continued to be wonderful for approximately ten minutes, wending its way through Byzantine bliss in the sunset, until Lauren's mobile rang again. Saiv thought she would explode.

'Don't answer it!'

But already Lauren was embroiled in some problem about a missing fax, a crucial fax apparently, the mother of all faxes without which the planet would combust. By the time the conversation came to its fretful, acrimonious end the mood was ruined and Saiv was seething.

'Lauren,' she demanded outright, 'is this going to go on for our entire holiday? Is that bloody phone going to ring morning, noon and night, day in and day out?'

Lauren had the grace to look a little abashed. 'Probably,' she admitted, 'but I'll switch the ringer off. It'll just vibrate silently and you won't hear it any more.'

'But I'll still hear the conversations! And ours will still be interrupted! This isn't fair to either of us . . . you need a break so badly and now they won't even let you have one.'

Wide-eyed, Lauren looked at her. 'But Saiv, my clients are my – my babies! I can't simply abandon them.'

'They are not your babies! They are grown adults and they have no manners, no consideration whatsoever.'

'Oh, come on, don't sulk. That was only a little flap over nothing . . . look, the moon is lovely now, a full crescent. Let's relax and enjoy it.'

Steeling herself, Saiv tried, but her nerves were primed, anticipating further shrieks and yelps from Dublin. Were Lauren's colleagues really so hopeless that they couldn't cope without her, or . . . ? Nastily it crossed her mind that maybe one or two of them might actually be envious of her holiday, deliberately interrupting it, or that perhaps some kind of power politics were coming into play, people calling just to remind her they could, that they had that right to her time, her endless attention. Well then, she thought, they're utter bastards; even if they don't know she's ill, they must know everyone needs a break. Especially from the likes of them. Talk about earning your living the hard way.

When she cooled off, she tried to make Lauren see the logic, and to also make her understand that she was concerned for her, wanted her to have the peace and quiet to which she was entitled.

'But' Lauren demurred, 'suppose we lost a contract because I wasn't contactable? Suppose my apartment was on fire or—'

'Or you had to pump water from the Venetian lagoon into your apartment in Dublin? Laurie, you're away! Someone else will just have to cope. Stop trying to rationalise rubbish.'

For the sake of peace they let it drop, but both were vaguely irked, Saiv not least because she wanted Lauren to shed whatever wearing responsibilities she normally carried, and get some good from her hard-earned holiday. The holiday that could well be her last, if she didn't ease up and start nurturing herself.

Sensing their mood, the gondolier did not sing or joke, and in silence they continued to weave their way through the silken water, quiet in the dusk, but not in harmony. Although Lauren didn't say another word, Saiv could see she was secretly perturbed, her mind flying to the missing fax, diving into drawers, already composing a new one in her head – to be sent, undoubtedly, the moment they got back to their hotel. With a major effort, she sat back on the plump velvet cushions and tried to savour what was left of their gondola ride, of their last night in Venice. It was late; surely Laurie would be left in peace at last?

Even as she speculated, Saiv stared disbelieving. The phone wasn't ringing aloud this time, but Lauren was plucking it discreetly from her pocket, murmuring surreptitiously into it.

'Shane' she mouthed, catching Saiv's accusing eye. Grimly, Saiv nodded, mulling on what she knew of Shane Jackson. Nice Shane, Lauren had told her after her fainting episode; kind Shane, concerned Shane. Married Shane.

Was he calling, at this hour, simply to enquire how she was? Or . . . did he know Lauren had broken up with Jordan White? Could he possibly be trying to cash in on that, use the moment to his advantage? He had already, if she remembered correctly, had some kind of fling with Lauren one night years ago . . . was he hungry for more? Might he be one of those callous creeps conveniently oblivious to other people's pain once they got what they wanted? Thinking of the anguish Lauren had already endured at the hands of Jordan White, of the devastation he continued to wreak, Saiv felt her heart hardening against Shane Jackson.

Not just against Shane Jackson, but against any man who had the power to hurt her friend, to do more damage and walk away from the fire he had lit. Lauren was ill, not in a position any more to embark on a new relationship however much she might want or need one, but did Shane know that? No, he didn't, because Lauren had confided the extent of her predicament to nobody. Shane had absolutely no idea what she was going through – but he knew she'd recently broken up with Jordan, and that she must be lonely. Lonely and grieving and, maybe, longing for a shoulder to cry on?

Sitting up, Saiv thought about it, and made a decision while Lauren was still talking to him. When she finally hung up, she started to explain what it was he'd wanted, but, cutting her short, Saiv simply smiled sweetly and held out her hand.

'Laurie, that phone is so tiny, it's amazing! Could I see it?'

Looking surprised, Lauren handed it over. 'Sure. It's a new one actually, a WAP, it can access the internet and everything.'

Pleased to see Saiv interested, she smiled back, and Saiv took the phone, held it aloft for a moment, studying it. Then, reaching her arm out over the side of the gondola, she dropped it into the water. With a plop, it disappeared.

For a moment, too shocked to speak, Lauren sat stunned. Calmly, Saiv waited, fully prepared to take whatever was coming. Lauren's mouth was open, her face perfectly rigid.

'A very cute phone,' Saiv agreed, 'but now, alas, gone.'

Gone! Had the gondola been struck by lightning, had it shattered and sunk under them, Lauren could not have looked more stricken, more aghast. Wrenching her gaze from Saiv, she swivelled it to the already closing ripple on the water, leaned over and plunged her arm in, gasping and grasping.

'Ah! My phone, my phone! Stop the boat, my phone has—!'

'Has drowned,' Saiv supplied, equably. Lauren leaped up, and the gondola began to rock wildly as she clutched at the boatman. 'Stop! Stop!'

Bewildered, the gondolier tried to peel her off. Standing with his back to them, he had not seen what had happened, and Saiv smiled calmly. 'Let go, Laurie, or you'll have us drowned. Your phone has gone to Davy Jones's locker and it's not coming back. I don't think they'll bother dredging the lagoon for it, do you?'

Open-mouthed, Lauren stared at her, lurching, looking as if she'd been stabbed. 'My phone! I can't *believe* you did this! I – I – my entire *life* is on that phone! My diary, my notes and appointments, all my numbers, my whole *life*!'

Sagely, with a feeling of immense satisfaction, Saiv let her fingers flow on the wash of the water, and the gondolier pushed on. 'No, Laurie, your whole life isn't on it. Most of your life is still here, in Venice with me, on its way to the isle of Murano tomorrow and the beaches of Rimini after that. We still have ten more days in Italy and, somehow, you're just going to have to soldier on.'

Still gaping, with a look of despair now as well, Lauren leaned back at the spot where the phone had vanished, as if a hand might suddenly shoot up waving it. 'Y – you bitch! I need it, I can't go on without it—'

'Oh, I think you can. Look at it this way. Michelangelo didn't have a mobile, did he? Yet his work is all done, still standing, a monument to his—'

'*Screw* Michelangelo! I'll have to get another one—'

'Mmm. Eventually. When you get home and have access to all your info . . . you didn't bring your briefcase with you, did you?'

'That phone *was* my bloody briefcase!'

'Oh. Well, if anything really urgent crops up, you'll be contactable at the hotel.'

'We're moving on to Rimini tomorrow!'

'Yes, well, ring them from there. Give Angie the new number. In case of any genuine emergency.'

For a moment Lauren looked as if she were about to jump into the water, dive to its murky depths and retrieve her precious lifeline. But the gondola drifted on, past the scene of the crime, and quivering with rage she clenched her fists, freezing into a glacial, furious silence.

But she'll get over it, Saiv thought unrepentant. She'll fume tonight, maybe tomorrow too, but then she'll adjust. She'll be her own boss for a change, rid of all these people who keep nibbling at her; things will be much harder for them and much easier for her. Now I'll have her to myself, and what's more she'll have herself to herself. Maybe we'll even have a long, real talk some day, and I'll find out how she's really feeling, what the hell is going on in her head.

'I'm not going' Lauren flatly asserted. 'You can go by yourself.'

'But Laurie, don't you want to buy some Murano glass? Hand-blown?'

Shopping, Saiv thought swiftly; that'll get her moving. I'll never make it to Murano by myself, in all those crowds, with a ferry to find . . . and it'd be a shame for her to miss it just because she's sulking.

'Hand-blown, huh? Well, guess what, Saiv. They can blow it out—'

'Laurie! It's an ancient craft, exquisite glass—'

'Glass my ass. I have to call the office and sort out this mess about the phone, buy a new one if the Italian system is compatible. You were a little hoor to do it and now you can take a hike.'

Saiv sighed, recognising futility in argument. Lauren's voice had a crusty edge to it, she was wearing the flinty face which said her decision was final. I wouldn't care to cross her in business, Saiv thought . . . still, I'm not sorry about losing that blasted phone. Even if she is punishing me for it.

'All right. I'll go alone, so.'

'Good. As in 'bye.'

Frostily, she turned away, leaving Saiv no choice but to depart with dignity, opening her guidebook as she went and trying to figure out its directions. But, after only a few hundred metres, she realised she'd already taken a wrong turn somewhere. Retracing her steps, she picked up the thread again for a while, making her way through a maze of back streets sliced with early sun and cold bars of shadow; it was only a little after eight, and Venice felt somnolent, barely beginning to stir.

Here and there a workman's café was opening, shutters were creaking back and 'buon giornos' were being exchanged in what seemed to be a residential neighbourhood, its inhabitants slowly coming to grips with the new day, scents of strong coffee wafting from unseen breakfast tables. Clutching her guidebook, Saiv caught sight of what looked like a large religious building of some kind in the distance, and felt a little relief; she hadn't much experience of finding her way around foreign cities, but according to the map that should be the Jesuit institution, leading onto the quay where boats departed for Murano. But when she got closer it turned out to be some kind of convent instead, one that shouldn't be there at all, and she was obliged to seek help from a waiter plunking down a minuscule cup in front of a man reading a newspaper.

The waiter was helpful, but too quick for her; all she caught was his first few gestures to left and right. Following those as far as she could, she found herself stuck thereafter, floundering in a warren of tiny side streets that seemed to have no beginning and no end.

Damn! This wouldn't happen if Lauren were here, would it? Glancing at her watch, she saw that she'd already been walking for half an hour, to no apparent avail. Where now? She had completely lost her bearings, didn't even know where the hotel was any more, much less the elusive quay. A passing man smiled at her, and she smiled back, feeling like an idiot. Feeling under some pressure, too; they were leaving for Rimini at three and she had to be back from Murano by then.

Concentrating hard this time, she asked directions again, grasped them and ploughed on, eventually sensing that she was nearing the open sea. Phew! Following her nose, she came at last to the edge of the water, but it was the wrong section of it, and fifteen further flustered minutes elapsed before she finally found the ferry point. It was teeming with people, hundreds of them all scrambling to board a bobbing boat.

Oh, God! She did her best, but she knew she wasn't going to be one of those who got a place on it, because she was simply useless at elbowing her way through thick crowds. Lauren would have elbowed, with a charming smile as she shamelessly jumped the queue – but this wasn't a queue anyway, it was a minor riot, led by hefty Americans and nimble Japanese, and the thought of fighting her way through them all made her quail. Feeling punctured, she watched while the most determined of them poured onto the vaporetto, leaving at least a hundred waiting for the next one.

No, she thought. No way, this is like the sales at Christmas. I don't need to see Murano badly enough to get squashed and flattened and . . . and that boat is so packed it looks as if it might sink. That'd really be great. My drowned body carted back to the hotel, and Lauren throwing her eyes up to heaven, dear Jesus, can Saiv Lovett do nothing right, not even be let out safely for one morning? Better abandon the whole project than carry on with this nightmare. I'll sit down and have a coffee somewhere, decide what to do instead.

Turning her back on the departing ferry and the hustling horde, she sought out a small café in a nearby side street, and seated herself with a mixture of gratitude and disappointment. After all, Murano hardly mattered, she had seen everything else she wanted; better to let it go than battle through that awful crowd. Only – only it was so annoying, to have to go back and tell Lauren she hadn't got there, couldn't even do this on her own! For a few minutes she sat mulling on it, her chin on her knuckles, thinking that really she was for the birds. Definitely not what Lauren would call 'management material', if she couldn't even manage a simple trip.

Yet she'd managed to write her book, hadn't she? Not only started but finished it . . . what were the publishers making of it, now that they had it? Suddenly she longed to know, to hear some news, some reaction – which she could easily have, it struck her with sudden irony, if she had a mobile phone. She could ring them here and now, and find out.

Oh, hell! As she sipped her cappuccino she began to ponder, to reflect on her aversion to the many things which could make her life so much easier, and her reasons for rejecting them. Was it really lofty disdain of technology, of living a kind of artificial life with all the stress it could bring? Or was it fear, cowardly pointless fear of engaging with the modern world, filled as it was with challenges, innovations, things that kept mutating before you'd even mastered them? Admittedly she had mastered a basic computer, but that hardly counted; the university had held a compulsory training course for faculty members and she'd had to do it. Under duress; yet the skill had enabled her to not only write her book but research it too.

The computer came under the same heading as the car, which she'd also resisted in her teens. But her father had insisted, made her learn to drive because 'a young girl is a sight safer with her own transport than depending on anyone else's, just get in there now and do it.' So she had done it, and nowadays couldn't survive without it. As for the television – another intrusion, another gizmo to decry, yet she'd avidly watched that fabulous documentary on Renaissance art. Planes? No way – except for the one that had flown her here for this wonderful holiday.

I'm all talk, she thought. I'm *precious*. High and mighty, living my hippy life in rural isolation, permanently hibernating while everyone else gets on with life, *lives* it. Everyone else will get on that boat to Murano eventually, I bet I'm the only one who's given up. I'm the kind of klutz who invites Lauren for a drink at the Gritti Palace and she ends up paying for it. I'm going to have to do better than this, if I'm not going to be a pest and a pain for the rest of our time here. I'll just have to toughen up, be what she calls more 'pro-active'. Start taking initiatives, instead of letting her do all the talking and organising. That's what she's here for – a break from all that. The last thing she needs is me hanging out of her apron strings. She'll despair, she'll wash her hands of me when I trudge back saying no, I didn't get to Murano actually, it was all too difficult, couldn't cope.

I can't go back yet. She's still mad over that phone, wants me out of her face this morning. So – what'll I do? Sit here till noon, drinking a dozen cappuccinos? Hang round the quay like a dead duck? Or go back to that hotel with something to show for my time, some small thing accomplished?

I know. I'll go shopping. If I can't go back with an armful of Murano glass then I'll go back with something else – maybe a little present for her, a peace offering. I will set off right now and keep going until I find the shops, buy something, produce an excuse for missing Murano. I hate shopping, but . . . if we're going to any more ritzy places like the Gritti Palace, a decent outfit wouldn't go amiss. Something up to scratch, so I won't look like Lauren's granny next time. I will buy something – something *hot*, as she'd say. A little number. Even Jung wrote that we should 'explore the daily will of God' – so, I'll explore. And pray that God's will extends to size fourteen.

God's will. That's what Emily Dickinson's poetry is about, basically. Fate, and how there's no escaping it. What joker left such stuff lying round the hotel for Lauren to find? What inspired her to pick it out, of all the books on the shelf? Usually she'd say poetry was for airheads. But she's been different lately . . . changing, thinking in a way I've never known her to. Looking at paintings, statues, art, stuff I thought would send her screaming round the bend. She's mentioned nightclubs but hasn't dragged me to any, she's talked about department stores but bought nothing. And now, here I am, going shopping! She'll laugh at that, but if she can do new things then so can I. Let's pay for this coffee and get moving.

Settling her bill, she set off, thinking as she went what a lovely, mesmerising city Venice was. But so lush . . . after five days of it she felt as if she'd eaten an entire box of chocolates, and was beginning to get indigestion. Beaches were not her scene in high summer, but maybe there was something to recommend Rimini after all, Lauren's next choice of destination.

Undoubtedly it would be touristy, with a lot of rampaging children and ice-cream parlours blaring pop, but there'd be fresh sea breezes too, clearer water and more of this delicious sun.

Lauren could toast herself on a lilo all day, while she walked on the sand and did a bit of meditating . . . would she be going back to the 'day job' at college in autumn, or could that book possibly change anything, point her life in a different direction? She didn't know; but she did know it was time for something new. If I were married, she thought, it'd be called the seven-year itch.

Married! Hah! That'd be the day. It's extraordinary how you can sense some things from the very start, from childhood, even then the idea of marriage was a non-runner. Marriage is for normal people. Lovable people. Attractive women who know how to flirt and be sweet, be amusing. Women with maternal instinct, who are happy to compromise occasionally and wash the odd sock, in return for warmth, love, security. Not that there's any such thing as security, but . . . they're optimistic about it, anyway. Whereas I, for some reason, have always been pessimistic. It never crossed my mind that anyone could possibly love or be attracted to me – and they never were. Not unless you count two brief relationships that fizzled out, one because we were physically incompatible and the other because I was more interested in books than baking. There just aren't many men around who feel they can compete with Carl Jung or Jean-Jacques Rousseau – nor can they. And I never encouraged anyone to think he could. If I die a withered old spinster it'll be my own fault. Partly, anyway. 'Woman found dead in Meath cottage with two starving dogs' – that'll be me, some day.

Good grief. What's wrong with me, on this beautiful sunny morning in Venice? I should be giving thanks that I'm well and healthy, in a much stronger and happier position than poor Laurie, who really is facing the possibility of death . . . what must it be doing to her, deep down? Was I wrong to throw away her phone, after all? Maybe she needs to talk to all these people, maybe they sustain her in some way? I might have misjudged Shane Jackson, he could be a genuine friend, platonically, no threat to her at all. I'm acting like her mother, and it might be over-protective of me? If I am, then she's right to be annoyed. I just don't want her hurt again, damaged any more by the likes of

Jordan White. Or Isaac Hyland. *He's* the one who started the ball rolling, really, and I'll never understand how he could dump such a lovely girl overnight, wound her like that when she was only nineteen. Really, men are a complete mystery. And yet, when you see these romantic couples gliding by in gondolas, kissing and smiling, you have to think that maybe there's something to recommend relationships. Something that's worth all the difficulties and disappointments and . . . something I've evaded, all my life. I have a stack of degrees and qualifications, yet I haven't a clue how you go about *living*.

Well, here's a little boutique. Let's go in and start living. Let's see . . . h'mm. How can they cram so many clothes into such a tiny place? I don't know where to start. But I will ask for help, and buy something if it kills me.

'*Scusi, signora, mi potrebbe aiutare?*'

With a friendly smile, the assistant, who was about her own age, emerged from behind the counter to help Saiv, and soon they were immersed in a kind of bilingual pantomime, taking clothes off racks, delving into stacks of shirts, scarves, tops, groping to describe colours and holding out their hands to approximate size. It was a quaint, vaguely eccentric boutique with something to suit everyone, and the first thing Saiv decided on was a bronze velvet scarf for her niece Gráinne. Beaming approval, the woman wrapped it in gorgeous gold-striped paper, and Saiv beamed in turn.

See, that wasn't so bad, was it!? Gráinne might want to be a mechanic but she's still a girl, she'll love this and it'll be a little good-luck present for her. Now, what about Lauren?

After much more rummaging and searching, a stretchy white top was extracted from a box, and Saiv knew straight away it would be perfect on slim, dark Lauren.

'Yes please, I'll have that too.'

And finally, something for Saiv herself. The assistant eyed her, sizing her up, thought for a moment and took a large, loose cotton dress from a hanger, raising a quizzical eyebrow. It was pale blue, but it wasn't right for what she was resolved on – a new look, brighter image.

'*No, grazie, vorrei qual'cosa più – più—*'

More modern, she thought, struggling to communicate. Younger, fresher – I'd nearly say sexy, if I knew the word and didn't think she'd laugh. Handing it back, she ransacked the rails, and finally found a dress of which, she thought suddenly, Lauren would approve.

'*Posso* . . . uh . . . try it on?'

The changing room was minuscule but she was ushered into it with a flourish and a smile, one that seemed to suggest this was going to be a waste of time, but if it amuses signora . . . I don't care, she thought defiantly, the label says my size so here goes.

It was a linen dress in dark chocolate with cream panels down either side, sleeveless, with a low square neckline. The minute she was in it Saiv felt transformed, and gazed astonished at her reflection; the design was incredibly slimming, the fit not tight at all. Good heavens, she thought, the Italians make dresses for people like me!

Tentatively, but optimistically, she emerged to seek the assistant's opinion. What was the Italian for 'do my arms look fat in this'? But the assistant didn't seem to think they did in the least; her instant reaction was a smile of delight, a look that said *mamma mia*, the lady is transformed!

'*Sì?*'

'*Ah. sì, sì! Certo! È bellissima!*' The woman's joy was such that she actually clasped her hands to her bosom, in a peculiarly Italian gesture of such emotion that Saiv laughed outright. She'd need new shoes to go with this dress, something with a heel of some kind, but what the hell. Presumably Venice had a shoe shop too.

'*Bene! La prendo!*'

Looking as pleased as Saiv felt, the woman took the dress, folded it reverentially in tissue and placed it in a carrier bag with the other items. Grinning triumphantly, Saiv took it and peered while the bill was totted by hand, presented in a majestic blaze of zeros. Millions of lire, it seemed . . . um . . . more money than she had on her. Blankly she searched her bag, knowing it wasn't going to yield two hundred pounds.

'Visa?' the woman suggested helpfully.

'Er – no.'

'Amex? Diner's?'

'Uh, no – *mi scusi—*'

Oh, God! Why didn't she have a credit card, why wasn't Lauren here to take charge and sort this out? But Lauren wasn't, and she felt a fool as she fought to ask that the bag be kept while she went to a bank. There must be a bank near here, yes?

Looking bemused, the woman eventually drew a map to indicate the nearest one, ten minutes away and ten minutes back, if one were not a hopeless idiot and didn't get lost again. Blushing furiously, Saiv sidled out and went to find it.

By the time she did, and a bewilderingly complex transaction was completed, Saiv's mind was made up; she was joining the modern world forthwith, getting a fistful of credit cards the instant she went home. There was absolutely nothing rustic or romantic about this sweltering, mortifying mess. And now, in her panic, she was in possession of far more cash than could be safe to carry, would probably be mugged on the very steps of the bank.

Serve me right too, she thought, hastening back to the shop, collecting her purchases with further mime of apology and embarrassment. But at least the woman was nice, laughed it off and assured her that the dress really suited her superbly. Yes, Saiv thought, and it's a miracle I've got it, because Italian banks close for lunch and if it had been any later I'd have had to go off to Rimini this afternoon with no shopping at all, no goodies for anyone.

Perspiring, still flustered, she backed out with multiple thanks, hastened to the nearest café and ordered an icy granita. Phew! The shopping had taken two good hours, the bank trip had added more and now, if she didn't embark on the mysterious route back to the hotel, she'd be late and they'd miss their train to Rimini. Lauren would eat her and, probably, throw the new top at her idiot head. Lauren would be all packed when she got back, ready to move, organised and immaculate.

And still fuming, still glacial? But no, probably not; one of the many good things to be said about Lauren Kilroy was that she didn't hold grudges. She just blew a fuse and then forgot all about it. She'd have forgiven the phone episode by now, be all smiles again.

Or so Saiv hoped. Gulping the granita, she set off at an anxious trot, getting hotter and damper by the minute as she negotiated a zig-zag route which, she suspected, was twice as long as it should be. By the time she finally pitched up, panting, at the hotel it was lunchtime, and she realised she'd forgotten to buy the new shoes without which the new dress was pointless. Oh, well, she could get those later, in Rimini; at least she was here with time to take a cool shower before she fainted.

Lauren was out in the courtyard, sitting under a parasol, looking fresh and chic in a short black dress, radiating panache. Catching sight of Saiv, she raised her sunglasses a fraction.

'What's this? A shopping bag? Am I hallucinating?'

'No! I – I've bought – phew – you – something – God, let me get my breath.'

Collapsing into a crumpled heap on a chair, conscious that being overweight didn't help when you were in a hurry, Saiv gasped for a moment, ran her hands through her hair and plucked loose the folds of her sticky, soggy blouse.

'Bought me something?' Lauren sounded suspicious, as if it were a joke.

'Yes, a – a present, to make up about the phone. I've been thinking about that, maybe I was wrong . . . did you get a new one?'

'No. I rang the office from the room, then I took a long bath and decided just to chill out for the rest of the morning. I'd kind of had enough sightseeing.'

'Oh?' Saiv frowned, wondering whether Lauren was feeling tired, feeling all right. Not that there would be any use in asking.

'Yes – anyway, how was Murano?'

'Uh – I never got there.'

'What? Why not?'

'Because there was a massive queue for the boat and I . . . I decided to go shopping for a change. I've had enough sight-seeing too, for now.'

Did Lauren look relieved? She thought she did. Glad she hadn't insisted on marching her to the Murano she'd never reached, Saiv groped in the bag at her aching feet and extracted the small beribboned package.

'This is for you. To say sorry.'

Not that I am sorry, she thought, if I've saved you from being plagued by pesky colleagues. I'm just sorry that I had to do it.

Curiously, Lauren examined the luxurious package, which was sealed with a small classy sticker, and opened it with one neat twirl of its ribbon. Extracting the white top, she held it up in amazement.

'But – but this is beautiful! My colour, my size, my style . . . Saiv, what on earth came over you?'

'I – I don't know. I just thought it was time to do something – different. Something unlike me!'

Laughing, looking fascinated at her, Lauren held the top to her upper torso and immediately Saiv saw that it not only suited her but would fit her too; at last she'd got something right.

'That looks perfect. But then everything always does, on you.'

'Oh, Saiv!' Impulsively, Lauren leaned over and planted a kiss on her burning cheek. 'This is gorgeous, and so kind of you . . . I'm really sorry if I was cranky this morning. It was mean of me to send you off by yourself.'

'It was no more than I deserved. And it was good for me, to have to manage on my own. I – er – I think I might get a credit card when I go home. They really are handy, aren't they?'

Lauren burst out laughing. 'Let me guess! You hadn't enough money and had to traipse to a bank – oh, Saiv! You could have used my card, if only I'd been there.'

'Well, you weren't. It taught me a lesson. I'm not half as self-reliant as I like to think. Anyway, I bought a dress as well, would you like to see it?'

'I certainly would.' Lauren sounded disbelieving. With the air of a warrior displaying the spoils of battle, Saiv ripped open her parcel, unfolded the dress and held it aloft.

'What do you think?'

'I think I – I'm going to pass out cold! That is *gorgeous*! Pure linen – let me see – low neckline for the cleavage you never normally show off – Saiv, this dress is *sexy*.' Lauren sounded astonished, looked quite dazed.

Saiv simpered. 'Do you think so?'

'Yes. Seriously sexy. You'll need heels with it, cream leather—'

'I know. I'd have got those too if there'd been time. You can help me choose a pair later.'

'Well, I – I certainly will! My God, Saiv, I think you're in serious danger here!'

'Danger? Of what?'

'Of – of getting a life! Of waking up and smelling the coffee!'

'Well . . . better late than never.'

Beaming, Saiv folded the dress carefully back into its bag, and sat back well pleased that she'd missed the boat to Murano. I might have missed that one, she thought, but I could be just in time to catch another. One that could take me who knows where, if I have the courage to wear this with – with *confidence*. The kind of confidence that Lauren takes for granted, that carries her everywhere.

JULY

'Laurie, you're crazy.'

'So? Have you a problem with that?'

Saiv gripped the rails of the ladder on which she was stuck, neither up nor down, and gazed at the water below.

'Laurie, I am a professor of philosophy. Professors of philosophy do not slide down water chutes.'

'Why not?'

'Because – because it's ten feet up and I'm scared of heights!'

'Saiv. You're blocking the queue. Holding everyone up, just like you did all those years ago in the college canteen . . . hurry up, there's a little boy here wants to go next.'

Quaking, Saiv took a deep breath, climbed higher and hesitated.

'Go on! It's great fun, you'll love it.'

In a rush Saiv clambered up, reached the top, sat down in the swirling water chute and, with an earsplitting scream, let it carry her off to the distant pool below. By the time she reached it her stomach felt as if it had changed places with her tonsils, her face was frozen with fright and her last thought before she hit the water with a crash was that everyone was staring at her, open-mouthed.

Splash! In she shot, down she plummetted, until her toes touched the bottom of the pool and gravity propelled her back up, to emerge gasping and floundering like a manatee.

Standing on the edge of the pool, sleek in a navy Speedo, Lauren applauded and, to Saiv's utter horror, several other people did too, cheering in raucous Italian. She had made a complete spectacle of herself. Spluttering, she swam to the side and hauled herself out. Laughing, Lauren clapped her on the back.

'Way to go! Wasn't that great?'

Shaking off water like a sheepdog, Saiv considered. 'It was' she said at length, 'absolutely fabulous! I never thought I could do it, but I loved it!'

'See, there you are. I told you you would.'

'I'd never have dared do it if you hadn't made me.'

'Then you'd have missed out, wouldn't you?'

Yes, Saiv thought, I would. I'd have missed out on this as I've missed out on so much, by not daring to do things it turns out I can do perfectly well. OK, maybe I looked silly and felt silly, but so what? This is a holiday and I can do what I want! God, Lauren is just great at making me enjoy myself.

'More! I want to do it again!'

'Then let's!'

Up they went and down they flew, several times more until, laughing, Lauren finally flopped down on a sun lounger, throwing a towel to Saiv as she reached the sun deck and sat down beside her. Rimini was a cheap-and-cheerful beach resort, and Saiv had recoiled from its gaudiness until Lauren had seized her by the shoulders and faced her square-on.

'Well, it's not my usual standard either, I'd be on the French riviera only you're the one who wanted to come to Italy. Rimini suits your budget and *I* proposed it so *you* could afford it, OK? So lighten up and don't be such a bloody snob.'

Abashed, Saiv had instantly determined to 'lighten up', whereupon she found herself enjoying it, starting to feel like a carefree kid as she licked ice-cream, kicked sand, swam in the warm ocean and, today, sampled the water park. Stretching out on her lilo, she was conscious of an incredible feeling of invigoration, healthy energy, her body glowing with sun, sea and fresh air.

'Laurie?'

'Mmm?'

'I feel absolutely great. Rejuvenated, like a teenager.'

'That's what happens when you put your mind in neutral and let your body take over.'

'Is your mind in neutral?'

Lauren reflected, lying on her back, gazing up at the infinite blue sky. 'D'you know, it actually is. Or idling in first, anyway. I've hardly thought about work all day . . . yesterday, either.'

'You mean – you don't mean to say there's life after Axis? Life without a mobile phone?'

Saiv grinned, and slowly, sheepishly, Lauren grinned in turn. 'OK. You win. It's a fair cop, officer.'

Delighted, Saiv smiled smugly, and Lauren smiled at her in turn, affectionately. 'It was a dreadful shock at first, like having my right arm amputated, but I have to admit I'm glad now you did it. Work seems more remote every day . . . I may even give up calling the office altogether.'

'What? Let it sink or swim without Lauren Kilroy?'

'Yeah. Let it. I'm only beginning to realise now how badly I needed to get away.'

'You really did, Laurie, you know. You had so much on your plate, were so stressed out . . . tell me something?'

'What?'

'Do you ever think of Jordan, now? Is he still on your mind, or at the back of it anywhere?'

Sitting up, Lauren wrapped her arms around her knees and gazed into the pool. 'No. Sometimes I get a flash of him, but it's just an angry flash now, a disgusted flash. I pride myself on being such a smart cookie, so how could I have been so stupid? Huh? For five years?'

'Because, I suppose, we all have our blind spots. My friend Jennifer, who is a brilliant historian as you know, has awful trouble with men too. Sometimes it seems that the better a woman is at her work, the worse she is at her personal life.'

'Yes . . . that kind of goes for you, too.'

'Me? But I – I'm not in any kind of mess, that I know of!'

'Sure you are.'

'Huh?'

'You're in a rut. Bogged down like a tractor in the mud. You had two lousy relationships and then you gave up.'

'I didn't give them up. They gave me up.'

Lauren shrugged. 'Same thing, sweetie. The end result is that Dr Saiv Lovett, spinster of this parish, hasn't dated a man since Columbus set sail for America. I don't know what's to become of you at all.'

Saiv flinched. She sometimes wondered the same thing herself. 'Well, I – it's not my fault, Laurie. They're not exactly banging down my door.'

'No, because you exude this aura of such ferocious independence. You have a look like an electric fence – danger, keep clear!'

'What?'

'Back off, don't touch! Genius at work!'

'That is not true, categorically not true—'

'It is totally true, whether you know it or not. You're so scared, you're standing in a trench ten feet deep. I bet you wouldn't go out with a guy if I served you up one filleted on a silver tray.'

'I most certainly would, if he was nice and he asked me.'

Suddenly, her eyes glinting, Lauren turned to look at her. 'Would you? If I could lassoo you one of these Italian Romeos, for instance, get him interested in you, would you go out with him?'

Saiv quailed. Lauren never started anything she didn't mean to finish, and she loved a challenge. Her eyes were sparkling dangerously.

'Oh, don't be silly. How would you do that, or why for that matter?'

'Well, I don't know how yet, but I'll tell you why. I've been thinking quite a lot since Dr Mallon sprang his little surprise on me, and one of the things I've been thinking about is you. I'm worried about you.'

'About *me*? Laurie, I'm the one who's worried about *you*!'

Impatiently, Lauren waved a hand. 'Yeah, well, there's no point in that, because I'll either sink or swim. But if – if I sink, where will that leave you? You'll be all on your own with nobody to look after you. Nobody to give you a laugh or a hug or any of the support you think you don't need. I've been racking my brains thinking about it.'

Astonished, Saiv sat silent, staring at her. Resolutely, Lauren went on. 'And then, the other day when you bought that dress, I said to myself, hey, there could be a window here. She's in a different frame of mind in Italy. I got her onto a plane and now maybe I can do this too. Fix her up with the kind of guy who – who I'd bag for myself, if I were in the market! Unfortunately I'm not in it, as you know, but finding someone for you would give me even greater pleasure, in a different way. Only—'

Hardly daring to speak, or able to, Saiv caught her breath. 'Only what?'

'Only, if I do, I have to be sure you'll respond. There's no point in doing it if you're going to go all academic and stand-offish, start spouting drivel about how you don't need this and then run a mile. You'd have to be *open* to it.'

On the point of protesting, Saiv found that she wasn't able to say anything, because even as Lauren spoke she felt her armour closing around her, clicking defensively into place. All her adult life she had lived alone, and after so many years she was . . . was fixed in her ways. Stuck in exactly the rut Lauren had described, protective of her space and privacy, her set way of doing things . . . and yet, when Lauren did persuade her to try something new, such as the scary water chute, or the plane for that matter, it seemed to work. Work like a charm, opening up exciting new horizons on a world that was fun, not nearly as terrifying as it looked.

'Oh, for heaven's sake, this is a completely nonsensical, hypothetical conversation. Men are attracted to you, not me!'

'See? There you go. Thinking negative already. Burrowing into your little bolthole. Sometimes I could strangle you . . . it may have escaped your attention, Saiv, but mine has been drawn to the fact that life is not infinite. Life is to be lived to the full – now, not tomorrow or next week or whenever it suits you, but *now*. Time is a luxury that can be whipped from your grasp overnight . . . and besides, you're not getting any younger, are you?'

Well, no. Saiv had to concede the truth of that. If she ever wanted to have a relationship, maybe even a family . . . the prospect was so remote it seemed almost invisible. Was that because she was pushing it away, convincing herself it was impossible so she couldn't be disappointed if it never happened? But it never would happen if she kept doing that. For several minutes she sat thinking about it, turning it over, thinking also that Lauren had a point. Time was not infinite, and it would be an insult to Lauren to pretend otherwise. Lauren was really putting her on the spot here . . . and yet, her concern was so generous, so touching.

'Laurie, you – you shouldn't be wasting your time worrying about me.'

'Jesus! There she goes again! Look, Saiv, I'll worry about you if I like, OK? Meanwhile, you haven't answered my question. Would you be open to meeting a man, or not?'

Guiltily, Saiv fiddled with the towel. 'I – I really don't know. I mean, they're so difficult, aren't they? They can kind of – kind of take *over* your life. I'd need one who—'

Drawing a deep breath, Lauren looked at her hard. 'I'm going to count to five. And then you're going to answer me: yes or no. One – two – three – four—'

'Yes! All right! I would!' There, Saiv gasped, I've done it. Taken the plunge. Jumped in the deep end and . . . and this is all going to come to nothing, anyway. There's no way Lauren can possibly contrive such a thing. At best, it'll amuse her, keep her mind off her own problems. She's always happy when she has a project to get her teeth into.

And sure enough, Lauren was beaming already. 'Great! Then we'll do it, we'll get you one!'

Sceptically, Saiv smiled. 'Will we? How? Do they sell them over the counter? D'you get a free one if you can recite "The Love Song Of J. Alfred Prufrock"?'

Lauren hooted laughing. 'Oh, Saiv! You *are* J. Alfred Prufrock . . . "I grow old, I grow old . . . I shall wear white flannel trousers and walk along the beach, and wonder do I dare to eat a peach . . ." Eat the peach, Saiv, while you can!'

'I didn't think,' Saiv retorted loftily, 'you were paying attention in college that day. I thought you were—'

'Busy dreaming up advertising slogans? Hah. That was just camouflage. I was listening, at the back of it all.'

'Mmm . . .' Glad of the diversion, Saiv surveyed her speculatively. 'I always thought you should have finished college, Laurie. You were a lot brighter than you ever gave yourself credit for.'

'Yeah, well, life snapped me up. Career girl.'

'Yes. Still, your career cost you, in more ways than one.'

'H'm? What do you mean?'

'I mean that . . . apart from losing out on your degree, you also lost out on family life. Your parents never seem to have accepted your job, and – and you were so busy, you only ever had time for a part-time relationship. That's why you said Jordan suited you, anyway.'

Lauren grimaced. 'Yeah, well, he did at the time. But now, signora, we are going to make up for all that and get *you* a much better man. A real relationship.'

'But – but even if such an unlikely thing were possible, that's still not much comfort to you, is it? You should have someone . . . I wish . . .'

'You'd be surprised' Lauren said unexpectedly, tartly, 'how much comfort it would be to me. I want to see you settled before I shuffle off this mortal coil.'

'Laurie! Stop it!'

'Sorry. Just kidding.'

'It's not funny.' Nor was it; Saiv felt a tightness in her throat, wished Laurie would tell her more about how she was really feeling. Was she loosening up, at all? Would she eventually be able to talk about it? Even as she wondered, Lauren put the side of her hand to her forehead, Red Indian style, shading her eyes as she scanned around the pool.

'Let's see . . . h'mm. Big into families here, aren't they? Mama and Papa and billions of little bambinos. I don't think this is good scouting territory . . . the art galleries might be better, if only I'd thought of it in Venice.'

Unable to take her seriously, Saiv was surprised to find herself agreeing; if she ever actually was going to meet a man, she'd like him to be the kind who went to art galleries. But then they were the kind who also went to dating agencies, weren't they? Sad lads who . . . oh, for God's sake, she told herself sharply, stop it. You should go to a dating agency yourself, if you had the guts, and do what Lauren says: get yourself a goddamn life. Take a flying leap off your high horse. Suddenly annoyed with herself, she stood up.

'Laurie, it's getting very hot. Do you think maybe we've had enough sun?'

Quizzically, Lauren looked up at her. 'I think maybe you've had enough of this conversation, and are chickening out of it.'

'No, I – I really do appreciate everything you're saying, Laurie, and your concern for me. I just don't want you throwing your time away on me, that's all.'

Reaching for her sandals, Lauren shook her head adamantly. 'I'm not planning to throw one minute away. I will use it as wisely as Solomon – only, you'll have to co-operate, OK? Work with me on this, and I tell you, it's a done deal. Fait accompli.'

Saiv had to laugh. 'What an optimist!'

'Yeah, well, one of us has to be.'

*　　*　　*

Having won her point, Lauren mercifully didn't pursue it, and Saiv was relieved. The last thing she wanted was Lauren trying to pick up men for her, dragging anyone into conversation who wasn't visibly moored to a wife or girlfriend. It was a gruesome thought; yet she knew Lauren was brazen enough to do it, didn't know the meaning of the word 'shy', would cheerfully tackle Attila the Hun if she made up her mind to do it. But Lauren said nothing more, and after a day or two Saiv began to relax. Maybe because of her own lack of enthusiasm, the project appeared to have been shelved.

One day they had lunch at a little restaurant on the beach, outside under parasols, on a deck facing the rolling ocean breakers. The sea air gave Saiv such an appetite that, while Lauren snacked on a salad, she despatched an entire plate of spaghetti carbonara, followed it with a chocolate ice-cream and then, over cappuccino, began to feel both full and guilty.

'Wow . . . I'm going to have to work that off! What are our plans for this afternoon?'

'I don't have any,' Lauren replied indolently, 'do you?'

Saiv was pleased to hear her sounding so relaxed. Her phone calls to the office had dwindled to virtually zero now, there was no further mention of getting a new phone, and Lauren's expression had taken on a newly drifting, almost dreamy aura. She looked as if she'd be perfectly content to lie on the beach for the afternoon, basking in the sun. But in Saiv's case exercise was imperative.

'No, but . . . how about getting bikes from the hotel and going for a cycle out in the countryside?'

Lauren looked at her. 'Moi? Cycle? I haven't been on a bike since I was ten years old.'

'Why not?'

'Because God invented cars! Cycling is for children, sweetie. Children and peasants.'

Saiv laughed. 'Oh, you're such a city girl. The countryside would be—'

'Would be dusty and ghastly. I'd much rather just stay where

I am, thanks, lounge on a lilo and maybe have a swim later. But you go if you like.'

'You wouldn't mind?'

'Of course not. I have a book to read and several fingernails to varnish. Might even do my toes too, if I get a burst of energy. You go off and do all the sweltering for both of us.'

'Well – all right then, if you're sure you'll be OK on your own.'

'Saiv, I'm not an invalid, or a child! Away with you.'

Lazily, she adjusted the brim of her baseball cap, and Saiv thought how gorgeous she looked, how golden and gleaming. How healthy, too, as if there were nothing wrong with her. For a split second she let herself hope that maybe there wasn't, that maybe she was going to be fine after all. Out in the sun on a beautiful day like this, anything seemed possible.

'OK. I'll try to do about twenty kilometres or so, and see you back at the hotel around six?'

'Uh huh. Have fun.'

Parting company, they set off in opposite directions, Lauren across the sand, leggy and barefoot, Saiv in the direction of the hotel where, she hoped, they could provide her with a sturdy bike.

Two hours later, after a blissful doze in the warm air, Lauren stirred and looked around her. It was still siesta time, that lull in which life seemed suspended, too hot for activity, and she let her abandoned book slide to the sand, sitting up a fraction as she reached for her sunblock. Normally a 'people person', she was surprised to find the quietude agreeable, even restful; all she could hear was the distant drone of a water-ski boat and the nearer surge of the rhythmically shushing rollers. Apart from a few toddlers paddling peacefully at their edge, nobody was doing anything at all.

Nothing, she thought. Absolutely nothing. For two whole hours I have lain here like a lady of leisure, not even reading, not lifting a finger. This is so different to any holiday I've ever been on before, with Jordan who'd be hauling me off to play golf, with Adèle who'd be in the shopping mall all day. Not that I ever objected to shopping malls. But . . . I must admit I'm getting on much better with Saiv than I'd expected. She's such easy company, and she's having a good effect on me. If there's one positive thing to be said for having hep C, it's that it has brought me closer to her. I know she's keeping an eye on me, not letting me do anything too exhausting, yet she isn't fussing. I was so mad at her, over that mobile phone, I could've killed her – but now I feel liberated without it, cut loose from all the damn stress and hype at that office. It's only when I stand back from it I can see how pointless so much of it is, how unnecessary . . . I wonder, if I were a man, would I be afraid that they might learn to manage without me, now?

Probably. Even today, in the twenty-first century, there's no room for women in business unless they're prepared to behave like men. Prepared to play politics and power games, participate in the theatre of war. That's how the guys see it; now that they're not hunter-gatherers any more, commerce is their hunting ground, it's all about outwitting the enemy and looting the spoils. I never even thought about that when I got into it, I just accepted the rules and got down in the mud with the rest of them. I was good at it, I loved it. But now . . . now I am devoutly glad to be lying here on this beach, with no demands, no crises, no noise, no screaming colleagues or clients to contend with. Saiv is right about the clients not being babies, but most of them act like three-year-olds. Spoilt, demanding, bad-tempered three-year-olds. If they were here they'd be roaring and raving, unable to believe that the world could continue to spin on its axis for two minutes without them. But, amazingly, it seems to be spinning on without *me*.

How long, I wonder, could it spin? If I played a game of make-believe and pretended that I wasn't going back to my desk at Axis next week, what would happen? If I didn't even get in touch, if I just vanished into thin air, would the company collapse? Or would they just send someone else in to bat for me, Bill or Shane or someone, and struggle along until further notice?

Of course, that's nonsense. Senior executives don't just disappear. Still, it's an intriguing thought. Just how indispensable am I, is anyone? If I – if I see that specialist and he confirms Dr Mallon's diagnosis, what then? What would happen at Axis?

Nothing. That's the unpalatable truth of it. Oh, sure, there'd be a flurry and a panic – and a lot of jostling for my job – but at the end of the day a new partner would emerge, a new name would go on my door and it would be business as usual.

Yet I've invested so much in that job, it's meant so much, been the focus of my entire life for nearly fourteen years. Nothing has ever come between me and it, I've even settled for a man who couldn't marry me because marriage might have distracted me, might have meant children and . . . and other priorities. You can't *have* more than one priority. I know so many women who try to juggle kids and jobs, but they're all exhausted, every single one of them. In fact I've even been impatient with them, nearly ate Angie alive that time her boy had his tonsils out and she had to take two days off . . . it was disruptive, it did cause inconvenience. But we just had to manage without her, and if I needed to take time out they'd just have to manage without me.

Do I need to?

I don't know. All I know for sure is that I've been bone-weary all this year, and for the first time ever I really, badly needed a holiday. If I – I'm not as seriously ill as that tiresome doctor thinks, then what's wrong with me? Am I getting stale? Bored? Too old for the cut-and-thrust, the swordplay? Is it possible to use up all your interest in one thing, and feel the need of something fresh?

Of course, money is a great motivator. But here on the beach in the sun, it doesn't seem so important. As Saiv says, you can live quite simply really, most of the time . . . so many of the things I've bought over the years have been just for show, to assert my status and prove my progress. My value to Axis, my worth . . . but if they can replace me as easily as I suspect, then I'm not invaluable. Not at professional level, and certainly not on a personal level. Apart from Shane Jackson, I don't have any good, trustworthy friends at Axis, anyone who'd miss me.

Who would miss me, if I died? Somehow I think Saiv genuinely would. In fact I know she would. She's not the kind of person who'd waste her friendship on anyone she *wouldn't* miss. She's one of those people who'd rather have a handful of close friends than dozens of social contacts, and that's one reason I've always hung onto her – she has the kind of integrity I've never found in anyone at work. Except Shane. Who might, or might not, have his eye on me?

Well, he's wasting his time, if he has. He doesn't know it, but my days of sexual cartwheels with married men are over. I've missed out on the chance of a close relationship and now, just when I need one, I can't have one. The thought of dying alone, without anyone to hold my hand or even care very much, is the most awful, empty thought in the world. And that's why I'm not going to let Saiv get into the same situation; if I can't have a partner then I'm going to find one for her, so she'll have someone to look after her when I'm gone. She needs someone – someone extrovert, to take her out of herself, liven up her life. She'll resist, but I'll do it. And then, apart from that, what else am I going to do?

If I see this damn specialist, and he says, quick, decide what you want to do with the rest of your time, then – then what *do* I want to do with it?

I want to see Caoimhe again, that's for sure. Caoimhe and her baby girl, my niece. No way am I letting go without that.

And – and I want to patch things up with my parents, too. I don't know how, but I do. I want them to understand why I quit college, why I took the job I did, worthless and all as they think it is. It *is* worthless, in many ways, but at least it made somebody of me: I became a success in advertising instead of a failure in university, in the academic life I didn't have the patience or the brains for. I'm smart, but I'm not intelligent, not in the intellectual sense that Saiv is . . . if only they could have accepted that, and accepted me. But they wanted the best for me, they meant well – God, I hate the way things are now, between us! I *hate* those polite empty lunches every other Sunday. I want to talk to them properly, even if it's only once, in the unexpectedly short time available to us. For years now Saiv has fulfilled my mother's role, in many ways, but she's not my mother – even if she might make someone else a good one, some day, she is not *mine*.

Ha! Wouldn't that be the funniest thing, to see Saiv Lovett rocking a baby! Pigs might fly, let's not carry fantasy too far – she doesn't even seem to like the kids she teaches. She's so shy, she's probably a bit afraid of them. But fear only makes things worse, so I will try not to be afraid of whatever is in store for me.

I'll try . . . and what else do I want to do? Read a real book, the kind she reads, and actually understand it? I'd love to do that. Even if it were only one, I'd be able to say to my parents, see now, I'm not so stupid!

I'd love to travel more, too. Italy has been a revelation. It's so much more enjoyable, more rewarding, when you've got time to look around you properly, aren't dashing between planes and meetings. Aren't being marched around by Jordan White, to things that don't interest you, pretending to love everything for the sake of peace. I spent so much time humouring that damn man! But now, I don't have to humour anyone. If I had the time I could stay here for ages, maybe go on down to Greece . . . I could get a camper van and wander all over, be a drop-out!

There she goes again, Mother would say. Dropping out of her career now, can't even stick to that. But hey, Mother, guess what? I'm dying! My days are numbered, so I'm going to make the most of every last one! Put that in your pipe and smoke it!

And there are other things I'd love to do. Crazy, zany things – bungee jump off the Cliffs of Moher, trek into the Amazonian jungle, dye my hair magenta, sing a duet with Rod Stewart, learn to fly a helicopter . . . some of those things are possible, so why have I never done them? How has my life got so pre-dictable, where did all the spontaneity go?

Anyway, that's my wish list. It's not really so much to ask, is it? There don't seem to be any diamonds on it, or yachts or playboys or mansions in Monte Carlo. I must be losing my grip! But, modest as it strangely seems to be, will I live to see any of it through?

I wonder if – if I could do it? Some of it, or all of it, or any of it? I seem to be spending this entire afternoon wondering, taking things off the shelves in my mind and turning them over. There's never any time for this kind of speculation at home, all I ever do is work and go to social events. For the first time I've had enough of social events – even had enough of work, for a while. What bliss it is to have an entire afternoon like this, all to myself, out in the air under the Italian sun. No schedule, no pressure, no impression to have to make on anyone.

It's a relief, if the truth be told, a huge, liberating relief. How lucky I am, here and now, to have this beautiful day to call my own.

It was a long cycle, and Saiv enjoyed it immensely, pedalling slowly along dusty roads between golden fields ablaze with poppies, interspersed with little farmhouses and tall dark cypress trees hiding the horizon, on which there were intermittent glimpses of rising hills, veiled in the hazy heat. Let's see, she thought, whether I can reach their foothills at least, even if it's too hot for slogging up into them.

As she went she pondered Lauren, back on the beach, lazily lying in the sun. In all the years she had known her she had never seen her so relaxed, so – so agreeably willing to go with the flow. Normally Lauren was the kind of friend who, on holiday, would be organising everything, ticking off lists of things to see and do, directing and controlling every little detail. She'd even have come cycling, on the grounds that Saiv would get lost without her, or get run over by a truck . . . but now, she seemed to be learning to delegate, take a chance on people being able to manage without her.

Not that I could manage without her, she thought, or want to have to. Our friendship used to be sporadic, but it was always there, and since the beginning of this year it has developed so much, grown closer and deeper. She listens to me in a way she never used to, pays attention, even seems to be thinking about some of what I say to her. I suppose that's what happens when you're ill – it gives you pause for thought. If she gets through this awful situation, I think she'll be changed by it; she'll never be so blithe, so brisk again. Meanwhile, she's coping so well, hasn't lost her sense of humour or her strength of character . . . she is mellowing, though, and I think it's for the better.

Why does something like this have to happen to someone like her? She's over thirty but she's still so bouncy, so vivacious, it's not fair and it's not right. The world is full of horrible, healthy people who'd be no loss at all . . . but if I knew why these things happen I'd be a philosopher myself, instead of merely purveying other people's ideas. If there is any kind of after-life, maybe there'll be some answers in it; this one only seems to throw up the questions. We're just cosmic children, feeling our way around, often snuffed out before we've learned anything at all. There's no logic, no rhyme or reason to this life, even someone as controlling as Lauren can't put any kind of shape on it. The gods must really laugh, sometimes, at our futile little efforts. Hateful bastards, if they exist!

Still, Lauren isn't the only one learning the hard way. I am, too. It has been forcefully brought home to me that time is finite, you can't faff around forever. I have to make some decisions about where I'm going, what I want. I could have throttled Lauren for dragging the truth out of me, about how I'd like a relationship – but I would. I still prize my independence, but being alone at my age gets to be less fun as you go along, especially when you don't have any other family, when all you've got is two useless brothers engrossed in their own affairs. It makes me mad that they make no effort, but maybe it's time I made some effort myself, to bring other people into my life instead. Not that men are the answer to a maiden's prayer, but if I could find a good one, a decent one, I'd take a chance. Give it one last shot! Lauren makes it sound so easy, as if you could simply pick one out and say yes, I'll have that, wrap him up! Of course it would be easy for her, she's so attractive, but in my case – I don't even know how you go about it, I'd sooner die than chat a guy up.

No. That's a lie. I would *not* sooner die. That's a glib, silly thing to say, cowardly too, an insult to all the people who really are dying and would give anything to change places with a fit, able-bodied person like me. I should be making the most of my life, seizing every chance, 'going for it' as Laurie would say. Her situation is a lesson to me and I am going to learn from it. I've already managed to write a book and if I can do that I can do other things too, take risks, tackle anything that might make me stronger, or happier or more fulfilled. I've been lazy, and it's going to stop. If Lauren Kilroy can face death, I can surely face life.

Rimini was a lively town at night and, feeling energised after her cycle, Saiv proposed a trip to the street market that evening. A long market apparently, running parallel to the beach, it would lead them eventually to a point near the town hall, where fireworks and barbecues were to be held to celebrate a local festival.

'Sounds fun' Lauren commented, 'are you sure you wouldn't rather stay at the hotel, read an improving book over a mug of cocoa?'

'No' Saiv retorted firmly, 'I would not. I would like to check out this market and maybe buy a few souvenirs, then see the fireworks and the street parties – who knows? There might even be music, or dancing!'

Lauren looked at her. 'Dancing, huh? I hope you've brought your best clogs.'

'I have my new shoes and I'm going to wear them with my new dress. I – I'm going to put on lipstick and perfume and *party*!'

'Good God. What a shame I don't have my phone, I'd ring RTE and tell them to put it out on the nine o'clock news. Saiv Lovett is getting a life!'

Defiantly, Saiv squared up to her. 'Yeah. You can put it that way if you like. Come on, let's go.'

Off they went, elbowing their way into the midst of the fun, the big noisy market that turned out to have hundreds of stalls touting everything from dolls to doorknobs, food to fine lace, heaped piles of weird and wonderful items. Resolutely, Saiv bought an unframed oil painting, a carnival puppet and three hand-carved African masks. Bargaining with all the vendors, eating candy-floss as she went, she showed every sign of enjoying herself to the hilt, and Lauren laughed.

'I thought you didn't like crowds or noise.'

'I don't. But I'm learning to deal with them. I am determined to have fun tonight and that's all about it.'

Although Lauren didn't buy anything, they did have fun, and eventually they emerged from the mayhem somewhere near the site of the promised fireworks, clutching Saiv's booty as they debated where to get the best view.

'Let's go over there, towards the harbour—'

'Let's go right down on the beach – here, let me put all this stuff in my backpack and take my shoes off, we can walk in the water . . . take yours off too.'

Bemused, Lauren removed her strappy sandals and carried them dangling in her hand as Saiv led the way to the beach, which was still warm even after dark. Barefoot, they picked their way over the stones onto the sand and began to walk in the direction of the harbour, watching for the first firework to go up. A few other people were also strolling on the beach, murmuring greetings, but it didn't seem to have occurred to many of the tourists that they could get a better view from here than closer up. Gazing at the starry sky, Lauren stopped for a moment.

'Look, Saiv. Isn't it beautiful?'

Lifting her face in turn, Saiv paused, squinting to pick out individual stars. 'Yes, isn't it . . . that's Orion's Dagger over there, and I think that's the Plough—'

'I wouldn't know one from the other. But they are all so exquisite . . . I've never really looked at them properly before, or seen them so clearly. In Dublin you can't see the stars for the city lights, not in town anyway, and it would never strike me to go to a beach at night.'

'You'd probably be mugged or murdered if you did! But in Meath you can see the night sky quite clearly, I often go out in the field to look at it.'

'Do you? All by yourself? How bizarre.'

'The dogs come too! I'll take you with me, next time you come to stay. Not that it's quite as romantic as this, or as warm . . . oh, Laurie, I absolutely love Italy! Thank you so much for making me come!'

Impulsively, Saiv turned to hug her friend, and at that moment there was a muffled bang. Raising their faces in unison, they were just in time to see a white jet of light shoot up, explode, and come cascading down in a shower of green and pink spirals, twirling in delicate plumes even as another rocket burst skyward to the sound of distant cheers from the street.

'Oh, wow! Magic!'

It was truly magical, and then music struck up too, a band playing the old Dean Martin song 'Amore' as the sky filled with a blazing ballet of colour, huge spumes of gold and silver, tiny fizzing flames of mauve and scarlet, whirling discs of jade, sapphire and orange. Grasping Saiv's arm, Lauren gazed enthralled, her face filling with such eager joy, such childlike delight that Saiv felt a pang, the sudden prick of tears, and could not speak. It takes so little sometimes, she thought; it takes so little to make us forget everything, and be happy.

The panorama continued to light up the night, a brilliant vista of sheer, sparkling beauty, and they stood transfixed, watching together, each knowing she would never forget this fabulous moment, on a summer night on the sands of Rimini. A night on which it felt wonderful to be alive, and life itself was tinged with starlight, twinkling and shimmering with an exuberance that left them dazzled, barefoot and breathless on the water's edge.

'I don't care' Lauren drawled, 'where we go today. Last night was the highlight of the holiday for me. I can't imagine anything more stunning than those fireworks, that fabulous music and dancing.'

'Nor I! But we still have five more days, and there are so many other lovely places to see.'

'Then let's rent a car and drive around – or are you mad keen to get your fix of Michelangelo in Florence?'

Briefly, Saiv considered. She'd adore to go to the Uffizi Gallery and the Casa Buonarotti – but Lauren seemed to prefer being out and about. For all its charms Venice had been daunting, exhausting, and Florence would be equally demanding. Glancing at Lauren, she made a snap decision.

'No. I don't think I can take any more hordes of Japanese tour parties. Why don't we head for some of the smaller towns – Verona maybe, or Padua or Urbino?'

'Wherever you like! I'm beginning to see what it is you love about Italy . . . it really *has* something, hasn't it?'

'Yes! It has joie de vivre, it has a heart and a soul, romance – Jesus, Laurie, did I really dance with that waiter at that café last night?'

Looking bewildered, Saiv flushed, and Lauren laughed. 'Yes, you did, between all the tables, you were a smash hit. Unfortunately he was a bit young for you, but I must say it's an encouraging start. There's hope for you yet, Dr Lovett.'

'Stop calling me that, it makes me sound like a wizened old bag! Last night I felt like – like Sleeping Beauty, waking up! Not that I can ever be accused of beauty, but—'

'But beauty is in the eye of the beholder. You looked great

to me, and to him too or he wouldn't have done it. Stop putting yourself down.'

Saiv reflected. 'D'you know, I think I will. For some reason I feel very – very confident this morning!'

'About time too.'

But, half an hour later when they were standing on the forecourt of the car rental agency, Saiv's heart suddenly sank. She had forgotten that driving in Italy would be back-to-front, with the wheel on the left on the wrong side of the road.

'Oh, Laurie – oh, no – I can't do this. You'll have to drive.'

'I'll do my share. And you'll do yours.'

'But – I – we'll be killed!'

Gritting her teeth, Lauren smiled charmingly at the man who stood holding the keys, took them from him, opened the boot of the car and threw in her suitcase. Wishing them a pleasant journey, he handed them a map and left them to it. Saiv quailed, and Lauren shot her a look like steel. 'Get in and get used to it. I'll drive this morning and you'll do this afternoon.'

Oh, God. Feeling very disorientated, Saiv sat gingerly into the passenger seat and Lauren started the engine, reversing out of the parking space with easy, gliding grace.

'See? Any fool can do it. Open that map and tell me where we're going.'

Well, Saiv thought, that's a reversal all right. Time was when she'd be telling *me*. Lauren Kilroy seems to be tearing off her dictator's epaulettes. But then it's two weeks since she's been in her office, giving orders right, left and centre. She's really starting to relinquish the reins . . . maybe she won't even make me drive?

Wrestling with the map, she studied her options. 'How about Urbino? That looks like an easy start, it can't be more than a hundred kilometres.'

'H'mm. Do we know anything about it?'

'Well, *I* know that it's where Raphael was born.'

'Who he?'

'Raphael, Laurie, the painter! Raffaelo Sanzio, great rival of

Michelangelo, preening peacock, social climber and money-grabber!'

'Sounds like my kind of guy. Tell me more.'

So Saiv told her more, and she listened intently, apparently able to drive on the right and listen at the same time. Saiv was impressed, and apprehensive. The Italians drove like lunatics, speeding, smoking, gesturing and yakking on their mobiles, all at once. This was going to be the dodgem ride from hell.

But Laurie gave as good as she got, hooting and swearing at anyone who tried to bully her, zipping merrily along as if born to it. It must be great, Saiv thought, to be such a *natural*. After a while, she began to relax a fraction, take an interest in the swiftly passing scenery.

'Look, a lemon grove! Fields and fields, full of them—'

'Yeah. Do we take a left here, or what?'

Hastily Saiv returned her attention to her job as navigator; if she made a mess of it Laurie might well pull in, she thought, and say here, swop places, *I'll* do it. Which would leave her, Saiv, in the driving seat.

'Yes, left and then off to the right, up that hill – Jesus, Laurie, not so *fast*!'

'I'll drive my way and then, later, you can drive yours.' Airily, playing the gears like a piano, Lauren drove on, out into open countryside bright with golden crops, glossy with the jasper leaves of summer. Through the air-conditioning vents Saiv could smell the wafting scent of oregano and thyme, a herby perfume which, she thought, she would forever associate with Italy. It was a hot cloudless day, and as the car wended its way up into the foothills of minor mountains she sat back and resolved to enjoy the journey. The Rimini traffic was behind them now, and beautiful houses were beginning to sporadically appear, tinted old tones of ochre, umber, washed yellow and faded lilac; here and there she could see a donkey, an ash-white olive grove, a straw-hatted worker in the fields. Timeless, she thought; timeless, and so tranquil. This is my kind of territory.

After an hour or two, just when it began to look as if they

might be running out of road, Urbino suddenly materialised in the distance, an ethereal vision of ancient grandeur. Perched high on a hill, it looked like a massive fort, castellated and profoundly *pink*. Lauren grinned.

'Looks like some gay boyo lost the run of himself here.'

'That must be the Ducal Palace. God, it's huge.'

'Mmm. You could throw quite a party in that lot. But I'm not going near it until I get a cold drink.'

Saiv was thirsty too, and when they reached the upper slopes of the hill on which Urbino stood they ditched the car; by all accounts trying to park any higher would be a waste of time. Setting off on foot, they peered upwards, realising they were in for quite a climb.

'Tell me if you get tired, Laurie.'

'Say that once more and I will smack you.'

Saiv hadn't actually said it for several days, but the point registered; Lauren was simply determined not to be tired, not to be reminded of even the possibility. Touched by her resolve, Saiv surveyed her slender resolute frame, and fell silent. After a lengthy trek, they eventually reached the gateway into the fortified, lofty little town.

'Oh, cobblestones! Gorgeous!'

Lauren scowled. 'Huh. Whoever invented cobblestones didn't wear stilettos. They're lethal when it rains, too.'

'Oh, come on . . . where's your sense of romance?'

'It's in that shop, yanking an iced can out of the fridge.'

A little anxiously, Saiv went into the shop and bought cold drinks; she didn't want Lauren getting dehydrated. Or mulish.

'Now. Let's see. The guidebook says we should start right where we are, make our way up the hill to the main square, then Raphael's house is on the left further up, there's great view it says from a picnic area at the very top.'

'H'mm. Big into hills here, aren't they?'

Yes. Very. Saiv hoped it wasn't all going to be too much. Normally Laurie could skip up hills like a mountain goat, but . . . but it was nearly noon, the heat was becoming weighty, crushing.

'We'll just do a bit at a time. Look, there are little shops along the way, we can browse and take it slowly.'

'Yeah, why not? Urbino looks to me like a town that was built to last. It's not going anywhere and neither are we, if we don't get to see it all today we can stay overnight and do the rest tomorrow.'

What, linger, adapt their plans to suit the situation? *Dawdle?* Never had Saiv heard Laurie suggest such a thing before. It was bemusing, and she mused on it as they began to make their way up the first part of the hilly street, hugging the shade. Laurie looked as crisp as ever, and undoubtedly her business brain was still sharp as a sword, but she wasn't forging briskly ahead, nor darting into every shop. There was something easy about her today, some comfortable aura that said hey, no rush, let's enjoy this and see it properly.

Urbino was a university town, and even in summer there were students around, but they seemed somehow subsumed into the antiquity of the architecture, sitting on steps, lounging round the fountain, idly chatting in the sun. Instinctively, Saiv felt drawn into the atmosphere of the place; unlike Rimini it had substance and dignity, it was a centre of learning. Soaked in history, the thick walls seemed to ooze with character, the whole town was as tawny as an old, dusty bottle of port.

'I think I'm going to like Urbino,' she said, and Laurie nodded in unexpected agreement.

'Me too. It's not Milan or Miami, but it . . . it's different.'

It took them an hour or more to make their way up to the top, where in a parched park that looked more like a field people were lying stretched in the sun, here and there, the older ones snacking on fruit and the younger ones murmuring, embracing, one or two of them kissing indolently, their ardour tempered by the heat. Gathering her skirt around her, Saiv sat down on the grass, gesturing to Laurie to do the same. Dubiously, she looked at it.

'It's like straw! My clothes will be ruined!'

'So what? You can change later . . . come on, you can't just stand there!'

As if she were being invited to jump over a cliff, Laurie inspected the site and then, grimacing, abruptly sat. 'Uh, hard as a rock! I haven't sat in a field like this since — since I can't remember when.'

But gradually she eased herself into a comfortable position, stretching out until, to Saiv's surprise, she was lying on her back, her arms clasped under her head, looking up at the occasional puffy, floating cloud. Propped on her elbows, Saiv lay looking at the view, thinking how blissfully peaceful it was until, after ten minutes or more, she looked down at Laurie to find her not only supine, but fast asleep.

Asleep?! It was so comical she had to stifle a laugh, resist the urge to take a photograph of Lauren Kilroy, catching flies; undoubtedly her colleagues would howl with laughter if they could see it. Oblivious, Laurie snoozed on, her hair dark against the dry grass, her lips half-parted, smiling at what seemed to be a very pleasant, engrossing dream.

For a long while Saiv left her in peace, until at about two o'clock people started packing up their picnics, moving away, and it dawned on her that they would see nothing at this rate.

'Laurie?' Gently, she shook her shoulder. 'Come on, wake up. Let's go see Raphael's house.'

Sitting upright, Laurie was wide awake in a flash, glancing at her watch. 'Oh, look at the time! You must have dozed off! Come on, Saiv, shake a leg.'

Grinning, but saying nothing, Saiv got up, thinking that the nap would do her good. Sheepishly, Lauren brushed wisps of hay off her silk top, and they made their way back out of the field to the cobbled street, turning down the hill towards the house. From the outside it looked like any other; inside it was unexpectedly large, and deliciously cool.

'Now, where do we start?'

A custodian gave them directions, and they set off into the depths of what turned out to be a beautiful house, with thick stone walls and mullioned windows, polished floors and sparse furniture. Raphael had only lived in it for a few years of his early childhood, but Saiv was entranced.

'Well, I never did like the sound of the man, but his house is gorgeous!' Sitting down on a deep stone window-seat, she draped her skirt around her, and beamed at Laurie. 'Do I look like a Renaissance Madonna? Would he beg to paint me, d'you think?'

They were both laughing, when a solitary, resonant voice replied from the doorway: 'Yes, signora, I believe he would.'

Jumping with fright, they gazed into the shadows, and a large, bearded, bespectacled man emerged into view. Carrying a camera over his shoulder and a pamphlet about the house in his hands, he appeared to be a tourist like themselves, the only other one in the spartan, cavernous building. For a moment, they gazed uncertainly at him, Saiv flushing and feeling extremely silly.

'Oh – I – sorry, I was just talking to my friend here.'

Looking vaguely amused, he smiled at her. 'But talking is allowed. This is not a museum. This is Raffaelo's home.'

Raffaelo? Glancing at each other, they caught his accent; despite speaking English he must be Italian. For Lauren, one look at his shoes confirmed it; only Italian men wore glossy loafers like those.

'Hello' she said airily, recovering her composure with ease, 'we didn't think there was anyone else here. Great house, isn't it?'

Thoughtfully, the man looked around him. 'Yes. I was afraid it might be precious, like the painter himself, but it isn't.'

Precious? His English seemed to be perfect. And he seemed to hold the same opinion of Raphael as Saiv did herself. Rising from the window-seat, she turned in the direction of the one fresco, on the far wall, alleged to be by the painter.

'Do – do you happen to know whether he painted this? There seems to be some debate about it.'

Turning also, the man did not reply, but stood studying the fresco, examining, assessing, seeming to weigh the odds.

'Well, the experts have never been able to agree whether he did or not. Some say his father did it, and that his mother was the model for the Madonna, the boy himself was the model for the child. My own view is that he may possibly have done it, but if he did then it was a very early work. It doesn't have the fluidity, the assurance of his later work, does it?'

Did it? Trying to remember the paintings she had seen in Venice, in Rome years ago, Saiv found she couldn't decide, couldn't judge this one against them. Uncertainly, she fell silent, and the conversation teetered on the brink of a void.

'Probably the guy did do it' Lauren cut in cheerfully, decisively. 'He was a precocious little brat by all accounts – so my friend here says, anyway.'

With a wide smile that made him look like a slimmer version of Pavarotti, the man surveyed Saiv. 'So – you know something of Raffaelo, then?'

Seized with shyness, Saiv shook her head a fraction. 'Oh, no, not really . . . all I know is that I much prefer Michelangelo, whose life he made a misery at times.'

Loudly, heartily, the man laughed. 'Yes, he caused Michelangelo some grief! There was a lot of rivalry, envy on Raffaelo's part I think . . . but you are right. Michelangelo was a much stronger painter. He understood the architecture of painting.'

'Yes!' Surprised by the vehemence in her voice, Saiv felt herself blush, but she also felt compelled to reply. 'He did, he knew about draughtsmanship and how to structure a painting – but I think his sculptures are even better. His Madonna in the Casa Buonarotti would knock this one here for six, have you seen it?'

'Yes, many times. It is an Italian's duty to see as many Michelangelos as possible.'

The man's tone was grave, but his eyes were twinkling, lightly teasing. For a moment they all looked at each other, and then Lauren bestowed him with her most charming, disarming smile.

'Are you from Florence, then? That's where the Casa Buonarotti is, isn't it?'

God, Saiv thought, does she have to get personal? It's none of our business where this man is from.

'No, I am not Florentine. I am from Verona.'

'Really? We're thinking of going there, tomorrow or the day after! What's it like? What should we see?'

'Hah! You should see all of it! Especially the Arenà, of course, where the opera is held – in August unfortunately, you are too early. But go there anyway, and go to the Giusti Gardens, they are in full bloom – up a steep hill, like this house, but worth the climb.'

'We certainly will. My friend here loves gardens – don't you, Saiv?'

Was Lauren emphasising her name? It sounded as if she was? Mortified, Saiv murmured that yes, she did. Blithely, Lauren continued.

'And what else should we see? Can you recommend a hotel in Verona? We're kind of touring round, we—'

The man opened his mouth to reply, and at that moment there was a beep from his pocket. Taking out a mobile phone, he answered it, and put his hand over it to politely excuse himself.

'Forgive me, ladies. I will not disturb you. Enjoy the rest of your visit.'

With an almost imperceptible bow, he turned away and went to take the call outside the house. As the heavy tread of his footsteps echoed down the stairs, Lauren clenched her fist and punched the wall.

'Damn! Hell and bloody damnation!'

'What? What's the matter?'

For a moment Lauren stared at Saiv without answering, looking at her as if at an inexplicably babbling idiot. 'What's the *matter*? He's gone, is the matter! Are you *dense*?'

'I – I must be. What's your problem?'

Throwing her eyes to the ceiling, Lauren sighed profoundly.

'My problem? My problem is that I'm saddled with an utter dimwit, who doesn't even recognise the man of her dreams when he plunks down from a spaceship, stands six feet in front of her and says yes, Raphael would beg to paint you, signora!'

'The man of – my dreams—?'

'Yes! Yours! Not mine, because he's no movie star, but yours, because he is interested in art and knows about Raphael, about your chum Michelangelo – he's a big beefy bear but he's chatty and charming and his shoes are shiny and he's *not wearing a wedding ring!*'

Astonished, Saiv subsided back onto the window-seat, unable to believe she had registered so little while Lauren had registered so much. The man had been very likeable, but it had never for one moment entered her head he had even *seen* her. Men simply never did, especially not when Laurie was around. And yet . . . he had made that remark about Raphael painting her – hardly in jest, to a total stranger? He must need new glasses.

'Laurie, your imagination is running away with you.'

'It is not! In another two minutes I'd have got all the information I needed out of him and now he's gone – oh, hell's bells! How are we going to find him again?'

'I – we – we aren't! Anyway, a wedding ring doesn't mean anything, maybe Italian men don't wear them—'

Lauren peered at her. 'Jesus. You really don't see anything, do you, apart from paintings and statues? They *do* wear them! But this guy . . . Saiv, trust me. I can tell a single man at a hundred paces. And I tell you this one is – is perfect for you!' Groaning, as if she'd missed the last plane to paradise, Lauren sank down on the seat beside Saiv and gazed wretchedly at the spot where he had been. Her expression was so tragic that Saiv had to laugh.

'Well, perfect or not, he's gone! I didn't even realise you were chatting him up, for my benefit.'

'No. You just stood there like a dork, blushing and mumbling instead of making use of Michelangelo . . . I could brain you. The guy *liked* you!'

Firmly, Saiv stood up. 'Laurie, get a grip. The guy exchanged a few civil sentences with us – both of us – and that's all. Anyway, he said he lives in Verona. I live in Meath. So that's that. Come on, let's get going.'

Frowning darkly, her expression speaking volumes, Lauren got up and followed her out of the house, scanning the street immediately she was in it, squinting against the blinding sunlight. But the man was gone. 'Too bad', Saiv shrugged; but her casual tone belied the disappointment she felt, suddenly, tugging at something in her heart. As ever, she had made a mess of things, and now it was too late to remedy them.

Moving on, they went to see the Palazzo Ducale, but the rest of the day was thrown into shade, and neither of them deemed it a success. Mentally kicking herself, Saiv found herself wondering what the man's name was, what he worked at, what age he was and whether, by any miracle, Lauren could have been right about his not being married. 'There' she said crossly, 'what did I tell you about mobile phones, huh? They ruin everything.'

'Yes' Lauren conceded glumly, 'you have a point this time, all right. Especially as we didn't even get his number.'

That evening, feeling inexplicably drained, Saiv rebelled. She was not, she informed Lauren, in the mood for taking her turn to drive the car. Admittedly they had seen most of Urbino and could go on to Ravenna before nightfall, which would put them in striking distance of Padua tomorrow – but it was rush hour, and soon it would be getting dark. She was tired and she would, frankly, much rather find a hotel here, have a warm bath, a meal and a good night's sleep.

'OK. On condition you do your share of the driving tomorrow.'

'I will. Provided I get a stiff drink and a big hot plate of pasta tonight.'

Lauren raised an eyebrow. 'You should try to take it easy on the pasta.'

'Oh, what does it matter? I'm starving and I want spaghetti alle vongole! Open that guidebook and see what it says about hotels.'

But they had left it rather late, and had to try four hotels before, finally, they found a small unappealing one, where Lauren discovered to her horror that her hair-dryer wouldn't work.

'Oh, what matter, at least we have beds for the night. Just let it dry naturally, Laurie, there's no need to doll yourself up tonight. Any old pizzeria will do us.'

Somehow Lauren still managed to emerge looking lovely, unlike Saiv Lovett who let her washed hair frizz back into shape at will, threw on a nondescript old dress and pronounced herself ready to go. Lauren eyed her.

'In a bad mood, are we?'

'Certainly not. Just tired and hungry.'

But Saiv was conscious of vague irritability as they went out, found the first bar to hand and ordered drinks. With increasing difficulty Lauren was still sticking to mineral water, but Saiv was unable to offer moral support tonight.

'A gin and tonic, please.'

Longingly, Lauren eyed it when it came. 'I'm getting so fed up being good . . . I'd give anything for one of those.'

Suddenly abashed, Saiv stared into it. She had absolutely no business being snappy, had absolutely no excuse for crankiness when Lauren, who had, was being so perfectly pleasant. Picking up the glass, she passed it to her.

'Here. A little sip won't hurt you.'

Encouragingly, she smiled, and Lauren did have a little sip, looking nostalgic and somehow sad. 'Mmm . . . that is *good*! Was there really a time when I'd drink two of those before dinner without a thought?'

'There was . . . d'you miss it, Laurie?'

'I do tonight. I'd love that whole glass, followed by a big velvety red wine with our meal . . . oh, well. If it's the price I have to pay for staying healthy, getting to see Caoimhe at Christmas – that's life, huh?'

Yes, Saiv supposed, but what quality of life? Would it always be like this for Lauren now, no drinks, no rushing round, no relationship without risk? Thinking about all the constraints she was facing, Saiv was acutely conscious of her own many freedoms, and the unfairness of the whole situation. Picking up her glass, she emptied it in a rush, and the gin swirled dizzyingly to her empty stomach. In seconds, she realised she was very slightly drunk, just enough to make her feel relaxed, and much better. What the hell! She was a very lucky woman, to be here on holiday in her favourite country with her favourite friend. Tomorrow would take care of itself.

'So, let's find somewhere nice to eat.'

Oh, said the waiter when they asked him, that would be the Pizzeria Tre Piante, where the food was wonderful and the view, from a terrace cantilevered into the hillside, was to die for.

'That's for me, so' Lauren said cheerfully, leaving Saiv speechless; she could actually make such a terrible joke, laugh at her own predicament? Moved, and propelled by the gin, she squeezed Laurie's hand, and they laughed giddily together.

The terrace of the Tre Piante turned out to be, they thought, the most romantic restaurant either of them had ever seen. As the sun went down in a violet sweep, the valley below began to twinkle with distant lights like fireflies, and the scent of pine and oregano floated up, a night fragrance headier than even Lauren's French perfume. Seated by the balustrade with the valley to their right, they sat gazing rapturously down into its umber folds, unwilling to speak for fear of breaking its mesmerising spell.

'*Bella, eh?*' a cheery waiter nodded at them, '*E abbiamo anche della musica questa será.*'

'What'd he say, Saiv?'

'He said they have music this evening too . . . later, I suppose. God, how lovely can it get!'

On his suggestion they ordered some bresaola to share, followed by spaghetti for Saiv and, recklessly, a pizza for Lauren. 'Why not?' she wondered aloud with a sudden defiant grin. 'I could be dead in the morning.'

'*Laurie!*'

'Well, I could. Let's enjoy ourselves tonight. I'll have anchovies on that — and please bring us a carafe of your house wine. Red.'

Piccolo, the waiter enquired, or *mezzo* or *grande*? *Mezzo*, Lauren said laughing; her friend here loved her wine, and this looked like the kind of place where you'd trust the house hooch. With a friendly smile, he went off to fetch it, and Saiv sat back feeling suddenly, expansively, blissfully happy.

'This is divine . . . I feel *much* better now.'

'Mmm . . . it was a pity about that man, wasn't it? Unwittingly, he kind of spoiled your day. Maybe I shouldn't have said anything.'

'Oh, never mind, it was my own stupid fault. I'm a hopeless idiot and I'll deserve to be a miserable old maid when I'm ninety.'

But Lauren looked at her, askance. 'No, Saiv, you won't. You'll find someone right yet and I'll help you . . . only fair, since you've helped me so much.'

'Have I? But how? What have I done?'

'You've been sweet and kind to me, you've been patient and positive, thoughtful and helpful . . . this is such a different holiday to the one I had last winter with Jordan in Florida. Or that excursion to France. He was so selfish . . . treated me to the best of everything, but there was always a price to be paid. He was sex-mad. And he'd never have let me loll on a beach for five days the way you let me in Rimini. Everything had to be to his taste and his schedule. This is the best time I've had in — in years!'

'Is it, Laurie?' Pleased and touched, Saiv smiled as the waiter lit a candle between them, and it began to glow gently in the still night air.

'Yes, it is. I'm only sorry we didn't do it years ago, and often since.'

'So am I. My fear of flying is absolutely pathetic, and I'm never going to let it hold me back again. Neither literally nor metaphorically – I should have flown at that lovely man, this afternoon! But I've learned my lesson, and won't let another chance like that slip through my fingers, should I ever get one.'

'You will. You'll see. Never say die!' Brightly, Lauren laughed, and Saiv laughed with her as she raised her glass of wine. 'Here's to you, Lauren Kilroy. Never, ever say die.'

'I'll drink to that! Pour me enough that I can.'

Gladly, Saiv poured her a little wine, and Lauren clinked the glass to Saiv's before tasting it with a look of rapture. 'Ooh, nectar! Up yours, Dr Mallon!'

Giddily, they laughed, and were still laughing when the first of their food arrived, glistening with pungent olive oil. As they started to eat a guitar began to play from some unseen point within the restaurant, its music undulating out onto the terrace amidst the other diners.

'Look . . . the others are all couples, Saiv. Male-female, ripe for romance. If ever there was a place for it – ! But I don't care. I'm happy to be here with you.'

'And I with you, Laurie. I wish we weren't going home on Saturday.'

'Do you?'

'Yes. Italy is so – so me! I can't explain why, but I feel so much at home here, so happy and comfortable. I'd love to live here, wish I'd been born in that valley down there. Feel, in some weird way, as if my spirit was.'

'Hah! Maybe you were Italian in some past life . . . do you believe in other lives? Reincarnation, and all that?'

Was Laurie looking for – what? Reassurance, of some kind? Something in her tone suggested to Saiv that maybe she was, and that it would be a kindness to be . . . well, philosophical.

'The Buddhists believe in it, and I have a lot of respect for Buddhism. My attitude is that nothing is impossible. We know so little about life, about its nature or purpose . . . it's probably wise to be as kind to each other as we can be, in case we come back as something vulnerable next time!'

'Yeah. Maybe. Maybe I could be a better person myself . . .

I've stabbed a few backs along the way, in my pursuit of Mammon.'

'Have you?'

'For sure. Pulled deals from under rivals' noses, by dint of telling porkies. Assassinated a few characters. Padded a few bills. Pushed all kinds of rubbish products . . . I'm wondering whether maybe it isn't time to put a stop to all that.'

'Are you? Like, how?'

'By quitting my job.'

'What?!'

'Mmm. For a while, anyway. Would you think I was mad?'

'No, I wouldn't, but . . . but how would you do it?'

'By renting out my apartment. That'd pay the mortgage on it, while I freewheeled around for a while.'

Winding spaghetti, Saiv paused to consider. 'Well – it would. But what would you live on?'

'I dunno – my wits, I guess! Any old kind of work would do – barmaid, waitress, whatever. In that market in Rimini I was even thinking I could sell stuff myself . . . I'm good at selling! But all I know yet for sure is that, as long as my health holds out, I want to do something different. And I want to see more of the world. And I *don't* want to be stuck in that damn office any more, playing petty politics, jostling for contracts, spending a fortune on fripperies and on – on just going to work, looking good so I can sell *myself*! That's the one thing I don't want to sell any more, Saiv. Myself.'

'H'mm. I know what you mean by that . . . nobody's life really belongs to them as long as someone else is bankrolling it, huh? The piper gets to call the tune.'

'Usually, yes. But – you know, Saiv, what you were saying about reincarnation? I reckon it doesn't have to be confined to the next life. It can happen in this one too. If I stop working, I might fall down a few rungs on the career ladder. But in return I get the opportunity to regenerate. To really *live*, in a way I'd forgotten is possible. You took a break and it didn't do you any harm, in fact it did you good, and now I'm wondering whether my own life needs to be so – so structured. If I don't have as much left of it as I'd always assumed, now's my chance to go into freefall. Jump off the conveyor belt and see where I land.'

'Where would you like to land?'

'Oh, I don't know! In a clearing in a South American jungle, swinging from a length of creeper, wearing nothing but a grass skirt? In bed on a private jet, joining the mile-high club with Daniel Day-Lewis? Singing karaoke in a Tokyo nightclub? Paddling my canoe down the river Nile? It's loopers, of course, but it's all out there, all to play for.'

Saiv smiled. 'Yes. It surely is. And if you feel you can go for it, Laurie, then I think you should. Take a break, reinvent yourself – even if you lose your job you'll always get another, you're so smart.'

'D'you think I would, in my thirties?'

'Yes! You're bright and beautiful, experienced, eminently employable. The only thing you need to worry about is whether your health will let you do it. If it does, then go for it.'

'Yeah. I know I'm going to have to keep my side of the bargain, see that damn doctor when I go home – Jesus, Saiv, what if he says no, I can't do anything? What if—?'

Putting down her fork, Saiv took her hand across the table. 'Don't. Don't think about that. Not tonight. It's a beautiful night and you're entitled to enjoy it, enjoy your dreams. To-night is a night made for dreams, Laurie.'

'Mmm.' Looking briefly misty-eyed, Lauren let her atten-tion wander from the food before her, turning to gaze around the candle-lit terrace.

'It is, isn't it? It's so – *Saiv!*'

Startled by her suddenly urgent tone, Saiv blinked. 'What?'
'*Don't look now!*'

Instantly, magnetised, Saiv turned to look, to see whatever it was that was causing Laurie to hiss like a snake. And there, standing directly behind her, waiting while the waiter cleared a table for him, was the man from Raphael's house.

'Oh – oh, my God – Laurie—'

For five or six seconds they stared in unison. A split second too long; the man caught sight of them, and nodded a surprised, courtly salutation. In a flash, not allowing herself time to think, Saiv astonished Laurie by getting up and going over to him.

As she went her mind took a photograph, one she knew would be indelibly vivid for the rest of her days, of this man she was about to invite to join her. Why he should be alone she had no idea; all she knew was that no-one should have to eat by himself in a place like this on a night like this, under a sky full of glittering stars. Patiently, he was standing with his hands in the pockets of navy cord trousers, a leather pouch slung over his shoulder Italian-style, his beard neatly trimmed, his dark eyes assuming a look of quizzical anticipation as she neared him.

'*Buona sera!*'

'*Buona sera, signora.*'

He sounded formal, but – but for once she was going to do something without Laurie's help, without analysing or debating it. Taking a deep breath, she faced him and smiled.

'Are you alone?'

Slightly sardonic, he gestured at the empty space around him. 'Yes, I—'

Maybe he was going to say he wanted to be alone? But she wasn't going to give him time to.

'Then why don't you come and join our table? We have this lovely one with a view down over the valley.'

She raised her arm to indicate it, and he looked over to where Lauren was sitting, trying to look nonchalant.

'*Grazie.* That is very kind. But I would not dream of disturbing your meal.'

Was that a put-down? Shyness? A yearning wish for solitude, perhaps, after an aggravating day? She didn't care what it was.

'Oh, but you must! It's a view to be shared, and we – we don't know any Italians. We'd love to talk to you, if you'd enjoy the company we would too.'

Briefly, he frowned, considering. 'You're sure it would not be an intrusion?'

'It would be a pleasure. Please come.'

'All right! I will come.' Suddenly he beamed at her, and she was bedazzled by a mouthful of strong white teeth, molten brown eyes full of warmth and friendly humour. He was around forty, but she thought there was something youthful about him, something lively. Close up, she could smell the freshly laundered cotton of his white, short-sleeved shirt.

Signalling to the waiter, he communicated the change of plan and followed Saiv back to her table, where as she sat down she silently cursed herself for having worn this rag of a dress, for having let her hair curl like a fistful of bedsprings. Damn! But at least she had achieved her goal, she had got this likeable, appealing man where she wanted him. She'd done something spontaneous and hey, it had worked!

A chair was furnished and he sat down, taking Lauren's outstretched hand and surprising them both by not shaking but kissing it, in a way that was charmingly Italian.

'Good evening, signora. I hope I am not interrupting, but your friend has—'

'We're delighted you can join us! I'm Lauren Kilroy, and this is Saiv Lovett. We're on holiday from Ireland.'

Good old Laurie, Saiv thought gratefully; while I'm racking my brains wondering what to say next, she'll chat away, it won't be a bit awkward.

'From Ireland? And what draws you to Italy?'

'Art,' Laurie said immediately, firmly. 'Saiv loves it. She loves everything about your country, the sun and the food and the music – don't you, Saiv?'

'Yes' Saiv agreed, catching Laurie's determined look, one that said she was to catch this ball and run with it. 'I – I was just telling Laurie that I sometimes think I should have been born in Italy. Maybe one of my ancestors was, because I feel so at home . . . but you're from Verona? What brings you to Urbino?'

Sitting back, the man raised the glass of wine Lauren offered him and looked into it. 'Business. I am an interpreter. I specialise in ecology, and there is an eco-conference in progress at the

Palazzo Ducale. I was on my lunch break when I met you earlier today. My name, by the way, is Vittorio Scalzini.'

The waiter intervened with a menu, but he didn't study it; he would have some melon and then some osso buco. With some more wine, please, whatever the ladies were drinking. During this interlude, Saiv caught Lauren's look; it clearly said 'ecology, huh? You're on a roll here, go for it!' Nodding imperceptibly, she was amused to see Laurie silently wrestling laughter.

But she wasn't going to give Laurie anything else to laugh at, she was *not* going to blow this second chance that had, undeservedly, fallen into her lap from the skies. Vittorio Scalzini was no Greek god, no lithe toyboy, but he was big and solid, there was something chunkily strong about him, and very personable. Anyone who was into ecology had to have, in her book, something going for him.

'Tell us about your conference' she invited with genuine interest, and he waved an exasperated hand, laughed aloud.

'Oh, it's insane! Full of fighting factions, like all big bureaucratic gatherings. This is the third day of four, and so far they have done nothing but squabble. I never cease to be amazed by the way this urgent subject gets hijacked by lobby groups, vested interests . . . but it is the same all over the world. The Italians just make more noise than most. That is why I went out to Raffaelo's house at noon, to get away from all the politicking and power-factions. They are like children, shouting, refusing to listen to each other.'

'What kind of ecology is it about?'

'Forestry, mostly. But I will not bore you with the details.'

'You certainly won't bore Saiv' Lauren interjected, 'because she feels very strongly about ecology – don't you, Saiv?'

'Yes, I – did you know that Ireland is actually the least-forested country in Europe, Vittorio? The government planted a tree for every person in the country in 2000, to mark the millennium, but it still isn't nearly enough.'

Thoughtfully, he looked at her as the waiter brought his

melon. 'Yes, I have heard that this is true – are you involved in the subject?'

'No, I teach philosophy. But I live in the countryside and ride a bike wherever possible, recycle everything and—'

'She's an eco-warrior! She drags me out on these awful walks with her dogs, up hill and down dale, everything in her house is made of natural fabrics, our Saiv is a country girl and no mistake.' Lauren smiled affectionately as she said it, and Vittorio looked at Saiv approvingly.

'Good for you. Our children will inherit the earth and we must try to see that it is livable for them – do you have children, signora?'

Surprised by the personal question, Saiv flushed. 'No, I don't – do you?'

It was equally cheeky, she supposed, but she wanted to know. Wanted to find out all she could about this man. Proudly, he nodded.

'Yes, two, a son and a daughter. Michele is fifteen and Gina is nearly thirteen, they are at school – it was Gina who telephoned me today while I was speaking to you. My phone is switched off while I am working but she knows she can get me at lunchtimes – she fusses when I am away!'

'Are you away often?'

'Yes, quite a lot. I used to do international conferences, but now I only travel within Italy or nearby, for short periods. Their aunt looks after them, but I do not like to burden her for more than a few days.'

Their aunt? Saiv and Lauren exchanged glances. But it was Lauren who spoke. 'Their aunt? Why? Is their mother away working too?'

Finishing his melon, Vittorio sat back to survey the slopes of the valley for a moment, in thoughtful, vaguely wistful silence. 'Their mother, sadly, is dead. She died in a boating accident on Lake Garda when they were only small, seven years ago. It was a terrible loss for them, for us all.'

Lauren didn't look as if she thought it was, at this moment;

glimpsing her appallingly smug smirk, Saiv looked away in horror. The poor man, his poor children! She felt instant, genuine sympathy.

'And – now? Do they remember her, still miss her?'

'Oh, yes. Particularly Gina, who was only six when it happened. She still talks of her mama. But . . . tell me about yourselves, and about your holiday.'

Eagerly they obliged, embarking on a long enthusiastic conversation that began to flow with the wine, with the gradual recognition that they had stumbled on a very nice, very affable man with whom Saiv had much in common and to whom Lauren also found herself warming. A fluent, easy conversationalist, he was also a good listener with a sense of humour, and by the time they were all ready for coffee tentative camaraderie was beginning to evolve between them, tiny buds of friendship were opening out on the warm night air.

But the heavy stillness had turned clammy, and Vittorio was not the only man reaching into his pocket for a large handkerchief with which to mop his brow. Suddenly, in one swift flash like a zip, a streak of lightning shot down into the valley, and after a startled second there was a massive, deafening roll of thunder.

'Oh, how magnificent!' Saiv was entranced by the glowing drama of it; but even as she spoke a raindrop hit her head like a bullet, and all the Italians leaped up shrieking from their tables as, within seconds, a violent downpour cascaded over the open terrace. Racing out, waiters ran to retrieve what might be damaged, and everyone poured hastily into the restaurant within, laughing and exclaiming amidst the mayhem.

'I am sorry, ladies' Vittorio apologised as if it were his fault, 'but this is Italy. Especially in summer, we are prone to violent storms. Happily, they do not usually last very long.'

Lauren hoped not; she had caught the worst of it and her clothes were soaked. But Saiv was euphoric. 'Oh, this is beautiful! What a *torrent*! Look at it, it's so – so *power*ful!'

Obediently looking, from inside the open glass doors,

Vittorio grinned. 'Yes. It has a certain beauty. But you have a lot of rain in Ireland too, no?'

'Not like this. Nothing so – so *elemental*! It's like a fury . . . and yet it's still so warm, still such a magnificent night.'

'Nonetheless, I think we had better close the doors, or the water will come in. Let me find us some chairs.'

Everyone was scrambling for them, but eventually most of the milling throng was seated and, perhaps to soothe their nerves, the guitarist began to play again. Neither Saiv nor Lauren knew the song, but many of the locals evidently did, joining in with humour and gusto as they mopped their wet clothes with table napkins. Thinking she heard Vittorio humming beside her, Saiv looked up at him; he was gallantly standing while she and Lauren sat on the last two available chairs.

'Can you sing, Vittorio?'

Steam was rising in the room, there was an aura of besieged congeniality in it as he looked down at her, a raindrop falling from the edge of his beard onto her hair.

'Yes, I like to sing, sometimes.'

'Then do! We'd love to hear you.'

Leaning against the wall, he didn't immediately comply, humming gently while other people sang, accompanied by the guitar and the thundering rain, impromptu amidst a litter of coffee cups and battered, salvaged desserts. The restaurant's domed ceiling lent it a cavernous air, and its acoustics were perfect; Saiv felt as if she were suddenly sitting in the midst of a choir. Funny, she thought, how storms or such adversity can have this effect on people, bring them together in such a spontaneous, harmonious way.

After the first song everyone clamoured for another, and this time Vittorio did begin to sing, in a deep tenor voice that made people gradually lower their voices as his flowed over their heads, warm as chocolate. Even Lauren, who'd been bantering with a waiter, was hushed as she turned to look at him, amazed and impressed: he had an utterly beautiful voice, and slowly the others died away, leaving him to sing a solo. Unlike the first cheery communal melody, it was a slow, poignant song, demanding ability from its singer and attention from its audience, swirling among them like a river, wending its way into every crevice. Riveted, Saiv sat gazing up at him, fighting to follow the lyrics, and although she didn't succeed she did, suddenly, grasp two things.

One was that this was the most ethereal, wonderful night of her life, this Italian night unexpectedly filled with sunsets and stars, thunder and rain, music and friendship. Like a painting, she knew it would hang in her mind forever, and that she would look at it often, pause to remember its colours and contours, its rich fragrance and sensuous bounty. The other was that the empathy she felt with Vittorio Scalzini was, at this transfixed moment, melding into a feeling that transcended anything she had ever known before, the notes of his song dancing down her spine, bringing out a kind of beauty in him that was uniquely in the eye of the beholder. As she listened and watched, the rain polished her vision of him until it gleamed with the pure brilliance of a diamond.

This man, she thought disbelieving, is doing something to me, something nobody has ever done before. He's almost a stranger, but his voice is revealing something I've waited all my life to hear. I am attuned to him, and we are on a wavelength, one we've found by the sheerest fluke.

Looking up at him, she sat fascinated as the last notes of his song floated down like falling leaves, but he did not look at her, and suddenly it hit her with the sharp stab of an ice-pick: I am invisible to him. If he sees either of us, in the sense that a man *sees* a woman, it will be Laurie. It has always been Laurie.

AUGUST

Three weeks later, on a damp Saturday afternoon, Lauren sat
with arms outstretched at Saiv's kitchen table, critically inspect-
ing her nail varnish as it dried.

'If you don't, I'll cancel Dr Richards.'

Her tone was languid, but Saiv's head shot up from the notes
she was writing, her curls flew furiously round her face.

'No! You will *not*! You can't do this to me again, it's
blackmail and I won't stand for it!'

'Look, pick up the phone and do as you're told. I'm ill and
you have to humour me, or I might take a nasty turn.'

'Lauren Kilroy, you are a nasty piece of *work*! I'm not having
this, and I am not making a fool of myself.'

'You'll be a fool if you don't.'

Saiv banged her pen down on the table and faced her,
flinty-eyed. 'Lauren, two things. The first is that if Vittorio
wanted to talk to me, he would have called me. The other is
that Dr Richards, as we have discovered, is an extremely busy
man and you were damn lucky to get an appointment with
him, even if it is nearly a month off. You're going to see him
and that's that.'

'Yeah. I'm going to see him and you're going to call
Vittorio.'

'Jesus! I am *not*! I have a mountain of work to do and he – he
has my phone number. If he wanted to use it, he would have.'

'Maybe he's shy, same as you.'

'If he was shy, he wouldn't have sung in public in that restaurant, would he? Besides, he hasn't called you either, which is the far more likely scenario if he wanted to speak to either of us.'

'Why's that?'

'Because – because you looked lovely that night, as usual, while I looked like something the cat dragged in. God, I could *kick* myself for not having worn my new dress.'

'You wore it the next night.'

'Yes, but the damage was done. Now, if you don't mind, my publisher wants all this bloody stuff rewritten and then I have to take the dogs for a long walk, so why don't you leave me in peace to get on with it.'

Tartly, Saiv returned to her paperwork, and Lauren returned her attention to her nails, idly buffing them for a few minutes, Elmer's shaggy head resting incongruously on her lap. Since she had become a regular visitor to the cottage the dogs had accepted her, and unexpectedly she had finally accepted them; there were even signs of mutual affection between all three. After an interlude, she looked up.

'Did I tell you that the partners went ballistic?'

Saiv nodded. 'Yes. You did. At least three times already.'

'Well, then. If I can do something so radical as inform them that I'm taking six months' leave from my job, if I can live with their shouting and screaming, if I can rent out my apartment and start running up credit card bills without the least idea how I'm going to pay them, why can't you make one lousy little phone call?'

With a sigh, Saiv put down her pen again, cupped her hands under her chin and sat thinking, with an aggrieved air of resignation. All right. So Lauren Kilroy had made a risky decision, had faced up to the wrath of her colleagues, installed some stranger in her beloved apartment and come here to live in what she called 'outer space', with no income beyond whatever expensive credit her bank would supply. So, Lauren had dropped out of the rat race and was now planning, if this specialist Dr Richards permitted it, to work her way down to Turkey on an ocean-going yacht next month, masquerading as a galley hand. She knew nothing whatsoever about either yachts or galleys, but she had airily assured its owners that she did. So, did that mean Saiv Lovett had to telephone Vittorio Scalzini?

Wretchedly, Saiv recognised that yes, it did. Lauren would badger her mercilessly, make her life a misery until she got her way and her master plan was en route. Her 'master plan' involved telling Vittorio a brazen lie, namely that she, Saiv, had decided to return to Italy for the opera festival in Verona two weeks hence, and would love to return his generous payment of their restaurant bill by inviting him to dinner.

Never in a million years would it have crossed Saiv's mind to think up such a pushy, devious plan, and the thought filled her with dread. Unlike Lauren she was no actress, had neither the nerve nor the talent to carry it off – and besides, what was the point? Vittorio had shown no particular interest in her. He might be busy with his work or with his children or both. He might resent being put on the spot in such a way. And he might – possibly if not probably – have some woman in his life already, in which case she, Saiv, would expire of complete and utter mortification.

Furthermore, there was the added complication of having to fly. Fly alone this time, without Lauren to cajole her, reassure her, drug her to the eyeballs and drag her from one end to the other. While the return flight from Italy hadn't been quite such a tortuous prospect as the outbound one, it had still involved three stiff drinks, a fistful of Zimovane and a sleepless, panic-stricken night before. Without Lauren, there was no way she could have done it – nor could she do it again, single-handed this time. The whole lunatic project was out of the question.

'I tell you what' she groaned at length.

Lauren looked up. 'What?'

'You do it. You ring him, from here where I can listen in, and we'll play it by ear. You tell him you just called to say hello, and see where it goes from there. If he asks for me, I'll speak to him. If he doesn't, you can just say I send my best wishes and that'll be the end of it.'

Looking gratified, Lauren beamed. 'Great. I knew I'd talk you round. He's mad about you, you know.'

'No, I don't know! You have absolutely no grounds for saying that.'

'Sure I do. I can spot these things a mile off. You're just not – not on radar at all, Saiv, you miss all the signals from men!'

'Such as? No phone call, no e-mail, not a cheep out of him for three whole weeks?'

'Trust me. I said I'd find you a man and Vittorio Scalzini is the perfect one. He's going to revitalise your whole life, he's going to love you and look after you and, this time next year, you are going to present him with bambino Scalzini, the first of five I trust. Italians like big families, you know.'

'*Lauren!* I—'

'I know. You're scared stiff, as usual, you're afraid even to dream of getting what you've long wanted and needed. You think if you ignore him he'll go away and you'll be safely back in your rut. Well, I—'

'Excuse me,' Saiv curtly interrupted, 'but may I say you're a fine one to talk about ignoring things in the hope they'll go away. I even had to make your appointment with Dr Richards for you!'

'Yeah, well – now I'm going to make yours with Signor Scalzini. Where's his number?' Briskly, Lauren dug it out, picked up the phone and punched it in with airy assurance. But, when it was answered, her grin turned to a look of horror, and she thrust the receiver at Saiv.

'Quick! Take it! It's a child, speaking Italian!'

As if it were a burning coal, Saiv reluctantly took it, summoned up some revived words of Italian and said hello, she was calling from Ireland, could she speak to Papa, please, if he was there? Politely the child replied that she could, just a moment please. In the interim, Saiv threw the phone back at Lauren.

'That must be his daughter! Gina . . . oh, God, Laurie, this is really biting off more than I can chew.'

But, her composure returning, Lauren took the phone and beamed into it. 'Hello, Vittorio! No — it's not Saiv, it's Lauren. Yes, we had a great time in Padua, thanks, but we never did get as far as Verona. Yes, we'd love to have seen you too. So we just thought we'd call you and say hello — yes, Saiv is here beside me, would you like to have a word with her?'

Already!? Cringing, Saiv took the phone, ignoring Laurie's triumphant wink. What to say, now that — 'yes, thank you, I'm very well . . . yes, it is a pity, but we just hadn't time . . . yes, we'd love to come back some day. You should come to Ireland too, some time — oh, really? In Sicily, with the children? Did you enjoy it?'

Beside her she could see Lauren's face lighting up; so that was why Vittorio had not called. He had been on holiday in Sicily with his children. Relieved and encouraged, she felt Laurie nudge her in the ribs, took a deep breath, and the plunge.

'Actually, I — well, I don't know what your plans are, but I've been thinking . . . I'd love to go to this opera festival in Verona . . . if I went over, would there be any chance of getting tickets? No, Lauren won't be with me, I'd be travelling alone — oh, really? And would he be able to do anything, do you think?'

Alternately grimacing and nodding, she turned towards the window, leaving Lauren unable to read the rest of the conversation, which eventually ended on what appeared to be a speculative note.

'Well? Tell me!'

Looking thrilled, but apprehensive, Saiv turned back to her. 'Phew! What an ordeal! I felt like such a fake. But, Laurie . . . it seems the opera festival has already started, and it's sold out.'

'Oh, no!'

'Yes. But – but he sounded delighted to hear I was thinking of coming over for it, and says he knows some man on the local council, who might be able to wangle tickets. He's going to call back later to let me know.'

Lauren punched the air. 'Yes! I knew you could do it, if you'd just seize the chance!'

'I haven't done it yet.'

'No, but you will. You'll see.'

'But – but I have all this work to do, I can't really afford the time, or the fare, or . . .'

'Jesus, don't start! You've got this far and you're not turning back now. If you're broke, then get this credit card you've been talking about and use that. You can pay it off later when you go back to work.'

'You mean, get into *debt*?' She looked aghast. Grimly, Lauren nodded.

'You got it. Speculate to accumulate. Keep the banks in business. Somebody's gotta do it.'

'Oh, Laurie – I – I'll end up as bad as you! I don't want to go back to teaching, yet I do need some money to get back to Verona . . . Vittorio sounded as if he'd like me to, he – he was enthusiastic.'

With a laugh, Lauren hugged her. 'Then you shall go, Cinderella, and have a ball.'

Suddenly, hugely grateful to her, Saiv hugged her back with all the warmth she'd once reserved for her dogs. '*Thank* you. Thank you so much for making me do all these things I'm afraid to do. I don't know where I'd be without you, Laurie. I really don't.'

Even as she said it, her heart clenched against it, and she murmured some choked excuse to leave the room.

The following morning, Lauren sat on the edge of her bed, absently studying Duster the dog, who had inexplicably gained entry to her room and was lying on the floor, studying her in turn. Biting her lip, she looked at him.

'OK, so it's written all over me, huh? You can tell, with that extra-sensory vibe that Saiv says dogs have? You know I'm in trouble here, huh?'

Duster looked at her as if to say yes, that was exactly right, and Lauren sighed, picked up a pillow and clutched it to her.

'Well, maybe I am. Breathe a word to your mistress about it and you're Chinese takeaway. But my mind is made up, pal. I'm going off on this adventure to Turkey no matter what Dr Richards says. Unless he actually handcuffs and hog-ties me, hauls me into hospital on the spot, I am going to do it. If my health doesn't hold out and I end up expiring in some awful Turkish hospital, well – tough. At least by then I'll have had my adventure, I'll have chosen my own manner of departure. If I take a bad turn before then, if it happens while we're on the boat – well, death at sea is highly romantic, don't you think? They can hold a prayer service and then chuck me over the side, toss in a wreath to mark the spot. So there you have it.'

Duster gazed at her.

'Yeah, yeah, all right. I'll put it in writing, make a will and leave instructions. It'll clearly be all my own fault – and you'll be in clover, because I'm going to leave my apartment to your boss. She can sell it and then she won't have to worry any more about going back to work. I reckon that's a pretty good plan, huh?'

Dubiously, Duster thumped the floor with his tail.

'Oh, don't you start! Saiv Lovett is worrier enough, she can do all the worrying for both of us. If she had her way I'd spend my last hours lying on her sofa, embroidering a sampler while she dabbed my forehead with lavender water. She'd eat me if she thought I was going to do things my own sweet way, regardless of what the medics have to say about it. But I will *not* snuff it in some hospital, pumped full of drugs and tubes, is that clear? I will not have my parents or sister standing around any damn bed, wondering whether to pull the plug . . . I do not want to die, Duster, but above all I do not want to die like *that*. Maybe you think it's stupid, but each to her own. If I'm going to go then at least I get to choose the manner of my going – meanwhile, I get to choose how to *live*. If these are my last months then – then they're *mine*. Mine to do whatever I like with. One way or the other, I'm going off on this voyage of discovery. So there's no point in lecturing me about my job or my parents or my responsibilities, you can save it, OK?'

Duster's tail swept gently back and forth across the floor, his gaze never leaving her face. From somewhere in the depths of the cottage, she could hear Saiv moving about, running a shower by the sound of it.

'Yeah, I know. You're thinking, what if it turns out that I'm not so ill after all? What if I'm jeopardising my career to flit off like a gadfly and it costs me my place on the corporate ladder? Well, I tell you, dog, I don't care. Status and money don't matter to me the way they used to matter. I've been playing Monopoly with my life, jumping around the board, acquiring stuff I no longer need nor even want. It's time for some changes here. And, whether I'm on my last legs or not, there are going to be changes. Got that?'

Duster shifted position, laid his head on his front paws and, Lauren could have sworn, looked at her exactly the way Saiv would look.

'Yeah, well, Saiv's no saint herself! She wants to make a few changes now too – only in her case we'll have to listen to a litany of ifs and buts and maybes first. Fussing and dithering . . . but the end result will be the same, because she knows it's now or never, for her just as it is for me. She's got a chance here, a chance of real happiness if you ask me, and I'm going to see she takes it. What's the point of worrying and procrastinating, eh? She'd simply miss the boat to Vittorio, and I'd miss out on whatever hope I have left of enjoying my life, of doing something totally different if only with the dregs of it. If I get into debt, they can deduct it from my estate when I'm gone. If I get into trouble on the high seas – well, I'll deal with that when it happens. The only thing I refuse to do is waste my time worrying. It's valuable time you know, *precious* time. So there's no point in banging on about how I should be resting or having counselling or exploring my medical options. This is my decision and I'll thank you to accept it.'

Something about Duster suggested that he didn't accept it at all, and suddenly Lauren laughed, dropped the pillow and went to stretch beside him on the floor, pat his head for the very first time.

'Come on, don't cry for me, Argentina! If it all ends in tears, shed them later! Today is for living – well, for taking my parents to lunch actually, so you'll have to excuse me while I get dressed.'

Half an hour later, she emerged in full warpaint to find Saiv shuffling around in her dressing gown.

'What, not dressed yet? What's keeping you? It's a lovely day, snap to it!'

Looking woebegone, Saiv didn't answer. In an instant, Lauren sussed the problem. 'Vittorio? Vittorio hasn't rung back yet, is that it? Oh, Saiv! He's probably having to go to all kinds of lengths to get these tickets, pull in favours all over Verona – but he'll call, you'll see! Meanwhile, why don't you put on that nice new dress of yours and come to lunch with me?'

'Because – you're going to meet your parents. It's a family gathering.'

She sounded somehow sad, and Lauren laughed. 'Yeah, Sunday is dysfunctional family day! I suppose your niece hasn't even called to thank you for that scarf you sent her, huh?'

'Actually, she called just this morning, before you were up. She loves the scarf. And she says she'd like to come to see me – only her father won't let her.'

'Why not?'

'Oh, because – because he's a sulky bastard, holding a grudge against me for encouraging her to become a mechanic! She still wants to do it. But he's still all against it. So I'm being banished as a bad influence.'

'Then I'll lend you my family instead. My mother can't be any worse than your brother. Come on, say you'll come.'

Saiv glanced at the phone. 'But what if Vittorio rings?'

'Do him good! You don't want him thinking you have nothing else to do only hang round waiting – leave a voicemail saying you'll be back later.'

Saiv plucked at the sash of her robe. 'But Laurie, it's your day, with your family – I don't want to intrude.'

'You won't be intruding. You'll be a blessedly welcome diversion at this ritual which, normally, is set in stone. Vegetable soup, followed by roast chicken, roast potatoes, soggy peas, followed by sherry trifle – Jesus, just come, and order caviar! Lobster, champagne, anything for a change, for the love of God! We usually talk about the neighbours and the weather, but you can talk about terrorists and earthquakes and whether there's life on Mars – hurry up, we meet at one o'clock on the *dot*.'

Reluctantly, Saiv smiled. 'All right. I can't concentrate on work anyway, until Vittorio – Laurie, do you think he'll ring? Really?'

'He will, and spend the rest of his day wondering what hunk you've gone out with. He's not to know my father is a fifty-eight-year-old defeated doormat. Now, linen dress, high heels and be quick about it.'

Saiv trudged off to her room; but by the time she reappeared twenty minutes later she looked much brighter. 'Am I presentable? I haven't seen your parents for years, I don't want to make a show of—'

'Wow' Lauie whistled, 'you've lost weight!'

'Have I?'

'Yes! Three weeks of pining for Vittorio has worked wonders!'

Perhaps it had, Saiv silently conceded – still. She didn't want to lose weight until she was as thin as Lauren. Mrs Kilroy would be shocked, and worried, when she saw her daughter.

'OK. I'll just leave a message on the phone in case – anyone – calls, and then let's go.'

★ ★ ★

En route to the seaside hotel, Saiv began to waver. 'Laurie, what if . . .?'

Lauren did not take her eyes off the road. 'What if what?'

'What if . . . Vittorio can't get tickets?'

'Then we'll have to think of some other excuse to send you over.'

'Mmm . . . if I can face flying by myself.'

'You will.'

'But Laurie . . . what if . . . the plane did actually . . .?'

'Then you'd be dead and your worries would be over.'

'Oh, *Laurie*!'

'That's the fact of it. Speculating won't change it.'

'But . . . what if Vittorio is just being polite, and doesn't really want to see me at all?'

'There's only one way to find out.'

'I – I suppose. But . . . what if his – his children don't like me? He said Gina still talks about her mother all the time—'

'Are you hoping to marry Gina?'

Edgily, Saiv laughed. 'No, but –! I mean, what if she – might resent—?'

Exasperated, Lauren changed gear, put her foot down and shot the car through what she called a 'pink' traffic light. 'Saiv, tell me something.'

'H'mm?'

'What if the Eiffel tower blew over in a gale and flattened five hundred people? What if Mount Etna erupted and swamped Sicily? What if a falling meteorite crashed onto the Pentagon?'

'Huh?'

'Or what if I whipped out an axe and lopped your head off? Because I swear that's what I will do, any minute now, I'll find a hardware store and get one if you don't stop all this bloody *fretting and fussing*!'

She looked suddenly so incensed that Saiv fell silent, feeling chastened, groping for some other topic of conversation.

'Sorry. Maybe I – I'm just a bit nervous about Vittorio. Tell me about your parents instead, I can hardly remember what they look like.'

Saiv had not in fact seen them since she and Lauren were students, when she had been invited to their home one evening for 'tea'. They had been nice to her, as she recalled, interested in her studies, but it was a long time ago, a very blurred memory.

'They look like Darby and Joan. Dad is still a sweetie, in his way, but he's kind of ground down, if you ask me, by life with Mother. She's the boss. You'll love her – a real fusspot, like yourself. She'll give you the third degree and be *terribly* concerned about your current desire to down tools, your distaste for your *excellent* job. The kind of job she thinks I should have.'

'Well, she'll be a lot more concerned when she hears about yours! Does she know yet what you're planning to do?'

'No. But I'm going to tell her today, and you are going to back me up.'

'Me? But – but maybe it would be better to say nothing for the moment, Laurie. Not until you've seen Dr Richards and have a clearer idea of the – situation.'

'I have a very clear idea of it. Unless Dr Richards says he can perform some instant miracle which will restore me overnight to full health, I am going off on this trip to Turkey. Six months. Unpaid leave. Apartment rented out. Career on hold. *Voilà.*'

Anxiously, Saiv turned to look at her stony profile. 'Oh, Laurie . . . are you sure? Is this wise?'

'Yes, I am sure, and no, probably it isn't wise. It may well be madness. But there you go. If I worked the way you do, I could waste what may well turn out to be my last few months on this earth worrying and wondering. But I'll be thirty-three years of age next month, and I didn't get this far by faffing around. I got a great job and made lots of money by being able to make decisions, *fast*, and take responsibility for the consequences. So that's exactly what I'm going to do now.'

A dozen arguments instantly arose in Saiv's mind. But Lauren's face said that she didn't want to hear any of them. Thinking how stubborn she was, and how brave, and how foolhardy, she decided to let the matter lapse for now, until they heard Dr Richards' prognosis and had something definite to go on.

Lauren fell silent in turn, also thinking. Sometimes – frequently – she would dearly love to wring Saiv Lovett's neck for her. *How* could a grown adult be so anxious, so indecisive, so unsure about everything? Was that what the study of philosophy did for you, turned you into a world-class worrier? For all her academic qualifications, she thought, Saiv didn't have a clue about reality. She had absolutely no street-smarts, she was naïve and gullible and horribly vulnerable to anyone who might ever take a notion to brainwash her for whatever purpose. She could be manipulated and abused and horribly, horribly hurt if she didn't wise up, toughen up.

I wish I could make her, she thought, because the last thing I want to do is leave her open to unhappiness after – if – I go. Vittorio seemed like a nice guy, a decent guy, but who can tell, after only two days with him? Neither of us really has any idea about him, what baggage he might have, what complications or complexities. I certainly don't want to throw cold water on him – quite the opposite, I want it all to work out wonderfully for her – but I wish I could get her to see the real pitfalls, instead of all these imaginary ones. Forewarned is forearmed, and she needs to develop a harder hide, a healthy degree of cynicism.

Only then she wouldn't be Saiv Lovett, would she? Then she'd be Lauren Kilroy. Whose own romances have not, notably, ended in rainbows.

Courteously, Eoin Kilroy stood up when his daughter walked into the hotel lobby, accompanied to his surprise by another woman, one he did not recognise. Betty Kilroy remained seated, trim and prim in a Sunday-best suit, her hands folded in her lap and her handbag parked upright alongside, as if in case of sudden attack. It was a stiff white leather one with a brass clasp, the kind associated with British royalty, and as she looked at it Saiv was horrified to experience a sudden, terrible desire to laugh. In front of her, primed waiting for their inexorable Sunday lunch, was the couple Lauren archly referred to as 'Moan and Batty'. Shaking hands with them, she had to clamp down hard on the wicked mirth welling up in her; this event, Lauren seemed to feel, was never any laughing matter.

Briskly, Lauren introduced everyone, and a waitress arrived to take what was evidently their regular order for apéritifs. A half of lager for Eoin, a cream sherry for Betty, ginger ale for Lauren and – 'what would you like, Saiv?'

She thought of her instructions for sedition. A pint of stout? The cocktail she'd seen on a list in Rimini, so fetchingly called A Slow Comfortable Screw Up Against A Wall? Catching Lauren's eye, Saiv was suddenly on a wavelength with her, conscious of their common stifled laughter. But she didn't want to alienate the mother Lauren felt she had already irretrievably alienated, herself.

'A dry sherry, please' she said demurely, and Lauren pouted surreptitiously at her. Yet Lauren hadn't ordered anything very daring herself. Despite everything, Saiv sensed that Lauren was on her best behaviour, like a little girl anxious to please and ingratiate. Could that be, when Lauren was so dismissive of her parents – when they were not around? Saiv wondered.

Over drinks they made small talk, mostly about their Italian holiday and the senior Kilroys' plans for a trip 'to Devon, perhaps' in the autumn. Quietly, Lauren murmured that she would give them a contribution to the cost of it, and again Saiv wondered. Always so generous! But what was she trying to achieve here? To please them, or to get rid of them, assure their departure? Catching her eye, Lauren looked away, too quickly Saiv thought; it wasn't false modesty, it was guilt. The guilt of someone who said one thing, and was doing another. Even though Lauren would certainly rubbish the suggestion later on, she could not disguise her wish, her almost palpable need, to please her parents.

Yet she hadn't pleased them, Saiv thought as they finished

their one allotted drink apiece, which clearly never varied or extended to two. She had, thirteen years ago, done her own thing, gone her own way. Surely she couldn't still be trying to make up for that, atone for her one unforgivable sin? Lauren Kilroy, so adult, so assured, so brash and breezy, kow-towing to this grey suburban couple? It would seem, Saiv thought, there's more going on here than meets the eye.

At precisely one-thirty they went to take their seats in the dining room, at a table they apparently always occupied, by the window overlooking the sea. Saiv was struck by how cold, how metallic the sea looked in contrast to the exuberant blue waves of Rimini, and thought with unexpected nostalgia of that lively resort. It had not been historic or dignified or classy in any way, but it had been vibrant, and she had very much enjoyed it. Remembering the water chute and her screams as she splashed inelegantly down it, she smiled to herself.

'Indeed, yes' Betty was saying with what also appeared to be fond nostalgia, 'I do remember that, Lauren. You brought your friend here home to tea and Eoin and I thought she was quite charming – didn't we, Eoin?'

Lifting his soup spoon, Eoin confirmed that they had, and Betty pressed on. 'You were in first year then, Saiv, studying philosophy – and went on, I hear, to graduate with distinction, to make an excellent career for yourself in the groves of academe.'

Groves of academe? Saiv thought of her regional college with its surly, shaven-skull students, its losing battle against graffiti, its malcontent grizzling staff.

'Er, yes, well, I do lecture in philosophy now. But I've been on a year's sabbatical.'

Betty beamed. 'Yes, so we hear! To write a book, Lauren says. How very interesting! Is it finished yet?'

Not 'what's it about?' Was it possible that Lauren actually knew, and had told them? Lauren had always seemed so offhand about that book . . . yet it appeared that her parents knew its contents. Either that, or they were indifferent.

'It is finished – sort of! I'm revising some sections, it's taking a bit longer than I'd expected.'

'Aren't you dedicated! I'm sure it will be a huge success.' Betty's tone was nakedly admiring, even eager, and with a jolt Saiv realised why: she thought – hoped – she was lunching with someone whose acquaintance might be worth cultivating. Someone whose name – unlike her daughter's – might be distinguished some day? For a moment, Saiv sat reflecting.

'My publishers are only a little outfit in Kerry. They seem to think there could be a market for it – limited, of course, but then that's not why I wrote it. I was simply interested in the subject.'

It was Betty's cue to discuss the subject. Instead she patted Saiv's hand, approvingly. 'Oh, I'm sure there'll be a wide market for anything written by a girl as clever as you.'

A girl? Mrs Kilroy, she thought, I'm thirty-four. Please don't patronise me. And by the way, why are you keeping your hat on over lunch? With that handbag standing sentry beside you? Is this some kind of morse code, to signal your intention of leaving if anyone displeases you? You look like a powdery sort of woman, with that pale pink outfit and matronly bow-tied blouse, but do I detect a ramrod spine in there somewhere? Your husband has yet to utter a full sentence, and Lauren is as subdued as I've ever seen her. Jesus, if you only *knew* about Lauren! She'll never tell you, never ask for your help or even sympathy, but I wish you knew how badly she needs both. Wish you could sense it, before it's too late.

Abruptly, Saiv looked at the almost untouched bottle of wine sitting in a chiller bucket beside the table, picked up her glass and held it firmly out to Eoin, who was nearest to it. 'Mr Kilroy, would you mind . . .? Lauren is driving, and I do love Sancerre! May I call you Eoin?'

Yes, he said like a startled rabbit, of course she may. Would anyone else care for some wine, while he was at it? Demurely, Lauren and Betty shook their heads; defiantly, Saiv drank from her refilled glass, lifting it aloft a little.

'Well' she continued, 'whether the book gets anywhere or

not, I have your daughter to thank for encouraging me to do it. Lauren is the most positive, encouraging person I've ever known. She's made me do all kinds of things I never thought I could do. She's the most inspiring friend, and you're very lucky to have such a terrific daughter. I congratulate you on her.'

Raising her glass in a sudden, solo toast, she drank again, and they all looked at her in surprise, a kind of collective apprehension. But why? All she'd said was that Lauren was great. No need for Lauren to flush, no need for any little tremor between the parents.

'Yes' Eoin said suddenly, desperately, 'Lauren is quite a daughter.' His tone was the anxious tone of a man who wanted peace, was trying to placate without taking sides. Dipping his head, he focused on his lunch, and resumed it.

In that flash Saiv saw two things: he was proud of his daughter, but mystified by her, and afraid to say so. He was afraid of his wife, and under her thumb. It was Betty she needed to concentrate on; his responses would follow automatically, in step with his wife's.

For a while Saiv held her fire, said no more, mulling on what she suddenly realised was her strategy. Lauren might not have enough time left for any real rapprochement with her parents, the three might never really get to know each other – and she, Saiv, had no wish to cause a scene. Yet it was Lauren who had empowered her, Lauren who had made her take that plunge in Rimini . . . Lauren who clearly craved her parents' approval so surprisingly, so very much. Lauren who might not be around this time next year, for another polite pointless lunch with them. And Lauren, it struck her, who had insisted she come along to this one, saying she must order 'caviar, champagne', anything she liked . . . was that Lauren's way of telling her she wanted change, wanted her to break the deathly pattern of this weekly ritual? She couldn't do it herself, because Eoin and Betty were her parents; but there was no reason why Saiv Lovett should collaborate in the brittle vacuum.

Biding her time, she listened to the trickle of conversation for a while: Eoin mentioned something about his vegetable garden and then Betty interrupted to denounce the 'disgraceful behaviour' of a politician who was 'openly flaunting' his mistress. Needled, Saiv thought of Jordan White, who had so long camouflaged *his* mistress – and what would you have to say about that, Mrs Kilroy, if Lauren had ever felt able to tell you?

As the meal progressed Saiv gradually abstracted herself from it, observing from what felt like an increasing distance until she was sure she was not imagining things; but no, she was not. She was taking a growing dislike to Lauren's parents, especially her mother, and feeling slow sadness for Lauren who, for no other reason than blood bonding, seemed so anxious to stay on good terms with them. Or *get* on good terms, despite all lack of common ground. It was not the cheery, irreverent Lauren she knew, and Saiv suspected her colleagues wouldn't recognise her either if they could see her demeanour today.

By the time they were ready for dessert Saiv's mind was made up, and all she was waiting for was an opportunity. For Lauren's sake, she was going to *do* something about this. If she was blamed for interfering – well, it was worth the risk. Clearly Lauren had been trying for years already, in vain, meeting only with vague, unvoiced disapproval.

Eventually, commanding Lauren to order tea for her without even saying please, Betty stood up and announced her intention of visiting the 'powder room'. Steeling herself, Saiv also stood up. 'Good idea, I think I'll come as well.'

Betty glanced askance at her, but there was nothing she could do about it as Saiv followed her out. When they reached the 'powder room' she opened her handbag and extracted her comb, her lipstick, began patting at herself in a way that made Saiv, to her astonishment, want to deck the woman with a punch that would floor her on the tiles. Gritting her teeth, she smiled at Betty's reflection in the mirror.

'So, Mrs Kilroy, I hope you enjoyed your lunch?'

'Oh, yes. We always do. This hotel does the best roast chicken in Dublin.'

The statement was so flatly authoritative that Saiv yearned, again, to punch her. Who gives a damn about the fucking chicken, you stupid woman, what about your *daughter*?

'Mmm. If you say so. But Lauren didn't eat very much of it, did she?'

Betty blinked. 'No, she didn't. She's always dieting. I don't know how often I've spoken to her about it. But of course she never listens.'

Dieting? Saiv drew a deep breath. 'Actually, Mrs Kilroy, Lauren isn't dieting. She has the kind of metabolism that doesn't need to.' And you'd know that, she thought, if you knew the first thing about her.

Not looking pleased to be contradicted, Betty frowned at her. 'Oh, Lauren has always been fussy about her appearance. She says it's important to this job of hers.'

'Perhaps. But that's not why she's so thin now. Haven't you noticed?'

Pausing, lipstick to mouth, Betty did not reply, but looked sharply at her. Embarked on her mission, Saiv carried inexorably on. 'Lauren hasn't wanted to worry you, Mrs Kilroy, but the fact is that she hasn't been very well lately.'

Swivelling her lipstick down, Betty snapped it shut. 'I beg your pardon?'

'She – she's been very stressed. Under a lot of pressure. As you know, she isn't the type to complain. But I'm . . . concerned about her. I think it might be helpful if you could get her to talk to you about it.'

There, Saiv said to herself, you've done it. That's enough. Stop now and leave the rest to Lauren.

'Under pressure? But she thrives on pressure. It seems to be one of the things that attracted her into the – the advertising business.'

Betty sounded as if she were sucking a lemon, and Saiv looked at her. 'Yes, well, perhaps it did. She has a lot of energy to give . . . or had until recently. But she – she's very tired, now. She's always been a very giving person, by nature, and it would be helpful at this point if she got something back in return.'

From you! Are you getting the message here, Mrs Kilroy, or do I have to take that lipstick from you and spell it out on the mirror? Your daughter n-e-e-d-s you!

Betty drew in her stomach and smoothed the collar of her blouse. 'Well, she's just had a restful holiday in Italy. I'm sure that will help. And I'll have another word with her about eating properly.'

Eating? Suddenly Saiv wanted to weep. This isn't about eating, you idiot, this is about nutrition! Nourishment, of soul not body! Clenching her fists, she stood silent for a moment, digesting the fact that she was wasting her time.

'Yes. Well, she wants to have a word with you too, actually. She's thinking of making some changes in her life . . . good ones, I think. I'm trying to give her all the support I can.'

And why don't you try too, was her unvoiced addendum, why don't you try too? But Betty simply packed up her cosmetics, clicked her bag shut and decamped with an aura that said she did not appreciate any comment on, much less advice about, her own daughter, thank you very much.

It was after she had insisted on paying the bill – with merely token protest from her parents – and they were all toying with the last of their tea and coffee, that Lauren dropped her bombshell. Dropped it very softly, as if it were a bag of flour.

'Mother,' she said softly, almost pleadingly, 'Dad – I – I have something I want to tell you.'

They looked at her in unison, their expression conveying that Lauren did not tell them things very often, and maybe it would be better if she didn't now.

'I – I've taken leave of absence from my job.'

Betty gasped. 'What? But – but what are you going to live on?'

No, Saiv shouted silently, that's the wrong question! The

question is *why*, Lauren! Why, when you've always loved your job, would you want to do that? What's the matter, love, is there something we can help with?

'I – I'm not really sure what I'm going to live on. I'm going to rent out my apartment, so at least the mortgage will be paid, and I'll be staying with Saiv until . . . I . . . I'm thinking of going off on a boat, working my way down to Turkey.'

There was the eerie silence that follows an explosion. Agog, the senior Kilroys looked at each other, looked at their daughter and then, in unison, sighed heavily.

'Well,' Betty said eventually, flatly, 'I know that selling cola and crisps and such things is hardly the ideal job, but really, Lauren, just when you've got a promotion?! Less than a year ago – and now you want to go gadding off?'

'It – it's not entirely gadding off, as such. It's a – a break. I feel I need a change of scene and – and climate.'

'But you're an executive now! And you've just had a break, in Italy!' Betty's eyes were huge with horror. 'Saiv has just been telling me that you're a little tired, but – but will your job be kept open for you if you take leave? What about your pension? Your insurance – how will you keep up all the payments?'

Looking crushed, Lauren shrugged. 'I – I suppose I'll have to borrow.'

'What? Get into debt? But you can't do that!'

'I'll manage.'

'But – Lauren, this is nonsense! People don't simply flit off on boats to Turkey! Have you taken leave of your senses?'

Betty's hand flew to her throat, and Eoin looked beseechingly at his daughter. 'Your mother is right, Lauren. This really is a rather irresponsible idea. If you're feeling a bit under the weather, why don't you go to one of those clinics – health farms – have a massage, a weekend away? Surely that would help?'

Plucking at the tablecloth, Lauren shook her head. 'No, Dad. It wouldn't help. Not enough. I need to do something more – more fundamental.'

Baffled, with slight desperation, Eoin turned to look at Saiv, as if she might be able to explain this. Firmly, she spoke up.

'It probably does sound strange. But, as I've just been telling her mother, Lauren needs a break. A complete break. She – her – her health has been suffering.'

Eoin frowned. 'Has it?'

'Yes' Saiv continued, 'she's been under both physical and mental strain.'

Sitting back, she waited for them to turn to Lauren and make enquiries. What strain? About what? Since when? It was the opening they needed; but neither of them took it. Eoin looked nervous, and Betty looked incredulous, as if anyone as resilient as Lauren could possibly have any kind of problem. But then, to everyone's surprise including apparently his own, Eoin cleared his throat and moved his hand in Lauren's direction across the table.

'Well – I'm very sorry to hear this. And I think it's very rash of you to run off and leave your job, Lauren, even if they keep it open for you this could be held against you in the future.'

'I'll take my chances, Dad.'

'Yes – well, I hope everything will work out. In the meantime, let me know if you – if you need any financial assistance.'

He blurted it out, and his wife froze as he said it, but Lauren looked both heartened and touched. 'Thanks, Dad. I hope I won't need any, but it's very good of you to offer, and I'll bear it in mind.'

Across from them, Saiv was pleased too, but still wondering. Could neither of Lauren's parents bring themselves simply to ask her, straight out, what the matter really was, why she was doing this, what was *wrong*? Apparently not; their body language was defensive, saying that communications had somehow lapsed long ago, and now nobody knew how to resume them. But then Lauren could be prickly at times, adamant about things she set her mind to . . . and maybe her own presence was inhibiting, too. With as much reassurance as she could muster, she smiled around the table. 'Don't worry. I'm sure Lauren will be fine. She'll tell you more about her trip before she goes off on it – won't you, Laurie?'

Gratefully, Lauren nodded. 'Yes. I will.'

Betty looked as if she didn't want to hear any more about it, but Eoin smiled with a kind of relief. 'Yes . . . please do, Lauren. Drop in home some evening and we'll have a chat.'

Have a chat? At last, Saiv felt maybe things were getting somewhere, moving an inch in the right direction. Even if Betty remained hostile, Eoin sounded open . . . perhaps Lauren might be able to tell him about her illness, as soon as Dr Richards gave her some more definite information about it. Both parents looked somehow armour-plated, but Eoin's armour seemed to have a chink in it. Clearly he was baffled by his daughter, and restrained by his wife's disapproval of her, but under all that Saiv thought she sensed affection.

As they stood up and prepared to leave, that feeling was confirmed. Eoin helped Lauren on with her coat and, when she was enveloped in it, patted her briefly but somehow encouragingly on the shoulder. Noting his quick, almost surreptitious gesture, Saiv though that maybe where there was life there was hope.

'So' Lauren asked without taking her eyes from the road, 'what did you think of them?'

Saiv turned it over in her mind. 'The truth, the whole truth or nothing but the truth?'

'Yeah. Shoot from the hip.'

'Well – I thought he was henpecked. I got the feeling he'd have had questions to ask you if you'd been alone with him. But frankly she seems to call the shots and I think he's afraid of her. I also think he – he might be fonder of you than you give him credit for.'

'Do you?' Lauren still didn't turn around, but something in

her tone plucked at something in Saiv, something that sounded eager despite her apparent cynicism.

'Mmm. I'd say you've got him worried. He'll go home now and spend the rest of the afternoon out in his vegetable patch, digging and rooting into the conversation, trying to figure out what it is exactly that could be sending you off on this insane odyssey. He seems to be a bit of a wimp, but he also seems to be concerned. I got the feeling you'll be hearing more from him, if you give him half a chance.'

Saiv looked sidelong at her as she said it, but Lauren betrayed nothing. 'And Mother? What did you make of her?'

'I nearly made mincemeat of her! God, Laurie, I don't know why you bother . . . she's obtuse and she's a snob and I was amazed by the effect she had on you.'

Lauren's grip tightened on the steering wheel. 'What effect?'

'So – so demure, so stifled! You're a grown woman, a successful executive, yet you sat there like a little girl, the perfect dutiful daughter! *Why?*'

'I . . . Saiv, I don't *know* why. I can play hardball in business but for some reason I've just never been able to play hardball with her. She – she's my *mother.*'

'Well then she should act like one. And you should stop acting like a convent girl, being good, taking her out to lunch on her terms at her chosen venue, talking only of things that interest her. Next time, go somewhere else, discuss – I don't know, drugs or international finance or something! – and let her pay the bill for a change.'

'Pay the bill? But why? I've always earned plenty, I always pay it.'

'Yes, and she assumes you will! Lets you do it, as if it were your job and your great honour! I tell you, Laurie, she looked to me like a woman who takes her daughter – and her husband – completely for granted, as if you were her handmaidens. It was my fervent wish to sock her in the jaw.'

Lauren spluttered, laughing despite herself. 'I wish you had! I've so often longed to do it myself . . . and yet, the moment I'm in her company I'm checking to make sure my shoes are polished, watching every word.'

'Yes. Tom has that effect on me, too. He assumes this lord-of-the-manor attitude. The only time I've ever stood up to him has been to do with Gráinne. He makes me feel like – like a *failure*, somehow.'

'Well, maybe you are a failure, on his terms, just as I'm one on Betty's terms. Now that I think about it, I wonder why either of us puts up with it.'

'I suppose we put up with it because, quite naturally, we crave the love and approval of our families. And we're women . . . it's ingrained in us, this desire to please. But after having met your mother, I wonder whether we're not being exploited.'

'How so?'

'They're taking advantage of us. Your mother knows she has you where she wants you, she senses your need of her and, as long as she keeps withholding it, you'll keep trying. It's exactly the same with Tom. He knows I love Gráinne and that's his weapon, he thinks I'll play things his way in return for being "let" see her. Right now he's punishing me for going against him by not letting me see her – even though that means she's losing out, too. God, they are selfish bastards, the pair of them!'

Quizzically, Lauren glanced at her. 'You're annoyed, aren't you? Placid, innocent, sweet Saiv Lovett is suddenly pissed off?'

Vehemently, Saiv nodded. 'Yes. Yes, as a matter of fact I am. It made me furious to see your mother's attitude to you today, and I am starting to see the same syndrome in Tom's attitude. What's more, I'm starting to think that if they don't like us the way we are, then they can go fuck themselves.'

'*What?!*' Astonished, Lauren gaped. Saiv never swore.

'You heard me. They're both banking on the fact that we're not married, we don't have other sources of love or approval. We have to rely on them for all the things a husband or children would normally supply. They sense their *power*, and they use it to keep us under their thumb. Well, I have suddenly had it with all that. It was a real eye-opener, observing your mother as an outsider. I suddenly saw the whole strategy, and I didn't like it. Didn't like *her*. If I were you I'd let her go to hell.'

Amazed, Lauren didn't immediately reply, concentrating on her driving as they headed out of the city into the countryside. Could Saiv possibly be right, could her own mother really be 'exploiting' her? Admittedly, Betty had always been difficult, been disapproving and distant, but . . . surely it couldn't be *deliberate*? Could it?

Even as she thought about it, a memory came welling up from the depths of her mind. A very youthful memory, from when Caoimhe had been born, and she had come running in one day to see her new sister. She'd been at kindergarten, and Caoimhe had been sleeping, perhaps a week or two old at the time. In her babyish enthusiasm, she had hurled herself at the cot, inadvertently waking the infant. Caoimhe had not cried, but Betty had come dashing in nonetheless to scoop her protectively up into her arms, away from her thoughtless sister.

'You stupid little girl, you'll wake your sister! So noisy, so selfish!'

And Betty had whisked Caoimhe away, crooning, shutting Lauren out completely. Even today, the memory was hurtful . . . but never before had she analysed it, thought that there might be anything *to* analyse. All she knew was that it had made her feel clumsy, unwelcome, disapproved of. While her love of her little sister had never wavered thereafter, it had been a defining moment in her relationship with her mother. For the first time, she had been given to understand that love could be withdrawn. Could be doled out like sweets, not as a right but as a treat. It was something you had to earn . . . and keep on earning, apparently, all your life. You earned it by being co-operative, by playing according to the beloved's rules.

Was that what had happened with Isaac Hyland? Suddenly it hit her with the resounding force of a hurley. She had lost Isaac by *trying too hard*. She had worshipped him and he had sensed her adulation, let her do all the giving and caring, and lost interest in her when he knew his power to be complete. Fourteen years after the devastating event, she had cracked the mystery, saw with certainty what had gone wrong. Hungry for love, she had loved too much, failed to offer the kind of challenge that kept a man interested.

And Jordan . . . Jordan had pulled her strings too, manipulated her emotions, taken advantage of her need for a 'safe' relationship after the pain Isaac had inflicted. Jordan had read her like a book, played her like a piano.

Scorched with sudden anger, shocked and seared by it, she turned to Saiv, her profile sharp as a knife. 'Saiv, d'you know something?'

'Do I know what?'

'You're right. You are absolutely right, have hit the nail bang on the head. Your brother *is* exploiting you, and my mother is exploiting me. They are playing power games with us both. I can see it, and I think it's high time I started doing something about it. *She* can start making the effort for a change.'

Saiv was delighted to hear it. 'Bang on. Exactly. That sounds much more like Lauren Kilroy! I tried to tell her, you know, in the loo . . . I mean, not to tell her you're ill, which is up to you, but to plant the seed in her mind, so that she might enquire further. It fell on rocky ground, though.'

'Yeah. She *is* rocky ground. From now on I'm going to concentrate on Dad, who is being somehow trampled as I have been trampled, and if Betty doesn't shape up she'll simply find herself excluded. Now that I'm on to her game, I'm thinking that two can play it.'

'Yes. I'm starting to feel the same way about Tom. He thinks I'll crack when I don't get to see Gráinne, but I won't. Gráinne will simply lose an aunt who adores her, that's all, which will be a sad thing for her. Or, if she is as fond of me as I secretly suspect, she'll find her own ways of staying in touch. Either way, I'm not going apologising or kow-towing back to Tom. As family goes, both of my brothers are useless. They give so little yet they expect so much . . . I think what I actually need is to go out and get myself a *new* family. One of my own choosing, for a change.'

Saiv looked so suddenly assertive that Lauren would have laughed if she hadn't seen, just in time, that Saiv wasn't joking; she meant it. A new Saiv seemed to be taking shape, here in the car this Sunday afternoon. Belatedly, Vittorio flicked across her mind, and Lauren felt a taut pang of curiosity: would he have phoned, when they got back, would Saiv get this slim chance of love from another source?

Saiv didn't even attempt to dissimulate. As soon as they got home she flung herself on the phone with naked, urgent desire to hear whether there was a message. Evidently there was, and Lauren stood waiting eagerly to hear what it might be; as Saiv listened to it her face began to look like slowly melting ice-cream. Eventually, blankly, she put down the receiver.

'Well? Was it him?' Lauren was almost hopping, excited as a child.

'No. It wasn't him.'

Saiv's voice dwindled, disappointment seemed to ooze from her pores, and Lauren ran to put her arm around her as she sank, looking extinguished, onto the sofa.

'Oh – but maybe he'll call later, then. Who was it?'

'It was Gina. His daughter. Saying that her papa asked her to call and tell me that he wasn't able to get tickets for anything. He was sorry but he couldn't talk to me himself, apparently he had to go out on business.'

'Business? But – today is Sunday—?'

'Yes. It is. People don't normally work on Sundays, do they? Oh, Laurie . . . he must have just been making an excuse, didn't want to talk to me himself.'

Lauren was bewildered. Why would Vittorio get his daughter to call? What business could he have, where could it be on a Sunday afternoon? Loyally, her arm tightened around Saiv's sagging shoulder.

'Oh, Saiv. I'm so sorry. But don't lose heart . . . maybe something urgent cropped up. He might ring back, later.'

Saiv looked at her, and in her eyes Lauren read profound distress, the rejected look of a woman whose hopes had risen too high, too fast. It was clear to her that Saiv was very, very attracted to Vittorio – and now, terribly disheartened. Lauren felt a sweep of sadness for her as she rested her head on her friend's shoulder, deeply desolate.

'I should have known . . . he's not interested, Laurie.'

'No! Don't quit! It's too soon, this is just some misunderstanding . . . give the guy a chance, Saiv. It's early days yet.'

But Saiv sighed, roused herself a fraction and sat staring into the empty grate. 'No. I may as well be realistic. It's probably less painful, in the long run, to accept it. He didn't find me attractive, I imagined whatever vibe I thought I felt. I probably only felt it because I – I *wanted* to feel it.'

'Well, I think you're being negative. I think you should give him until close of play tonight, at least. If he doesn't ring back by – say by ten o'clock, we'll review the situation then. After all, you can still – you could—'

'What? I could be the one to ring him back?'

'Yes! To thank him for trying to get the tickets – even if he didn't manage to get any, you should thank him just the same.'

'Oh, Laurie. What's the point in – in prolonging it, in making a fool of myself? I know you think I'm not pushy enough, but I – I won't throw myself at him. All I can do now is let go with whatever tatters remain of my dignity.'

Uncertainly, Laurie bit her lip. She wouldn't accept that this was the end of Vittorio, but neither did she want to hold out false hope. After a long moment, she stood up.

'I'm going to make you a cup of tea. We'll take it out into the garden and read the Sunday papers. Just switch your mind off Vittorio for a little while.'

Faintly, despite herself, Saiv smiled. The idea of Lauren making tea was novel, and comical . . . the entire kitchen was a mystery to her, she'd probably end up brewing it in a vase or bucket or something. Wanly, she nodded acquiescence.

'All right. The kettle is on the worktop, the cups are in the cupboard behind the door and the tea is in the canister on the windowsill.'

Lauren's laugh floated out from the kitchen. 'Yeah, and the water is in the tap! Give me credit, Saiv, I'm not *that* bad!'

In due course the tea was made, quite drinkable as it turned out, and they went into the garden with it, installing themselves in a sunny corner with the papers, at which Saiv stared unseeing.

Oh, what kind of idiot am I? How could I let myself think for one moment that Vittorio Scalzini would be remotely interested in an overweight, ill-dressed, *mess* like me? He probably didn't even *see* me. Lauren would have completely eclipsed me. I was invisible to him and that's all there is to it. He's a nice man – a very nice man – but he was just being polite. He hadn't really the least interest in seeing me again. It's better to face the facts and . . . and forget about him.

For a long time she sat thus, the dogs lying quietly at her feet, letting the newspaper sections slowly slide to the ground. Lauren, in possession of the financial section, seemed to be actually reading it, concentrating in the way she always did on matters of business interest; but after half an hour or more she reached the end of it, and put it down.

'D'you want the fashion supplement? Or the travel?'

'No, thanks.'

Idly, Lauren sat looking out over the sunlit meadow, and they lapsed into contemplative silence, each absorbed in her thoughts. Overhead, small clouds scudded in the azure sky, at the end of the field a rabbit bobbed into view, paused irresolute and then bobbed away again; from one of the apple trees a blackbird carolled distantly. It was a tranquil vista, but neither friend felt soothed by its serenity. Eventually, at nearly six o'clock, Saiv stirred herself a fraction.

'Penny for them?'

Slowly, Lauren turned to her. 'Oh . . . I was just thinking.'

'About what?'

She hoped Lauren wasn't going to say 'Vittorio'; but she

didn't. Instead she dipped her head and gazed down at the tufty, buttercup-spattered patio.

'About my mother.'

'What about her?'

'Oh . . . just that . . . that I've tried so hard, for so long, to please her! To *relate* to her. I wish she'd respond, just once.'

Saiv wished so, too. But – 'Well, now is her chance. People don't normally chuck their jobs, she must know something is going on. After she's had time to think about it, maybe she'll phone you.'

Lauren smiled slightly, wryly. 'Let's open the betting! Who'll call first – Vittorio or Betty?'

'A tenner says it's Betty.' Saiv smiled in turn, but it was an empty smile and, she feared, an empty hope. Certainly a remote one. Normally Lauren was the one who did all the calling and contacting. But maybe Eoin would pick up the phone for a change and speak to his daughter, start drawing her out on her reasons for quitting work?

Lauren sighed. 'I want to tell her about the – the situation, Saiv. I *need* her to know. But I can't unless she gives me some encouragement, some signal that she's interested, and concerned. And then, if she does, I want her to *listen*. Listen properly, ask questions, not start into any lecture about how I've brought it all on myself. Recrimination is such a waste of time, and I – I may not have enough time for all that.'

'Well, we'll know more soon, after you see Dr Richards. But still, Laurie, I think you should hold out. She is your mother, after all, she must surely have your best interests at heart. If she hasn't, then do as you said you would in the car earlier, and cut your losses. If she's really so cold, so egocentric, I don't want you worrying about her or chasing after her.'

'No, but – Saiv, I don't want to die without having made my peace with her.'

Laurie's voice was a whisper, and Saiv thought she suddenly looked very pale. So pale that she was ashamed of herself, for fretting over Vittorio when Laurie had something so much worse to contemplate. Resolutely, she sat up and reached out to touch her friend's hand with her own.

'Laurie, you're not going to die. I won't allow it. You're going to get the care and medical attention you need, at last, and then you are going to be fine.'

Eagerly, Lauren allowed herself a glimmer of hope. 'Do you think so, Saiv? Really? You're not just saying that to – to lull me?'

'No, Laurie, I'm not. You have always been a strong woman, by far the strongest I know, and you are going to fight this. There may not even be anything *to* fight, you could be one of the many people who live for years and years with hep C, experiencing no symptoms or problems at all. One way or the other, we're going to find out and tackle it from there. Facing it is the biggest hurdle and probably the worst – once you know what you're up against you'll start feeling stronger. Besides, you've already got this far, eight months since Dr Mallon's diagnosis. That's a promising start, isn't it?'

Lauren looked uncertain. 'Yes, it is.'

'Well, then! Think positive!'

Reluctantly, Laurie grinned. 'Hah! That's rich, coming from you! You've been in the depths of despair yourself all afternoon.'

With some determination, Saiv spread a glossy smile on optimism she did not feel. 'Well, maybe you're right, maybe Vittorio will phone yet. But never mind him, for now. I'm much more interested in *you*. I tell you, Laurie, if I could strike any kind of bargain with the gods, I'd gladly exchange Vittorio for your health.'

Looking moved, Lauren eyed her. 'Would you?'

'Yes, of course I would! I only have the potential to love him, but I already love you! And I'll say it aloud, here and now, throw down a challenge to the gods – take Vittorio, keep him, if you can make Lauren well in return!'

Saiv upturned her face to the sky as she said it, glaring fiercely into the heavens, her voice so defiant that Laurie looked long and hard at her.

'Well, I don't think it works quite that way. I certainly hope it doesn't, because I would hate for you to be called on to keep such a bargain.'

Saiv thought she would hate it too, felt a tremor even as she thought about it. But she had thrown down her gauntlet to the gods, to fate or whatever amorphous deity might exist, and she was fully prepared to keep her word, pay the price. If it cost her Vittorio, then so be it.

SEPTEMBER

On the morning of her appointment with Dr David Richards, Lauren awoke with a feeling of the purest dread. Aching and exhausted after a sleepless, tormented night, she pulled the duvet up over her head in Saiv's guest bedroom and decided, no. She would not, could not go through with it.

How could anyone go through with it, face the prospect of a death sentence? Since discovering that life might be limited she had also begun to discover its preciousness, its rich and unexpected potential, its tantalising divergence down new paths, ones that were leading her far away from her former self. Despite living in this uncouth rural outpost, despite being short of money and sometimes short of physical strength, she felt new resources developing within her soul and her psyche, uncovering so many new and priceless pleasures: the serene silence of a sunny morning, a wild flower glowing with vibrant colour, the books she had begun ransacking from Saiv's shelves. Although she could not name or specify what it was, she sensed some corner waiting to be turned, if only her life would last long enough to reach it. She was outgrowing her old skin, ready now to shed it and don another, to depart for formerly undreamt-of destinations.

To where, to what? She had no idea; all she knew was that the things that mattered to her now were intangible, something to do with her state of mind. Money had become unimportant beyond the bare minimum, clothes no longer counted, she didn't even care what became of her apartment. What she valued now was a poem she read one day, a long engrossing conversation she had with Saiv one evening, a walk one starry mauve night out across the fields with the dogs in tow, a deep and increasing sense of fulfilment. Although her friends Adèle and Gemma still kept in touch, were mystified by her sudden seclusion, it was Saiv to whom she had drawn closer then ever before, Saiv who had shown her how to live life in a new light.

And now, Dr Richards was going to rip it from her grasp. With sudden, certain despair, she knew he was. He was going to force her into a hospital, where doctors would take control of her body and drugs would take control of her mind; she would no longer have any power over, or any say in, her own destiny. *No!*

Burrowing down into the bed, she stifled a sob. She had lived a bad life, before, and now she was to be punished for it. She had been vain and selfish and shallow, cossetting her body while neglecting her soul . . . but did she deserve to die, for that? Was there no way to make amends, was it too late for forgiveness, and change? She *wanted* to change. But Dr Richards was not going to let her. This illness was going to be outed, and take over. She was going to die without forging any new bond with her mother, without any love, Saiv's friendship would be the only thing to sustain her.

Not now, she pleaded silently, not now! I'm waking up, I'm changing, I'm learning! I wasted so much time on my worthless work, on loveless sex and superficial people – give me another chance, please! Let me prove what I can do, let me dig into my depths and find out who I really am, let this terrible day not *happen*!

There was a soft knock on the door, and Saiv came in upon it, pale in her bathrobe. 'Laurie . . . are you awake? Come on, it's time to get up.'

No response. Moving closer to the bed, she gently shook the inert bundle in it. 'Come on . . . you promised me you would do this, and now you must. It's your duty to keep your bargain.'

Slowly, very unwillingly, Lauren sat gradually up, pulling the duvet defensively around her. If bargains were to be kept, maybe, just maybe she would stand a slim chance today, because Vittorio Scalzini had never contacted Saiv again. Since the day his daughter had left that short decisive message, he had completely, inexorably disappeared. Guilt mingling with all her other emotions, Lauren forced her eyes open and looked at Saiv, who had never mentioned him since.

'Yes' she muttered shamefaced, 'all right, Saiv. I will keep my side of the bargain.'

'Good. I'll leave you to get up and ready, then, while I make some breakfast.'

'No – please, not for me. I don't want anything.'

'You'll have some coffee and toast. And juice.'

Quietly but firmly, as if speaking to a child, Saiv glided away, leaving Lauren to hug the duvet around her for a few final, desperate moments. In that brief time, a hundred warring feelings assailed her, she thought of everything including escape through the window; and then, finally, she got up to face the day.

By the time she presented herself for inspection Saiv was also dressed, sitting at the kitchen table toying with a piece of fruit. Immediately Lauren felt the tension in her, sensed that this was going to be an ordeal for her, too. But at least it would be a shared ordeal. And it would, briefly, distract Saiv from the new sadness she never voiced.

'Well, here I am. Do I look OK?'

With just the faintest tinge of envy, Saiv smiled at her, sleek and so slim in a green gabardine suit, a soft silky blouse. 'Yes, Laurie. You look lovely, as always.'

'Then let's go. Let's go and get this nightmare over with.'

Pausing only to release the dogs into the garden, Saiv gathered her things and made her way outside to the car, so purposefully that Lauren guessed they shared the same attitude:

just go, no point in stalling. Feeling as if she was being led to the guillotine, she got into Saiv's car, and they set off for the doctor's office in Dublin.

For the first few miles there was silence between them, a tight laden silence that seemed to lock them inside walls of glass. Eventually, unable to bear it any longer, Saiv strove for something to say.

'Did you call Shane Jackson back?'

Shane Jackson had been plaguing Laurie with calls, demanding to know how she was, know more about her shocking decision to abandon her work. But for some reason Laurie did not seem to want to talk to him, and in response to his latest call yesterday, she had asked Saiv to tell him she was tired and would get back to him when she was feeling up to it.

'Yes. Yes, I did, finally, I rang him at home last night.'

'And?'

'And I – I told him to ease off the inquisition. I said I appreciated his concern, but that I needed space, would rather be left alone for the foreseeable future.'

Saiv frowned. 'What? Why did you say that?'

'I said it because . . . because, at long last, I have come to recognise the signs.'

'The signs of what? He's been a good friend to you, and he seems—'

'That's just it. He's not what he seems, and now I have learned to tell the difference. I have learned to read between the lines of what a man says. What Shane is saying is that he's a nice guy, a good pal – but that isn't what he means.'

'Isn't it?'

'No. What he means is that he wants me – has been chasing me ever since I broke up with Jordan. He's a charmer, likeable to the point of irresistible at times, and he thinks I am now ripe for the plucking. I – uh – I have something of a reputation, amongst my colleagues, for dating married men. I stupidly gave Shane a bit of encouragement, one night years ago, and now that Jordan is out of the way he thinks he's got a green light to pick up where we left off. His recent sympathy has been very touching, but entirely self-interested.'

There was an edge to Lauren's voice that made Saiv wonder. Could Shane really have such an ulterior motive? He always sounded so pleasant, so plausible over the phone.

'Oh, Laurie. Are you sure of this?'

'Yes. It's only from a distance, since leaving the office, that I can clearly see it. In a way, you could say I only have myself to blame. But it infuriates me that he should think I'm so – so *available*. I am no longer available, to him or to any other married man.'

She looked so indignant, so primly righteous, that Saiv laughed with a mixture of amusement and relief. So, Lauren had learned something from her experience with Jordan – and was, apparently, continuing to learn? Well, better late than never.

'Good! Dr Richards will be safe, so, from your predatory clutches!'

Crookedly, Lauren laughed in turn. 'Yeah. He certainly will. I'll be making sure his nurse is present throughout our consultation.'

Her tone held the zealous fire of the newly converted, but in it Saiv also detected defiance; Lauren was holding the whole spectre of Dr Richards at bay. She thought before replying.

'Yes. And I'll be there too, Laurie. Waiting for you whatever the outcome – which I'm sure will be far more optimistic than you think.'

She had no basis for saying it, but she was determined to keep morale up, their joint spirits as high as possible in today's daunting circumstances. Had she not sacrificed Vittorio Scalzini, so that the outcome of this long-deferred consultation *would* be positive? Of course, that was a completely ludicrous way of thinking, unworthy of a philosopher who'd studied logic, but still . . . the gods had better keep their goddamn bargain.

As they neared the city she sensed Lauren's stress level rocketing, saw her knuckles whiten as she gripped the ends of her scarf, and groped for distracting conversation.

'So when are you having that get-together with your Dad?'

'At the weekend, if . . . if everything goes OK today. Just him and me, we've decided to go out instead of meeting at home. We're going to a pub for supper and a – a chat.'

'Without Betty?'

'Yes. She can come the next time, if she likes, but for now it's only the two of us. Better half a loaf than no bread, huh?'

Nodding, Saiv agreed. If Lauren could establish any kind of improved communication with even one parent, it was a start, it would cheer her up. But, as the consulting rooms on Fitz-William Square approached, Lauren began to pale and perspire, her breathing rapid and shallow.

Scouting for parking, Saiv glanced at her. 'Come on now, Laurie. Chin up. You'll get through it, you'll see.'

Lauren didn't answer, her body taut, her eyes suddenly very frightened, very vulnerable. Feeling monstrously cruel, but utterly determined, Saiv found a space, pulled in and switched off the ignition. 'Well, here we are. In time and all. Let's go.'

She unbuckled her seatbelt, but Lauren didn't, clutching it instead, as if it might save her in a way the manufacturers had never calculated. 'No.' Her face was ashen. 'I can't, Saiv. I – I cannot go in there. I can't go through with it. Take me home.'

Her voice was a pleading whisper, so childlike that for a split second Saiv almost relented, felt sheer pity for her. But then she braced herself.

'Lauren Kilroy, you are going to see this doctor if I have to throw you over my shoulder and carry you in. You made *me* face *my* fear and look how that turned out!'

'What?'

'The plane, to Italy! I had refused to fly for nearly ten years, I was petrified, but you made me do it – and it worked. I had a wonderful time in Italy and now you are going to have a – well, maybe not exactly a wonderful time with this doctor, but a *productive* time. Is that clear?'

Glued to her seat, Lauren whimpered. 'No. I – I've changed my mind. I'm not going to see him.'

Getting out, Saiv marched around to the other side of the car and whipped the passenger door open, her face ferocious. 'Get out this minute, and get in there! You promised you'd do it and you damn well *will* do it! If you don't move, pronto, I will drag you in by the hair, I will make an unholy scene and Dr Richards will have to treat you for multiple injuries! Move it, *now*!'

Looking up at her, Lauren assessed the extent of her resolution; and then, meekly, silently, she got out of the car.

'That's better. Now, put one foot in front of the other, it's that red door over there, quick-march!'

Her voice was the bark of a sergeant-major, and Lauren gazed at her accusingly. 'You're a bully.'

'Whatever.'

In grim silence they reached the doctor's door, and Saiv gripped Lauren's wrist in one hand while she rang the buzzer with the other. The door swung open, they were admitted, and it swung shut behind them. Lauren looked ready to faint.

'Sit down there, and I'll deal with the receptionist.'

While Saiv went through the form-filling with the cool, starched receptionist Lauren sat, staring at her with the aura of a martyr, ready to go on hunger strike, chain herself to the railings, whatever would make her protest heard. With her back turned, Saiv ignored her. They were going to see this through.

The wait felt endless; but in fact it couldn't have been more than five or six minutes before an inner door opened, and a cheerful, cherubic blond man came out, holding a file.

'Ms Kilroy? I'm David Richards. And which one of you ladies is—?'

Saiv indicated Lauren. 'This one.'

Left with no choice, Lauren stood up and, very begrudgingly, shook hands with him. Reassuringly, he patted her shoulder as he steered her into his room, and smiled as he shut the door behind them.

Only when Lauren was out of her hands did Saiv realise what a battle she had fought, how terrified she had been that Lauren might actually bolt. Sinking onto a chair, she picked up a magazine, but her fingers were shaking and its pages were a blur. It was a plush waiting room, with original oil paintings, a coffee perker and wafting music, but she felt shut into a cell, ice-cold.

How long? How long was it going to take, this awful verdict? For the first time she glimpsed how prisoners must have felt when they were up on charges in Jordan White's court, awaiting the decision of a hanging jury. Except that death sentences weren't passed in courtrooms nowadays, only in rooms like these.

Time dripped by like a leaking tap, and after a while she got up, poured a coffee, put it down and began to pace the room, studying the paintings with absolutely zero interest; they might as well have been posters for Lola Cola. Lauren, she prayed, just be all right; please come out of there and tell me there's hope, some kind of future for you. *Please.*

But the consultation seemed to go on forever, and her spirits plummetted with every passing second, so low that she could barely stutter a greeting to another arriving patient, had to be asked twice whether she minded if the window was opened. The receptionist seemed to think it was a very warm day, but to her it felt arctic. *What* could be taking so long?

It was nearly noon before, finally, the door opened and Lauren stood framed in it, swaying slightly, clutching the wall for balance. As the other waiting patient was summoned out, she came in, bone-white, and collapsed onto the nearest chair, her teeth chattering violently.

Speared with fright, Saiv stood rooted. 'Laurie – oh, God – what—?'

Laurie's head fell forward to her chest, her hair swung down and she burst into tears, sobbing hysterically.

'H – h – he says—'

She couldn't breathe, couldn't articulate, and Saiv stood mute in turn, frozen to the floor, unable even to go to her.

'He – he says I—'

Locked in anguish, she sounded as if she were trying to communicate from a million miles away.

'He – I – oh, *Saiv!*'

Her face was buried in her hands, and with sudden desperation Saiv flew to her, knelt down in front of her and wrenched them away. The news, clearly, was as bad as it could possibly be.

'Laurie, please tell me! We – we'll handle it, but just for Christ's sake *tell* me!'

Lauren's face jerked up, tears cascaded down it and the silence tensed like a tightrope until, finally, in a rush, she blurted it out.

'He says I – might – be going – to be – all right!'

A wall of dizziness hit Saiv, her legs buckled under her as she sank into the carpet, the blood sluicing in her veins like a mountain torrent.

'Ohh . . . *Laurie* . . .'

To her horror her own eyes flooded with tears, her throat knotted and she was unable to speak in turn, only grip Laurie's hand to breaking point. Then, beyond caring, they wept on each other's shoulders.

It was the striking of some distant, sonorous clock that eventually roused them, what felt like aeons later; but it was only striking noon. Gasping, Saiv struggled upright, and pulled Laurie with her.

'Come on. Let's get you out of here. I think you're in shock.'

She certainly was herself, and together they tottered out, forgetting even to check back with the receptionist before leaving, gulping down air when it hit them on the steps outside. For several seconds they stood irresolute, looking around them at the world as if it had just been created.

'Let – let's go into the park, and sit down.'

The park was normally locked, but a resident of the square was just going into it, leaving the gate ajar for long enough that Saiv could squeeze through, dragging Laurie after her.

'T – there's a bench. Now, sit down, calm down and tell me exactly what he said.'

In tandem they sat, side by side, and Lauren began to hiccup as she rummaged in her bag for a handkerchief, dabbed at her eyes with it. She was still hideously pale, but two bright patches of colour were rising and blazing on her cheeks.

'Well . . . I've to go for tests . . . to a hospital . . . I have a letter here in my pocket he gave me for outpatients.'

'Which hospital? When?'

Sitting back, Lauren strove for her shattered composure. 'St Audoen Clinic. Right away, this afternoon. He rang them and spoke to someone, he seemed to have contacts there.'

Right away? Saiv suppressed a shudder.

'He said it was because I'd waited so long already – actually, he said I was a damn fool. He – he absolutely ate the face off me!'

Suddenly Laurie began to laugh like a scolded schoolgirl, and Saiv saw that she was light-headed.

'Go on.'

'Well, it all got a bit technical, something about a thing called a Riba test and another called El – Elisa? Anyway, it's all written down here.'

She patted her pocket, from which a white envelope protruded, and Saiv waited.

'Seemingly Dr Mallon did one of these tests already, whichever one you do first, and it indicated that I do have hep C, but not an acute kind. Dr Richards wants it done again to double-check, and then the other one, and then depending on the outcome maybe a third one, called a PCR. But Saiv – he says that while he can't give me any guarantees, he's very hopeful! There's no sign of deterioration since I saw Dr Mallon months ago, and I've obviously been taking good care of myself . . . if I continue to do that, and let him monitor me from now on, he thinks I could be fine for a long time yet. For years!'

Her eyes glistened again, but a kind of devout smile rose simultaneously to them, and she mopped at her face with something close to elation. Guardedly, Saiv smiled back.

'And what about taking time off work? Your mad sailing plan? What did he make of all that?'

'He thought I'd done perfectly right to take a "career break", as he put it, and that Italy had done me good too. But – uh – I – I didn't tell him about the sailing thing.'

'Why not?'

'Because – Jesus, I didn't dare! He's such a nice man, but he really read me the riot act. Said I was a total idiot and that I was never to let such a long time elapse again before seeking help, for *any*thing. It was a bit, er, embarrassing.'

Mutinously, she grinned wickedly, and relief made Saiv twang with rage.

'And he was bloody right! Those eight months might have cost you your life! If I had the strength I'd beat the daylights out of you!'

Sheepishly, Laurie hung her head. 'I know. You might as well eat me too, and then we can get it all over with, have a cup of tea somewhere and go on to the hospital. God, I'd give my right arm for a double brandy.'

Drained, Saiv stood up. 'You can whistle for your double brandy. *I'm* the one who needs one, after that nightmare.'

'Yeah. I know. I'm sorry, Saiv. I really am. I didn't even realise I was keeping you in awful suspense, as much as myself . . . as Dr Richards said, I've been stupid and cowardly and every ridiculous thing under the sun – but I tell you truly, I couldn't have faced seeing him even now if you hadn't made me. I was ready to run this morning, from here to Australia in five minutes flat.'

'Well, now you've cleared the first hurdle you're jumping the next. After we pull ourselves together we're going straight to that clinic, and you're having your tests and that's that. I don't want to hear another cheep out of you until we get home this evening.'

Abruptly, Saiv pulled her coat around her, threw her bag over her shoulder and headed for the car, leaving Lauren to follow in her wake, unaware of the vast smile of gratitude that followed her out of the park.

* * *

By the time the first of the three mooted tests had been done and they got back to Meath late that evening, Lauren was exhausted. Saiv knew by the look of her that she needed to rest, and with only token protest Lauren let herself be put to bed early, with a mug of hot chocolate and a kiss that took Saiv by surprise as it fell softly, affectionately, into her hair. No sooner had it fallen than Lauren evaporated like a wraith, her unvoiced thanks drifting on the air behind her.

After she had gone Saiv settled into the sofa, no less exhausted, to lie back absorbing the turn events had taken. Somewhere in the midst of her relief that all had gone so well some small misgiving gnawed at her, and without much success she tried to suppress it. Nobody in their right mind could hope for any more, for any better outcome than today's; it would be absurd to expect a *miracle*. And yet, persistently but pointlessly, that hope had long lain dormant, not only in her mind but in her heart. Deep down, she had clung to the remote, million-to-one chance that Dr Mallon's initial diagnosis had been mistaken, that there had been some terrible muddle, and Lauren didn't have hep C at all. Dr Mallon might have got his files mixed up, or he might be ill himself, or he might, at a long shot, have conceivably been mad, an aspiring Dr Shipman. Now, it was evident that he had been perfectly right. In the long term if not the short, Lauren was facing a very fraught, uncertain future.

But at least it sounded as if she had one, of some description! And how delighted she had been, how grateful for hope. Somewhere between the consulting rooms and the hospital, she had turned Dr Richards' words of cautious encouragement into gold nuggets in her mind, was already halfway to believing that the worst was over, instead of yet to come. As she saw it, she had been granted a huge reprieve, no danger was imminent, and now she had everything to play for. She had *years* to live, she enthused euphorically, and was she ever going to live them! There was a huge world out there and she was going to explore every possible corner of it, try every experience, taste every flavour! Never again would she get trapped in any tense, seething office, wasting her precious time on politics, on trashy products, on fripperies or illusions or the mad pursuit of money. She'd been a fool and now, she asserted with almost religious fervour, she'd seen the light. Massaging every nuance out of every word that had been said to her, she had already embraced the firm conviction that everything was going to be great – more than great, fabulous, superb! As her confidante and closest friend, Saiv wondered whether perhaps a little counselling might not go amiss – not only for Lauren but for herself. She could see a roller-coaster looming somewhere up ahead, and could not imagine how to deal with it.

But maybe tonight was not the time to worry about that. Maybe they should leave that until they came to it and, in the interim, just live one day at a time? After all Dr Richards would not have offered hope if there was none, and already things looked infinitely brighter than they had this morning. Suddenly suffused with gratitude, Saiv decided to pour herself a glass of wine, and toast Lauren's health with it.

'It's a pity you don't drink,' she told Elmer as she stepped over him to reach the sideboard, 'or you could raise your glass with me in thanksgiving. We haven't quite got Laurie back yet, not for sure or forever, but our chances seem to be rising rapidly. I'm only going to drink one glass tonight – just in case – but if Laurie's tests turn out the way I pray they will, I tell you, I'm going to fill the bath with Dom Perignon and *swim* in it. I am going to do something completely insane and celebrate like a lunatic!'

Elmer eyed her, and she smiled; she must be fairly loony already, to be talking like this to a dog. But who else was there to talk to? At moments like this it would be so wonderful, so comforting, to have a partner with whom you could discuss it all, a strong shoulder to snuggle into, a repository in which to leave the day's worries. Today's stark truth was that Lauren was not out of the woods yet, the specialist had said no more than the bare encouraging minimum, but for now it was all she had to cling to.

At least there was hope for Lauren, which was more than could be said for Vittorio. Feeling some bittersweet emotion, Saiv swallowed a mouthful of wine, abandoned the rest and went off to her wide, empty bed.

Although the private clinic was speedier than a hospital, it still took two days to process the tests, throughout which Lauren's feet scarcely appeared to touch the floor. Saiv couldn't make out whether she was floating on premature joy, or whether she was levitating with anxiety. But she was incredibly talkative.

'How's your book coming on?' she demanded to know next morning, as if she were Saiv's boss waiting for a report to be typed up.

'It's nearly finished' Saiv replied, 'but if I'd known what I was getting into . . . ! It's really been a full-time job, much harder than I'd imagined – and yet, I wouldn't have missed doing it for anything. It's been so – so *stretching*.'

'Are you going to do another one?'

Saiv sat back and considered. 'I don't know. I'd love to do something on Descartes, maybe, or Sartre. But college opens the first week in October, I have to go back to work and start earning again. I can't afford to do another one.'

'Why not? Won't you earn anything from this one?'

'Maybe – or maybe not! I won't know for ages yet. But I do know that the demand for philosophy biographies isn't exactly frantic. It's really a kind of luxury career, I could only consider it full-time if I had a second income to back me up until I got established.'

'You mean, like, if you were married for instance?'

'Mmm, for instance. But let's not hold our breath for that.'

Eyeing her, Lauren reflected. 'Well, no. Let's not. Still – I wish you'd call Vittorio. There must be some explanation for—'

'Yes, there is. And we both know what it is. If you don't mind, I'd rather not discuss him again.'

There was such finality in her tone that Lauren recognised

defeat. But she couldn't accept it, couldn't sit still this morning; waking after the best night's sleep she'd had in months, she felt full of restless energy.

'OK. Then let's play with the computer. Let's look up Turkey on the internet, and find out about yachts too, I don't want to appear a total dork on this trip.'

Saiv still couldn't believe she was really serious about going. It was just a chimera, a goal to cling to, until she had her test results and could make more rational plans. But if it would humour her, she supposed, keep her mind busy . . . all right.

In the end they spent hours on the computer, finding out all kinds of fascinating things until even Saiv began to wish she could embark on such an exciting venture; Laurie's daring and curiosity were so contagious!

'But what if Dr Richards says you can't go?'

'I *will* go.'

'Regardless?'

Lauren nodded defiantly. 'Yes, regardless! It's only for six weeks, I'll be back before he even notices I've gone. Don't be such a killjoy. And don't dare breathe a word to him, you hear me?'

Part of Saiv wanted to rush to the phone and call Dr Richards immediately: help, she's losing her marbles, spinning out of control! Another part urged Lauren to go, just to run off and do it, have a wonderful time and to hell with the consequences. If only I had the courage of my convictions, she thought, I'd do something equally radical myself – contact Vittorio, or quit my job to write another book, or both. But I just don't have Laurie's vision, her determination or her insouciance. I'm one of those wretched women who was born to keep the home fires burning. I'm a thinker, not a doer. I'm stuck with some endless, ridiculous sense of responsibility – even though I'm not a parent, don't have anyone to be responsible *for*. Or to, since my own parents died. But there it is, I can't help it.

God, it's going to be so quiet around here when Laurie goes. I'll be back at work, back in the same old rut I was in last year, teaching a class with a drop-out rate of seventy per cent. The kids only take philosophy as a stop-gap until they figure out what they really want to study. They don't take it seriously, or me. And why would they? They're far more interested in sex and cars and rugby and holidays, in living their lives than analysing them. They're Lauren, when she was young. If they change their minds later . . . well, I'll be an old lady by then, they won't even remember my name, never mind anything I ever taught them. I'm wasting my time. Even now with Lauren here beside me, living proof that time isn't infinite, I'm still wasting it. I just can't think what else to do, or how to do it.

'Come on Saiv, let's go out for a walk.'

Once Lauren had taken to walking she had taken to it with a vengeance, and over the following few days they walked miles, to the tops of hills and the ends of beaches, absorbing the last of the summer sun, throwing sticks for the dogs, rubbing their hands against the evening chill and lighting fires when they came home, marvelling in unison at the beauty of the harvest moon. Despite whatever turmoil seethed within her, Lauren was visibly falling into harmony with nature, attuning to its frail but tenacious rhythm in ways she never had before.

And then, on the morning of the third day, Dr Richards called. Guessing who it was, Saiv dived for the phone, but Lauren beat her to it. Standing taut, braced and upright, she gripped the receiver in one hand, the sash of her flimsy robe tightly in the other.

'Yes . . . yes, this is Lauren Kilroy . . . yes, I see—'

For a split second, time stood stalled. And then her face detonated with joy, exploding in dazed, dazzled delight. As Saiv stood transfixed with terror, Lauren clenched her fist and raised it over her head, triumphant as an Olympic gold medallist crossing the tape.

'*Yes!*'

Oh, God, she had done it, she had beaten the odds! Close to collapse, Saiv almost wept, but Lauren put down the phone wreathed in smiles, gushing thanks at the doctor she'd been so reluctant to see. Then, in one bound, she was wrapped around Saiv, engulfing her in a hug so tight it hurt.

'I'm OK – oh, Saiv, I'm going to be all right – for ages, they think! The tests show that my condition is static for now and should respond well to treatment in the future – he said something about proteins and drugs and stuff but I couldn't take it in, it was all long term, years off – but for now, I'm all right! I've got my life back and I can live it normally, live it fully! Oh, Jesus, it's a miracle!'

Lauren's faced glowed like a bonfire, ablaze with kindling emotions of all descriptions, and Saiv thought crazily of her vow to fill the bath with Dom Perignon and swim in it. She was so overcome, she felt like carrying it through, felt like climbing up on the roof and dancing on it. Oh, thank you God, thank you, *thank* you! Or Buddha or Siva or Allah, whatever your name is!

It was worth it. It was worth swopping Vittorio, for this. I made a bargain and the bargain has been kept.

What happened next neither of them could later remember, all they knew was that it involved a lot of giddy celebration, excitedly barking dogs and the most profound, overwhelming sense of escape. A falling hatchet had missed Lauren's neck by a hair's breadth, and only now did they feel free to confess the abject terror they had both felt – been feeling separately and together, for eight months. It had been like living on the edge of a crumbling cliff.

'Oh, Saiv – you know – there have even been moments – when—'

Lauren could barely speak, and Saiv felt drunk with relief. 'When?'

'Moments – when – I even thought – thought about what I might do, if the worst came to the worst.'

'W – what do you mean, Laurie?'

'I mean – I – I didn't know whether I'd be able to face it. Wasn't sure if I'd have the strength, physical or mental. I'd been working out ways . . . wondering whether you'd . . . help me out, if I needed helping out.'

For a moment Saiv didn't understand; and then, in a shocked flash, she did. 'Oh, Christ, Laurie, you can't have been thinking . . .?'

'Yes. I can, and I was. Litres of whiskey, bottles of pills, razor blades, products labelled X for poison – whatever would be quicker and less painful than slow, agonising, useless treatment – I tell you, I've thought of them all.'

Saiv was stunned. Never once had Lauren confided any of this; on the contrary, she had appeared to be thinking about anything and everything except her predicament. Unable to face the reality of it, how could she have faced such resolution? Had the one engendered the other? Urgently, she gripped Laurie's wrists.

'Well, you're never to think of them again. *Never*, Laurie, do you hear me? Today is proof that where there's life there's hope.'

Manically, Lauren beamed. 'Yes! It is! I can't believe this – oh, I'm going to go to Turkey now and have the time of my life!'

Now above all, Saiv did not want Lauren to leave, could not bear to let go of her. And yet simultaneously she did want her to go, anywhere and everywhere, to the ends of the earth if it would make her happy. Reluctantly, but resolutely, she looked at her, absorbed all her throbbing, palpable joie de vivre.

'Then – then go, Laurie. Board your yacht and set sail, and may every fair wind go with you.'

'Come with me, Saiv! Come with me!?'

It was a reckless impulse. Soberly, sensibly, she resisted Laurie's suddenly pleading look. 'No. Don't be silly. I have a job to go back to. You – you just keep in touch along the way, and let me know how you're getting on.'

'But Saiv . . . you've been so wonderful . . . how will I ever manage without you, after all we've been through?'

'You will!'

'But . . .' A sudden cloud scudded across Lauren's radiant face. 'But even if I do, how will you manage without me? You'll be back where you started, all on your own. You'll be lonely!'

Saiv knew she would. 'No I won't. I have Elmer and Duster, my friend Jennifer, my eco-work and faculty meetings and—'

Dismissively, Lauren grimaced. 'Saiv, there's got to be more to your life than all that. There's got to be.'

'Well, I'll just have to make do for now. You won't be away forever, will you? Meanwhile, maybe I – I'll join a chess club or something, a bridge class—'

With the flat of her hand, Lauren thumped the table. 'Oh, bugger that! If I'm getting my life back, it's time you got one too!'

From anyone else it might have sounded patronising; from Lauren, Saiv knew it came from the heart. Her once-selfish friend had changed so much, in ways that were some more subtle than others. As had their relationship. Once patchy, it glowed now as steadily as the logs in the fire, warm and crackling.

'I'll be fine.'

Lauren pouted. 'I don't want you to be fine. I want you to be *great*. I want you to be – to be ecstatic, the way I feel now!'

Saiv laughed. 'Yes, and look what you had to go through to get there! Thanks very much, but I'll settle for a quiet life for a while. It's joy enough to know that you are going to be well, that you're going sailing instead of into hospital – Laurie, don't tempt fate, don't wish for the sun as well as the stars! Just calm down, and promise to bring me back a box of Turkish delight.'

Her tone was arch, and airy. But Lauren's was vehement, and rebellious. 'Huh. You're getting more than that. I don't know what yet, exactly, but I can assure you it will be more than that, Saiv. It will be a hell of a lot more than that.'

Normally Saiv's heart ached for the luckless creatures at the animal sanctuary where she occasionally helped out as a volunteer; but today for no apparent reason she felt flashes of impatience with them, darts of rage at the selfish morons who had neglected and finally abandoned them. Trudging round in wellies and mud-spattered jeans, hefting bales of straw, wrestling a recalcitrant whippet and smarting where a goat had bitten her through her sweater, she recognised today for what it was: a thoroughly bad-hair day. Waking up to low grey cloud, she'd been in a matching mood ever since, and thought it was just as well she wasn't cooped up in the small cottage with the ever more effervescent Laurie.

Lovely Laurie, lucky Laurie, the one for whom everything seemed to go right in the end. In the days since she'd got her medical reprieve she'd been blossoming almost by the hour, burbling with bliss while she, Saiv, gradually deflated like a burst balloon. Why? Because, now that the drama was over, or shelved at least, it was dawning on her just how much time, how much care, how much effort she had put into Lauren Kilroy over the past eight months. Not that she begrudged it; on the contrary, she would not have had it any other way, but it had been hard going. It had been wearing and worrying and it had consumed a colossal quantity of emotional energy, as well as placing Laurie firmly in the limelight where, in any event, she had always believed she belonged. Every action, almost every thought, had had to be taken with Laurie foremost in mind, leaving Saiv Lovett a very tardy also-ran. Not that any of it was Laurie's fault – irritatingly, her burden had been even greater – but God almighty, it had been draining.

And now, here was Lauren happily heading off to Turkey, while Saiv Lovett slaved over a lot of mangy animals, painstakingly rewrote bits of a book that nobody would give a damn about – did Lauren even know *what* it was about? – and faced up to a future that was going to leave her exactly where she had been to begin with. For Lauren the world had magically expanded; for Saiv it had constrictingly shrunk. As she cajoled a flea-infested poodle to eat the food with the antibiotics concealed in it, she suddenly felt like ramming the dish down its throat, and leaned back with a feeling of unreasonable but pervasive impatience.

Well, there were days like this. Days on which, for no good

reason, you woke up out of sorts and felt low, hard done by, invisible to the rest of the entire human race. Days when you wondered what the hell it was all about, what was the point of anything when you were going to get no thanks, no recognition? Oh . . . Lauren was grateful, of course she was. But still, she wasn't the one living this half-life out in the muddy middle of nowhere; when she came back from her sailing adventure she'd probably take up right where she'd left off, merrily partying once again, turning the head of every man she met, flirting and having fun more resolutely than ever. Even if her illness did leave some long-term questions to be addressed, her immediate future glowed with all the radiance that Saiv Lovett's did not.

It wasn't fair. It just wasn't bloody fair.

Why had Lauren Kilroy been born with all the beauty, while Saiv Lovett only got the brains which, in today's image-mad world, not only counted for nothing but were a social liability? Men were wary of women with brains, didn't want to know about them or have anything to do with them . . . even your goddamn brothers resented you when you were smarter than they were. Resented you and avoided you and patronised you to mask their own feelings of inadequacy, even quarantined their daughters lest they be contaminated. Gráinne had been in touch, but only by phone, cautiously conscious that her father Tom could pull the plug on any number of projects if she alienated him. Until she was old enough to be fully independent, Gráinne would always choose her father over her aunt and, while Saiv understood that, she resented the whole stupid, miserable situation.

As for Vittorio . . . brusquely, Saiv picked up the poodle, carried it back to its kennel and thrust it in without any of the usual endearments she lavished on the orphan animals, thinking what a prize idiot she'd been. What on earth had persuaded her that she had the faintest hope of getting anywhere with a man like Vittorio Scalzini? A charming, attractive man like him would want a charming, attractive woman – someone like Lauren – to amuse and flatter and entertain him, brighten his life visually as well as in every other way. Probably he already *had* such a woman; the whole pathetic project had been doomed from the start. For a totally unreasonable moment, Saiv thought she'd never even go to Italy again, never set foot on the soil that grew such rich bounty only to snatch it out of reach. You might as well try to steal a Michelangelo, it was all so futile.

So. What did that leave to look forward to? Two collies to be wormed, a Shetland pony to be fed, a bad-tempered Scottie to have its injured paw disinfected. After that, dinner tonight with Lauren, only cooked of course by Saiv Lovett, because if Lauren peeled a potato she might chip her nail polish. On the domestic front, Lauren was about as much use as a porcelain doll, a pretty ornament who, in her own apartment, had always had a cleaning lady to look after her. It struck Saiv that she was getting very tired of Lauren's domestic laziness, and that if she went home tonight to a cold grate and empty kitchen she would divest herself of a piece of her mind over it.

Maybe, after all, it was just as well that Lauren was leaving soon? On the one hand, Saiv knew she would miss her, miss the company and diversion of having her around; on the other, the cottage was really too small for the pair of them, especially since Lauren had crammed it with so many bits and pieces from her rented-out apartment. Where was all that stuff supposed to go, while Lauren swanned off sailing? Saiv didn't know, but she hoped Lauren bloody well knew, because she was tired of having her wardrobes jammed with clothes that didn't belong to her, the bathroom stuffed to the ceiling with cosmetics that were – were so maddeningly *unnecessary*. Lauren needed such gilding like a hole in the head.

I'm tired, Saiv thought reluctantly, resentfully. This whole business has worn me out. I'm cranky and hungry and I – I've had enough. Not that anybody knows, or cares. Lauren's problems are my problems, but my problems are mine alone. It's unbalanced and unfair and that's the way this damn world always has been, always will be.

*　　*　　*

Lovingly, all but purring with pleasure, Lauren extracted her new mobile phone from her pocket and caressed it in the palm of her hand, savouring its slim, sleek contours. She didn't dare tell Saiv about it, would endeavour to conceal its existence for as long as possible, but . . . there were some things a girl simply couldn't live without, and this was foremost amongst them. Her brief conversion on the road to Damascus was over; finally, inexorably, the road had only led as far as the nearest Speakeasy shop. With a new lease of life tucked under her Gucci belt, she was raring to enjoy it with a vengeance.

Besides, she had calls to make, and was it not better to avoid running up a bill on Saiv's landline, which might cause conflict? Something in Saiv's face and manner, as she'd gone off to her animal sanctuary this morning, had signalled caution: for some unimaginable reason, Saiv had seemed to be in a tetchy, scratchy mood. Lauren thought a Tisserand massage and a Clarins facial would do her the world of good, but of course you might as well try to persuade Saiv Lovett to pluck her eyebrows with a pair of white-hot pliers. Never, in all the years they'd known each other, could Lauren remember Saiv ever doing anything indulgent, anything she would classify as 'pampering' or 'pointless'.

Well, there you go. For better or for worse, that was Saiv: her own worst enemy more often than not. In Italy she'd shown some brief flicker of promise, been on the brink of mellowing a bit, but since things had fizzled out with Vittorio Scalzini she'd closed over again, battened down the hatches. Lauren thought it was a shame, and proposed to do something about it.

But first – bip bip bip – there was the yacht's skipper to call. You could hardly just sail off to Turkey with a man you'd never even met. A whole caboodle of men you'd never even met, actually . . . h'mm. It was a pity she was off men at the moment, but still – the demographics of the group promised more fun than might be expected from, say, a posse of Benedictine nuns. You could always study the menu without eating everything on it.

So, Carl Delaney, answer your phone! As she waited Lauren speculated, anticipating their long-delayed rendezvous, arranged by e-mail for after her test results and green light from Dr Richards. Not that Dr Richards was to know of her plans, any more than Carl Delaney was to know of her tests. But it was time she put a face on the man, met him in person and assured him of her many outstanding talents. He'd been a tantalising blur for quite a while now, ever since she'd chanced on his website . . . not that he was ever going to find out how she'd happened on that. Surfing the net one day, dreading what Dr Richards might be going to disclose, she'd been drawn to its name: www.waytogo.com. And there, instead of finding what she'd been looking for, she'd discovered that the *WayToGo* was a boat, heading off on an adventure cruise, skippered by one Carl Delaney, who needed a cook to feed the crew.

He'd sounded great on the internet, said she sounded great too, just the kind of person they were looking for, adventurous and lively, yet organised and businesslike. Provided they got on well when they met in person, the job was hers, which to Lauren meant it already was. Carl Delaney would be no more able to resist her charms than any other man had ever been.

He answered his phone and the meeting was soon fixed: pub lunch tomorrow at the Chocolate Bar. Lauren hadn't been in Dublin for ages and her heart lifted at the thought of it, the welcome prospect of bright city lights again, even if only fleetingly glimpsed. Undoubtedly all this country air had done her good and she had in many ways come round to its benefits, but still . . . there were times when it smelled of *manure*. Now that she was going to be in town, she might as well take the chance of popping in to David Marshall and getting her hair done before meeting Carl. Her highlights urgently needed retouching.

Next, Eoin Kilroy. Briefly, Lauren braced herself before dialling her parents' number, wondering what she'd say if Betty answered. What *did* you say, to a mother who didn't even know you'd been ill and could not therefore participate in the joy, the relief of a good prognosis? Not, perhaps, that the prognosis was indefinitely good, but it was good for long enough to put the whole issue on the back burner. Lauren didn't propose to think about hep C again for as long as the subject could possibly be avoided. Tomorrow, as good old Scarlett would say, was another day. One that would, hopefully, take care of itself.

But, undoubtedly, she'd had a bad fright. Bad enough that she wanted now to rescue whatever she could of her relationship with her parents – which boiled down, basically, to Eoin. It saddened her that things should be thus, but there was no point in wasting any more precious time on Betty, whom even Saiv recognised to be a lost cause. In fact, now that she thought about it, Saiv had in many ways almost *become* her mother, caring for her in ways that Betty never had. Betty had an attitude problem, and that, ultimately, would remain Betty's problem. Mulling it over, Lauren felt regret, coupled with a certain coldness. But that was no reason to lose Eoin as well.

However, it was Betty who answered. Lauren steeled herself.

'Hello, Mother, how are you?'

Betty said she was very well, hoped her daughter was too?

Yes, very well, considering. Better than you'll ever know, because there's so much you don't want to know. So much I could tell you, would love to tell you, if only we'd ever been able to communicate. But we haven't, and we're never going to have any Hollywood-type reconciliation; if there's one thing I've learned in this life it's to face facts when there's no altering them. If you worked at Axis, if we had a business relationship I'd *sack* you.

'I'm great, thanks.'

But still not back at work, no? Still jeopardising your career, taking time off to goof off on this crazy––?

'Yes, still goofing off. Is Dad around, by any chance?'

Yes, Betty said, Eoin was there, would Lauren like her to give him a message?

'No thanks. I'd like a word with him in person actually.'

Oh? About anything in particular?

'Nooo . . . nothing much. Just put him on, please?'

Thwarted in what Lauren suddenly recognised as her eternal quest to know everything, control everyone, Betty went off to fetch her husband, and Eoin came on the line.

'Lauren? How are you, dear?'

Lauren thought he sounded touchingly concerned, and somehow hopeful. 'I'm fine thanks, Dad. I'm just calling to firm up our drinks date, down at your pub?'

Oh yes, Eoin said, he was looking forward to that. But . . . well . . . maybe he should bring Betty along too, if there was to be no Sunday lunch?

Lauren braced herself. 'No, Dad, please . . . I hope you don't mind, but I'd rather you and I had a chat by ourselves. Just the two of us.'

Well – if she insisted, was sure – but—?

'I'm quite sure. Mother doesn't like pubs, and anyway I – I'd like to talk to you. On your own. You don't have to do everything with Mother, do you?'

Sounding as if it had never occurred to him before, Eoin conceded that no – no, he didn't actually. Very well then, eight o'clock at Byrne's?

'Perfect. Looking forward to it. 'Bye, Dad.'

There was equal affection in his own adieux, and as Lauren clicked off she thought of him with a kind of amused warmth. Probably he'd toss and turn until he saw her, wondering what it was all about – while Betty, undoubtedly, would wonder even more. But Betty, if she wanted in on the new terms of this filial relationship, would have to do more than merely wonder. Lauren would never slam the door on her, but neither would she hold it open for her to sail through. If Betty wanted entry, she would have to nudge the door open for herself, inch by inch. It was a pity, but at least Eoin could be salvaged, and half a loaf was better than no bread. Betty was the kind of mother you could try to please till Doomsday, without ever succeeding. What made people like her the way they were? Was it a genetically cold streak, or was it some warped chilly relationship with her own mother, or what? Lauren had no idea, but she was distinctly sure of one thing: henceforth, she wanted warmth in her life. Some kind of giving, caring warmth, the kind Saiv normally radiated.

Was that what was wrong with Saiv, in fact, today? Was she upset that, soon, she would have nobody to care for any more? Turning it over in her mind, it seemed to her that perhaps this was possible, that maybe Saiv had got used to having a recipient for her naturally generous nature, an outlet for all her frustrated affections. Well, that couldn't go on forever; much as Lauren appreciated all her help and concern, it was time now that each of them stood on their own two feet again. And time, too, that Saiv received in turn some tiny modicum of all she had given. Without hesitation, Lauren picked up the phone again and keyed in yet another number.

Jesus. Saiv would kill her for doing it, so it had better work. It *would* bloody well work. Lauren prided herself on being able to read a man like a book, and she had definitely read all the signs in Vittorio Scalzini. Shyly, but distinctly, he had looked at Saiv the way a man *did* look, when he liked what he saw. His subsequent silence was a mystery, but there must be some reason for it, and Lauren was determined to disclose whatever that reason might be. Without even knowing his name at the time, she had promised Saiv this man, and you didn't renege on promises to someone as good, as honest and trustworthy as Saiv Lovett.

It was lunchtime, and there was every Italian chance that he would be at home. Only please, Lauren prayed as the phone rang, don't let him be at home with some other woman, don't let me discover that he's been happily partnered all the time. He can't be, or he wouldn't have had those big brown eyes for Saiv. I wouldn't be doing this if I didn't reckon the odds were good; I've often gambled in business on no firmer basis than body language, and it's always paid off. Well – ninety per cent of the time, anyway.

'*Pronto?*'

Yes! He's at home! Great! 'Hello, Vittorio? This is Lauren

Kilroy, in Ireland – you remember, we met one day in Urbino and had dinner with you that night?'

'*Ma* – yes, of course I remember. How are you, Lauren?'

Fractionally, Lauren hesitated. Instantly, politely, he was switching to English, but did his tone sound a little guarded? She thought it did. 'I'm very well, thank you. But I'm calling because we were wondering how *you* are. We haven't heard from you at all – I hope we didn't do anything to upset you?'

Carefully, she kept her tone light, almost playful, and spoke in the plural – *we* are wondering, Vittorio, both Saiv and I. There was a slight, reticent pause.

'Well, no, of course you did not – but apparently *I* did something to upset *you*.'

He was that kind of man, she guessed, frank, unable to blithely dissemble. But what on earth did he mean?

'You upset us – Saiv and me? How could you have done that?'

'I failed to get the opera tickets for – for your friend. I am very sorry, but it was impossible.'

'The opera tickets? Oh, Vittorio – they were such a long shot, at such short notice! It was very kind of you to have even tried.'

'I did my best. Please tell Saiv I am sorry she was disappointed.'

'She was sorry too. But not so much about the tickets . . . more that she would have liked to see you again. And Urbino – she fell in love with it, you know!'

Steady, Lauren. Not too much, too fast. Just enough to tantalise.

There was another pause, vaguely puzzled. 'Did she? That was what I thought, at the time. But then she – she did not come back. She did not even return my phone call.'

'Your phone call? But – Vittorio, she said it was your daughter who called.'

'Yes. My daughter Gina, because I had to go out in a hurry – I asked Gina just to let Saiv know that the tickets were unavailable, but to please call me back if she would like to come anyway.'

'What?'

'So, when I did not hear from her, I assumed she was not interested in coming for any other reason than the opera. I must have misunderstood her interest in – in Italy.'

Slowly, assembling the pieces of the picture, Lauren exhaled into the phone. Could this possibly be what it was starting to dawn on her it might be?

'But – Vittorio, Gina didn't tell Saiv the latter half of your message. The part about coming over anyway, tickets or not. All she got was a message via your daughter, that you sent your apologies, which she – she interpreted as a rebuff. She felt she'd been a nuisance, and didn't want to be one again by ringing you back.'

A much longer silence, suddenly: one in which she could almost hear the cogs turning in his head. When he finally spoke again, it was in the low sheltered tone of a man who feared being overheard.

'Oh, *dio mio*. For an interpreter, I seem to have made a very bad job of this communication. Perhaps we had better start over again, from the beginning.'

'Yes. I think maybe we had. Do I understand that you would have liked to see Saiv, even without going to the opera?'

'Yes. I would. Very much. And now, may I ask you a question in turn?'

'Certainly.'

'Would Saiv, do you think, have liked to see me?'

'Yes. I think she would. I have reason to believe that.'

'Then – then Lauren, I am very glad you have made this phone call. And I think I had better explain something to you.'

Lauren thought she could probably guess what it was. But, waiting, she said nothing.

'My daughter, Gina – she is a very sweet girl.'

'I'm sure she is.'

'But she – she is a little – how shall I put this? She is a little over-protective, at times, of her papa. She still remembers her mother, and misses her acutely.'

'Yes. I remember you telling us that.'

'So, it can be – a little problem, for her and also for me. She does not like any other woman to come near her papa, even to talk to him. Her mother is sacred to her and she guards her memory like a soldier. It is the cause of some difficulty between us – which is why I remain unmarried! Clearly she has – um – edited the message I sent to Saiv.'

Unexpectedly Lauren was seized with a pang of some sharp emotion. What an awful thing Gina had done – and yet, how wonderful to love your mother so fiercely!

'It would seem that she has. But Vittorio – don't be too hard on her, please? She's probably just turning into adolescence, all mixed up—'

'*Sì*. It is my view that she truly needs a mother, now more than ever, yet she rejects – Lauren, I have to tell you that she is not an easy child. My son Michele, now there is a nice boy. But Gina . . .'

He sighed aloud, and Lauren laughed. 'Is a handful?'

'Yes. Sometimes I am almost in despair. But today, you have made me feel much better. And today, if it is not too much trouble, perhaps you will do something else for me also?'

'Of course.'

'You will tell Saiv all this, what has happened? You will give her the part of my message she did not receive?'

'Yes. Indeed I will, and if you like I'll get her to call you tonight.'

'Thank you. That would be wonderful – if she is not too discouraged by my dreadful daughter, I would love to hear from her.'

'You will. She's out right now with her animals, but stand by! About nine o'clock, your time?'

'*Perfetto*. I will be waiting, and arrange that Gina is not here. Thank you very much for this, Lauren.'

Elated, she grinned into the phone. 'It's a pleasure, Vittorio. Ciao for now.'

They hung up, and Lauren sat back, nakedly delighted with herself. Now there was a good day's work! Saiv probably thought she'd been lazing around doing nothing, but she'd have to eat her words when she heard about this. She was going to be thrilled, and Lauren was thrilled for her; even if Vittorio came with what sounded like a very difficult, determined daughter, at least he was, after all, available.

Available and, by the sound of him, interested. Very interested. There had almost been an element of camouflaged desperation in his voice, and Lauren recognised it, liked that in a man. Unwittingly Saiv had managed to treat him mean, and that was how you kept the bastards keen. Hopefully Vittorio was not a bastard, but increasingly Lauren was forced to the conclusion that most men were. Even the delightful Shane Jackson, given half a chance, would have . . . but he had not got the chance, and Lauren was pleased to think that she might, at last, be learning something.

'Sweet God! Could you not even have thrown some pasta in a pot? Do I have to do every last little thing myself? I'm out slaving all day—'

'Voluntarily.'

'Slaving! Filthy, exhausted, bitten by a bloody goat, and this is what I come back to! You are the most thoughtless, selfish, useless – I don't know why I *bother* with you! The sooner you trek off to Turkey the better! I need my space and you're clogging it *up*!'

With a violent slam of the door, Saiv stormed off to shower, leaving Lauren both amused and bemused. Admittedly she hadn't got round to cooking anything, but she had opened a bottle of the wine she no longer drank, to breathe entirely for Saiv's benefit – was that not thoughtful, or what? Hopefully Saiv would cheer up after a nice soothing shower, especially on the day that was in it — surely she couldn't deliberately be ignoring the date? Besides, she was a much better cook, there was no point in dabbling in things you'd only make a mess of and then get eaten for having tried. If Saiv wanted to let off steam, fine — Lauren was used to explosions in the office, over things that had nothing to do with the ostensible catalyst — but please let it blow over soon.

Saiv needs Vittorio, she thought; today's handiwork isn't a moment too soon. Meanwhile, I'll have a stab at rustling up a salad, after all I am supposed to feed the crew on this boat next week.

Eventually Saiv returned, still looking mutinous. Lauren smiled brightly.

'Feeling better?'

'No.'

She glowered darkly, and Lauren pulled back hastily: maybe she'd better save her news of Vittorio up for dessert.

'Lauren, you don't *chop* lettuce, you tear it.'

'Really? Oh, here then, why don't you do it. You're the expert.'

'Yeah. So I get to do everything. Take the eggs out of the fridge and I'll make a fucking omelette.'

Lauren laughed aloud. It was a rare joy to hear the saintly Saiv swearing like a sapper.

'Here you are. No need to beat them, one look will do it. Meanwhile, why don't you have a glass of this excellent Amarone I have selected for madam's delectation?'

Grudgingly, Saiv accepted the offered glass, and glared into it. 'How much did this cost, and who or what is paying for it?'

'My bank manager has been permitted the pleasure. Chill out, Saiv, if you don't feel like cooking we can always order in a—'

'Lauren, in case you hadn't noticed, this is the *country*! Chinese takeaways and pizzerias do not bloom on every ditch! The nearest one is in Navan and it charges a fortune to deliver — which is why we're having a blasted omelette, OK?'

'God, you fret so much about money, for someone who isn't interested in it. Anyway, you'll soon be back at work, earning a steady salary again.'

Yes. That was another thing on Saiv's long list of woes, this evening; back at work, soon. Steady, sensible Saiv. Seizing a whisk in one hand and the eggs in the other, she cracked them viciously into a bowl and proceeded to beat them senseless. Idly, Lauren sat down at the table to watch.

'So. Tough day out on the ranch, huh?'

'Yes. On top of your complete lack of consideration.'

'And your PMT, or whatever is eating you.'

'Nothing is eating me, apart from—'

'Apart from your terminally ill friend who, now that her future has brightened up again, you actually wish would bog off and die, after all.'

Saiv gasped, her face whitening as it jerked up. 'Lauren *Kil*roy! Don't say that!'

'Why not? I can see that my welcome is running out and I can see why it would. I have taken up a great deal of your time and space, I have imposed myself mercilessly upon your generosity, and now the time has come for me to waltz off into the sunset. It's OK, Saiv, I'm not taking offence. *Au contraire*. You are perfectly right. You're a very private person and I'm a space invader. A very lucky one, to have been tolerated for so long. You have no idea how grateful I am, and always will be.'

Saiv banged a frying pan onto the hob and hurled the eggs into it. 'Don't talk nonsense. I only did what any—'

'What most people wouldn't do in a fit. What my own mother wouldn't do unless a gun was put to her head, amidst endless inquisition, nagging and lecturing. What my other friends wouldn't do without having the news out all over the country – hey, guess what Lauren's lover did to her! What Jordan White would never have done, for all his pretty promises. You're one in a million and I—'

'And you couldn't even make a bloody bite of dinner.'

'Yes, well, I do have other talents. And I have been busy.'

'Really? Doing what, may I ask?'

'Tell you later, after you've eaten and downed a few more glasses of that wine.'

Lifting her glass, Saiv stared suspiciously into it. 'What's that supposed to mean? You're trying to get me drunk, is that it, before springing some hideous surprise on me? You poisoned the dogs while I was out – ordered a sun bed – wide-screen tv – Jesus, don't tell me you *tidied* my *desk*?!'

'I never laid a finger on it! Come on Saiv, let's enjoy our meal and relax.'

'I'm perfectly relaxed.'

Yeah. Right. You're about as relaxed, Lauren thought, as a steel girder. You're exhibiting every one of the symptoms of a crabbed old crone who hasn't . . . well, maybe I haven't either, lately, but it hasn't been *that* long. We're not talking millennia, in my case.

Defensively, Saiv sat down eventually to eat, leaving Lauren to talk about Carl Delaney and the Turkish trip, her demeanour conveying that it couldn't begin soon enough for her. Aware of the vibes but deflecting them, Lauren chatted blithely on, unwilling to disclose the sharp tingle she was experiencing. This evening, Saiv unexpectedly, but definitely, seemed to want to be rid of her.

Finally, after pouring her another glass of Amarone to go with the chilly looking cheese, Lauren drew breath and embarked on her mission.

'Well – guess who I called today?'

'I neither know nor care, so long as it wasn't on my phone at my expense.'

'No, actually it wasn't. I – um – I bought a new mobile.'

Half pleased, half quaking, Lauren produced the offending object and Saiv glared at it in disgust. 'I see. Lovely. Now you can natter on round the clock about all the trivia in creation.'

'I'll need it when I go to Turkey. A phone will be indispensable. But that's not the point.' God, was Saiv's opinion of her really that low?

'Oh? So what is the point?'

'The – the point is that I called Vittorio Scalzini.'

There was a long, long silence. Stunned, stricken, it seemed to emanate from within Saiv's suddenly glacial core, freeze the very air around them. When at last she spoke, her face and low voice were arctic.

'You what?'

'I phoned Vittorio. Just to say hi. But as it turned out—'

'Jesus!' Saiv's palm slammed down on the table, her face flared with fury. 'I don't believe this! I told you not to interfere, Lauren, I *told* you *not* to!'

'Yes, I know, but I thought—'

'It wasn't your business to think! It was *my* decision, not yours!'

Her stance was such that Lauren cringed involuntarily, dodging the wine she thought was about to be thrown over her. 'Saiv, would you calm down and just listen! There's been a misunderstanding! His daughter never—'

Flinging back her chair, Saiv stood up, threw her plate at the wall and watched for the split second it took to smash to splinters. Then, with a cry halfway between a sob and a shriek, she flew out of the room so fast that it seemed to Lauren her feet never touched the floor. Two seconds later, the quivering silence detonated with the sound of her bedroom door slamming off its hinges. Aghast, Lauren sat transfixed, unable to believe the shortness of the fuse to which she had unwittingly touched a match. Clearly Saiv had been taken with Vittorio from the start, but – but *this*?

Nonplussed, she waited for the dust to settle. And then, into the seething vacuum, she shouted after her: 'Saiv! Listen to me! Gina only gave you half the message, because she doesn't want any new woman in her father's life – but he wants to see you! You're to phone him at nine his time, he's waiting to talk to you!'

No answer. Over the next hour Lauren tried again, several times, knocked in vain on the locked door, but nine o'clock came and went without response.

OCTOBER

It was a cold morning, with a sharply autumnal edge to it, when Saiv emerged from her room next morning, looking exactly like the distraught harridan she felt. Sleepless, alternately tearful and incandescently angry, she had tossed as if on a bed of nettles, assimilating the audacity of what Lauren had done, wrestling her will to believe the shouted messages through the door.

Vittorio Scalzini did *not* want to see her. If he did, he would have contacted her in person long ago, never relayed all these remote communiqués through either his daughter or Lauren Kilroy. It was a ploy on Lauren's part, she was sure, yet another of the ruses she so artfully deployed to manipulate people – the *lies*, that she so cutely dismissed as 'little porkies'. Only this was no 'little porky', it was a whopper of unforgivable dimensions, one for which she would never speak to Lauren again.

How could Lauren, after all she'd done for her, have exposed her to such an agonising situation? Did she honestly think that, just because she was so shallow herself, everyone else was too, had no depth of feeling whatsoever? Had it never for one moment dawned on her that people were not her personal playthings, that people could get *hurt*? If she had done what Lauren wanted, fallen into the trap that had been set for her, she would not only have made an utter idiot of herself in the eyes of

Vittorio Scalzini, but suffered the agony of hearing him say no, he had no idea what this was all about, why was this Irish leech of a woman contacting him yet again? Whereupon, Saiv knew with certainty, she would have expired in utter mortification, in the sheerest misery. Would, arguably, have run down to the river and thrown herself in.

But of course Lauren saw it differently. Lauren thought all she had to do was throw the two of them together and – presto! – wedding bells would ring out in Verona tomorrow morning. Lauren thought that, because everything always turned out fine for her, it would on her mere whim turn out fine for everyone. Lauren, endowed as she was with such wealth of beauty and confidence, had no *idea* how it felt to go through life without possession of either.

Lauren was a perfect *bitch*.

Wretchedly, clutching her towelling robe around her, Saiv trudged into the kitchen and went, on auto pilot, to make a pot of tea. Her interest in the new day – the new month according to the calendar – was nil, but the dogs had to be let out, let back in, fed and watered. Alone amongst all the creatures on this earth, they were the only ones to be trusted, to give or to receive the slightest modicum of affection. Wearily, she patted their heads and opened the door; but, sensing her mood as Lauren had never done, they loped rather than bounded out, looking quizzical.

So. Sunday. October first. In three more days, college would open and she would be back at her post, Dr Lovett, present and correct. Good morning young man, and what is your name? Howya, I'm Sid, just doin' yer course until I get into bleedin' commerce. (And a right old bag you look.)

Vittorio! Suddenly the thought of him hit her like a hammer, so hard and fast she clutched the worktop, almost swaying under its force. In her inner ear his voice resounded, richly Mediterranean; in her mind his warm, articulate words reverberated; on her heart his image stamped itself indelibly, heavy as lead. And through all this the Italian sun rose, diffusing its rays far across the vista of what might have been, illuminating a life she knew would never be – had never been – within her grasp. Fleetingly, searingly, she had an urge to snatch up the breadknife and slash her wrists.

The kettle boiled, and as she poured from it the scalding water splashed her hand, its hot pain welcome, beneficially shocking. She must find some Vaseline for the burn, pull herself together. There was a jar, as she dully recollected, in the drawer of the kitchen table.

The liniment was in the drawer, but she never retrieved it, never applied it; instead she stood mesmerised, staring at a piece of paper under the fruit bowl, a note in Lauren's airily sprawling hand. For several moments, she was unable to read it, not because it was illegible but because her eyes refused to focus. Pulling her spectacles from her pocket, she put them on, thinking that her eyes were going, as soon all the rest of her would start to go.

Saiv—

I'm so sorry. Please forgive me. I went about the whole thing with all the sensitivity of a bull in a china shop. I am a thoughtless klutz and it's no wonder you're not speaking to me.

But I didn't lie. Please believe that. For once I told the whole, unvarnished truth. Vittorio does want to see you, only his daughter doesn't, and if you get in touch with him – now! this minute! – you'll be forearmed with the knowledge that she's hostile to you. It's an obstacle, but don't let it be insurmountable.

Thank you again for everything you've done for me. I deserved none of it, but I love you for all of it.

Lauren.

Bewildered, Saiv dropped the note and whirled round. What – why was Lauren writing to her, when she was sleeping in the bedroom next door, they would see each other any minute? But, even as she hastened to it, some sinking intuition told her what she was going to find: an empty, carefully stripped bed. The room was hollow, Lauren was gone.

But –! Dashing to the bathroom, she raced into it, and it was denuded too, all the jars, all the lotions and potions vanished except for one, apparently overlooked by Lauren in her stealthy speed. Despite thinking that she had not slept, Saiv realised that she must have briefly at least, because she had heard none of this. Rebuffed and chastened, Laurie had crept away like a thief in the night, taking her laughing, maddening friendship with her. Desperately Saiv ripped open the curtains, and the drive disclosed only one car, her own decrepit Citroën, no longer embarrassed by Laurie's shiny, state-of-the-art vehicle.

Slowly, her head spinning and her heart thundering, she returned to the kitchen, picked up the note again and sat staring at it, unseeing. As if from a million miles away, it shouted at her to get up – 'now!' – and go to the phone, call Vittorio, accept everything it was saying to her. Accept that there were, against all her suspicions, despite all her disbelief, at least two people in the world who did, after all, care about her. There was Lauren Kilroy and there was – incredibly – Vittorio Scalzini.

Was there? Was that possible? It must be . . . Vittorio didn't just want to talk to her, Lauren said, he wanted to *see* her. In the flesh, plenty of it as there was; it seemed a more remote possibility than she could ever get her head around. Only – only Lauren wouldn't lie, not like this, in writing, when she already felt covered in guilt. The note had a ring of utter truth about it.

Where was Lauren? A sudden electric charge shot up Saiv's spine, and she stiffened like a pointer, seeking her quarry out of its burrow. Where could she have gone to ground? Not with her parents – she never stayed under Betty's roof – not with her friend Gemma, who had a family and no space to spare. Her other friend, perhaps, Adèle? Adèle what, what was her second name? Goddamn, that she couldn't remember! And Goddamn it entirely to hell, that she had not asked Lauren her new mobile number! If only she had, she thought with wretched irony, she could contact her now within seconds.

Surely . . . surely not Shane Jackson? No. The old Laurie might have gone to him, accepted whatever compromising refuge he could offer, but the new one hardly would. Besides, Shane was married, his wife would certainly query a gorgeous brunette turning up on their doorstep. Sitting immobile, Saiv tried to marshal her wits and think it through.

But rational thought eluded her completely; instead feelings flooded through her, terrible, guilty feelings about her horrible behaviour last night, her mean spirit, her childish tantrum, her persistent silence and hostility. I have been, she saw with clarity, a graceless, nasty, hateful *witch*. Now I've lost my best friend, and I deserve to lose her. She was only trying her best, and I—

Oh, Jesus! Appalled, Saiv clutched her throat as an even worse thought hit her, the worst, most appalling offence of all: after all Laurie had been through, all she had endured and survived, she had forgotten what date yesterday was. September 30, the last day of summer, and Laurie's birthday. The day they had promised themselves they would celebrate with such joy if Laurie lived to see it; and miraculously she had lived to see it. But they had not celebrated. They had quarrelled, and parted in enmity – one-sided enmity, exclusively on Saiv Lovett's side. Laurie, had she held a grudge, would not have written this note.

Overcome with the horror of it, swamped in self-recrimination, Saiv let the note slide from her hand, unable even to think any more of Vittorio much less tackle him. Having driven away one person she loved, she could not go now in pursuit of another; not when Lauren was out there somewhere, driving alone through the dawn, feeling so hurt, so rejected, as she surely must be feeling. And all because she had tried to help.

I don't deserve her, Saiv swore vehemently. I am incapable of handling any relationship of any description, and I don't deserve *any*one. That's the first thing I'm going to tell her, when I find her.

Where is she? Where *is* she?

It was difficult, alone in the car with a Bob Dylan track mournfully playing on the radio, to deny the bleak sense of betrayal that washed through Lauren as she drove into Dublin, feeling as she had done only twice before in her life: when Isaac Hyland dumped her and when Jordan White duped her. They'd been men, with a sexual agenda, but – stupidly? naïvely? – she'd always felt women were different, especially when they'd been friends as long as she and Saiv Lovett had been.

Rationalising, refusing to let emotion cloud her vision, she could understand some of what Saiv had said and done. She could see why Saiv might be feeling put upon after having furnished care and shelter for so long; why she might resent the imbalance between the attention they were proportionately exchanging; why she'd be grouchy about having to resume a job she didn't enjoy, and, especially, why she was so upset about Vittorio, the only man on her horizon in an arid desert.

That much made sense. Her home had been colonised and she'd had to look after two people instead of one, was unused to sharing and impatient with someone who, admittedly, was more of an ornament than a contributor. Accustomed as she was to assessing business situations, Lauren readily acknowledged all of these factors, could even smile at some of them. But . . . the crack about the phone, about using it to 'natter on about trivia round the clock' . . . that stung. Did Saiv really think her so superficial, such a feeble airhead? And then the comment about not running up bills on the landline – amongst all her faults, Lauren would not have thought she had ever been mean. On the contrary, she flung money around like confetti, had provided the wine Saiv had been drinking even as she made the remark, had fallen over herself making sure she chipped in more than fairly to the household budget.

But, above all, it was the birthday. Logically, there was no reason to remember each other's birthdays in their thirties, but logic had never come into it before. They'd always made a point of remembering and giving each other gifts, gifts that sometimes spoke volumes. Always, Lauren had had the feeling that Saiv gave her things intended to somehow *improve* her – books she'd never read, music she'd never otherwise listen to – and Saiv was the only person who got away with doing that. She set high standards, and in recent months Lauren had formed the impression that at last she was beginning tentatively to rise to them, to slowly evolve into a better person than she'd been before.

Well, that wouldn't be difficult! She was aware of her shortcomings, aware also that she'd always fall shy of Saiv's lofty ideals, but she thought she'd at least been trying. Had definitely been trying, because her illness had shed light on numerous new ways of looking at things. And yet here was Saiv dismissing all her efforts, ignoring her birthday as if to say 'oh, forget it, I can't be bothered with you any more.' That was the part that really hurt, and try as she might Lauren couldn't accept that Saiv might have simply forgotten the date; she'd never forgotten it before, and she kept note of everything in her leather diary in true professorial style. Her house might be cluttered, but her mind never had been.

Well, then. It was better to get out of Saiv's house, out of her face and out of her life for a while. Better to leave quietly without any big dramatic scene about it, and let Saiv simmer down in her own time. Maybe, if she believed the note on the kitchen table and acted on it, she'd discover through Vittorio that no lies had been told, that all had been done in good faith and good friendship.

But *would* she contact him? Or would she sit there persuading herself, as usual, that no man could ever want her? Of all Saiv's habits Lauren found this one the most exasperating, her perpetual need to be convinced to do things, to believe that they could go right, to be smacked and shaken till her teeth rattled. There were times when Lauren yearned for a cattle prod.

Pondering it, feeling both upset and enraged, she gritted her teeth as she came into Dublin's early traffic, reached for her bag to get her lipstick and brighten her face. She felt like crying but she wasn't going to cry, she was going to get her hair done and then meet Carl Delaney looking like a girl who hadn't a care in the world. He wouldn't want to spend six weeks cooped up on a boat with a moaning Minnie, wouldn't take anyone weepy on such a daunting voyage. He wasn't to know that she now needed as well as wanted to go on it, because – of all the ludicrous things – she was effectively homeless. Of course Adèle would put her up if asked, but then she'd have an awful lot of explaining to do to Adèle about why she'd been incommunicado for so long, why she'd rented out her apartment . . . it might be better just to check into the Morrison for the few nights before the yacht sailed, and worry about the Visa bill later. As for the stuff she'd left at Saiv's house – well, she'd cleared out the bathroom and wardrobe, surely Saiv wouldn't dump her few bits of bric-à-brac out in the field?

Reaching town and finding parking eventually, Lauren ditched the car and headed off with her head held high. She didn't believe in going to even the most discreet of hairdressers looking anything other than up, up, up. And besides, when you made the effort to look good you could sometimes find yourself actually feeling good. When she treated herself to a few tears over Saiv it would be later tonight, in private.

After a few futile hours, Saiv gave up. She was wasting her time trying to concentrate on her book, and anyway it was as finished as it was ever going to be. No point in tweaking at it until Doomsday. From here on in it was the publishers' baby, out in the world where it would just have to make its own way.

And yet, when it was finally despatched in a flurry, she felt no satisfaction. She felt the anxiety of a mother sending her child off on its first trip to school, where it might be bullied or beaten or, worse, dismissed as hopeless. Pacing round the kitchen table, she drank several cups of tea, sat down, stood up, sat down again and eventually acknowledged the truth: she felt bereft of her baby.

God, the house was so quiet, without Laurie! Even Duster and Elmer seemed to have picked up on her absence, were lying forlorn on the floor as if missing her. Well – enough of this. They couldn't lie around moping like damp dishcloths all day. She'd take them out on a long walk and it would do everyone good.

But it didn't. The faster she walked, down long country lanes and round the edges of the farmers' fields, the faster her mind flew, racing in circles like the dogs. *Where* had Laurie gone? Where was she going to sleep tonight? Would she remember to take her medication and eat fruit, get vitamins? Would she phone, get in touch to divulge her whereabouts at least, or was she sulking somewhere, grieving, hurting? Would she ever even speak to her again?

At first Saiv determined not to fret. It was only a silly row, it would blow over, Lauren's sunny nature could be relied upon to prevail. In the interim she'd drop in on her friend Jennifer and have a chat, after all the entire planet did not revolve around Lauren Kilroy, there were other people on it. Maybe she'd even do what Lauren had been suggesting for ages and go to the beauty salon in the village this afternoon, have a facial or – something.

But when she reached Jennifer's house, about four miles from her own, she did not go in. For some completely obscure reason she walked right past it, and was halfway home before she figured out why: if she told Jennifer what had happened, Jennifer might say, well, is it any wonder, your friend tried to help you with this Italian man and you flew right in her face, naturally she's furious with you? You're prickly as a cactus, Saiv Lovett, it's a miracle Lauren ever put up with you for as long as she did. Now she's seen the light and washed her hands of you.

Oh, God. Saiv felt she could walk forty miles, fifty, walk to Canada and back without exorcising the guilt and misery gnawing at her – Lauren's birthday, above all! The special day that had nothing to do with ageing, in which neither of them believed, but with surviving, achieving, *growing*. Lauren had done all of those things in the past year, only to receive a slap in the face for her pains, no recognition, no celebration. She'd been left on her own all day yesterday, while her oldest friend went about her own business, came home in a filthy mood and took it all out on her – while she'd been playing Cupid, to boot.

I *am* an old boot, Saiv muttered as she strode along, indifferent for once to the loveliness of the autumn landscape, to the golden hay in the fields and the friendly farmers out on their tractors, the gulls wheeling low in the rock-grey sky for scraps. I can understand the nature of human existence perfectly well in a book, on paper, but I can't handle it for five minutes in person, in reality. I shouldn't be let *out*.

Vittorio would hate me, if he knew what I'm like. He has no idea what a narrow squeak he had. He seemed to have such a sweet nature but I'd have soured it for him in no time, he'd have gone mad living with the likes of me. He'd never have sung another note, except maybe at my funeral after he'd throttled me. No jury would convict him.

Could it possibly be true, what Lauren said about his daughter not having told me his full message? Did he really want me to go back to Italy, without the pretext of the opera? That was Lauren's idea too . . . she really did do her best to help us, to get us together. For all the thanks she got.

Would she forgive me, if I tried to make it up to her now by doing what she wanted? If I somehow summoned the courage to phone that man, risk whatever rebuff or difficulties might be looming? If his daughter is as tricky as she sounds, she might hang up on me, or not give her father my full message in turn. She might . . . if I got as far as going to see Vittorio, she might cause major trouble, not only for me but for him.

To push the scenario to its limits, Gina Scalzini could be a serious obstacle, a long-running bone of contention between her father and myself. Or, on the other hand, she might be just a lost little girl, with all the potential in her that Gráinne has, if I could only draw it out of her, convince her that I don't aspire to take her mother's place . . . do I?

Do I? No. Not now. Right now the only thing I dare do – if even that much – is maybe phone and say hello to her father, apologise for not having phoned when apparently I was supposed to. He'll think I'm rude and unreliable, apart from everything else. And, since I don't want to start off with a lie, I'll have to tell the truth, explain that I was busy having a row with Laurie. That'll sound endearing, all right.

Is he the forgiving type? Well, here's my chance to find out. At least he'll know from the start that I'm no picnic. And I'll know whether he is capable of overlooking my – my stupidity. If either he or Laurie ever pardons me, I'll try to be a nicer person in future.

She will. She must. By the time she gets in touch I'll be able to tell her that, apart from being abjectly sorry about her birthday and the awful things I said, I've also done what she wanted me to do, had a bit of backbone for a change. God, I'll even get on a plane, *fly* to Italy if need be. I can't keep on wimping out for the rest of my life – especially not now that we both know how short life can suddenly threaten to be. She's making the most of hers and I must make the most of mine.

All right. I will. I'll do it. I'll ring him this evening at a time when he's likely to be home with his kids. I'll come clean and admit that yes, I'd love to see him. Which, after all, is no more than the truth. I really would . . . if only he gives me the slightest encouragement. If he does that, then I'll allow myself to believe the truth of what I kept so blithely telling Laurie: where there's life, there's hope. What a cliché, it must have driven her nuts! But she needed to hear it, and now I need . . .

I need Vittorio. I'm petrified of him, of his daughter, of

risking the safe solitary life that has become my armour, but . . .
it's now or never. I haven't had a chance like this for years and
I'll probably never get one again, never meet anyone as — as
appealing as this man. He's no oil painting but then neither am I,
and besides image has never fascinated me the way it fascinates
Laurie. Appearances matter for nothing compared to what's
underneath, and although I barely scratched Vittorio's surface in
Italy I liked what I found. He's interesting, he's educated,
articulate, generous, and a man who sings the way he sings
has to have depth to him, as well as a romantic streak. Does he
still miss his wife, I wonder? Probably he does . . . there was
something in his face, when he spoke about her. I'll never be his
first love, and I'll never be Gina's mother.

But, if I succumb to the opportunity, grasp it and make the
most of it, maybe I can be *some*body. Some other, warmer,
rounder person, with love and joy in her life, giving and
receiving . . . living, in full, at last?

It's a long shot. But I'm going to give it a try. Lauren Kilroy is
not the only one who can be reborn, reinvent herself. Lauren
Kilroy is . . . is showing me, this fine morning, what life is like
when you have nobody in it, nobody to love. She's only been
gone a matter of hours, and already there's a crater full of empty
space, a hollow echo where she used to be.

I'm going to fill it up. Hopefully with her again, eventually,
but with Vittorio and his children too, if they want me, if they'll
let me. Jean-Jacques Rousseau has gone on his way, and now it's
time to start tackling real people.

'Wow' Carl Delaney whistled with frank delight, 'I wasn't
expecting such a stunner.'

Crossing her legs to best advantage, Lauren allowed him the
benefit of her gleaming smile. 'Thank you.'

'The pleasure's all mine. Though I wonder how ten red-
blooded men are to be kept in check in cramped quarters with a
girl like you around!'

As he took off his coat and sat down opposite her, Lauren made a mental note already: he was one of those men who called women 'girls'. She never took issue with them, but she knew how to handle them. Carl would respond beautifully to a little ego-stroking, she'd wind him round her finger on a silken thread. Even as a sailor, he'd never see his resemblance to a floundering fish.

'Tell me about the red-blooded men, and then I'll tell you about me?' She beamed invitingly, and he nodded agreeably.

'Sure. But first, where's a waitress? Would you like some white wine, perhaps?'

'Thanks, but I don't drink. A Ballygowan would be lovely.'

Approvingly, he nodded again, a haywain's hank of topaz hair falling over his forehead as if off a pitchfork. He was attractive in a confident, chunky way, crisp and solid with lively, clear green eyes. Lauren guessed maybe a company director, or architect or consultant of some kind. Like herself he was in his early thirties, and she put him down as direct and uncomplicated, a rugby fan or maybe still even player. When he ordered their drinks, it was in the easy manner of a well-travelled man, with money and a polished education – the Jesuits? – under his belt.

Steepling his fingers, he sat back and regarded her. 'So, you don't drink, huh? Well, that's good news for a start. The guys all drink like camels at an oasis.'

'I'm sure they do . . . but not on duty. On a trip like this, I'd say it will be a case of work hard and play hard, in that order. Everything in its place, right down to the toothpaste cap.'

'You've got it. Discipline will be the key to us all reaching Turkey intact. Most of them are pretty experienced – oh, and there's one other girl too, by the way, her name is Sara. Her father was on the Irish Olympic team.'

Ah, yes. Daddy's status was assuring Sara's already. Lauren guessed that this crew would be made up of financially sound, gung-ho, middle-class men, enlightened by their own standards, prepared to take on board a token woman with a good sailing pedigree – plus one to cook for them. They'd laugh and call her 'darling' and try to seduce her, brag about succeeding when they failed. With the right attitude, she'd have great craic with them. And, if the weather got rough or the chips were down, they'd be protective, reliable, tough and good-humoured; you didn't get to go sailing at this level unless you'd already proven all those qualities. Not unless you were a pretty girl with equally proven ability to lie through her pearly teeth.

'Tell me about her. About all of them.'

'OK. I'm the skipper, as you know, and I work as an engineer in private practice. Then there's Sara, the youngest, she's a physiotherapist at a sports clinic. The other nine guys are mixed in age, from twenty-five to forty, there's a solicitor, a dentist, a pyschologist, a chef, a freight haulier, an electrician, a golf pro, a pharmacist and a civil servant. We've all been friends, in various combinations, for years, and we're all members of two yacht clubs. This project is for fun, without any competitive element, but naturally it has to be taken seriously.'

'Naturally. But why isn't the chef doing the cooking?'

'Because he wants to get away from cooking! That's where you come in . . . maybe. I do have another appointment with another candidate this afternoon, she's very keen, but . . . tell me about your cooking and sailing experience?'

Lauren tossed back her newly done hair and smiled radiantly. 'Oh, I'm not a professional cook, but my dinner parties are famous' (all catered by Party Planners) 'and I used to sail a Scorpion at college' (Isaac Hyland took me out on his on three sunny days).

'H'mm. Done much sailing since?'

Yes, Lauren thought airily; right through life, pal, right through.

'Oh, lots. But I thought you wanted me to cook, not crew?'

Carl nodded. 'Yes. You won't be called upon to rig the sails or haul sheets or anything, but you'll need your sea-legs. You'll also need, obviously, to take charge of supplies and source fresh produce in a hurry whenever we put into port. Everyone is contributing equally to the budget and your keep will come out of that kitty. No pay, but lots of fun and adventure. I hope you have a sense of humour?'

'I certainly have!' (Anyone living with Saiv Lovett would need one.)

'As for gear – one duffel bag per person, no more. Space is at a premium.'

Lauren thought of her car full of junk. What . . . ? It would just have to stay in it then, parked in Temple Bar for the duration. Thank God she hadn't rented out her space in the garage!

'Right. I'll just bring my lipstick and my mobile phone!'

Carl held up his hand. 'You can bring your mobile, but you can't charge it on board. Between us we have twelve mobiles and they'd eat precious power. So we've decided that mine is the only one we'll use, except when we're in port. That OK?'

Lauren swallowed. Her lovely new mobile! But . . . she had managed without one when Saiv insisted. She'd just have to do it again now.

'Yes, that's fine. Very sensible.'

'Good. So, tell me more about yourself.'

Briskly Lauren told him, emphasising her business experience and the amount of organisation she had to do. Organising food would be a breeze by comparison.

'Indeed. And why do you want to come on this trip?'

She was ready for that. 'Because I'm too young and energetic to stay shut up in an office for the rest of my life! The time off will cost, career-wise, but you have to take chances and opportunities when you get them, don't you?'

She guessed that this was his own philosophy, and was not surprised when he smiled in warmly approving agreement.

'You sure do. Everyone on this trip feels that way. If we decide you're the right person for the job, would you be free to meet us all on Wednesday night? We're having a final planning meeting at the Royal Marine hotel.'

'Absolutely. I'd love to. But, tell me, Carl, why have you left it so late to sign up a cook?'

'We had one, but she dropped out – went and got pregnant on us.'

'Oh, dear. Well, you needn't worry about me doing that!'

He grinned wryly. 'I certainly hope not. Can I take it that you are totally fit, in perfect physical condition?'

She didn't even blink. 'You can indeed. Tip top.'

'Good. Now, let me show you our route, some photos of the boat . . .'

Unfolding paperwork from his briefcase, he got down to details, immersed in the project which, she saw, was very dear to his heart. He was taking leave from his work along with all the others, and she found herself feeling empathy; everyone would be, so to speak, in the same boat. She wasn't the only drop-out. Most of these people, she guessed, had enough money not to have to worry about it for a few months. And maybe the others would be like her, simply flying by the seat of their pants. She was looking forward to meeting them.

'So, any other questions?'

Nearly two hours had gone by, and he had informed her fully. 'No. The only thing I wonder is why you'd consider taking on anyone other than me!'

He laughed, but didn't commit himself. 'Give me your number and I'll call you tomorrow, one way or the other.'

She gave it to him, and turned her parting smile up to full voltage. 'It's been wonderful meeting such an adventurous man, and I'm sure we're all going to have a great time on this voyage!'

Warmly and courteously, he shook her hand with a final thought. 'If we do take you on, be ready to buy all the supplies and have them loaded up by Friday night. High-protein obviously, vitamin-rich, we don't want anyone getting scurvy!'

I'll buy a book, Lauren thought. I'm going out to buy one

right now, and a duffel bag as well. I wonder if Vuitton does a nice one?

Trembling, Saiv lifted the phone, dialled the Italian code and put it down again.

She couldn't do it. Couldn't imagine this crazy call going anywhere beyond polite pointless small talk, the uncomfortable exchange of trivia between two people whose paths had briefly crossed three months ago, and diverged again immediately afterwards. It would all fizzle out.

Lauren's voice rose in her ear. 'And if it does fizzle, so what? At least you'll have tried. You'll know where you stand and be out of your misery.'

Only that's wrong, she thought. I won't be out of it. I will be as wretchedly disappointed as a teenager, as one of those silly girls I teach who are always falling in and out of love. I've never been in love, and now I'm investing this encounter with colossal importance, because it has such huge potential to change my life. It's a time bomb.

It could blow up in my face and leave me permanently scarred. I'm sufficiently attracted to this man that he has the power to do huge damage – or huge good, if by any miracle things did go right. How could they, when we don't even live in the same country? How would we manage the logistics of it? What if I got on well with him, but not with Gina?

What if. That's what Laurie would say: what if there was an earthquake, Saiv, or the Leaning Tower of Pisa fell over, or we were all struck by a thunderbolt? What if I got a reprieve from a fatal illness, what would that teach me – or you, who is already a teacher? Do you only teach, or do you ever learn?

All right! All *right*! I'll do it.

Once the phone was in her hand it felt glued to it, and she waited rooted to the floorboards, vaguely noticing that they needed waxing. Ring, ring, nobody home, thank—

'*Pronto?*'

Her tonsils felt caught in a pincers. 'Hello? Vittorio?' It sounded like the squeak of a rusty hinge, and she winced: he'd think some looper was winding him up.

'Saiv! *Come sta?* How are you?'

I'm in tatters, Vittorio. I'm a nervous wreck, sorry for wasting your time, I'll just say goodbye now.

'I – I'm very well, thank you. I – I'm just calling to apologise – apparently there has been some misunderstanding—'

That's it, Saiv. Start out with an apology, and take it all downhill from there.

'Yes, there has. I am so sorry. I have spoken to Gina about it, and she too is very sorry.'

'Is – is she?'

'Yes, she is. She has understood that what she did was – how do you say it? – was out of line.'

Oh? Saiv was taken aback. It had never occurred to her that Gina might be in trouble for what she had done, that Vittorio could be firm with her. But it sounded as if he had been.

'Oh, I'm sure she meant well. Don't be cross with her.'

'Cross?'

'Angry.'

'But I am angry. She withheld important information and caused a problem for us both. If Lauren had not telephoned . . . but let us forget about it now, and move on.'

Move on? She liked the sound of this: evidently he didn't sulk or harbour grudges. 'Yes. Let's. How have you been since – since last we met?'

'I have been thinking about you! It was such a pleasure to meet a lady who appreciates my country, its art, its food and music . . . I would very much like you to see more of it. When are you thinking of coming back?'

A lady? Saiv was caught off-side. She was a woman, an academic, but surely not a lady, with its ring of feminine delicacy? She was a *person* who, if things hadn't gone awry, would have adored to go back to Italy while she had time, with

Laurie ideally, to hold her hand on that petrifying plane. Now, both Laurie and time were gone. College was about to resume.

'I don't know, Vittorio . . . maybe at Christmas, if it's not too cold and dark then?'

'Christmas?! Yes, it is cold and dark then! You must come sooner, while the evenings still linger a little – what are you doing next weekend?'

Next weekend?! She was stunned, thrown completely. 'I – am starting work, a new term—'

'But not on Saturday, surely, or Sunday? Do you not have two days off, a five-day week in your country? I have been doing some research on Ireland, and—'

'Well, yes, we do work a five-day week. But—'

'But what?'

'Next weekend is – is too soon!'

'Why? Have we not already wasted enough time?'

Good God. He couldn't be *this* keen to see her, surely? Nobody in their right mind could possibly be. Maybe he was a murderer, that was it, eager to lure single women into his clutches, from which they never emerged alive.

Only murderers didn't usually have twelve-year-old daughters living with them, did they, or young sons? Children would get in the way of homicide. And murderers didn't sing the way Vittorio Scalzini sang, with such rich, profound emotion.

'Vittorio, I – I'm not sure – let me think—'

'All right. You will think and I will telephone the airline, book you on a flight and into a nice hotel. Can you get away on Friday night?'

Saiv wondered whether she might be going to faint. He would organise everything, all she had to do was somehow board that plane, and go?

Great, Lauren's voice said in her head. A weekend is just long enough that, if it doesn't work out, no harm is done. And this weekend is so near you'll scarcely have time to fret about flying. Your doctor will give you a sedative. *Arrivederci.*

'I – I—'

'*Va bene*. I will call you back with the details and pick you up at the airport on Friday. I am looking forward to showing you Verona.'

His voice was both eager and decisive, and she strove to sound in command of herself in turn, without entirely disclosing her equal eagerness. She was too old to *throw* herself at him.

'Yes. I'm looking forward to seeing it. If a flight and hotel are available at such short notice——?'

'They will be. Since I failed to get the opera tickets, I will succeed with this! You will be my guest, in my lovely city.'

'Your guest? Oh, Vittorio, no—'

'I insist. You will be mine in Italy, and I shall be yours whenever you ask me to Ireland. I hope you will ask me, some day.'

What was there to say? 'Yes, of course I will, some day!'

'*Benissimo*. Now, let me set about making these calls.'

With what sounded like a laugh – a cheery, optimistic laugh – he was gone, leaving Saiv staring at the dogs. They stared in turn, looking somehow reproachful she thought. Giddily, she grinned at them.

'Well, lads, pack your bags! You're being farmed out for the weekend!'

Suddenly seized with euphoria, she reached automatically for the phone again to tell Lauren this wonderful news. But with a sickening thud she remembered she didn't know where Lauren was, and didn't have her new number.

One comprehensive cookbook and one elegant holdall later, Lauren made her way to Byrne's pub where she was to meet her father, smiling grimly at the irony of it: two pubs in one day, and not a drop to drink! Not a stitch of shopping either. What would be the point, when this voyage only required jeans, sweaters, maybe shorts and T-shirts when they neared Turkey? Besides, she wasn't earning, and a girl in that position could hardly hit Brown Thomas. For the first time in adult memory, economy was called for, and it felt very odd to emerge from Grafton Street having spent less than a hundred pounds. Plus the hairdresser this morning of course, but you could hardly call that a luxury, could you?

Eoin was already in the pub when she arrived, sitting quietly in a corner with a half of lager, and she surveyed him as she went to him, thinking how nearly invisible he looked, just an ageing suburban man in an overcoat, grey compared to the vibrant twenty-somethings in the noisier part of the pub. Jostling her way through them, she reached the back and bent over him, surprised him with a kiss.

'Hi, Dad.'

He smiled with wary pleasure. 'Hello, Lauren. How are you? Let me get you something to drink.'

'Thanks. A coffee would be great.'

He waved at a distant waitress, and was ignored. Hopefully, he tried again, in vain. Stifling a sigh, Lauren sat back.

'Never mind. Someone will come eventually. We're not in any hurry, are we?'

'No. Well, I'm not anyway. But you always seem to be!'

'Do I? Then let's take our time tonight.'

'Yes. Though I did promise Betty—'

'What, that Cinderella would be home by midnight?'

He smiled slightly. 'By ten, actually.'

'Oh, Dad! You probably will be, but what does it *matter*? There isn't a war on, no curfew that I'm aware of.'

'No. But you know your mother.'

Lauren reflected. She was determined, this evening, to have some kind of meaningful conversation with at least one of her parents. 'No, Dad. I don't think I really know her at all actually, and she certainly doesn't know me.'

Startled, looking as though some worst fear had been confirmed, he took an anxious sip from his glass. 'What – what do you mean, Lauren?'

'I mean . . . oh, Dad. I'm so tired of this pretence, of playing happy families when we're no such thing. We don't communicate properly, we – we're dysfunctional, in some weird way. All we've ever talked about for at least the last decade is the weather and the price of eggs.'

He blinked. 'Eggs?'

'Yes, you know, trivia! That's why I wanted to see you this evening. I wanted to find out whether we're never going to have anything more to say to each other, or whether maybe you and I can establish some sort of – of dialogue, with Mother or without her.'

The waitress arrived to save him, but only temporarily. When she whirled away there seemed to be a kind of vortex in her wake, into which he gazed dismayed. 'But, Lauren, I thought – I thought you were happy.'

'I am happy, in my own right, my own life. Lately I've found reason to be happier than ever, depending . . . depending on how you look at things. But I'm not happy with our relationship. It's stagnant, it's empty – pointless, really. I wish you'd stop being polite for at least this one night, and tell me how you really feel, what you really think.'

'A – about what?'

'About us, as a family! I know you miss Caoimhe and we're all looking forward to seeing her at Christmas, but when we do, what are we going to have to say to her? To each other? Will we all go off for another of those glazed, brittle lunches at that ghastly hotel in Howth, will that be the height of family communication?'

'Ghastly hotel?'

'Yes, ghastly! Prim and proper, stiff and starched, chosen by Mother for its tedious respectability. Why do we never go for a picnic or to a jazz brunch or have a barbecue or do anything *different*?'

'I – I didn't know you wanted to.'

Her coffee arrived, and Lauren seized it, drank thirstily. 'Well, I do! Don't you? D'you really want to keep on trudging out there for the next twenty or thirty years, every blessed Sunday?'

Studying the depths of his beer, Eoin did not immediately reply.

Resolutely, Lauren pressed on. 'Dad, I'm going off – probably – on this sailing trip to Turkey on Saturday. I haven't time to beat about the bush. What I'm trying to say is that it's time for a shake-up in the Kilroy family, time to throw open the windows and let in a good stiff blast of fresh air. And somehow I feel you might be more open to doing that than Mother is likely to be.'

His next remark surprised her. 'Lauren, what is this sudden problem with your mother? She loves you, you know.'

'Does she? Then why is she forever critical, or distant, or both? Why does she always make me feel I'm not living up to her expectations, not living on her terms? Why does she treat me like a *child*?'

'But . . . to her, you are her child. I think most mothers feel that way about their daughters. The unmarried ones, anyway.'

Lauren paused to think. 'Oh. Is that it? I'll be a child until I'm a mother myself? Well, she needn't hold her breath for that, Dad. I'm sorry to tell you this, but I'm unlikely to ever make you grandparents. You'll have to make do with Caoimhe's kids if that's what you want.'

His eyes clouded over, looked sad. 'But – why? Lauren, you're a pretty girl, a clever attractive—'

'Non-runner! Dad, if you only knew what's been going on in my life, the wretched relationship I stupidly got into . . . but I've never felt able to tell you. Not with Mother around, anyway. She'd *disapprove*.'

She made a moue, and Eoin surprised her again by laughing faintly.

'Well, yes, maybe she would. I know she does tend to disapprove of quite a lot of things.'

'Of everything that isn't nailed down, everything that doesn't fit into her boxed set of values. Apparently I don't fit into it, but I've never known why.'

Eoin drained his glass, sat back and looked at her. 'Are you asking for my opinion why?'

'Yes. I am. Let me order you another drink – a pint this time.'

He fiddled with the button on his overcoat. 'Well, if you want my honest opinion, as apparently you do, I believe your mother may be – be a little jealous of you, Lauren.'

She was stunned. 'Jealous? Of me? Of what?'

'Of your lifestyle. Her generation didn't have the freedom you girls have today, nor the money either. She had to scrimp and scrape until well after you and Caoimhe were born. She didn't have the same – same options. There was never any question of buying a new car or flitting off to Paris for a weekend, of new clothes on a whim or a lovely immaculate apartment like yours. And – and I think—'

Lauren leaned forward. 'You think what, Dad?'

'I think it annoyed her that you started earning twice what I was earning at half my age.'

'But – but she should have been delighted! I mean, I've never been tight-fisted, have I? I've always tried to share with you and her, treat you to—'

'Yes. I know you have. You've been more than generous. But that made Betty feel – well, that she couldn't compete. Made her feel maybe a little inadequate, because she knew that neither she nor I could ever attain the things you attained – the status – while you were still very young. Neither of us went to college, even for a year, we – we just don't have the temperament you do. We're not as smart or as confident or . . . well, I'm just a plodder, really, and you showed me up for what I am. Showed her up too, as the plodder's wife.'

'Oh, for God's sake! You earn enough to support her decently, and she could earn extra herself if she didn't have this fixed view that a married woman's place is in the home.'

'But that is her view. Plus, she's not qualified to do anything very lucrative.'

'She could do a course then, couldn't she, adult education in computers or languages or interior design or—'

Eoin sighed. 'Lauren, are you listening to me? I've just told you that Betty doesn't have *con*fidence. The Church, or someone, beat it out of women of her generation. She's completely susceptible to what other people think of her and she thinks you think of her as some dreary duffer.'

'But I've never – she's the one who—'

'I'm just telling you how things are, since you want to know. The truth is that Betty . . . resents you, even if she may not realise it herself. That's why she's distant and domineering, on her own turf. She wishes she could be more like you and is angry that she can't, that it's too late for the likes of her. That's how she sees things and that's why there's this lack of communication between you. She'll never discuss anything serious with you because she thinks you're smarter than she is, that you'll win every round if she ever strays off domestic subjects.'

Amazed and incredulous, Lauren considered. Eoin had always been a man of few words, but apparently he'd long been a hurler on the ditch, watching everything.

'Is it a question of winning, Dad? Is this some kind of competition, that I never even knew I was entered in?'

'Yes. You could put it that way. She sees you as a winner and thinks it's only a matter of time before you marry some rich glamorous husband who'll put her own husband to even greater shame. She – she's very protective of me, in her way.'

'Is she? Is that why you never—?'

'Say anything to her, contradict her? Well, maybe it is. She's a good wife and she didn't have an easy life, not when she was young anyway, your age. All I can do now is try to make that up to her, as best I can. But I'll never be a high-roller like you, earning megabucks.'

His tone made Lauren laugh suddenly, his unaccustomed slang, his wry dismissal of his own prospects. Which, at fifty-eight, were probably limited right enough. Yet *he* didn't seem to resent her at all. Reaching forward, she touched his hand.

'Maybe not, but you gave me a good education, Caoimhe too, you were prepared to go without so we could go to college – and then I merrily threw it up and went my own sweet way. Were you disappointed in me, Dad?'

He drank a long draught from his fresh pint. 'No. I wasn't. I was glad you'd found a good job and were able to use your head in a way that I, as a civil servant, could never use mine. I knew you'd travel further and faster than I ever could, and I was happy to know you'd never need to depend on any man for your income – unlike my own poor wife. I'm not much, but I'm all she's ever had.'

'Dad! You're my *father*, and Caoimhe's, you made such sacrifices and Mother should be so proud of—'

'She made them too. Don't forget that, Lauren. She made them too.'

Yes. But what had satisfied Eoin had embittered Betty, left her discontented and envious. So that was where the problem lay. Lauren felt immense gratitude to her father for having enlightened her, for having been honest. How strange, but how hugely refreshing this conversation was turning out to be!

'Thanks, Dad. Thank you for telling me all this. I had no idea. But now that I have, maybe I can do something about it, I can work on it.'

'Maybe. But the answer doesn't lie in extravagant gifts or offers of trips or anything like that, Lauren. It lies in Betty's own mind, in her perception of herself, not her attitude to you. That's a symptom, not a cause. You must try not to take it so personally.'

'Nooo . . . from now on, I won't. I might lay off the lunches and expensive presents and start giving her some – some encouragement, instead. D'you think she'd ever come to like me, if I did, or is it a lost cause?'

'Lauren, whether she likes you or not, she loves you, as I said before. Please remember that. She can't help half the hurtful things she says or does.'

'But then, why does she never say or do them to Caoimhe?'

'Because you were the one who showed her up. Caoimhe got married and settled down, was never a threat to Betty's status or authority. Caoimhe was also younger, unluckily for you – the eldest always has the hardest time of it. Parenting is like anything else, you get more relaxed and better at it with practice.'

Crossing her legs, Lauren sat back and reflected. Caoimhe had indeed always been adored by everyone, had conformed and become a mother herself, was now treated with respect as well as being sorely missed. Yet, despite the much easier time she had had of family life, Lauren could feel no animosity to her, no envy.

'Well . . . look, Dad. I'm going to be away for the next six weeks, maybe seven or eight, but when I get back I'll see whether anything can be done to improve things with Mother. If they can, if she'll meet me halfway, let's try to have a really nice Christmas when Caoimhe gets home, huh? Will you work on Mother for me in the meantime, try to prepare the ground a bit?'

'Yes. All right. I will, as much as I can. I must say it has given me no pleasure to watch your relationship deteriorating with her, nor hers with you.'

'So you have been aware of it?'

'Oh, yes. I may only be a pen-pushing functionary, but I'm not blind . . . tell me, Lauren, when are you ever going to put on a bit of weight? I've been worried – and what is all this about taking leave from your job, about being tired yet setting off for Turkey? What's going on?'

She sucked her lip, hesitated. He had been candid with her and she didn't want to lie in turn, but didn't want to worry him either, especially not now when the problem was shelved for the moment. He would be horrified that she had not told him before, and Betty would be – be vehemently accusing, gasping, fussing.

'Well, the truth is, Dad, I've been a little under the weather. I had a – a small medical problem. It's fine now, but it did give me a fright. It made me realise I don't want to spend *all* my time at my desk. That's why I'm setting off on this – this voyage of discovery!'

'I see. Well, you don't have a family to support, you can afford to do the kind of things I never could – not when I was young enough to do them, anyway. I hope you enjoy your travels, dear. But are you sure you're well enough, if you've been ill?'

Delicately, he did not ask the nature of the illness, and Lauren felt gratitude to him. 'Oh, yes, Dad, I feel great now! All I have to do is watch my protein intake and get enough sleep – my partying days are over! Or radically curtailed, at any rate.'

'Well, that won't do you any harm. Now, dear, it's a quarter to ten . . . will you come home with me and say goodnight to your mother? Say goodbye to her I mean, before you go gadding off on this trip? I told her you would and to keep some quiche hot for you, she made a lovely one this evening.'

Poor Eoin. As he stood up and began to carefully button his overcoat, Lauren felt a huge wave of sympathy for him, for his well-meaning mildness and stoic silences. But maybe he wouldn't be quite so silent in future, now that some start had been made on new communication? If he seized it and she seized it, perhaps Betty would even participate in turn some day . . . as Saiv had so frequently and maddeningly said, where there was life there was hope.

'Yes, Dad, of course I will. I was going to do that anyway.'

He smiled gratefully, and as they left the pub together she put her hand through his arm, feeling closer to him than in many years, sensing both rapprochement and potential. Even if Betty was a warped woman, he was a good man, quiet but kind – a much better man than any other she'd ever known.

Opening the door of her car to let him in, she hugged him spontaneously, and he looked up at her with the devoted affection which, she suddenly thought, was as much as any woman needed from the man in her life.

Feverishly, Saiv hurtled from one end of the village to the other, ransacking its half-dozen boutiques and shoe shops in a frothing panic, begging all the assistants for advice. What would be suitable for a trip to Italy at this time of year, what did they have in her size and her colour, pale blue?

Only one of them was frank with her. 'Lose the blue' she counselled candidly, 'it's too cool for autumn.'

'But it brings out my eyes' Saiv pleaded, desperate to highlight her best feature.

The girl was the youngest of all the assistants, not more than twenty, but she stood her ground firmly. 'Maybe. But you can have too much of a good thing. You're not the Virgin Mary, are you? If I were you I'd go for something warmer . . . rose, apricot, we have a gorgeous silk blouse in old gold. A wool coat, too, in a caramel colour that would be great with your hair. All you need is a few blonde streaks and you're in business.'

Saiv glanced in the mirror. Her hair was sandy already, but did she dare go *blonde*? And could she afford . . . ? Oh, the hell with it. Her plastic would bend, just as Lauren said – horrified, she had a startled flash of herself actually turning into Lauren Kilroy. Profligate, brazen, vain: she was going to have to be every one of those things today.

'Yes. I think you might be right. Please show me the blouse and the coat . . . I'll need a skirt and a dress as well . . .'

By the time she got home evening was falling, and it took two trips to carry all her packages into the house, where she caught sight of herself in the hall mirror and stared open-mouthed. The blonde streaks were stunning, *wonderful*. And, somehow, to be lived up to. Dr Rhattigan would faint when she sailed in to get her Zimovane prescription.

But . . . slowly, chillingly, an awful realisation sank to the pit of her stomach. If she gobbled pills or alcohol before embarking on the plane, she would arrive cross-eyed in Italy, semi-conscious like the last time. Without Lauren to guide her she would be totally lost, confused, and Vittorio would be appalled, think her some kind of junkie. Without Lauren, she couldn't afford to indulge in any kind of anaesthesia.

Oh, Jesus. This was going to be a nightmare. If she didn't embark like a zombie then she was going to disembark like a lunatic, a gibbering knot of jangling nerves. One way or the other, she'd swoon into Vittorio's arms and he'd have to give her mouth-to-mouth resuscitation.

And what was wrong with that? Frozen in front of the mirror, she laughed suddenly, manically – poor Vittorio didn't know what he was getting into. She'd clutch at him like a drowning woman and never let go. She could think of nothing on the entire planet she'd like more than to taste his lips on hers. She was losing her marbles, turning into a slut even *worse* than Lauren Kilroy.

Well – if a choice had to be made, better a sober slut than a drugged, drunken slut. Somehow, marshalling every last gram of her strength and willpower, she was going to have to do this trip cold turkey. In just four days' time, she was going to have to get on that plane and . . . and fly.

Desperately she ran her hands through her newly-gleaming hair, and they were quivering already.

Jennifer tried to reason with her. One colleague confessed to his own terror of flying, another explained how he'd done a terrific course that had entirely eradicated his fear. But nothing worked. By the time she tottered through the first three days of term and departed for the airport on Friday evening, Saiv was speechless, strangled with fright.

Carrying her bag as if it contained congealing concrete, fumbling and stammering, she checked incoherently in, and waited as if for a sword to slice through her. Only one good thing, she thought, could be said for this ordeal: such was her all-consuming angst about the flight, it was completely subsuming her other angst, about meeting Vittorio. In person, at last, the dream leaping to life! Of course it would all go wrong, collapse in ignominious disaster, but that no longer mattered if only the plane would somehow, miraculously, land safely.

It had the last time. But nobody could be that lucky again. This time she was on her own, and she was doomed. Just like her parents. Wretchedly she thought of Lauren, wishing not only that she was here but that she'd got to say goodbye to her. Why hadn't Laurie been in touch, rung even once so they could part, this fateful day, as friends?

Because she'd driven Laurie away. There you are, Saiv, you brought it on yourself, and now you've brought this on yourself too. Your choice, your cosmic mistake.

Finally, after about six years it felt, the flight was called. Saiv staggered to her feet and looked round for the exit. She could run, she could escape, she could do here to New Zealand in five minutes flat.

But . . . Vittorio. At this moment he would be already getting into his car, leaving home for the drive to Milan airport, which was nearly as long as the two-hour flight. He had organised this whole journey, gallantly and extravagantly paid for the ticket, would be there waiting for her with open arms – into which, if she ever reached them, she was going to faint. She couldn't back out now, leave him there in Milan wondering what had become of her. Unfortunately, she couldn't move, either; her legs felt as if they were planted three feet deep in the concourse.

'Lovett . . . last passenger, please, for Milan Malpensa. Your flight is closing at gate fourteen . . .'

Oh. She was holding things up. Everyone else had boarded. If she stayed where she was, she could save them all. Better stay, then.

'Ms Lovett?' A hand touched her shoulder, and she all but

ricocheted into orbit. A man's face smiled down at her, enquiringly. 'It is Ms Lovett, is it?'

She gazed at him. He was wearing an airline uniform. She parted her lips, and an unintelligible squeak emerged. Brightly, he smiled again.

'We're ready for departure, ma'am, you're our last passenger – please hurry now. Or is something the matter?'

Imploringly, she looked at him, forced her mouth to move. 'No – yes – it's just that—'

His expression was friendly, seemed to invite her confidence. 'Just what? Is there a problem, can I be of assistance?'

'It's just' she blurted in a babbling whisper, 'that I'm a little nervous.'

Incredibly he didn't laugh, didn't shout the uproarious news to his waiting colleagues. Instead he nodded gravely, took her hand and smiled reassuringly.

'I see. Well, you'd be surprised how common that is. Tell you what, I'll escort you on board myself. You just hang on to me now, and you'll be right as rain. The flight's only half full this evening, I'll find you a nice comfortable seat with lots of space and tell the cabin crew to take special care of you. How's that?'

She couldn't answer as he eased her into motion, steered her slowly but firmly to the gate, through it and down the ramp. All the way down, onto and into the plane, where there was some exchange of conversation with a steward; it might have been in Chinese for all she knew or cared. And then, irrevocably, she was seated. Seated and buckled in, like a child, because her fingers wouldn't work.

The kindly man evaporated, and as the doors closed behind him panic flooded through every nerve in her body: she had to get out, she had to, *now*!

Another uniformed man appeared, sat unexpectedly down beside her and clicked himself into the seatbelt, turning to her with an aura of casual calm. 'Good evening, Ms Lovett. I'm Michael, your chief steward this evening. I'm going to sit beside you for take-off and then, when we're airborne, I'm going to bring you a nice cup of tea. Tell me, how do you take it, with milk or sugar or both?'

Wildly, she stared at him with the dawning sensation of being irrevocably trapped; to escape now she would have to climb over him. Normally the crew sat at the front for take-off, but apparently this Michael was to be her bodyguard. Prison guard. They were afraid she might storm the cabin and shoot the pilot.

The engines revved, the plane reversed and Michael beamed at her. 'Beautiful evening, isn't it? You'll have a fabulous view of the bay – do you live in Dublin, or did you have a long trip to the airport? I hope the traffic wasn't too heavy?'

She knew it was only diversionary small talk, but even the smallest, silliest reply was beyond her. Nodding idiotically, she gripped the arm rest, beading with sweat, exhaling every breath in her body. The plane was turning onto the runway.

Lauren, she thought, I'm so sorry. And Vittorio – I'm so sorry about you too. You went to so much trouble, and I would have loved to have seen you.

Whoosh! With demonic force the plane gathered speed, tore down the runway and – no, oh Allah, oh *no*! – soared up into the clear, vast, empty sky. The enormous expanse of nothingness, with nothing whatever to hold it up.

'Have you been to Milan before?' Michael was speaking again, in Arabic or Urdu. 'Great shops. And great restaurants. We're all going out for supper tonight to Tarantella. Lovely little bistro, we go there whenever we have a layover. And what are your own plans?'

It was still up. Still in the air. Until any minute now – 'Verona' she breathed.

'Sorry? Didn't quite catch that?'

'V – Verona. I – I'm going there.'

'Oh, divine! Verona's just a little bigger than Kilkenny, a little smaller than Galway maybe . . . we get quite a lot of people going over for the opera in August. Do you have friends there?'

Did she? 'J – just one—'

'Well, maybe you'll make more this time! Or' – he grinned cheekily – 'is it a special one? Someone you're really looking forward to seeing?'

Abruptly Vittorio's face swam into her mind, and she couldn't decide whether to laugh or cry.

'Yes . . . someone I . . . really am . . . looking forward . . . to seeing.'

Conspiratorially, he winked as he unbuckled his belt. 'Ah. Do I detect romance in the air? In that case, maybe you'd prefer a glass of champagne to a cup of tea? Let me get you one – be right back!'

Chirpily he stood up, and she gasped; he was going to unbalance the whole plane, tip it over into perdition. As he walked, sauntered nonchalantly down the aisle, her eyes remained riveted to his back. Nothing happened.

She scarcely drew breath until the champagne arrived, whereupon she seized the glass and emptied it in one long, gasping gulp. Michael raised an impressed eyebrow.

'Just the one, for luck! Now, do you have something to read until I come back with your snack? It's salmon tonight, or pasta – I'd go for the salmon if I were you.'

Somehow she managed to stutter some kind of thanks, and he settled a pillow behind her head before leaving her with the air of a baby-sitter who would be keeping a close eye on his charge. Quaking, she glanced at her watch. Mother of God, another hour and forty-five minutes more of this!

But somehow an hour went by, minute by agonising minute, and the plane remained inexplicably airborne. After a false start Saiv even managed to eat her salmon, speculating that it might, after all, reach Italy intact. Other people were chatting and walking round the cabin, and she forced herself to take comfort in their faith. They wouldn't be so relaxed if there was any—

Whump! There was a terrifying thud, the horrific feeling of hitting air or cloud as hard as a brick, and Saiv grabbed at the seat as the seatbelt sign glowed red, a man's voice floated into the sudden, icy silence.

'Small storm . . . quite common over the Alps – please fasten—'

Alps? As in *mountains*? Soaring jagged peaks that would rip the guts out of – twisted metal spattered for miles—?

Materialising at speed out of the gruesome mirage, Michael sat down again and strapped himself in beside Saiv. 'Hi. Thought I'd just ride out this little hiccup with you. It happens nearly every time. Be through it in about ten minutes, captain reckons.'

Whump! Another wallop, another plummet, and although Saiv had pulled down the shutter on her window she saw a flash through the opposite one, a huge zig-zag hideously illuminating a sheer, solid wall of black cloud outside, so dark it was like a coal mine.

So this was it. She had been right after all, and this was the end. Reaching out, she embedded her fingers in Michael's arm and, alarmed, he turned to her; but there was no way to read what was in her face.

It was a magnificent drive through the most brilliant, flaming sunset, and even by Italian standards Vittorio was impressed with its drama: the backdrop was positively operatic. What a perfect evening for Saiv's flight! Of course it would be dark by the time she arrived, but the view before that must surely be spectacular.

At the airport he went straight to arrivals with his bouquet of arum lilies, and was disconcerted to find a notice on the screen announcing that the plane was delayed. Damn! Delayed by what? Late departure, probably; that was what they always said, anyway, as if one unpunctuality excused another. Oh, well. He might as well go and have a cup of coffee.

Three cups later, he found his impatience melting slowly but inexorably into curiosity, and a sensation he reluctantly recognised as anxiety. It had started to rain outside, rain quite heavily in a way that indicated the cloudburst would soon be over, but surely that wasn't enough to delay a jet? So would somebody mind telling him why Saiv's plane was now thirty minutes late? After all, he had waited three months for it already. He would go and enquire, and there had better be a good reason.

No, said the girl at the desk, just 'operational reasons'. And what exactly, he demanded, did that mean? It meant, she replied, that he should just sit down and calm down, wait with the rest of the gathering throng for further information.

Left with no alternative, Vittorio found a seat and sat, grasping his flowers, feeling both faintly conspicuous and naggingly uneasy. Was that a rumble of thunder he heard, or was his imagination taking over? There had been thunder that first night too, the night he dined with Saiv and Lauren on the terrace in Urbino, and they had marvelled at the beauty of the valley when it was illuminated by lightning. Now he had the less romantic suspicion of glimpsing lightning again, and shook it firmly off: it was probably just the swivel of lights on the control tower, the thunderous rumble merely the reverse thrust of some incoming aircraft. Maybe even Saiv's, at last!

But the sign remained overhead: delayed. Blast! He had wanted everything to be perfect tonight, and now, at the very least, they were going to be late for the restaurant he had booked back in Verona. They wouldn't get there until after ten, and be lucky to be served at all. If there was one thing he couldn't abide, it was eating in a hurry, under any kind of pressure; tonight above all nights, it was unthinkable. Tonight, he wanted to sit and savour his first sight of Saiv, revel in it, slowly dissipate the shyness he had sensed in her that first time, explore that lovely beguiling gentleness she emanated. In a world full of strong strident women, he wanted to roll her reticence around his mind and heart like a mouthful of old, old Amarone.

While Lauren did most of the talking, it was Saiv to whom he had felt drawn, sensing some smouldering core in her. There was, he thought, a profound femininity in her; although she earned her own living and appeared adamantly independent, he had responded to her sweet softness, a softness that was embodied in her rounded, voluptuous contours. Unlike Lauren and so many other women, she ate her food with enjoyment, her appetite promising appreciation of all kinds of sensual pleasures. Certainly, music made her face glow, his own voice had brought a gleam to her eyes like a beacon, drawing him magnetically to the eager chord that seemed to resonate in her soul.

She was a lovely lady, a luscious creature he had been unable to forget since, and he was ardently looking forward to seeing her, embracing her and getting to know her. What in heaven's name could be keeping her?

Another ten or fifteen minutes dripped by, during which his nerves slowly began to reverberate like violin strings, gradually reaching an unbearable pitch. Apparently the other waiting friends and relatives were coming close to breaking point too, because they were beginning to converge and buzz around the information desk like bees around a honeypot. Standing up, clutching his flowers, he went to join in the attempt to extract information. Where in *hell* was this plane?

Defensively, the girl at the desk huddled behind it. 'I am sorry,' she said without emotion, 'but all we know is that this flight has encountered some turbulent weather and had to change its course. We will call you when there is further news.'

Turbulence? Vittorio swiped his hand across his brow and found it damp. A frequent flier, he knew that planes did not divert out of minor weather-walls; whatever was happening must be major, and very frightening for those caught up in it.

It was serious. And that was how he knew, as if someone had thrown a brick at him, that his feelings for Saiv Lovett were serious. Little as he knew her, his heart leaped with fright, with throbbing concern for her, he felt an insane urge to grab somebody or something and demand that she be brought to him, immediately, intact and unharmed. Around the flowers his fist tightened, as if around Saiv's shoulder, and every protective bone in his body stiffened for combat. At all costs she must be safe, she must come to him!

His free hand slammed down on the desk. 'Changed course?' he barked, 'For where? Where *is* it?'

'I do not know, sir. If I did I would tell you – will do so, as soon as somebody tells me.'

So. They were into 'somebody' now, were they, that mysterious omniscient being who always knew, but never divulged, the answers? Vittorio made up his mind. He would demand the president of the airline if necessary, have him frogmarched to this desk to explain himself, clarify every detail and produce Saiv Lovett.

Glancing at his watch, willing time to move and gather momentum, he began to pace up and down, up and down under the woman's nose, conscious of mounting tension in every muscle. Other people were gathering in little knots, murmuring and muttering, but he couldn't bring himself to join them, to take any comfort in their company.

Not now. Not this time. This was what had happened the last time. A few people standing on the shore, a sudden ripple spreading amongst them, first suspicion, then shock, then disbelief. And then, his wife's body, brought in bloody and bruised, laid gently on the grassy side of the lake. Everything that had happened after that was a blur, but the moment of recognition would never leave him: the moment at which he had been brutally forced to accept that yes, this could incredibly happen. Had happened, to Claudia.

No! Not twice, not after seven years, to Saiv as well! Saiv whom he scarcely knew, and yet knew intimately, in the way that one lost and pilgrim soul knew another. Her face was the face of every painting he had ever studied, every sculpture, its serenity that of a Madonna, wistful and reflective. Since Claudia there had been no other woman, not one who ever moved him in the way the mere memory of Saiv's face moved him now. If it were possible he would take flight and go to her himself, claim her and wrest her from whatever malevolent force thought to possess her. He would do *any*thing, if he only could.

But all he could do was pace furiously, impotently, his heart booming in his chest, his veins tingling as the blood surged through them, everything knotting and choking inside him. In an explosion of rage he threw the flowers in the bin – what matter, when they were wilting, and he would need both hands free to seize her! Meanwhile, if news did not come soon, he would need them to punch somebody.

He was on the point of screaming aloud when, after an eternity, he realised that people were moving past him, gathering speed as of one body, and he joined them, rushed frantically to the desk.

The plane was safe. It had diverted to Bern out of a violent storm and landed there, where the passengers had been given a choice of re-boarding later or travelling on to Italy by coach. Some, apparently, had not wanted to re-board the aircraft.

'Lovett,' he shouted over the throng, 'is Signora Lovett on the plane or on the coach?'

The girl went through an alphabetical list, taking hours it seemed to reach L for Lovett. 'She is' she said finally, indifferently, 'on the plane. It is due to take off again at midnight and reach here just before one o'clock.'

Unable to speak, he went to a chair and slumped into it, shuddering, crumbling with relief, his legs unable to support him. Without subterfuge, he raised his hand to his eyes and wiped away the tears that would, if he let them, turn to a torrent.

Saiv he thought, oh, Saiv. I knew I cared, but never until this moment did I realise how much I care. How deeply, how terribly . . . and now, you have to go through it all again. When you arrive, I will take you in my arms and never let you out of them again. Never, do you hear? Never!

Immobilised by the force of his emotions, he let the night drift off around him, heedless of the hour, of everything after the dreadful fright she had given him, so searing and yet so little compared to what she must have endured herself. On the one hand he fervently wished she had taken the safer option of the coach; on the other the plane would get her to him quicker. If the storm was really over that was, and there was no danger this time. *If.*

Just after midnight, Vittorio went to the window and stationed himself at it, his hands clasped behind his back. There he remained, staring fixedly out into the dark for the next forty-five minutes, contemplating over and over what he was about to regain, and what he had so nearly lost. Did Saiv, at this moment, feel the way he felt himself? If she did, then there was no more to be said, words would be redundant when they met, because for him this terrible drama had sealed his decision. He never wanted to be parted from her again. After seven long, lonely years fate had brought him this gift, bestowed this woman on him, and nothing or nobody would ever wrench her from him.

But did she feel the same way? *Did* she? Whatever she felt, she must feel it strongly, every emotion must be sharpened almost to snapping point after what she had been through. Even as he willed the plane on something in him held it back too, held it at bay, because if she could disembark calmly, speak normally, shake his hand and say hello, he would know he had made the worst mistake of his life. He would go out and throw himself under the wheels of the nearest passing car.

And then, at last, he saw it. Saw the lights glimmering like stars in the black distant sky, saw them coming nearer, lower, knew with absolute certainty that it was Saiv's plane, bringing her to Italy, to him. As if a torch had been lit under him he raced to the arrivals area, elbowed his way to the front of the milling crowd and planted himself facing the doorway, waiting, waiting, waiting.

A cheer went up as the arriving passengers finally emerged, but Vittorio stood silent, immobile as marble, hardly daring to breathe. Every nerve in him froze, everything constricted until she was in his arms, with the sudden force of a hurricane, locked irrevocably into them, her tears swamping his shirt.

Not one word, one syllable did she utter as her arms chained themselves around him, but at last he found his voice, heard it burrow into her hair.

'Saiv,' he said, 'my Saiv.'

NOVEMBER

A brisk resolute breeze ripped Lauren's hair back from her face, and she gripped the salt-sprayed rail, looking out over the distant toe of Italy with one ear straining to hear her name shouted over the wind. The guys were always hungry, always calling on her to rustle up snacks now that she could be trusted not to whip out a fistful of Mars bars. At first she had almost been the cause of a mutiny, there had been demands that she be put ashore at the first port of call, but she had ridden out that storm, promising swift improvement even as she relied on Carl, whose own status depended on it, to fob off the ravenous mob for as long as it took her to learn how to fry a dozen steaks. Under the furious tutelage of Jeremy, the chef, she had learned fast, sitting up in her bunk every night racing through her cookbook. She was still only one page ahead of the posse, but it was enough to satisfy them; even Jeremy grudgingly conceded that potatoes, while not exactly haute cuisine, tasted good with lots of butter and a stiff sea breeze. Grinning, she'd even persuaded him that they were better unpeeled, that the skins were chockful of valuable vitamins.

With Jeremy brought to heel, the others soon fell in line behind him, like children really, happy to consume mountains of sausages and beans with a look of boy-scout bliss. For the businessmen amongst them, Lauren reckoned such fare was a secretly welcome change from the fancy, faddish food around which their expense-account entertaining revolved. Now, three weeks into the voyage, they were happy campers, and Lauren was enjoying herself enormously.

Never in her life had she worked so hard, because they sailed in shifts and she was in demand from dawn to midnight, pumping endless fuel into them, but they were fun and the laughter was loud around the table, which had a brass rail to keep the plates from flying off. Twice the weather had got rough and there had been a heavy swell, towering waves that made her gasp in awe, but the men relished the challenge, showing off their skill with contagious confidence. If Sara was ever scared she never showed it, and Lauren was glad to have one other woman along for ballast, even if the cool Sara wasn't very chatty. They had not become particularly friendly, but Lauren had warmed to Declan, a dentist with a wicked sense of humour, and to George the civil servant, who kept everyone amused with his tales of political intrigue. Reserved at first, George had gradually shimmied out from under his polished mantle, and was now unashamedly having the time of his life, climbing the mast like a monkey, telling jokes even smuttier than everyone else's. He flirted constantly with her, winking lewdly, and even though he was the oldest of all the men, bald as a plate, she found his aura of released energy attractive.

Carl had laughed when she confessed her fondness for George. 'What? Not Joe, our pin-up boy?' No, she replied firmly, not Joe: he might be George Clooney's twin, he might be a rich successful golf pro, but he was vain and bossy, she didn't care for him at all. Carl was surprised, but she was adamant: she'd met Joe's type before, and she wouldn't count on him, in a crisis, to help everyone else with their life jackets before securing his own. Surveying her thoughtfully, Carl had said no more.

Carl himself was good company, easy-going but assertive, smart enough to let everyone establish their own hierarchy while remaining firmly in charge. Even though Lauren's awful cooking had shown him up, he forgave her deceit once she improved. 'And what' she asked cheekily, 'would you have done if I hadn't improved?'

'Chucked you overboard' he replied in the manner of a man with whom you didn't mess twice. Grateful to him, she made sure he got the fullest plate and tastiest treats after that. But of all the guys her favourites were Desmond the electrician and Luke the pharmacist, who shared a fondness for chess and were teaching her to play. Small and stocky, freckling fiercely in the open air, Desmond looked like an urchin and swore like the seasoned sailor he was, but Lauren had gradually discovered that his gritty surface camouflaged a kind heart, a generosity of spirit such as she'd never encountered before. He had been several times to Romania back in the nineties, driven relief trucks into its war zone and, on one occasion, smuggled out a little boy whom he and his wife had subsequently adopted.

'Had to' he said gruffly, 'can't leave orphans wandering the streets, dodging the bullets, can you?'

Thinking that Joe probably would have – and Jordan White certainly would have – Lauren gave Desmond full marks for that, and made sure he got his full share of the carefully rationed beer. In return he began to teach her chess, with amused impatience at her inability to 'see further than the end of her nose', and doggedly she persisted, charming Luke into teaching her too. Luke was far more patient, quiet and calm, as dark as Desmond was gingery. Something in him reminded her faintly of Saiv; often to be found reading off-duty, he had the thoughtful air of a loner, and once or twice she teetered on the brink of asking him whether he could explain anything to her of the book she'd smuggled on board, the one about Zen she'd snaffled from Saiv. But thus far she had held off: what if he knew every line of it, and made public fun of her clandestine efforts to understand it?

In private Luke was sweet, almost shy, but there was another side to him too, one that fitted well into the crew, lending ballast to their boisterous high spirits. Lauren thought that if it ever came to a crunch or a crisis, he was the one you'd rely on; nothing ever panicked him, and he was skilled at brokering peace when rows broke out. Thus far there had been several squabbles and – while Carl could command peace – Luke could get it simply by raising an eyebrow, one that suggested he expected higher standards.

Luke and Desmond were unlikely chess opponents, but well matched, Luke a patient strategist, Desmond smart and unpredictable. Sensing something impressive about them, some kind of integrity, Lauren had lately taken to mothering both men in little ways, and in return they were protective of her; it was a trio entirely without sexual charge or tension, and she found its platonic bonds refreshing. No agenda, for a change! Both Luke and Desmond were happily married, decent guys – unlike one or two of the others, who were in the throes of messy divorces or muddles. Sensing that she might not be the only person on board with an ulterior motive for sailing to Turkey, Lauren accepted what information she gathered, but didn't ask too many questions. Mercifully nobody was nosing into her business, and she was not going to enquire into theirs; when you were at sea yourself, you didn't ask what anyone else was doing sailing alongside of you. In the cramped space privacy was at a premium, but still she was managing to take Dr Richards' prescribed medication undetected, and if anyone else was doing anything clandestine in turn, she wasn't going to snoop into it.

Why bother! She was getting what she'd come for, which was fun, distraction, a refuge from angst and a sense of liberating adventure. Even though her work as cook did not make demands on her mind, it kept her physically busy, with no time to brood on either the past or the future. Up at dawn, on her toes, she had no time or inclination even to think about her illness, and in any event she felt fit as a fiddle, revelling in all the fresh air and invigorating company. At night, in the tiny cabin she shared with Sara, she was asleep almost before she hit her bunk.

Only now, in these unexpectedly free few minutes, did her mind drift homewards for the first time, and as the large, graceful yacht rounded the tip of Sicily, heading from the Mediterranean into the Ionian Sea, she found herself thinking of her parents. Although her conversation with her father had not left her with any warmer feelings towards her mother, it had left her with some better understanding of Betty, and she wondered whether it might be within their common power, some day, to effect some kind of reconciliation – or modus vivendi, at least? If they could all just respect each other as adults . . . but she did respect Eoin already, far more than before; he was not entirely the doormat he'd always seemed to be. He was a loyal, decent man who'd never got much of a break in life, never got to do the kind of exciting thing all the men on this boat were doing. One or two of them were running away from their wives, but he'd chosen to stay with Betty, and she saluted his fidelity whatever the reasons for it, because it must be difficult at times. How much easier, and more fun, to run away to sea! Whether Betty acknowledged it or not, she was a lucky woman, with a husband who loved and understood her, honoured his wedding vows.

For his sake, Lauren thought, I'll try. Saiv said I should just abandon ship, give up on Betty, and I agreed at the time. But it would make Dad so much happier to see his wife and daughter getting along better, and so, for him, I'll give it a shot when I get home. Six months, anyway, and see what happens. Mother and I didn't exactly fall into each other's arms that night I went home with him after our talk, but at least I did go, and said a civil goodbye to her. Even a peck on the cheek – and she didn't say boo about what a mad mistake this voyage was going to be, although I could see it nearly strangling her. He must have warned her. Thanks, Dad . . . I'll call you again when we stop off at Corfu, and have a civil chat with Mother. How's that, for a start?

I'll call Saiv again too, although I seem to be wasting my time. I rang from Lisbon and again from Gibraltar, last weekend and the one before, but no answer . . . where can she be? I hope she got my messages anyway, and I hope she's cooled off. I was only trying to help, never realised she was so sensitive about Vittorio or would get so angry. But I'm the one who should have been more sensitive, and I'll tell her so when I get hold of her. After all I was touchy once myself, when Isaac ditched me, I know the crazy things that love can do to you. She won't admit it, but she is in love . . . I have to find out what's happening. Where is she? She can't be gone far, she'd never leave the dogs – Christ, I hope they didn't get at that note I left, didn't eat it or tear it up! Surely she read it . . . but did she do anything about it? Did she get her damn butt in gear and ring him? Surely – surely that can't be where she is? In Italy, on this very length of land I'm looking at?

No. She'd never do anything that spontaneous. If they made contact, they're probably planning to see each other at Christmas – by which time he'll have forgotten who she is, and she'll be in a flap and a panic, running round like a squawking chicken. She'll need to be stunned with a mallet to get on the plane . . . want me to go with her, probably, and then I'll be left playing gooseberry. But if that's what she wants, I'll do it. I owe her, big time, for all she did for me. It's just a question of organising Christmas so I get to see Caoimhe too, I'm not missing that for anything. Or my new baby niece, either! This is going to be one *happy* Christmas, this year. I can't believe I'm actually going to live to see it, after all. But, since I am, I will fit in with everyone, do whatever anyone wants to make it absolutely lovely. I may not have a man in my life any more, but I have a family and a great friend. Maybe that's as good as it's ever going to get. If it is, then I'll make the most of it. You don't get a second chance twice – God, I still can't believe I even got one. I'll never be able to thank Saiv enough for making me see Dr Richards, for being so strong, having such faith . . . I'd never have made it on my own. Never.

And I don't want her to be on her own. I want her to get it

together with Vittorio, make a life for herself. I want her to have tons of babies – triplets to start with, since she's left it so late – and I want to share that joy with her. I know I'll never have children of my own, now, but maybe it's just as well. I'm not cut out to be a mother, I'm way too selfish, but playing auntie would be fun. If she has girls I'll take them straight to Louise Kennedy for their christening outfits.

Hah! Wouldn't that be hilarious, Saiv a mother! She wouldn't know what hit her, her entire life would be turned inside out. She'd be reading them philosophy instead of fairytales . . . not that I've ever been able to tell the difference myself. But then Saiv has always understood stuff that I haven't. I'm only street-smart, but she's intelligent. God only knows what she sees in me.

Or used to see, before she blew up. I have to keep trying, and I have to get in touch with her. She'll make a horse's ass of this romance otherwise, never manage Vittorio without me to guide her through.

After all, I know all about men, don't I?

Drowsily, in a kind of daze, Saiv rolled over into some soft warm glow that fell on her face, and opened her eyes just enough to see the light of dawn illuminating the thick curtains, suffusing their red velvet folds with hints of mauve and amber, promising a day of rich warmth for this time of year. Snuggling deep into the heavy duvet and fat pillows, she wondered idly what day it was actually, or what year for that matter; all she knew for certain was what she could see, hear and feel around her.

Beside her, Vittorio lay supine in sleep, cocooned in it, his arm around her waist, his rhythmic breath fluttering on her neck, the weight of his body solid at her back, enveloping her like an all-consuming cushion. Weighted with sleep, he did not move, and she smiled dreamily; they had worn each other out last night, drawn every drop of everything they had to offer each other.

It can't be, she thought. Even now, I'm dreaming it. I can't be here in this bedroom, this apartment in an ancient Italian palazzo, lying in the arms of my lover. This is what happens to sluts, not to professors of philosophy. There's been a mistake, and I've woken up in the middle of a Franz Kafka novel.

But if there is a mistake, I want it to continue. I want it to go on and on forever, for the rest of my life. I want to stay here in this massive room, wrapped in the arms of Vittorio Scalzini, safe inside these thick walls, surrounded by all these beautiful things, these soft fabrics and jewel-deep colours. I want to just lie here holding and being held, dreaming on, and on . . .

This is the third time, in four weeks, and I still can't believe it. Wasn't it only last night that I fell off that plane, into his arms? Isn't it only hours since he gathered me into them, brought me back here to Verona, both of us almost silent in the car, and stopped in the hall, at the end of the stairs?

He held my hand, and he looked into my eyes. 'Say yes,' he said, 'tell me yes?'

I didn't have to say anything, tell him anything. I simply held his hand in turn, leaned into him, and we came up the stairs to this room, and a bolt of lightning struck my life. Everything else vanished, all the fear I might have felt, all the awkwardness, the shyness that might have held me back if that plane had not flown into that storm. The moment when I was sure it was going to crash – that was the moment I knew nothing else mattered. The moment when I turned to that steward in terror, and saw Vittorio's face instead; I knew then that if I lived it would be for him. Nothing could ever frighten me again as much as the thought of losing him, being wrenched away just as I was reaching him at last.

That was how I was able to get back on the plane, later, and come the rest of the way. And that was how I knew, when I saw his face, that he felt exactly the same, had been thinking and feeling everything I'd been thinking and feeling myself. It was relief that silenced us after that, all the way back to Verona, the realisation that life had been miraculously restored to us. Like Lauren, I have been given a second chance, and Vittorio has been given one too. He knew he had almost been bereaved a second time, and now, in spite of all that separates Ireland from Italy, we will endeavour to live the rest of our lives together.

Still – to leap into bed with a man I scarcely knew! But I did leap, over the cliff, and I was airborne, I flew. I opened my eyes and found a new land stretching out in front of me, filled with love and passion, surging with power, rising up out of an ocean of emotion. If I live to be a thousand, I will never forget that first night with Vittorio Scalzini.

Thank God the children weren't here, that he'd sent them to stay with their aunt when the plane was delayed! I couldn't have faced them the next morning, because it must have been tattooed on my forehead in scarlet – this woman is a tramp, a floozie, an utter harlot! Only I didn't feel like any of those things. I felt wonderful, as if I had come home after wandering adrift for years.

I wanted to do it again. And again and again. And we did, as if we were starving, couldn't get enough of each other. It hasn't even mattered that we've had to stay in the hotel, sometimes, since then, because we couldn't flaunt such steamy, nakedly blatant sex under the noses of young children. As Vittorio says, Michele is at an impressionable age, and Gina would be shattered. But . . . they know something is happening. Something irrevocable. We're going to have to tell them eventually, and start breaking the ground in the meantime.

What are we going to tell them, exactly? We haven't discussed anything yet, made any plans. We've just been living from week to week, I've been racing to the airport on Fridays, flying back to Ireland on Sundays . . . not home, any more, but back to Ireland, to work, to the dogs. There's so much to sort out. But for the moment I don't care, this is enough; to make love, to wake up with the man I love, to talk and walk around Verona, getting to know each other. I used to think sex was a travesty with someone you barely knew, but in this instance I was completely wrong. Far from feeling profane, it has been sacred, as great a sacrament as anything ever celebrated in any of these churches. The gods made us for each other, and we are blessed that we have found each other.

I never could have done it if things hadn't worked out the way they did, if we hadn't both been so overwrought, so charged and vulnerable after that terrible flight. But that flight cured my fear of flying, because after I'd survived it I knew I could survive another, survive anything that would bring me to Vittorio. I am simply destined to be here, and I think even Claudia would approve . . . Vittorio says she would, and I have to believe him, since he knew her so well. I'm glad he's left her photos around the place, not felt obliged to sweep them away. That wouldn't be fair to her, or to the children, and I don't want them to worry that I might try to usurp her in any way.

But I do want to take my place – not hers, but mine. This is where I was born to be, in this vast bed with the Vittorio who has grown into being since his wife died seven years ago. Does he want to marry again, is he ready for it? Or are we simply going to be partners? Wouldn't Laurie laugh, if she heard that – Dr Saiv Lovett, shacked up, living in sin! I wish I didn't keep missing her phone calls, but I'll leave a message with Vittorio's number next time, and meanwhile it's a huge relief that she's been in touch, sounds so happy and vibrant. And so forgiving, as if she's already forgotten the cruel things I said and did to her. Selfish and shallow as she can be, she has this other endearing side too, her ability never to hold a grudge. I'm grateful to her for that, and I love her for it.

And I owe her now, big time. I wouldn't be here today if it wasn't for her. She made me come to Italy, last summer, her confidence inspired me to invite Vittorio to join us for dinner . . . and then, last month, she made me get in touch with him when I thought he didn't want me. I'd never have done it, never had any of this, without her. She has, effectively, saved my life. Saved it and revived it and given me a gift beyond measure. I can't wait to talk to her – not just on the phone, but properly, when she gets home!

I'm still not entirely sure what's taken her on this crazy cruise to Turkey. The lure of a yacht, of the sun, of lots of men to lech after her? Those would have been her reasons once . . . but maybe now she just needs time to think. Maybe she still can't face what she's ultimately going to have to face . . . or maybe she's attracted to the challenge, to doing something more than what she'd been doing at her desk. She could find new strengths on this journey, new horizons . . . delve into her own resources and see what she comes up with. Maybe she'll rediscover some of the things she ditched the day she ditched college . . . there's always been that bit more to her than ever met the eye. Not that she ever wanted anyone to see it! If only she hadn't gone off so suddenly, if only I hadn't alienated her, maybe she would have told me what it's all about. But I'll ask her when she gets home – from Istanbul, of all the peculiar places!

I don't know much about Istanbul. But it can't be a patch on Verona, because this is the most beautiful little city on earth, and I've fallen in love with it just as I have with Vittorio. Like him, it's not young, but it's quiet and mature, it has dignity and charm, sometimes a quirky sense of fun. Juliet's house . . . honestly! But the legend is lovely, and maybe there was even once a Romeo who stood underneath that balcony. Maybe Romeo walked with Juliet in the Giusti gardens, maybe they drank wine by moonlight under the walls of the Arenà, just as we have done? Since I've been with Vittorio I've lost my academic detachment completely, come to believe that anything is possible. There are moments when I feel like a teenager, no older than Juliet Capulet and every bit as madly in love.

Vittorio is sleeping so deeply this morning, so peacefully. I don't want to wake him, but I have a plane to catch tonight, we only have today . . . it's funny, he says he's forty, but he looks younger when he's sleeping. I can see how he must have looked ten years ago, or more . . . never handsome, but always beautiful, in my eyes. Even now he looks boyish when he laughs – and he makes me laugh, so much! Life is so different when it's shared, and even young Michele has made me laugh, with his remarks about Papa being a baby-snatcher. I'm only six years younger than Vittorio, but I must look even younger, and I certainly feel it. I also feel that Michele and I could become friends, that he's happy for his father, even if Gina will be another day's work. Not that either of them guesses the extent of it yet, I hope. Vittorio was right to let them stay with friends last night, it gives us all breathing space, and we need that.

Maybe, if we handle things carefully, Gina will come round in time? Vittorio says it's a question of being firm but gentle with her, not alarming her or rushing into—

'Saiv?'

Vittorio's lips touched the nape of her neck, luring her out of her reverie, and she turned smiling to him as he emerged from sleep, snuggling into him, sliding her arm under the weight of his body. Waking fully, he kissed her again, and she felt as if the rising sun were igniting the room, drenching it in molten gold.

'*Buon giorno, caro mio.*'

'*Buon giorno . . .*' She could feel his warm breath on her hair as he buried his lips in it, drawing her to him, their bodies meeting with a leap of liquid flame. Looking into his eyes, she found them bright and eager, filling already with everything it was too early to say. Everything they did not need to say, in either language. Pulling her even closer, wrapping himself around her, he found her mouth and kissed her with such ardour, such depth that his tongue seemed to reach every nerve in her body, at such length it felt like a kiss outside of time. And then, lifting his face a fraction, he raised one enquiring eyebrow.

Sì, Vittorio. *Sì, sì, sì*! But there was no need to say it, her fingers were already doing the talking, her skin was shouting aloud, their bodies melding and merging into another dimension, another being; a being that only they, uniquely, could create together.

'Hello, this is Saiv Lovett. Sorry I can't take your call just now, but please leave a message after the beep – unless it's Lauren Kilroy calling, if it is then please ring me at this number Laurie, I'm in Italy.'

Italy? Yes! She's done it, Laurie thought, she's with him! Quick, give me the number!

The recording recited it and, all but dancing with delight, Laurie inserted fresh coins into the Greek payphone. A different ringing tone this time, and then a young male voice answered.

'Yes – no – I am sorry, but Saiv has just left for the airport with my father.'

Damn! Thanking him, Lauren hung up and consulted her watch. But too late: by the time Saiv got home the yacht would have sailed again, on the night tide, and she would have to be aboard it. If only Carl would let her use her mobile! But she couldn't charm her way around him on that, he had firmly said that if he agreed then everyone would want to start making personal calls, and they simply didn't have enough power to start charging all the phones. It had been settled from the outset, and that was the end of it.

Frustrated, plunging her hands in her trouser pockets, she made her way along the quay to what looked like a main street, dotted with shops. She needed to buy groceries, fresh fruit and vegetables, arrange for the boxes to be delivered to the boat before nightfall.

Milk, meat, fish, and don't forget the papers for Jody's roll-up cigarettes, Declan needed a new strap for his watch . . . when they put into port it was her job to go off with the guys' shopping list, while they hit the bars, went sightseeing or found phones to make calls of their own. The yacht had arrived yesterday in Corfu, but she'd learned to leave the shopping as late as possible so that everything would be as fresh as it could be when they sailed again. Even if she didn't see much of any port, it was fun to visit briefly, haggle with the shop-keepers in sign language, glimpse the busy life of each new country. The Lauren Kilroy who'd worn glamorous suits in a glassy office was unrecognisable now; this Lauren lived in jeans, hefting sacks of oranges and onions, stuffing wads of cash into the fists of merchants who bore no resemblance at all to the suited, shaved, shiny colleagues she'd left behind. Without realising it she had come to love the smell of the sea, of the crates of fish in the sometimes scruffy ports, the salty tang of her whole new life; a life in which her nails had not been varnished for fully a month. What point, when the first thing you had to do in every port was lug a sack of laundry to the nearest launderette, and stuff the whole lot into a row of machines which, as often as not, fought back? When your hands were permanently dry from salt water, nicked where knives had slipped, red from washing dishes by the dozen?

Never before could she have envisaged visiting anywhere without investigating the boutiques, buying clothes, but that was out on this trip, there was no space on the boat to store anything and purchases were forbidden. Astonishingly, she was discovering that Saiv had been right, that it was actually possible to live without shopping, without spending anything on luxuries – without even missing what seemed, in retrospect, to have been a form of occupational therapy.

Now she was learning, instead, to select the freshest fish, the firmest vegetables, the brightest fruit, and she was savouring the unexpected pleasure it gave her when any of the crew complimented her on her eye for quality, her acquisition of anything that might have proved hard to find. As yet nobody had actually mentioned her cooking, but they ate what she provided, and there was satisfaction in all the empty plates, the requests for second helpings, the . . . the sense of nurturing, of giving, sustaining other people. It was a simple life she was living, and she was slowly coming to love it, to wonder how she would ever, next spring, go back to being a high-heeled executive who took taxis for fear of damaging her Ferragamos.

Not, she thought, that I could be a galley girl forever, dream of taking this up as a career. Sooner or later I'm sure I'll start hallucinating about designer clothes and nice restaurants, be ready to sell my soul for a cocktail party or a set of Descamps sheets, but for the moment . . . living with Saiv prepared me well for this trip. All the walking got me fit, and the dogs meant I couldn't be too precious about my clothes, and space was cramped just like it is on the boat . . . the *WayToGo*. I like that name. I'll be sorry to leave her and the guys behind, wish I'd signed up for the return voyage as well. But they're taking on someone else, and anyway staying on would mean missing Christmas in Ireland, missing Caoimhe, which I do not want to do. But it's been great, challenging and stimulating, physically rejuvenating, and I'm going to enjoy the few weeks we have left.

Meanwhile, I'd better set my mind to rounding up these supplies and getting them on board. If I get it done in time I might even be able to grab a quick pizza – oh, the luxury of not having to cook tonight, for once! The guys are probably glad of the break too, stuffing their faces in some restaurant somewhere . . . but they're good guys, and I'm getting very fond of them. Some of their habits would drive you mad, but I've just had to learn to be tolerant, the same as they tolerated my awful cooking in the beginning. That kind of give-and-take would never have happened in the office, everyone got bawled out for any mistake they ever made – and I was often the one who did the bawling out. From here on in, I might try to be a bit more patient. After all, everyone has to learn, start somewhere.

Let's see. Those courgettes look good . . . dammit, that I missed Saiv! But at least I got to talk to Dad and to Mother. Funny, she actually sounded a bit anxious, worried about how I was weathering the trip. I'm weathering it really well, but it's nice to know she cares – and that she could ask without fussing, without silly questions or a pall of doom and gloom. She just asked, and I just answered that everything was fine. That, by our standards, is progress. Maybe, some time in the next decade or two, we might even start to communicate, after a fashion? I'll leave the door open on it anyway, and see what happens.

Now. There's a tobacconist, I'll get Jody's roll-ups for him. I wonder if he needs tobacco too? Let's get some, just in case. And there's a newspaper in English, they'd all kill for that. Corfu looks like a nice place, pity there isn't more time to explore . . . but if I don't do my stuff the guys will starve, and hey, I'm kind of responsible for them.

It makes the weirdest change, to be responsible for anyone except myself. It's like looking down the other end of a telescope. And the weirdest part of all is that I like the view.

It was a mild day, for mid-November, with an almost spring-like softness, and Saiv was thrilled to be spending yet another weekend in Italy, walking down the Via Mazzini towards Verona's oval heart, the Piazza Brà, with Vittorio and his children, en route to a café famous for its ice-cream.

But this couldn't go on! Could it? In the long run it couldn't, nobody could commute back and forth forever, and apart from the chaos it was causing at home Saiv wondered how much longer she could accept Vittorio's generosity, the welter of expensive plane tickets he was showering on her. She didn't want to insult him, or hurt him, but she was making up her mind: she would accept no more of this after Christmas. What would she do then, instead?

She didn't know, but she would figure it out later. For the moment, all she hoped was that her almost giddy sense of reeling sensuality wasn't visible to Gina or Michele, that they couldn't tell for sure that she had rolled out of their father's bed barely an hour ago. It had required some subterfuge to hide the fact, and she harboured the hideous suspicion that she was walking now like John Wayne.

But was it worth it! After the first frantic burst, the first firecracker nights, Vittorio had mastered himself, refined his sexual pace and slowed it down; the slower he went, the further she flew. Whatever he might once have had with his wife, she sensed that what they were sharing now was unique to them, that his only thoughts were of her, and she smiled as he took her arm, steered her into the café that was a favourite treat for his children.

Seating themselves around a table under an outdoor heater, they studied the list of delicacies, and Saiv was careful to accept Michele's recommendation, a raspberry sundae. A friendly youth, blond and olive-skinned like his mother, he grinned at her; Gina sat back at a little distance, looking unimpressed. Small and dark, she was more like her father, and Saiv felt faintly sorry for her. At twelve, she was on the brink of chaotic adolescence, as well as having to face the fact that her father had a new woman in his life.

'What's your favourite, Gina?' Saiv asked in English, and Gina pretended not to understand. Saiv knew she did understand, because Vittorio had taught both children excellent English.

'Gina' Vittorio said firmly, 'answer the question, please.'

'Mint' she replied, with an indifferent shrug. Saiv persisted.

'And what other things do you like? Who's your favourite pop star? What's your favourite colour?'

'I don't like pop music. It's silly. I only like the songs Papa sings.'

She glowered darkly, but Michele intervened helpfully. 'Well, I like Robbie Williams. And the colour blue. And soccer. My favourite thing is cars. Will you ask Papa to buy me a Lamborghini? He won't listen to me, but he might to you.'

Vittorio laughed aloud. 'In your dreams, Michele, in your

dreams! If I could afford my own favourite, it'd be a classier model, maybe a Bentley . . . but then, if I were rich, I'd have to take you two to Disney World first, wouldn't I?'

As the ice-creams arrived this gradually led into a discussion of their favourite things, and Saiv began to learn more about the Scalzini family. Michele's enthusiasm for cars reminded her of Gráinne's, and it struck her that the two were around the same age. Michele seemed younger by comparison with Gráinne's evolved personality, but they might get on well nonetheless – at the very least, Gráinne would love a trip to Italy. Maybe next summer, if . . .?

Vittorio was not passionate about cars, but she discovered other tastes: a love of horses, which he had not mentioned before, a fondness for the music of Aretha Franklin and Andrea Bocelli, an enduring memory of a childhood trip to London, where a Buckingham Palace sentry had frightened the wits out of him by suddenly moving.

'I thought he was a toy, never suspected he was alive!'

Everyone laughed except Gina, and Saiv tried again. 'What's the funniest thing you can remember, Gina?'

'I can't remember anything' she said shortly. There was an uneasy silence. Vittorio looked at Saiv, and she caught the support in his eyes.

'Tell the kids about you, Saiv. What's your favourite thing?'

'A glass of Amarone' she grinned, 'and my dogs Elmer and Duster. And walks on the hill of Tara . . . and my niece Gráinne . . . and my friend Lauren.'

Unexpectedly, Gina sat up, challengingly. 'My best friend is Paola.' Her tone suggested that there was only room for one close friend in this conversation, and Saiv smiled. 'Is Paola in school with you?'

'*Sì.*'

'How old is she?'

'*Dodici.*'

'Would you let me meet her some time?'

'*Non lo so.*'

Vittorio frowned. 'Gina, your English is much better than Saiv's Italian, so please speak it.'

Saiv put her hand on his arm. 'No, Vittorio. Gina is right. This is her country and her language, and I'm the one who has to make the effort. My Italian is very rusty, but I'll work on it, I promise.'

Looking satisfied, Gina nodded. Evidently she felt she had won this small battle. Letting her savour her victory, Saiv said no more, and after they'd finished their ice-creams Michele looked at his watch.

'Papa, I have soccer practice at three, will you excuse me?'

Vittorio nodded, and as Michele stood up Gina stood also, slid her hand into her brother's. 'Michele, I want to go too, will you take me to Paola's house?'

Michele glanced enquiringly at his father, and Vittorio sighed. 'Very well, Gina. You may go. I will pick you up at five.'

The pair departed, and Vittorio groaned. 'Saiv, I am so sorry. I can see she is going to be hard work.'

She slipped her hand into his. 'Yes. But, as you said yourself, let's not rush her. In fact, I'm just thinking . . .'

'What?'

'That maybe, if their aunt would look after them next weekend, you could come to Ireland instead?'

He looked alarmed. 'Oh, Saiv, please don't let Gina discourage you from coming here—'

'No. It's not that . . . Vittorio, I don't want to be in their faces every weekend, don't want them feeling I'm colonising their home. I think it would do them good to have a break from me, have their friends over instead. Besides, I keep missing Lauren's calls, and I'd like to be there for the next one, she only seems to ring at weekends.'

'Oh. Well, then . . .'

'And, also, I'd like you to see my home, see where and how I live.'

He brightened. 'That would be good. I'd like that, very much.'

'Then will you come?'

'Yes. I will.'

'Great. I – well, I hope this doesn't sound too selfish, but I'd like you to myself just for once. I think . . . there are things we need to talk about.'

She was surprised when he didn't ask what they were. Instead he simply nodded, rather gravely. 'There are. Many questions, to which we perhaps do not yet know the answers. It is time to discuss them.'

For a moment they sat in silence, pondering this. And then his dark eyes twinkled. 'Meanwhile, the children are gone, the apartment is empty for two hours! Let us go back there, Saiv, and—'

She caught his drift, his eager tone. But – 'No, Vittorio. Let us stay here and have some coffee, and talk some more. I want to know more about you, and I want you to learn more about me.'

With only fleeting regret, he acquiesced immediately, and they sat there in the winter sunshine, a woman in a caramel-coloured coat, a man in a red sweater and olive corduroys, exchanging and eliciting from each other all the tiny details of their previous lives, which were the foundation stones necessary to the building of a new one. Overhead, a dove sailed high through the muslin sky, spiralled down and settled on the old, old walls of the Arenà.

In the very last week, when they were nearing the end of their voyage and almost within sight of Ilica, a storm blew up that sent the crew of the *Way To Go* hastening to their stations, and as the mainsail was hauled from its mast Lauren learned with a vengeance what it meant to batten down the hatches. At first the wind was merely fierce, but after a queasy, rocking interlude it gathered the force of a tornado, hurling torrents of water over the decks of the yacht, throwing it about like a die in the fist of a gambler. Several times the boat felt as if it was about to leave the surface of the ocean entirely, become airborne and slam back down with a smack which would shatter it to smithereens. Nobody said a word beyond the essential minimum, working together with interlocking precision, but Lauren sensed tension as she watched helplessly, knowing that this was professional stuff, there was nothing she could do.

Of course it had been a constant risk, one that Carl had clearly outlined before their departure. Was Lauren prepared for any weather, any eventuality? Yes, she was prepared, and so she stood her ground, experiencing a tingling thrill in spite of the apprehension, the lurching nausea. Over and over again the yacht was engulfed in water, so comprehensively she could see nothing, thought they must surely be blown off the face of the earth – and yet, there was a raw, eerie beauty that held her spellbound, fascinated.

So this was another way in which you could die! No hospital, no drips, no medication; just wham, instant annihilation. But some deep instinct told her she would not die, that her time had not come. She had survived hep C, for now at any rate, the doctor had said she had years to live, and she was going to live them. Hearing his words echo in her head, she felt immortal, embraced this opportunity to share the strength she felt in both mind and body.

White-faced, Sara staggered down into the galley, and Lauren saw immediately that she was frightened, that Carl must have sent her below, because fear was worse than useless. Declan fumbled down after her, looking for the first-aid kit; the boom had whipped round and snapped his wrist.

The break looked gruesome, but she tackled it, unrolled a bandage and bound up the splintered bone calmly, telling him and Sara not to worry.

'Actually' he said with a wan smile, 'I think this could be a very good time to worry, if we let ourselves.'

Sara gripped the brass rail around the table, so tightly her knuckles were almost transparent. 'Sit down' Lauren advised, 'and if I can – I – phew! – I'll pour you both – ah! – a stiff drink.'

Somehow she slopped brandy into plastic beakers; her two charges were clearly *hors de combat*. Declan downed his at a gulp, Sara's bounced off her lip and flew to the floor. 'So' Lauren asked casually, 'how many storms like this one have you sailed through, Declan?'

'Two' he gasped, 'in eighteen years. You tend to keep exact count. Laurie, do we have any Novocaine?'

She found him a couple of painkillers and wrestled with a foam sling, trying to aim his arm into it, stabilise the injury. Over the roar of the wind and water, he stared at her, shouted at her.

'You're very calm.'

'Isn't that what we're supposed to be?'

It was, but it wasn't easy; pain was turning Declan grey in the face, and in spite of her sympathy Lauren smiled a grim fraction: this was worse than anything his patients might dread he could ever inflict on them in his dental surgery. He would need to see a doctor as soon as – as soon as they reached shore safely.

With a groan, Sara groped for the wall as the boat flew aloft on a huge wave, missed it and was flung down on the seating banquette, her stomach hitting it with a whack. Dropping her head over the end of it, she vomited violently.

Somehow Laurie tottered to the sink, soaked a cloth and tottered back to her, wiped her face with it and took her head between her hands, steadying her as best she could. From some distant depth a memory welled up in her mind: her office in Dublin, her head plunged between her knees, Shane Jackson proffering icy water. She knew how Sara felt.

'Just lie still and ride it out.'

But an hour elapsed, another and another, in virtual silence apart from the roar of the storm: it was impossible to keep shouting over such a deafening thunder. But never once, not even when she heard the mast crack and saw it hurtle past the window, did Lauren believe that they would not survive. Fate had simply ordained her life otherwise, that was all, and everyone else would reach safety with her. The mast might snap, but her nerve would not.

And then, at evening, the wind began to spend itself, to retreat like an angry gangster, huffing in defeat. Cautiously, Laurie waited with Declan and Sara, until gradually the rollercoaster levelled off, and the *WayToGo* was merely rocking, regaining reassuring rhythm.

'Phew.' Declan's face was soaked in spray and perspiration, Sara lay utterly silent. 'Thank God that's over. My entire life was flashing before me.'

Lauren laughed. 'Mine too. It wasn't a pretty sight.'

Curiously, he looked at her. 'Wasn't it? I thought you lived a charmed life, that you were an overpaid executive who had it all.'

'Yes' she answered truthfully, 'that's exactly right. I had too much, and wanted more. Until this year, I was your ultimate material girl. Now, let's make you some hot tea, and see if we can get some Alka Seltzer into poor Sara.'

'Mmm. Still, I'd say after this little experience you'll be glad enough to get back to your nifty apartment and your life of luxury, huh?'

She thought about it. 'Well . . . I won't deny that I might still have my moments, that Brown Thomas might occasionally loom like Mecca in the future. Only shopping won't be the only thing in my life, any more, there'll be other things as well.'

'Such as?'

'Oh, I don't know.' She reached to fix his wrist more securely into its sling, and he winced. 'Maybe join the Red Cross or something. Think I'd be good in the broken-bones department?'

He grimaced wryly, and said no more.

★   ★   ★

It was frustrating and it was sad, but there was nothing for it: without her mast the *WayToGo* could not sail triumphantly into port at Ilica, complete her last lap under sail. It would have to trundle sheepishly in under engine power, and Carl was miserably disconsolate.

'Oh, what the heck' Lauren retorted briskly, 'so long as we get there in one piece, what matter?'

'You're missing the point,' he accused.

'The point is that we made it through that hellish storm, under your excellent direction, without loss of life or limb. I'd say that's plenty to be proud of.'

Muttering, he conceded that some other boats had not been so lucky, and she left him to mull it over. So long as you survived, what matter how you did it, reached your final goal?

And, when they did reach it, limping into Ilica with their shattered mast, there was cheering amongst the rest of the crew, delirious waving at the figures on the approaching shore. If they were not arriving in glory they were not arriving covered in shame either: after six weeks and four thousand miles or more, they were intact and they were hoisting the Irish tricolour triumphantly, if only on the prow. One last busy day still remained ahead of them, involving repairs and mopping-up operations, and then, Lauren promised, she would cook everyone a celebratory dinner on board this evening. It was a startlingly warm day for late November, muggy and dusty, but that meant they should be able to eat up on deck tonight, lapping gently by the quayside.

'Meanwhile, where's the champagne? I've been saving this – stand back, everyone!'

Shaking the bottle, she cracked it open, and everyone laughed as the froth flew over them, George clicking his camera to seal the moment. Lauren thought it would make a lovely photo, and looked forward to displaying it on her desk some day – see, I sailed to Turkey, on a wing and a prayer, I looked after this gang and we all reached our goal! Yes, that's me in the shorts and bare feet, with a smear of grease on my forehead!

The crew dispersed, some to see about repairs, others to check into the most comfortable hotel they could find, dying to sleep in a bed that did not rock. Once Lauren would have dashed to it too, but now she took a makeshift shower instead, slipped on fresh shorts and sandals, and went to suss out the Ilica area. Work wasn't quite over yet; she wanted to get some really nice ingredients for her feast tonight, and then have a look around.

But the town, when she reached it, was far from beautiful. It was gritty and grey under the cloudy sky, battered-looking, its atmosphere somehow muted and dented. Where was the exotic Turkey of her dreams, the white sand and blue bays, the bistros and belly dancers?

Well, it was winter, out of holiday season and mood, and this wasn't quite brochure territory anyway, it was a port chosen entirely for nautical reasons, its deep harbour and marine facilities. Over the next few days, as she made her way to Istanbul – by bus, Carl advised, it was the quickest and cheapest mode of Turkish transport – she would have a chance to see some more of this new and very foreign land. At the very least there would be Istanbul and minarets, some whiff of exotica before the five-hour flight back to Ireland.

Five hours! Was that really all? After sailing such a distance she could hardly believe it, it seemed so unreal, Ireland so very far away. Thinking of it, it occurred to her to send a postcard to Saiv, let her know she had arrived and show her where, exactly.

At a newsagent's stand she stopped to browse, select a card that illustrated Ilica under sunnier conditions, and went in to pay for it with the money Carl had given her. He supplied foreign currency as needed and it was part of her job to reckon it all up, account for every expenditure in a ruled ledger. Thanks to her business experience and hard nose for haggling, she had been able to get excellent value out of their kitty along the way, and she was proud of her performance, felt like tying up the ledger in pink ribbons before handing it to him with a flourish.

Paying for the card, she attempted conversation with the shopkeeper. Did he – she mimed a tiny square – did he have any stamps?

Dully, he shook his head. No.

Oh. She felt deflated. Almost all the other shopkeepers across Europe had been friendly, chatted with her or smiled at least. What was wrong with this guy, this port?

But, when she went on to the food shops, it was the same story; a flat listlessness in the air, a sense of some punctured atmosphere. Turkey, or Ilica at any rate, did not seem to be in a very good mood.

Eventually, after securing the rations for the boat with much difficulty, she found another newsagent, one who did have stamps and spoke some English. After a brief chat with him, she ventured to ask why everyone seemed so quiet, hoping he wouldn't be insulted.

Looking surprised, he raised an eyebrow. 'But . . . it is because . . . haven't you heard?'

She shook her head. 'No. Heard what?'

'About the earthquake?'

Huh? 'Earthquake, that has devastated our region! Our country! It happened last night, about two hundred miles east of here – thousands of people have been killed, thousands more are injured or missing. Whole towns are homeless, it is an enormous disaster for us.'

Oh, God. Oh, wow. 'No, I'm sorry, I've just come in off a boat, we got caught in a storm and didn't hear the news.'

He looked close to tears. 'It is a catastrophe. A terrible tragedy. We are hoping that international aid will arrive, it has been promised, but it is slow, nobody has come yet.'

Horrified, she thanked him and backed out of the shop, feeling oddly abashed. Of course an earthquake was not of her making, had nothing to do with her! But she felt he had been looking at her, as a European, to do something, to help or suggest something . . . or maybe he just couldn't believe he was face to face with such an idiot, who had heard nothing of such enormous disaster?

Well, that wasn't her fault, nor was the earthquake. But as she made her way back to the boat Lauren felt her balloon deflating, almost a stab of shame when she reached the *Way-ToGo*. Even without her mast she was a beautiful boat, a luxurious vessel in which a dozen well-heeled Europeans had lazily sailed the Atlantic, the Mediterranean and the Ionian Sea, for no other reason than the sheer fun of it.

And then, to arrive cheering, popping champagne corks, on such a day! Unwittingly, they must have deeply offended the local people. With fizzling enthusiasm, Lauren waited for her copious supplies of delicious food to arrive, and all but cringed when they did.

Evening was falling, puffy thick clouds were mounting as Lauren worked in her galley, preparing a meal for which her appetite had been blunted, and as she filleted a dozen silvery fish she heard voices up on the quay overhead. The men were wandering back, in twos and threes, from their various projects, the clink of bottles suggesting that beer was being swigged. But they did not board the boat; instead the voices remained overhead, and she guessed that they were sitting on the quay, legs dangling, chilling out for a while.

At first their conversation was of their day's pursuits, or of the voyage which had been so bonding, so satisfying despite its inglorious end. Not catching everything that was said, Lauren worked on, invisible to them in her galley below.

And then, idly, the conversation turned to herself. Hearing her name, recognising the voice of Declan the dentist, she glanced up, but could not see him.

'Not bad,' he was saying, 'turned out better than expected, once she figured her carrots from her cookies. Very cool during the storm, I must say, doc says she did a good job on my wrist.'

She was glad he'd found one and got it checked. Lazily, Joe's voice floated into the breach. 'Yeah. Cool lady, cute too, easy on the eye. Bit thin for my taste, though, not a pick of meat on her!'

There was ribald laughter, and she bit her lip; sexist bastard! Women were expected to look slim and trim at work, yet then men complained there wasn't 'a pick' on them? Jesus, you couldn't win.

'Well' George interjected, 'I wouldn't chuck her out of the bed for eating crisps . . . say she could be tricky, though. Bit of a pony, you know, preening and prancing.'

Hey? I beg your pardon?

'Yeah.' Astonished, she listened: could that be Luke she heard, agreeing with George? Nice, decent Luke? But it was. 'If you ask me, Laurie's more show than substance. Likeable, but not a lot of depth to her. Wouldn't want to be marooned on a desert island with her.'

Instinctively she knew he had a point, but she felt as if he'd slapped her face. Their laughter drove into her heart like a spear, and she tautened against whatever was coming next.

Carl spoke up, in his deceptively languid way. 'Oh, Laurie's all right. On the ball, learns fast. Love to know what took her on this trip . . . I reckon she's on the run. Maybe from the cops or something!'

More laughter, more clinking bottles, and then Desmond, the spicy-haired, peppery electrician of whom she'd become so fond.

'No . . . wouldn't say she'd have the stomach for crime. Tough cookie in business I'll bet, but not tough enough to play real hardball. Wouldn't hack it in a man-to-man situation – more likely to whip out the lace hankie and pout, wipe a little tear from those fluttering eyelashes!'

She couldn't believe her ears. Even Desmond . . .? It sounded as if none of them rated her very highly, that for the first time in her life she had failed to make any impact on any of the men around her. Nothing more than skin deep, visual, nothing that counted, that they would respect or remember her for?

Straining her ears, she listened for more, but even the very subject of Lauren Kilroy, apparently, did not hold their attention for long; their talk drifted off, to the new cook who would replace her, and to the voyage back. Jody and George were flying home, the others were returning with the boat.

Then Carl's voice, again. 'Hope these damn guys turn up tomorrow to fix this bloody mast. Awful hassle finding them. Half the town seems to have gone off to give a dig-out with this earthquake, wherever it is.'

'Yeah.' It was Joe she heard, the golf pro for whose taste she was too thin. 'Trust the Turks to get in a mess! They're so disorganised it's unbelievable – apparently there were warnings about the quake but nobody paid any attention. Fine fix they're in now, by all accounts.'

Poised over her fish, Lauren gripped her knife and listened as other voices added their tuppenceworth: it sounded as if some of them believed Turkey had brought this disaster upon itself, deserved all it got and was incapable of extricating itself from its predicament.

Mother, Lauren thought. That's who I'm hearing. That's exactly what Betty would have said if I'd told her I had hep C. It's all your own fault Lauren, if you get mixed up with a married man you must expect the consequences. Tsk, tsk.

Suddenly, her blood boiled. Was there not even one real man amongst all these macho guys, one who felt any sympathy for this poor country and these poor people, who could never in a million years afford to sail anywhere on a luxury yacht, whose only perceived use was to service that yacht and the rich lads who owned it?

Christ. If they thought she was worthless, they were even more worthless themselves, then; selfish and shallow, every bit as bad as she was herself. Even Desmond, who'd driven to Romania and rescued an orphan kid?

But then, even as she thought of him with surprise and

disgust, she heard him speak, his voice coagulating in the dusk.

'Oh, give it a rest, Joe. Turkey didn't ask for an earthquake. Even if there were warnings, what could anyone do about it? This country barely has tuppence to its name, communications are weak, resources are minimal—'

'Right.' It was Luke. 'And the zone is two hundred miles inland, hard to reach, even if the government sends aid there'll be chaos – Turkey's government is twisted as a corkscrew, we all know how it treats human rights issues, doesn't give a damn – half the aid money will end up in some bastard's back pocket, you can be sure of that.'

Really? Lauren had known none of this, but her attention was snared. So these people caught up in this earthquake were unlikely to get much help, even from their own officials? And international aid, the shopkeeper had said, was slow in coming . . .?

God. How much help I got, she thought, when I was in trouble. When I was down and out, afraid of dying, Saiv Lovett was there every inch of the way with me, for me. I couldn't have survived without the hand she held out to me, that pulled me back up on my feet.

Stiffening suddenly, she put her fish on the grill, washed her hands and removed her apron. Even now, after all she had heard about herself, she wasn't going to give anyone the satisfaction of serving them in an apron. She had her pride, she had her dignity . . . and she had a slowly coalescing sense of direction, of resolution.

Fixing her brightest smile on her face, smoothing her hair, she emerged out on deck, climbed the ladder up to the quayside and clapped her hands.

'OK, dinner's ready, to your stations! Luke, set up the folding tables and chairs, Joe, grab the cutlery – Carl, give me a hand to bring the food up here, will you?'

Startled, they blinked at her, unaware that she had been down below. In Luke's face she caught something whisking through, and saw that he was wondering how much she had heard. Obediently, they dispersed to their tasks, and demurely she asked Desmond to set about opening bottles of wine and beer. A little alcohol would lubricate her impromptu mission, and what was that old chestnut about the way to a man's heart being through his stomach?

She was going to serve them a banquet, and she was going to reach their hearts. Amidst it all, it bizarrely seemed that she might even be developing one of her own.

DECEMBER

Even as she led him into her cottage, Saiv wondered with sinking doubt whether she had made a mistake, whether Vittorio might gaze askance at its tiny cluttered rooms, take a dislike to the dogs or think that the meadow was a bog: in winter it got very mucky and ragged. But too late. He was here and, for better or worse, she was going to have to muddle through somehow.

His tall, broad bulk seemed to fill the entire living room, and the dogs held back, looking cautious. Saiv had never brought home anyone like this before.

'Sit down,' she said nervously, 'and I'll build up the fire, see about something to—'

He sat down, reached for her hand and pulled her down beside him, both of them still in their coats from the trip from the airport. With what looked like faint amusement, he began to unbutton hers.

'Relax,' he murmured, 'get comfortable, and I'll attend to the fire.'

'But—'

'We're not in any hurry, are we?'

Well, no. When she was with Vittorio, Saiv sometimes got the odd sensation of life having somehow been speeded up, moved onto fast-forward, everything happening in a glorious, confusing rush. But at other times – more often than not – she felt as if she were living in a dream, moving slowly, moving step by step with him into a hazy future which, thus far, remained vaguely veiled. Unsure of the extent of his ongoing attachment to the late, lovely Claudia, she was afraid to lift the veil, to speculate what might lie beyond. All she knew was that she wanted desperately to be with him, to be allowed to love him . . . not at the consuming pace of a summer flame, a candle that would burn itself out, but at her own pace, slow, steady, intense but quiet, and deep.

Was that too much to ask? Should she wise up, be more of a realist, acknowledge that the seeds of summer passion would scatter and disperse, that two very different countries and life-styles lay between them? Even now, after only two months, all the commuting was getting to be exhausting, disruptive, the phone bills were massive, it all felt muddled and messy, a battle which, in the end, even love might not be strong enough to conquer. Even love . . . finding it had been hard enough, but only now did she see that keeping it might be even harder. Like the fire, it needed constant feeding, could not be left unattended for a moment, its flames were filled with both intense warmth and incendiary danger.

It could gutter out, she thought with horror, or it could devour me, burn and leave me horribly scarred. I've never been this close to it before, and now I don't know how to handle it.

Removing her coat and his own, Vittorio caressed her shoulder, looked around him and let his gaze linger on the contents of the room, which in Saiv's eyes suddenly resembled a huckster's stall. A mish-mash mess, in some tatty bazaar, crammed way beyond capacity. Thinking of his own large, dignified apartment, with its chalky pastel walls and gleaming floors, its sense of space and light, she was more conscious than ever of the differences between them.

He's a man, she thought; a big, robust, capable man, and I'm just a little mouse in its burrow. I wish I could have taken him to Lauren's apartment, it's like a hotel, he'd have been much more comfortable there.

Standing up, he crossed to the mantelpiece and fingered an earthenware statue, a crude piece she'd bought years ago, because the vendor looked destitute and she'd felt sorry for him.

'Where did you get this?'

His smile was warm, but she felt shivery. 'In India, for a few rupees on a pavement. It's only—'

'India? What were you doing there?'

'I was – wandering! I used to love travelling, before my parents were killed, I was just getting started and then—'

'And then you were afraid?'

Silently, she nodded. She had told him what had happened, how many years she had spent marooned on her island, before Lauren blackmailed her into going to Italy.

'But finally you took the chance, you overcame your fear . . .' Putting down the statue, he knelt to kindle the fire, bank it up with logs and turf, coax it into life. Watching, she bit her lip, thinking how at home he seemed to be making himself, how readily the fire responded. When it was burning bright, he dusted off his hands and returned to her side, his smile very white in his dark, short beard. Taking her hand, he chafed it warm.

'Are you afraid now?'

'Now?' Nonplussed, she didn't know what to say. Yes, Vittorio, I'm petrified, this is all spinning out of control, you're filling up my entire little house and my entire little life?

'Yes, now. Are you thinking that perhaps you have – *come se dici?* – have bitten off more than you can chew? That it is one thing to visit me in Italy, another to bring me into your home? I think you are a very private person, Saiv, and do not let people easily into your life.'

'Yes' she murmured. 'That's true. I'm not sociable by nature, and don't have many visitors.'

'Well' he grinned unexpectedly, 'you have one now! I want to see all of this little cottage, I want to meet the people around it, walk the walks you walk, eat the food you eat, get to know everything about the way you live and the person you are. Sometimes I suspect I have only seen the tip of the iceberg.'

'*Ice*berg?'

'Yes! I don't mean that you are cold – on the contrary – I mean you are submerged, hidden, you only reveal as much as you think it safe to reveal. But, if we are truly to get to know and trust each other, you must not be afraid any more. You must open your mind to me, as I have opened mine to you.'

Even as he said it, she saw it – he had opened his mind to her, at considerable risk to himself. He had lost his wife, knew the anguish of loss, and yet he was exposing himself to it again, to the possibility that this passionate but tentative relationship might not work, never attain what he had had before, with Claudia. He might end up with only a pale, painful imitation.

Well, then. If he could take a chance, she must take one, meet him halfway. Thoughtfully, looking away from him into the fire, she drew breath.

'Vittorio. I am not an extrovert. I prefer to have a few close friends than many superficial ones. It takes me a long time to get to know people, never mind trust them. I normally keep strangers at arm's length and I don't know how you got past that point. Somehow my body and my heart seem to have flown light years ahead of my mind. But my mind is catching up, more and more every time we meet . . . please, try to be patient?'

Reflective in turn, he cupped her chin and turned her face back to him, looking into it as he touched her lip with his finger. 'Yes, I will try, am trying . . . so long as you promise me, Saiv, not to back off, not to feel I am coming too close?'

'Too close? Oh, Vittorio, I want you to come close, much closer . . . I just don't want you to do it too fast, that's all.'

'You're sure? You're not – regretting anything?'

She was puzzled. 'Regretting?'

'Yes! Regretting asking me here, regretting having . . . having let things move so far, so quickly, in Italy?'

'No! They wouldn't have, if I hadn't been so wound up, so jet-propelled, after that flight that first night. But I'm very glad they did. It might have taken months, otherwise, and we'd have missed so much.'

Satisfied, he kissed her nose. 'Yes. That's how I feel. We are not teenagers, not kids like Michele with all the time in the world. We have missed enough already, and I want to catch up.'

'Yes. But, Vittorio . . . how far can we go? Is there any point in going anywhere, as long as Gina is – is so hostile?'

He exhaled a long, slow sigh, and grimaced as he tightened his arm around her. 'Saiv, Gina is not hostile. She is defensive. It's not quite the same thing. It may take time, but I will win her around, and so will you. You may even find that she is worth winning, a sweet shy girl underneath it all – just like you.'

Like herself? Saiv had not thought of Gina in that light before. 'But – we will win her round to what, Vittorio? Should I try to get closer to her, when I live here in Ireland, all these miles away? It might merely upset her, in the end, all this coming and going, might be confusing and premature––'

'Saiv. Look. You may be only part-time in our family at the moment, but I assure you I would not have let you meet my children if I did not want you to be in it all the time. I know your work is here and your life is here, but we will find a way around this problem. I am determined to find a way, if only you––'

Only what? Listening intently, she looked up at him, wondering if he could possibly be so sure, be trying to say what he seemed to be––

Sudden and shrill, the telephone rang across the room, and she leaped up with a shriek, out of his arms, racing to it. Laurie!?

'Saiv, hi, it's me!'

'Oh! At last! Where are you, how was your trip, when are you coming home?'

'My trip was wonderful. I learned so much along the way, you wouldn't believe the half of it. Ten men and two women, on one boat – I tell you, it's not for the faint-hearted! We reached Ilica last week, but I'm in Eskiseher now, with Carl and Luke and Desmond.'

'Eskiseher? But – isn't that where the earthquake was?'

'Jesus! Don't tell me you've been watching television, for once!'

'It's been all over the media, even I couldn't miss it . . . Laurie, what on earth are you doing there?'

'At this moment I'm standing on a street corner, talking to you! The boat had to go into dry-dock to get its mast fixed, so I – well, myself and a couple of the guys decided we might as well come up here and lend a hand. We rented a jeep, it's only two hundred miles . . . they were very short-handed in the quake zone so – well, for Chrissakes, you can't just lounge around when people are dying, can you? We're just mucking in for a few more days until the boat is ship-shape.'

'But Laurie, isn't it dangerous?'

'Not a bit, safe as houses! The houses have already collapsed and there haven't been any more after-shocks, the experts say there won't be so we're not worried about that. It's just a question of getting down on our hands and knees in the dirt and maybe breaking the odd nail! I'll be booking in for a full manicure when I get home.'

Incredulous, Saiv could hardly absorb it. Lauren Kilroy, going into an earthquake zone? She must be hallucinating.

'But—'

'So, what's happening with you? How's Romeo? Tell me all!'

'I – I can't –' Cautiously Saiv lowered her voice, and instantly Laurie guessed.

'You mean he's there with you? Now, in your house?'

'Yes.'

'Wow! This must be serious! Oh, Saiv, I knew it, and I'm delighted for you! See, I was telling the truth that night.'

'Yes, you were . . . Laurie, I'm so sorry I didn't believe you. Sorry I exploded and was a miserable bitch and forgot your birthday—'

'Hey, maybe it's time we started forgetting them anyway, or shaving a few years off at least. We're not getting any younger, pal. Which is one of many good reasons to give Vittorio Scalzini your best shot and . . . is it going places, do you think? Is he keen as mustard?'

Saiv didn't know where to look, what to say. With Vittorio here under her nose, looking quizzically up at her as he stoked the fire, how could she describe the scene, tell Laurie that her call had interrupted something that had been sounding perilously near to a – a proposal?

But it wasn't a proposal. Not yet, maybe not ever. Better not count your chickens here, lady.

'Well, you could put it that way, but—'

'Oh, great! Can I be bridesmaid? Godmother to the triplets?'

'Laurie! Get a grip!'

'Get a grip yourself – on him! Anyway, look, I have to go. But I'll be home in about a week, max, and we'll have a long chat then, I'll come stay overnight.'

'Yes, but – Laurie, have you told your parents where you are, what you're doing?'

'You must be kidding. Betty would have a heart attack. I'll tell her and Dad when we get back to Ilica. By then they'll be so revved up about Caoimhe coming home for Christmas they won't give it a thought. Listen, Carl is getting impatient, I'd better move along here.'

Desperately, Saiv groped at her, across four thousand miles. 'Is Carl all right? And these other guys, will they take care of you?'

'Hah! I might take care of them, if they don't watch out! Yeah, they're good lads, Saiv, we'll all look after each other. They have useful skills for the situation – Carl's an engineer, Luke's a pharmacist and Desmond's an electrician.'

'And what are you?'

'Me? I'm just a pretty face! Ciao!'

In a flurry she was gone, leaving Saiv clutching at nothingness, wishing she could get more information, give more too, that Vittorio had not unwittingly inhibited the whole thing. But at least she had got to talk to Laurie, at last, and was hugely delighted to hear her sounding so well, so chirpy and confident. It sounded as if the old Laurie was back, in spirit, and would soon be back in person.

And when she gets here, she thought resolutely, I'm going to spoil her rotten. Make up for missing her birthday, for the ordeal she's been through, reward her for doing such a brave and extraordinary thing. Who or what could possibly have enticed her into such a situation, an earthquake of all the dirty, dangerous things . . . even if she says there isn't any danger, it must be gruesome, and hellishly hard work. Now I know what to give her for Christmas – a manicure, a facial, a massage, the works! She'll be exhausted, and need lots of pampering.

God, I love Lauren Kilroy! Full of surprises, daring to do all the crazy things I'd never dare to do. If she was here with a man like Vittorio she'd never be vacillating, thinking of all the ifs and buts, she'd have him pinned to the floor like a prizefighter, clinching him in her grip, he'd be Mr Kilroy before he knew what hit him. There she is grubbing in the rubble in Eskisehir, in a country she's never clapped eyes on before in her life, while I . . .

I need my head examined. If I let this lovely man away, leave him waiting and wondering, refusing to take the kind of chances Lauren takes, the kind he's taking himself, I should be certified. Locked up for the rest of my cautious, fearful, narrow, miserable little life.

'Vittorio? What were you saying, before Laurie interrupted?'

Frowning, he put his hand to his eyes for a moment, as if he had lost his train of thought. 'I was saying . . . that your life is here in Ireland, in this little cottage of yours.'

'Yes. It is little, and I – I've been cooped up in it. Feeling cramped, needing more space, room to breathe and grow. It's only since I've been visiting you, in Italy, that I've realised how small this place is, how isolated.'

'Have you, *cara*?'

His tone was full of concern, his look tender as he left the fireplace, crossed the room and came back to sit beside her, taking her hand once again into his grasp.

'Yes. Even the dogs . . . they're too big for this tiny house. I love them dearly, and it's not fair to them, they're shut indoors all the time I'm at work, farmed out to Jennifer when I'm in Italy with you . . . I think even Elmer and Duster are ready for a change. Need one, for their own good.'

For a moment he said nothing, weighing her words, reflecting on them. Her hand lay in his lap, and she waited, hardly daring to believe the audacity of what she was saying; as an interpreter, surely he wouldn't, couldn't misunderstand?

'Saiv. I think you know how I feel. We don't need words to express it, do we?'

'No, Vittorio. We don't.'

His eyes lit up. But his mind seemed to roam the room, thinking.

'*Dio* . . . I hardly let myself believe . . . but, Saiv, we must be serious, and responsible. I wish I could offer you a home in my apartment for your dogs, but it is full of children. I don't think – it would not be practical, or possible.'

She swallowed. 'No. I know that. Something would have to give.'

'Yes. And then – what of your work, your teaching?'

That was easier. She smiled wryly. 'What of it? Vittorio, my mind isn't on it, my heart isn't in it any more.'

'But it is your career. Your livelihood, and your independence.'

'Yes. But . . . Vittorio, I hadn't told you this, because maybe I – I'm a bit shy, only a beginner. But I've written a book.'

He looked astonished, and delighted. 'Have you? About what?'

'About Jean-Jacques Rousseau. It's obscure but it has been accepted, is about to be published . . . and I want to write another one. Maybe several. I don't know what might come of the whole project, but I'd like to find out.'

'Well – so would I! If you have a talent or an interest, you must pursue it. Growth is not possible otherwise, you would become frustrated and your soul would wither.'

She was glad he saw it the same way she did herself, did not immediately refer to money although he must understand it meant she would have none.

'What do your friends and family make of this book?'

'My friends think I'm nuts! Lauren doesn't even know what it's about, as far as I can make out, but she has been so encouraging, so supportive, so – so much more positive than anyone else. My family – well, I only have two brothers, as you know, and we're not very close. My only close relative is my niece Gráinne, who's around Michele's age – I'm very fond of her, though my brother rarely lets me see her.'

'H'mm. Why is that?'

'I'm not sure. Lauren thinks it's something to do with envy, maybe, some kind of insecurity that's sent him spinning off on a power trip. Or else he measures people in material terms, sees me as a failure and doesn't want Gráinne to go getting any ideas from me.'

'I see. Well, if Gráinne is Michele's age, she's old enough to start making up her own mind about things . . . I would like to meet her. And maybe she would like to visit Italy, some time?'

'Oh! She'd love it. But – what about Gina?'

'Saiv. Let me be frank about Gina. She is a troubled child. She has caused me much worry since her mother died, and if you are prepared to take her on then she will cause you much worry too. There will be times when you may heartily regret ever having met her . . . but I hope you will never regret having met me. If you feel strong enough to take her on, I will be eternally relieved and grateful to you, because – whether she believes it or not – she needs some maternal influence. This is not why I want you in my life, but it is a consideration, for both of us.'

'Yes. It is. It's a big project, and – apart from Gráinne – I have no experience of children whatsoever. The ones I teach are much older, not kids at all.'

'No. But still you are a teacher . . . I would very much like Gina to learn something from you. To come to trust you and, in time, to like and respect you. I will never ask her to love you, if she feels it is not in her power, but I will allow myself to hope, while loving you myself . . . even now I can scarcely believe such a thing is possible, but I fell in love with you the moment we met, in Raffaelo's house. And then, that night in the restaurant, out on the terrace . . .'

'When you sang . . . the moment I heard you sing, I knew . . .'

'Did you?' His voice was low, almost muffled by the crackling flames of the fire. Bracing herself, she took a deep breath, and the plunge.

'Yes. For the first time in my life, I knew I was in love. With you, with Italy, with life itself.'

His eyes widened. 'The first time?'

'Yes. I'd never loved anyone before, never allowed myself to hope that anyone could love me . . . but . . . Lauren gave me courage, made me believe in you, and in myself.'

'Then Lauren must be our guest of honour, and godmother to our children! Saiv, will you marry me, have children with me, help me care for the ones I have already? Will you love me, as I will love you, for the rest of the life that has been restored to us?'

His hand tightened on hers, his eyes looked honestly and hopefully into hers, and she reached up to him, taking the initiative, kissing his lips deliberately, deeply.

'Yes, Vittorio. I will. I will abandon my life here, move to Italy and marry you. I will marry your entire family, Gina and all, for better or for worse.'

Drawing her to him, he enfolded her in his powerful embrace, and his eyes gleamed in the flickering light.

'Oh, Saiv. My Saiv. After all these years, you make me feel so alive.'

Now, Lauren thought with satisfaction. That'll teach you. You guys will never be able to say another bad word about me, never accuse me of not being up to the tough stuff, of being a bimbo who'd whip out her lace hankie in a crisis and flutter her eyelashes like a helpless airhead. I'm the one who got *you* to come here, even if you'll never admit it, probably didn't even realise I was steering you into it. I buttered you up sweetly and shamelessly, I appealed to every macho instinct in you, and I got you to Eskiseher – not the whole lot of you, admittedly, but you three, the ones whose respect matters most to me.

And I've earned it now, haven't I? I've thrown all my weight – such as it is – into digging and hauling and wrenching, into carting buckets of water and crates of food, driving miles for drugs, rustling up meals out in the open air, ferrying people to the hospital, from the airport, doing anything and everything anyone possibly could to make herself useful. Lola Cola might not be much damn use to humanity, but Lauren Kilroy is, at this moment, and I know now why I didn't die of hep C. My life was saved so I could save someone else's, and I've done that, with your help; I've crawled into impossibly small spaces and I've got two people out from under, a man and his grandson, still living. Even if I'll never have kids myself, at least I've contributed to someone else's family, to somebody's wellbeing besides my own.

So there. Put that in your pipe and smoke it.

Jesus. How am I ever going to go back to Axis, after this? How will I sit at a desk in a cute suit, peddling cola and crisps, earning as much in a month as would keep any of these families for a year? I'll never be able to eat lunch at that hotel out in Howth again, talking about the weather to my parents . . . thank God I've already taken steps to get out of that rut, and now I'll certainly have something to talk about when I get back. Something real, whether Betty likes it or not, something interesting, and affirmative. Something that might even convince her I'm worth a damn, and get her respect. She seems so far away, at this moment, but she never is really, she's always there camping on my shoulder, telling me where I'm going all wrong.

But I'm not going wrong now, Mother! You'd never have wanted me to come here, you'd have fainted if you'd known, but it's the right place for me to be, the right thing for me to do.

I'll tell you all about it when I see you, and you'll have to agree, this trip to Turkey was more than just a silly jaunt. Even if being away is going to cost me career points, who cares – I'm young, and I'll make them up. If I feel like it, if I ever regain interest in posters and publicity campaigns. I might take on a charity account, when I go back, for Concern or Trócaire or something, that'd validate the rest of the rubbish. A bit, anyway. I'd feel there was more point to it all.

'Laurie!'

Standing upright, wiping her forehead, she left the woman whose tent she was helping to rig up, and looked round for Carl. He was standing some distance away, with Desmond; Luke had gone to a first-aid base to help dispense drugs.

'Yeah?'

'C'mere!'

His tone was bossy, commanding, and she smiled; he tended to shout only when he needed help with something he couldn't do himself. It was frustrating when you couldn't just fix everything instantly, as was your instinct, wave a magic wand that would restore the dusty destruction to pristine perfection. But the earthquake damage was going to take months to repair, maybe years.

'What's up?'

Sweaty and dishevelled, Carl pointed into the ground, and she saw nothing only a pile of bricks and earth, over which Desmond was kneeling, dangling some kind of electrical gizmo into its centre.

'Desmond thinks there's someone in here.'

'What? A body, you mean?'

Desmond glanced up at her, filthy, looking somehow intent and speculative all at once.

'No. Alive. The heat probe is giving a reading.'

'Alive?! But – there can't be. Not after a whole week. Anyone who's down there, buried under all this, is dead for sure. You said so yourselves.'

It had been agreed, between all the volunteers and helpers;

the last living survivors had been excavated four or five days ago, nobody else could possibly have made it. Not without food or water, for eight days.

Carl and Desmond exchanged glances, a Swiss worker said something she didn't catch, and everyone looked at her uneasily. After a hesitant silence, it was Carl who spoke.

'It seems impossible. Might not even be a person, could be a rat or some other animal. But something is definitely giving off heat. Something, or someone, we can't get at. The space is too narrow.'

Ah. So this was where she came into the picture. This was what she was good at, because she was so boyishly thin: shimmying into tiny vents, gullies, air bubbles under the debris. Six times already she had done it, locating four bodies and two living people, scrabbling with her hands from inside to clear space, widen it up so that they could be winched out. But it was agonising work, it tore at her mind as well as her body, kept her awake for hours on her camp bed at nights and then left her sweating, panting through nightmares. Twice Carl or Desmond had had to get up and come to her, comfort her after the trauma.

She wasn't going to do it again now unless they were convinced it would be worthwhile, that some man or woman might – incredibly – be still alive down there. Alive, and in agony, listening to their voices overhead, grasping at receding hope?

She turned to the Swiss man, an army despatch with professional experience.

'What do you think? Is it possible, after all this time? Could anyone survive?'

Frowning, he chewed his lower lip. 'It is unlikely. A very remote possibility. If anyone is alive, they are in very bad shape, clinging on by a thread.'

Carl looked at him. 'But it is possible? Just barely?'

'Anything is possible. Miracles can happen. What we must weigh up is whether it is worth investigating, risking someone's life to go in here at such long odds. Are we sure about the reading, that the equipment is not faulty?'

Looking up, Desmond nodded. 'I'm sure. There's definitely life of some kind down here.'

Again they all turned to Lauren, and she stood immobile, wondering. It was a very long shot. A dangerous shot, maybe for nothing.

Or maybe for something, for someone. Maybe she wasn't the only one the gods permitted to clutch at straws, to reach out to a life, to a future?

A surge of adrenalin shot through her, a sense of exuberant purpose gripped every nerve in her body, steeling her, tensing every bone to squeeze down between the breeze blocks.

'OK. I can fit. Let's go for it.'

Everyone stared at her, and then Desmond shook his head. 'No, Laurie. You've done enough. This one is too close to call. I'm taking a decision here. It's not worth it.'

She grinned at him. 'Desmond, it's not your decision to take. Your decision is that there's life of some kind under this lot, and mine is to find out who or what it is. Get me ready, give me a hand, I'll need the protective gear and a torch.'

Nodding, without another word, the Swiss soldier went to do as she requested. Uneasily, Carl ran his hand through his hair.

'Laurie . . . look . . .'

'Watch my lips! I said I'll do it, OK? Just keep a line on me and don't let go, or I'll have you keelhauled when I come up.'

Abruptly, he kissed her forehead, and nodded. 'All right. You're one cool cookie, I must say. If I wasn't married I might run away to sea with you.'

'Hah! Thanks, but I've had it with married men! Now, let's move.'

They assembled the gear, and when she was ready she lay down on the ground, stretching her arms into the air pocket as far as she could reach, waggling her fingers.

'Yeah. There's space down here, a kind of tunnel. Get a few of these top bricks off and clear as far as you can.'

In the sweltering silence they cleared, until there was just enough room to writhe through, down into the dark below. At the very last moment, Desmond put his hand on her arm.

'Laurie. You don't have to do this. You don't have to prove a thing.'

She smiled at him. 'I know. I've done it before, and I don't have to do it again. I'm just doing it because, as Joe said, there isn't a pick on me. Doing it because I can. And because, as Saiv says, where there's life there's hope. Keep that probe moving, and the ropes taut, or you're toast.'

He patted her shoulder, and Carl helped her down, until she was in the underground cavern, groping her way into the blackness, clawing at the sides of the earthen tomb and listening fiercely for any human sound, any sign of life.

The Scalzini family was assembled, the champagne was flowing and Vittorio was circulating with a bottle in either hand, beaming the beatific smile of a man about to be married, presenting his betrothed for the admiration of one and all.

Not married just yet, no date had been set, but Saiv wondered whether they should maybe fix one a bit sooner than Easter after all, because if her suspicions were correct she'd be the size of a prize pumpkin by then. It was just as well, she thought, that Vittorio had proposed and she had accepted, already given in her notice and taken a week's sick leave on the spot. You couldn't very well be dry-heaving all over your students.

But this was what came of rash unprotected sex, of falling madly in love with your man and madly into bed with him. This bambino must have been conceived the very first time, literally before they'd had time to think, and she blushed at the thought of it: this was the kind of thing her students were always doing! As an adult she was supposed to have more sense, to set an example.

But I am setting an example. I'm taking the chance life has

offered me, I'm learning and I'm growing – literally growing. I'll have to see a doctor here in Italy and then tell Vittorio. Will he be as astonished, as thrilled as I am myself?

Yes. He will be. He's a good father already and I know he wants this new life as much as I do. He will worship this baby and, if we handle Gina carefully, she might love her little sister or brother . . . we'll tell her we're giving her a present, that we made it specially for her. To some extent, it might even help to make up for losing her mother, she will have someone new to love. Meanwhile, I'd better keep an eye on her, make sure she feels included in these celebrations.

Making her way through the throng – how huge these Italian families were, they seemed to stretch into infinity! – she located Gina and said hello to Paola, the friend who shared everything.

'Hello, girls. Are you enjoying yourselves?'

Their mouths full, they nodded solemnly, and Saiv smiled at them.

'I have a question to ask you.'

'*Cos'è?*'

'I was wondering how you'd feel about coming shopping with me one day, getting some new dresses?'

'*Perchè?*' In spite of herself, Gina looked up; apparently the word 'shopping' affected her the same way it affected Lauren Kilroy.

'Because you'll need outfits for the wedding. If you'd like to be my flower girls, that is? Both of you?'

Her mouth ringed with cream, Gina turned to Paola to translate, and Saiv had to suppress a grin: she was still such a child really, munching her cake! Grasping the situation, Paola began to giggle, and then Gina giggled in turn, the pair of them looking like two little granny dolls.

'Paola says can we pick our own dresses?'

'Um . . . yes, all right, you're big girls now! Only promise me you won't pick anything in – uh – black?'

It wasn't impossible, because they were on the verge of their

Gothic phase like pre-teens everywhere. But Gina frowned at her, a trifle impatiently.

'Oh, no. I want pink. Dark rose pink. So does Paola.'

Phew. 'Then rose it is. Like your father, Gina, you have good taste.'

As does Italy, she thought; I feel so vibrant, so at ease and at home here. It's a beautiful, cultured country, and yet there's nothing precious about it, it has a warm heart and a lively soul. This apartment will be my new home, these people will be my family, Verona will be my new city and my new joy. I never liked cities, but this one has a river and heaps of history, it has a musical tradition and all these gorgeous, wonky old buildings . . . I'll miss Elmer and Duster, but they'll have a better life, and I'll have my new baby. My husband, and my child. My God.

Speculatively, unable to disguise her curiosity, Gina looked up at her. 'Why are we only to be flower girls? Why not bridesmaids?'

'Oh, because . . . because that's a job for my best friend. You have Paola and I have Lauren. You'll meet her after Christmas I hope, she's in Turkey now and first she has to go home to Ireland to see her family. She has a sister she's dying to see, and her mama and papa, and the sister has a new baby to show her.'

Gina perked up. 'Paola's mama has a new baby too. His name is Tommaso, he's Paola's brother.'

Saiv thought she saw a window. 'You mean Paola has a new brother, but you haven't? That's not fair!'

Gina tossed her head. 'I don't want a brother. I already have Michele. I want a sister.'

'Do you now? Well then, maybe your papa and I will see if we can get one for you.'

Gina grimaced. 'You don't *get* babies. You *make* them.'

Saiv grinned. 'Well, I wasn't sure whether you knew that! Anyway, we'll do our best, OK?'

'*Va bene.*' Gina nodded with the air of an approving house-wife whose grocer had promised some prime tomatoes, and Saiv smiled, deciding to quit while she was – just – ahead.

'All right. Now, where is your papa?'

Vittorio was way across the room, chatting with Donatella, the sister who was such a good aunt to his children. As she made her way over to them, catching their welcoming smile, Saiv absorbed his aura of genial wellbeing, the flash of intimate happiness that passed between them, the sense of unity that was already growing. I'm getting to know him, she thought, on that subconscious level lovers reach; I'd know he was near me even if I couldn't see him, I'd feel his presence, recognise his skin, his scent, his impact on the room around me. We're tuning in, the two components of a single entity. Why were things never this way in the Lovett family, why was there never this sense of communicating, belonging?

It's too late, now, for that. But at least Gráinne is enthusiastic, raring to come to the wedding and meet Vittorio, she's positive and pleased for me. Looking forward to meeting Michele, too, the boy who loves cars almost as much as she does herself . . . the family connection isn't entirely lost, and I'll fight to sustain it, foster it with her.

Winding her arm around Vittorio, she gave him a little hug. 'I've just promised Gina a present.'

'Oh?'

'Mmm. A baby sister.'

'Really! Then we had better see about getting her one.'

It wasn't the moment to tell him, not yet, but his wide smile, his cheerful enthusiasm warmed her heart. Like most Italians, he loved children. She felt as if she were being enfolded into this family, embraced and absorbed by it; after so many years of solitude, her life was starting to sing with vitality.

'Where's Michele?'

'In his room I think, probably watching television. You know how boys of his age are about social gatherings – painfully shy, for all their swaggering. Nonetheless, he must be polite. I will go and see if I can winkle him out.'

'Oh, let him be.'

But Vittorio departed purposefully, forging a path through

his friends and cousins and in-laws, including Claudia's brother Pietro who was there with his wife, Adua. Although it was a painful reminder to him, he kept in touch with Claudia's family for the sake of his children, who as he said did not deserve to be deprived of their uncle or aunt as well as their mother.

As he vanished from view, Donatella took Saiv by the arm and tucked her into a corner, whispering conspiratorially. Dark like her brother, slimmer but equally solid, Donatella was a congenial woman who, Saiv thought, might become a first new friend in Italy. Bubbly and gregarious, she seemed to be a lynchpin of today's relaxed, informal gathering.

'Saiv . . . I just wanted to tell you . . . I am so pleased. For you and for Vittorio . . . he has been lonely, you know. So lonely, for so long, since Claudia died.'

'Yes . . . Donatella, was she very different to me?' Prettier, more extrovert, graceful? Every possibility flitted through Saiv's mind.

'Yes. She was quite different. She was intense, fiery, sometimes a little impatient – a travel agent, and on the municipal council! Always busy, always on the go . . . Vittorio tells me you are a teacher, and a writer?'

'Yes. A biographer. Just starting, but keen to do more. If I'm asked! I've only done it once . . . but at least it's a portable career, I can do it anywhere. Work from home, which will give me more time with the – the children.'

'Yes. That will be a welcome change for them, and for me! An aunt can only do so much. I know Gina is difficult, but I will help you with her.'

'Thank you. I'd be very grateful.'

Nodding, Donatella took her by the hand and led her out into the centre of things, where as hostess she should be anyway. Entertaining on this scale was new to her, but she would learn, she would remember the names of all these twenty or thirty people.

Steering her round, Donatella took her to talk with each of them in turn, and she smiled at them all, chatting as best she could, half in their hybrid English, half in her dodgy Italian.

Were they saying it was a happy day, or that they wanted more pay? After a while she began to flounder, and wish that Vittorio would return to buoy her up. Where had he got to, surely he wasn't lecturing Michele or engaging in any kind of dispute with him? It was the wrong place and the wrong time, and she could sympathise with Michele's shyness.

But, when eventually he emerged from Michele's room, Vittorio's expression signalled immediately that something was wrong. All the light had drained from his face, he almost swayed to her side looking stunned, his eyes as dark as if it was raining in his soul.

'Saiv.' He grasped her shoulder and she turned into his.

'What kept you? Is Michele all right?'

'Saiv . . . please, come with me.'

'Why? Where? We can't leave our guests, your family, your friends—'

'Please. Come.'

His urgent tone forced her to excuse herself, and he led her away from everyone, into their bedroom. *Their* bedroom! Exulting as she looked around it, she sat down on the bed where, apparently, he wanted her to sit.

'Vittorio, what is it?'

Bewildered, she gazed at him, at this room which was so full of love, so richly inviting with its dense fabrics, its dusky walls, its tones of amethyst and amber burnished by the light flowing through the tall, ancient windows.

'Saiv, I . . . I am so sorry . . .' Sagging, he sank down beside her, lost for words. Her heart flipped and stalled; what terrible thing could he want to tell her? Had he changed his mind, decided he could not let go of Claudia, could not marry her after all? His eyes filling with ragged emotion, he was fighting tears, and her body iced with anticipation of impending horror. Breathless, she waited for the blade to fall, for the knife to plunge into her heart.

'I . . . Michele . . . on television . . . Saiv, there has been an accident.'

'A – a what?'

'Just as I went into his room, it came on the news . . . an Irish aid volunteer, in Turkey. She went underground to try to reach someone buried in the earthquake rubble . . . someone who had already died, only minutes before. The small cavern caved in on top of her – Saiv, it is Lauren.'

Stock still, she stared at him, her mind emptying, refusing to absorb what it could not absorb.

Desperately, as if each word was being dragged out of him, Vittorio ploughed on. 'Lauren Kilroy. They did everything they could, tried to save her, but it was not possible . . . it happened two days ago, but they have only now recovered her body and released her name. Saiv, Lauren is dead.'

Two days – Laurie was dead, had been dead *for two days*? Her mind slammed up against it, wrestled it, rejected it in a reeling, nauseous frenzy.

No! Laurie, no, hang on, I'm coming! *Laurie*—!

'Saiv, she – she gave her life, for someone else's. Gave it in vain, but gave it just the same.'

No!

Her hands were clenching into fists, Vittorio's were gripping her, the room was crumbling and dissolving around her, blurring into the fading haze of centuries.

Laurie!

She must have cried aloud, because Vittorio's grip tightened, held her upright, against his chest as if it were a wall, supporting her. Speechless, strangled by some searing fire in her throat, she clutched at his shirt, buried her face in it, feeling as if her mind was leaving her body and looking down on it from some other place, some great height. As if from a spring at the core of the earth, tears gushed up and poured from her, cascading over some cliff in her mind, the severed edge of her heart.

Maybe he held her for hours. Or only minutes, or weeks or months? Time evaporated, she had no idea how long she lay against him, gasping, weeping until she could weep no more, until he embraced her with such ferocity she was suffocating, ready to stop breathing and go to Laurie.

'Saiv, *cara* . . . what can I say, what can I do to help you through this?' His lips touching her hair, his eyes searching her face, his whole body was palpably yearning to help. But there was nothing he could do, nothing anyone could do. Lauren was dead. Numb, she did not respond.

'Do you want . . . should I arrange . . . if it would be a comfort, I will take you to Turkey. Now, tonight, to see Lauren, to be with her and accompany her on – on her journey home to Ireland.'

His arms did not leave her, but she felt him stiffen, gather his resolve and his resources as men did in a crisis, groping for some practical thing to do.

Ravaged, she lifted her face to him, and slowly shook her head. 'No . . . Vittorio, I can't. I can't go to her.'

She was barely able to whisper, and he whispered in turn, his lips brushing her wet cheek. 'Why not, *carissima*? Would it be too great an ordeal? I understand, if it would, but maybe later you might regret . . .?'

'No.' How could she tell him, how could this exquisite moment be so appalling, so unbearable? Stalling, she tried to refute it. 'Vittorio, are you sure? Absolutely sure, it was Lauren Kilroy's name they said, there is no mistake?'

'I am so sorry. But I am sure. There was a photograph, her face on the screen – I could not mistake it.'

No. Who could mistake Laurie? Lively, lovely Laurie? Her heart quivering and constricting, Saiv looked into Vittorio's old-new face, the face she had come to love so dearly, through Laurie, because of Laurie.

'Vittorio, if it were possible, if there were any way – I would do it – but I can't. I cannot go to Laurie, to Turkey.'

'Please tell me why, *cara*.'

Slowly, sitting up, she put her hand on his chest. 'Because I – I think – I am going to have a baby.'

His eyes flashed, his whole face flared with joy, shock and

delight blazing in the midst of his sorrow. 'A baby? A child, our child—?'

'Yes.' Oh God, what pain, what joy! 'Our child, that we made the night I learned to fly.'

Everything changed in him, some instant metamorphosis seemed to seize him, seal him protectively to her side.

'Oh, *Dio mio*. Oh, Saiv.'

For some time, neither of them spoke, a river of love and anguish flowing between them. When at length he moved a fraction, murmured into her neck, even his voice was different.

'Then you are right. It would be too arduous for you to travel so far, and the earthquake region is dangerous. I will not permit it. Instead I will tell Michele to inform our friends, ask them to quietly disperse, and I will take you to Ireland tomorrow. We will be there to – to receive Lauren, when she comes home.'

To receive Lauren. Lauren who had survived, and was now dead, after all? The force of it, the savage unfairness, ripped Saiv's breath from her lungs.

Laurie! Wait! I owe you a fiver! I owe you so much . . . I owe you everything. You can't go, you've to come to my wedding, you've to see my baby born . . . *no*. You can't go. You can't.

Vittorio was standing up, saying something to her, but Saiv did not hear his words, could no longer see his face through the tears that claimed her, took possession of her body and her soul, drowning her in a grief she felt would be eternal. Deep down in her heart some terrible struggle began, between her friend and her child, the old life and the new, the love that was lost and fighting for rebirth.

Three days later, on a winter's morning that was cold and clear as glass, Saiv stood with Vittorio at the door of Glasnevin crematorium, her shock masked, her pain subdued, shaking hands with the many people who had come to say goodbye to Lauren. For

Lauren's sake she had endured the ordeal of the ceremony; for her baby's sake she would survive its aftermath.

Leaving the chapel, their heads bowed, she could see Laurie's parents Eoin and Betty, and her heart went out to them; bent in unison, they wore the disbelieving, hammered look of loss, of a bereavement out of season, out of nature's course. Holding his wife's hand, Eoin was supporting Betty, guiding her through a ritual that appeared to be too much for her, and Saiv shivered, wondered what agonies must be assailing the woman's mind.

Behind them, their other daughter Caoimhe, come all the way from Canada for what was to have been a family reunion, a festive Christmas. Carrying a baby on her hip, wearing dark glasses, Caoimhe looked so petite, so appallingly like Lauren that Saiv gasped, had to compose herself before touching Vittorio's arm, leaving him for a moment to approach the family alone.

Yes, Eoin said, of course he remembered her, as did all the Kilroy family. His eyes were very bright, but his voice stayed steady as he introduced her to Caoimhe, to Caoimhe's husband, Betty standing silent between them.

'This is Saiv, Lauren's oldest friend, they were at college together . . . thank you for coming, Saiv, for being here today – and for being Lauren's friend.'

His tone was low and pained, but she was touched that he could say it, say anything at all. She strove in turn to speak.

'Lauren was my best friend, Mr Kilroy, the best friend I ever could have wished for. I loved her, and – and you must be so very proud of her.'

With a strangled sob, Betty put her hand to her eyes and turned away. Caoimhe turned with her, attempting to comfort her mother, but Eoin stood where he was, looking at Saiv with a kind of stoic calm.

'I can't tell you how proud, Saiv. I had no idea she was doing what she was doing, but I can tell you this – her death was not in vain.'

No. Lauren had not succeeded in what she had been attempting to do, but her effort had elicited admiration from everyone, heartfelt thanks from the family of the young Turkish woman she had tried to save; incredibly they had even managed to send flowers today, all the way from Eskisehir. Saiv could hardly believe the generosity of their gesture, their solidarity of spirit in the midst of their own distress.

'No. It had purpose, as her life had increasing purpose . . . her voyage to Turkey was a voyage of discovery. She never changed, as long as I knew her, but she was growing, had been growing all this year. Lauren was a lovely lady, and I was very lucky to have been her friend.'

Looking down, he said nothing, mastering himself, and then he looked up again, speculatively.

'Saiv . . . her mother and I, and Caoimhe . . . we've been wondering . . . where do you think would be a – a good place to scatter her ashes? Did she have some favourite spot, that you know of, where she was happy?'

His voice cracked, and she put her hand on his arm, struggling to keep her own voice steady.

'I think . . . maybe . . . the hill of Tara? Laurie and I used to go walking there – at first she hated it, but then she stopped protesting, which was her way of saying that she was enjoying it . . . even coming to love it, eventually. It would be a lovely place to let her go on the wind, so that her voyage can continue.'

He dipped his head. 'Thank you. I think that would be appropriate.' And then he turned away, looking old and sad, to find his wife, to Caoimhe his other child, to his little grandchild.

Looking for Vittorio, Saiv started back to where she had left him, but a hand touched her shoulder, and she turned to find two men behind her, dapper and respectful in dark yachting blazers. The taller of the two introduced himself as Luke Gallagher, and this was his friend, Desmond McFadden. She must be Saiv Lovett, of whom Laurie had so often spoken?

'Yes, I am . . . did she?'

Yes, Luke asserted, Laurie had talked about her many times, told them how much she was looking forward to seeing her again, to hearing all her news – some good news, that they were both hoping for?

Gratefully, Saiv smiled. 'Yes. I'm getting married, to the man Laurie brought me together with, wanted me to marry.'

Yes, Luke said, that sounded like Laurie – eager, optimistic, loyal and supportive. Uneasily, he glanced at Desmond, and she realised that they were badly rattled by Lauren's death, deeply distressed for men who had known her only a couple of months.

'We gave her a hard time,' Desmond admitted frankly, 'even though we liked her a lot, were teaching her to play chess and coming to respect her more every day, we said some things at the end of the trip that we – we wish now we hadn't said.'

He shuffled uncomfortably, and Luke flushed guiltily, in a way that suddenly told Saiv they wanted to tell her, to get it off their chest.

'What did you say?'

Again, Luke glanced at Desmond. 'Well – Desmond said he thought she was a bit temperamental, and I – I said I thought she didn't have much depth, wouldn't want to be marooned on a desert island with her. We didn't realise she could hear us, but we wondered afterwards whether she had, whether . . . that might have been what drove her on, to do what she did. You should have seen her in Eskisehir, she worked like a demon, she dug out an old man and a boy with her bare hands . . . I'd be proud now to be marooned anywhere with her. But she'll never know that, will she?'

Saiv saw the devastation in him, saw how, in some obscure way, he and Desmond were looking to her for pardon or comprehension of some kind. Sailors both, they were looking acutely uncomfortable, unused to articulating their feelings. Like Betty, they were left now holding a lot of baggage, and she marshalled her words carefully.

'No. She won't. But if that's what caused her to go to Eskisehir, then you gave her something she urgently wanted, and needed. You gave her a sense of purpose, of identity and direction.'

Desmond looked puzzled. 'Urgently – needed?'

'Yes. She'd been dissatisfied with her career, with her life, felt it lacked worth . . . and she was very ill. If she was going to die anyway, I think maybe this is the way she would have preferred to go.'

Luke stared, Desmond looked incredulous. 'She was ill? What?'

'Yes. She didn't want anyone to know, never fully faced it herself, but she had hepatitis. Hep C. She might have survived it for years, the prognosis was good, but . . . perhaps you helped to bring about something that was meant to be. Lauren was full of life, and she was living it to the full when she died. She'd have been very grateful to you for helping her to do that.'

Their expressions were dazed as they grasped what she was saying, clutching it almost tangibly to them, murmuring to each other as they thanked her and melted away. Following them with her eyes, she saw them join another man, a tall handsome man who must, she guessed, be Carl Delaney, the skipper of the *WayToGo*. Wearing dark glasses like Caoimhe, Carl looked shattered, gutted by the loss of a woman he had known for so short a time. Something in his bearing held Saiv at bay, repelled her from a man who seemed to be feeling the same intense anguish she was feeling herself, with far less claim to do so. As she looked at him, an elegant brunette, his wife no doubt, took his arm and led him away.

And then there was Shane Jackson, standing oddly isolated amidst Laurie's secretary Angie, her friends Gemma and Adèle; Saiv was unable to go to them either, unable to exchange the quiet words of condolence that decorum dictated. Suddenly, the only person she wanted to be with was Vittorio.

Sensing her need it seemed, he materialised at her side, and she took his hand, leaned gratefully into him.

He whispered into her ear. 'Are you all right, *cara*?'

'No, Vittorio. I'm not . . . I'm wondering how I'm going to live the rest of my life without my best friend, without my lovely Laurie.'

Tears trembled in her eyes, her voice faltered. But Vittorio's voice was firm, and strong. 'You are going to live it with me, instead. I will be not only your husband and your lover, but your best friend now as well . . . in time, I will bring the smile back to your face, my Saiv. I will make you laugh, and I will make you happy.'

Yes. Vittorio would make her very happy, and Laurie would want her to make him happy, in turn. Laurie would want her to do double the living and giving now, for both of them. Laurie would want her to be a good mother to the child she would never see, never hold . . . there was no end to the things Laurie would want her to do.

Lifting her hand to Vittorio's face, she touched it, and kissed him. With his help she had got through these terrible days, through Lauren's death and eulogies and this final parting this morning, the acceptance of a death that had been so sudden, in the end. So sudden; and yet Laurie had glimpsed it, from afar, had been given the chance to do something of value, a wonderful selfless thing for which she would always be re- membered.

Slipping her hand into her pocket, she felt in it and drew something out, handed it to Vittorio.

'This came this morning, just as we were leaving for the church.' He took it and turned it over, and laughed softly. It was a postcard, depicting a town in Turkey, with an X marked in front of a building on a street. On the back Lauren had scrawled 'Kilroy was here! Love, Laurie.'

'Sì, cara. I think Lauren had more love in her than she ever knew she possessed.'

Taking the card from him, returning it to her pocket, Saiv squeezed his hand, and nodded. Laurie had indeed loved, and in Turkey she had found a worthy recipient at last, of all she had to give. She had pushed the parameters of love to the limit, and she had lived, made her mark in a way that would live long beyond her. Without her Saiv was bereft; but a new soul was growing in her place, to live in turn and be dearly loved.

EPILOGUE

The summer's day was washed with sunlight, and Saiv lay basking in its warmth, propped up on her hospital pillows, her baby daughter nestling in her arms. Gingerly, peering down into the puckered little face, she adjusted the baby's shawl a fraction, her heart filling with love for the minuscule scrap of a girl. Her child was five hours old.

'Let me hold her' Gina commanded proprietorially, and Saiv handed her new sister to her, deliberately issuing no instructions, saying nothing inhibiting. Gina looked ready to stifle the child with clumsy affection, and should be allowed to express it.

'What are we going to call her? Are we going to call her Claudia, after my mama?'

Saiv and Vittorio exchanged glances, and he spoke gently to his elder daughter.

'We will give her two names. One of them will be Claudia, if that is what you would like. But Gina, it is not necessary.'

'Not necessary? What do you mean, Papa?'

'I mean that your mother is always with us, Gina, and will continue to live in our hearts. We do not need to remind ourselves of someone we will not forget.'

Saying nothing, Gina grappled with this, examining it in her mind as she inspected the baby like a punctilious little midwife.

'No . . . we will not forget Mama. But still, I would like my sister to have her name.'

Saiv smiled. 'Then she shall have it. But Gina, she will have another name too, the name by which she will be known. She will be called Laura.'

'Laura? Like your friend who died?'

'Yes. Like my friend Lauren, who died, only not quite the same. When people die, Gina, we cannot bring them back, cannot ever replace them exactly. We have to let them go a little apart, to make room for the new people . . . everyone is special, and everyone is different.'

'My mama was special.'

'Yes, and now your new sister is special. Will you let your mama move over a bit, to make room for her in your life?'

Gina thought about it. 'All right. A little bit. She's a very pretty baby.'

Saiv and Vittorio laughed in unison. By some quirky miracle their baby was very pretty, with a rosy, oval face, tiny translucent ears and eyes that had already flashed a glimpse of deep Mediterranean blue. Not that we care, Saiv thought, what she looks like so long as she has all the bits she needs, everything works and she's healthy. If only Laurie were here to see what I've done today.

She'd be so happy. And so happy to hear about my book, too, to know what's become of it. It vanished without trace in Ireland, never got anywhere near Europe, but hey Laurie, guess what? An obscure little American university somehow got hold of it, and has put it on its freshman philosophy course. All the students will have to buy and read it, I'll be able to write another . . . you never got to read it, probably never would have anyway, but maybe now you know what it's about, wherever you are.

Or maybe it doesn't matter, any more. Maybe you learned enough, in those last months before you died, to teach you everything you needed to know? You missed out on your education, you missed out on my marriage and my baby, you missed out on the family you might have had yourself. But you gained other things, in other ways. I think you died fulfilled, and happy, and profoundly enriched.

Cuddling baby Laura, Gina put her finger to her face and stroked it speculatively. 'Are we going to have more? Are you going to have lots of babies, Saiv?'

'No – not today, anyway! I think this one is enough to be going on with, and besides we already have Michele, and we have you.'

'Me? I'm not a baby.'

'No. You're a big girl, and a big job! Will you help Papa and me to look after Laura?'

'Well – OK. Sometimes. But I won't change nappies.' Primly, she made a moue of distaste, and Saiv smiled at the determination which, she thought, would always be Gina's hallmark. Fragile as she was, in many respects, she had a winning way about her, in more senses than one. Feeling some tinge of tenderness for the stalwart child, she reached to touch Gina's stoutly plaited hair.

'All right. We'll let Papa do that.'

Vittorio laughed, and Gina laughed with him, and at that moment Saiv caught some look in her inherited daughter, some grace note that resonated of Lauren: how lovely she was when she laughed.

Lauren brought us together, brought this smile to our family's face, and now my legacy is to keep it there, to keep this happiness alive.

LIZ RYAN

THE PAST IS TOMORROW

Shivaun Reilly has had enough. Still reeling from the loss of the only family she ever knew, passionately angry at the closure of her beloved hospital, she thinks her heart will break when solid, dependable Ivor – the man she always thought she'd marry – decides to give up his glossy career to follow rugged new paths in Spain.

Shivaun's ever-helpful lodger Alana finds the perfect solution: a job in America as a private nurse, away from all the politics and disappointments. She can't wait to go – and in a pretty New England town, she finds a whole new world of optimism and friendship.

But neither happiness nor unhappiness is that easy to leave behind. Helpful Alana had her own reasons for coming to Shivaun's rescue, and soon, her lies and evasions have led her into trouble. Though Shivaun meets new friends, including a fascinating Irishman, in New England not all of them are what they seem to be. And in Spain, Ivor has begun to re-think his rash decision.

Shivaun discovers both America and some important truths. Truths that are as challenging as they are liberating . . .

HODDER AND STOUGHTON PAPERBACKS

LIZ RYAN

A TASTE OF FREEDOM

Two young Irish girls, longing to taste life, escape to France to pick grapes for a month. Mary craves adventure before returning to marry Cathal Sullivan; Keeley only knows she wants to get away from her hopeless family.

Once there, Mary is enraptured by French cooking while Keeley discovers that in France she is considered intelligent and charming, not just a no-hope scrubber from the wrong end of town. She meets the irresistible Vincent, and begins a new, strange life; but a disastrous accident forces Mary back to her old imprisoned existence, made nightmarish by the destiny she cannot avoid.

Parted by circumstance, the two friends take separate paths until the years, tragedy and struggle bring them together again, to make another bid for freedom.

HODDER AND STOUGHTON PAPERBACKS

LIZ RYAN

A NOTE OF PARTING

When Aran Campion leaves her sleepy Irish fishing village for faraway London, she wants both to escape and to grow. Soon her job, her music, her Saturday market stall make her life too full for the love and marriage that once seemed to be her destiny.

Until she meets a struggling musician called Ben. Despite differences of race, religion, class and eduation, Ben and Aran seem destined for dizzying success.

Until Aran has to deal, alone, with the child who could spoil all her dreams.

HODDER AND STOUGHTON PAPERBACKS

LIZ RYAN

BLOOD LINES

Kerry Laraghy is the girl with everything: daughter of a lovely, loving Irish country home, she is destined to succeed her father as a trainer of world-class racehorses. But Kerry doesn't want Ireland or horses: she wants Paris, Africa and a man who can take her far away from her inheritance.

Brandon Lawrence, heir himself to a multinational corporation, is a loving father, husband of a glamorous wife, wealthy and secure. But under the smooth surface Brandon is secretly at war with himself.

When they meet, the consequences are devastating for them both, and for everyone they love, for decades to come.

HODDER AND STOUGHTON PAPERBACKS

A selection of bestsellers from Hodder & Stoughton

Liz Ryan	Blood Lines	0 340 62456 6	£6.99	☐
Liz Ryan	A Note of Parting	0 340 62458 2	£6.99	☐
Liz Ryan	A Taste of Freedom	0 340 67211 0	£5.99	☐
Liz Ryan	The Past is Tomorrow	0 340 72937 X	£5.99	☐

All Hodder & Stoughton books are available at your local bookshop or newsagent, or can be ordered direct from the publisher. Just tick the titles you want and fill in the form below. Prices and availability subject to change without notice.

Hodder & Stoughton Books, Cash Sales Department, Bookpoint, 39 Milton Park, Abingdon, OXON, OX14 4TD, UK. E-mail address: orders@book-point.co.uk. If you have a credit card you may order by telephone – (01235) 400414.

Please enclose a cheque or postal order made payable to Bookpoint Ltd to the value of the cover price and allow the following for postage and packing:
UK & BFPO – £1.00 for the first book, 50p for the second book, and 30p for each additional book ordered up to a maximum charge of £3.00.
OVERSEAS & EIRE – £2.00 for the first book, £1.00 for the second book, and 50p for each additional book.

Name . . . .

Address . . . .

. . . .

. . . .

If you would prefer to pay by credit card, please complete:
Please debit my Visa / Access / Diner's Card / American Express (delete as applicable) card no:

Signature . . . .

Expiry Date . . . .

If you would NOT like to receive further information on our products please tick the box. ☐